G000115673

30 DAYS

IN

BELFAST

"The gravitational pull of love has a sense of urgency that cannot be rebuffed."

— RITA A. GORDON

3● DAYS IN BELFAST

A Novel

Rita A. Gordon

12:56 a.m.

California

30 Days In Belfast

Copyright © 2023 by Rita A. Gordon

www.ritaagordon.com

Cover design by	Magdalena Karcz
Editing by	Sana Abuleil
Author's photo by	Abigail Huller
Interior design by	Olivier Darbonville

First Edition February 2023

Library of Congress Control Number: 2022923952

ISBN: 979-8-9853566-0-1 (hardcover)
ISBN: 979-8-9853566-2-5 (paperback)
ISBN: 979-8-9853566-3-2 (ebook)

Published in the USA by 12:56 a.m.
www.twelvefiftysixam.com

CONTENTS

———

To my late mother, Hildred, I feel your love.

We Have Time

*"If you love somebody, let them go, for if they return, they
were always yours. If they don't, they never were."*

– KAHLIL GIBRAN, *A Tear and a Smile*

"I'LL RACE YA," SHANNON CALLED AS SHE RAN PAST ROSE TOWARD THE
foam remnants of a forgotten wave on the shoreline.

Rose stopped scribing her initials in the sand heart drawing, a covert
confession of love to her celebrity crush. She jumped up and headed
toward the water. "Wait for me," she shouted to Shannon, who didn't
see her. The glare from the sun dancing on the waves mimicking a
million miniature mirrors distorted her view. Rose chased a wave and
jumped in the water, pushing through the powerful current. When it
subsided slightly, she popped up. "Shannon!" she called over the waves,
but didn't see her friend. Rose continued to push through the currents,
shoving the waves back with her arms that were growing sore by the
minute. With each breath she took, she became more panicked, still
unable to spot her friend.

Rose looked toward the shore to see if Shannon had made it back.
"Shannon, where—" Rose called out before being sucked under by the
current. Before it all became a faded memory.

Fifteen years later, the aftermath was fuzzy in her head. She remembered eventually getting herself to shore. The shock and overwhelming sense of loss she felt when she realized Shannon was not by her side finally came into focus as people crowded around her in the sand. An endless stream of questions rushed through her. The sudden end of a forever friendship stolen by sun, sand, and sneaker waves. Rose felt her face grow warm as memories of Shannon flooded her mind. Her heart started to race. Panic washed over her as she relived the day her friend died. All she wanted to do now was run.

"Rose, talk to me. I know it feels like it came out of left field. Tell me what you're thinking." The sound of Alejandro's voice sitting across the table pulled her out of her head. He was staring at her with a mix of concern and longing in his eyes. Shelved was the swoon-worthy smile that usually greeted her. The smile that made her melt after spending weeks away from her man. He reached his hand across the table.

Rose averted Alejandro's gaze and looked around his London flat, where they had just spent the last three evenings wrapped in each other's arms. Where they had made love for hours until they were both sore, satiated, and spent. Where they had shared rare stolen moments between their busy schedules. She was the one who convinced him to get the flat since he spent so much time traveling between New York and London. He was busy building his career as an international attorney, and Rose was recently promoted to COO. A reward for endless hours helping her father build his business and developing new technologies to innovate the company. Living on the west coast, paired with the busy travel schedule that came with her new position, meant they spent more time on video calls than in person.

Rose focused her attention on the modern, muted earth tones of the room. Her eyes were drawn to a painting she commissioned: A Black woman with a crown of flowers blooming from her head and partially covering her face. Rose remembered posing for the portrait with her chin turned toward her bare shoulder. "Think about your man," the artist had instructed her.

Now, she was sitting across the table from the man she thought she could build a life with. His words washed across her, pulling her down like the sneaker wave that snatched her childhood friend from her life forever. Stirring within her was the same sense of shock and sudden loss.

Rose sucked in a breath. "You sure about this?" she said, sounding as if negotiating a business deal—placing a wall around her heart and tamping the need to reach across the table to take his hand.

"No. But I do know we're both committed to our work. The time in between when we finally get together keeps growing. I'm torn between you and the job, and I don't want to ask you to bend for me. I respect that you're building your career, too. I want to make it work but can't see a way. You just got promoted and want to make a name for yourself away from your father's shadow. That's a tall order, and I'll use all my resources to support you in that effort. But trying to build something more between us is no small feat. Think about it. How many things did you and I have to shift to get these three nights together?"

"Quite a bit," she answered, hesitant to strengthen his argument.

"That's exactly the point. You and I know that you had to rearrange twice as much as me. I won't continue asking you to do that. Your father is my largest client. I know the demand he puts on me. I can only imagine how exponentially higher that is on you. I care about you, but I won't be the one to stifle your success. Let's take a step back and focus. Let's give ourselves a year." Alejandro leaned back in his chair and ran his hands through his hair.

Rose knew he was rethinking his words. But they were out, weighing heavy between them.

Was he right? Should they take a break, allowing time to establish themselves? Could they walk away and get back when the time was right? Would it ever be right?

The idea of them not being a couple made Rose feel like she did when she lost her best friend. The same emotions flowed through her all over again. She paused to think, unaware of what was keeping her from ending the conversation, putting her foot down, and refusing his suggestion.

Rose closed her eyes, inhaled, and opened them. Alejandro's gaze was still locked on her. "This isn't about something else. Or is it? You—" she started.

Alejandro stood, rounded the table, and pulled Rose to her feet and into a tight embrace. He planted kisses all over her face before touching his forehead to hers.

"Oh, Rose. Don't ever think that. I… I'd be hard-pressed to believe I could be with anyone other than you. You are the center of my universe, but I know I'm not yours. This is me setting you free—giving you time to do what you need to do. To be you without me interfering."

Rose listened intently, her breath becoming synchronized with his.

"I'm not saying it's just about you," he continued. "I also need to figure out why I haven't moved heaven and earth to be by your side. And for that, I'm at fault." Alejandro swallowed, then turned to look out the window. Rose held onto his hand, walked up behind him, and pressed her chin to his back.

"Okay." Rose paused. "We'll give it some time."

CHAPTER I

A Rose is Still a Rose

"What's in a name? That which we call a rose
By any other name would smell as sweet."

— WILLIAM SHAKESPEARE

"I'VE GOT EYES ON THE PICASSO," TROY, ROSE'S CHIEF OF SECURITY, said into his headset.

Troy surveyed the airport tarmac before opening the car door for Rose. Picasso was the security handle Rose chose because of her love for art. A love that led her to establish an art foundation in her name, and to open an art gallery filled with art she had curated. As far as Troy was concerned, Rose could refer to herself as whatever she wanted, granted she followed his endless list of security protocols.

Rose Ross was the thirty-two-year-old chief operations officer for Rick Ross Enterprises, and the daughter of Rick Ross, CEO of the company bearing his name. But unlike her father, who possessed a string of monikers—the country's richest Black man, Black billionaire, father, and husband—Rose had just one: daughter of Rick Ross, or Rick Ross' daughter, depending on who was talking. She winced inside every time someone referred to her outside her name. Rose loved her dad, but she wanted to be known as more than just the daughter of Rick

Ross. To not be swallowed in the shadow of the wealthiest man in the country. To pave a path that hadn't already been walked. That was why she was about to board a plane and fly over five thousand miles from San Francisco to Ireland to do a favor for a sick friend and host the annual patron of the art exhibition in Belfast.

"I'm about to board now, Mia," Rose said in her earpiece as she stepped out of the vehicle. "I'll check my rough draft as soon as I board. We'll make the timing work. Even if you're there for an hour. Anyway, who's to say that I can even pull something like this off in less than thirty days. It's never been done before." Rose put her hand in Troy's as he helped her from the car.

"Thank you," Rose mouthed to Troy. She touched his shoulder as she passed him and headed to the plane.

Once onboard, Rose greeted all the staff, sat at one of the tables, took off her earbuds, and put her phone on speaker. "Okay, I'm pulling up the schedule now," Rose announced, opening her laptop.

"I'm telling you I'll be cutting it close," Mia said over the speaker.

"You're right. It's close, but it's doable. You can fit in about an hour—maybe more at the exhibition before your flight. Looking at the photos, the main gallery has a domed glass ceiling. I need to account for the long days and push the event time out to take advantage of the night sky. I'm not sure how it'll play into the final plan, but that's why it starts so late," Rose said, pointing to her draft art exhibition outline on her screen as if her friend could see it over the phone.

"Don't worry. I'll be there. I'm so glad you're doing this." Mia's voice was cheery.

Rose looked up as Troy entered the plane and watched while he gave the crew instructions. When the door closed, Troy went to sit across the aisle from Rose in one of the leather seats near the window. She observed as he set up his laptop.

"Hey, if you hadn't introduced me to Brianna, I wouldn't be on my way to Belfast. The least I can do is ensure you're there to see it. Anyway, I have a lot to think about while I'm there." Rose scrolled through her screen.

"Please tell me you're not pulling double duty," Mia urged.

"A team member is filling in for me while I'm traveling, but I'll still attend key meetings via video, of course," Rose answered, glossing over the weight of her work as a major world provider of sophisticated machine learning platforms for artificial intelligence. Additionally, she was spearheading work on legislation to propose uniform standards related to data access, data sharing, and data protection. She shifted in her seat. "But that's not the issue. Dad's pressuring me on some things."

"I suppose stuff you can't talk about."

"Nothing you need to worry about," Rose said matter of factly. But in reality, anything related to her dad was a big deal.

"And I suppose there's a timeline associated with whatever it is?"

"I—" Rose stopped when one of the attendants approached her.

"Ms. Ross, we'll be taking off shortly. We have a flight time of ten hours and twenty-five minutes. The weather should be about sixty-five degrees when we arrive. Would you like anything to drink?"

"Nothing. Thank you," Rose replied. The attendant nodded her head and went to address Troy before heading back to her station.

"Rose?" Mia piped up over the phone.

"We're about to—" Mia cut Rose off before she could finish.

"Wheels up. I heard. What are you not telling me, Rose?" Mia asked, her voice filled with concern.

Rose thought about her call with her dad earlier that morning. The proud tone in his voice was etched in her brain when he told her he wanted her to succeed him as CEO. She hadn't thought about what was next for her at Rick Ross Enterprises. She had been hyper-focused on work and had given up everything—including her man—to focus on the business. Now, she felt she was finally in a place where she was firing on all cylinders, allowing her to pursue her passion in art on the side. Although it was inevitable that her dad would eventually decide to hand the reins over to someone, the timing felt odd. Did he accelerate his plans because of her—because of what she was doing in Belfast? She wanted to make a name for herself, not get lost behind his. She needed time to think.

Rose sighed. "I have three weeks to get back to Dad with a decision on something."

"Whatever it is, I know you got this. Just stay focused. Don't get distracted, and call me if you need *anything*," Mia said.

"Thanks, Mia. And if a distraction is your code word for men, don't worry. I'll be focused on the event. Anyways, I gotta go. I'll see you at the end of the month."

"I sent you a brief to review before we land," Troy said while tapping his screen, just as Rose ended her call. She had gotten used to his all-business-all-the-time communication style.

Rose pulled the documents he sent her up on her screen. "Give me the Cliff Notes, Troy."

"You need to read through what I sent. The folder labeled *staff* is the people who work in the house as house staff. The one labeled *trade* is the contract resources you requested. I included a layout of the grounds for the property and all the building schematics."

"And? I know you sent more than just what I requested. What's this?" Rose asked, clicking into a folder on the screen. "The one labeled *king*."

"Biographies. It seems your host, Brianna, has two brothers visiting her."

Rose scrolled through a list of articles and files detailing their backgrounds, and settled on a link to the King Enterprise company website. She clicked through to the founder section. "Are these her brothers?" Rose turned her screen toward Troy, displaying two well-suited gentlemen that could pass for billionaire book boyfriend male models.

"Yes. Those are the brothers."

❧

ON ROSE'S FIRST DAY IN BELFAST, SHE FELT A LITTLE ANXIOUS AS SHE drove up the private lane leading to the three-story gray house in the distance. It was a symptom of not sleeping during the whole day's plane ride across the pond. All her travel tricks failed, even in a private jet devoid of strangers. Even her attempt to read Darwin's *The Origins of Species* could not induce an appearance by the elusive sandman. There was a constant weight dangling in the back of her head, remnants of the unfinished conversation she had with her father before she left town.

"I need to name my successor before the end of the month," her dad had disclosed. "Don't make me put anyone but a Ross forward to the board." Rose felt a twinge of pain in her stomach as his words echoed through her mind. She had spent her whole life ensuring she never disappointed her father, and proved her allegiance by working alongside him, eventually becoming his chief operations officer. But since she was determined to carve a name for herself, distant from the legacy her father had created, she did double duty, managing his company while following her passion in the world of curating art. Between the two careers she led, well, there was no room for anything else, including distractions. For Rose, distractions meant men. She had already tried and failed on that front, surrendering to the notion that she couldn't have a man and run one of the largest companies in the world, all while trying to make a name for herself in her so-called spare time. Rose breathed a heavy sigh and tried to push the thoughts from her mind as she headed toward her client's house. Instead, she had to focus on the road ahead and a project that had the potential to change her career trajectory.

Rose turned her attention to the old, castle-like house at the end of the drive. Ornate and intricate hand-chiseled stone rosette detailing framed the enormous arched door and oversized windows lining the façade. As she approached the house, she instinctively made a mental note of her surroundings. It was a tactical move that her security adviser had taught her. Two cars were parked near the front entrance, an AMG, and a Maybach SUV, which Rose supposed belonged to Brianna Morrison's brothers. Born into wealth, Rose was all too familiar with the life of grandeur spread like a feast before her, which meant she felt simultaneously at home yet not at home at all, noting the unfamiliarity of the building before her, and the distance she had travelled to get here. Rose was a visitor, and these weren't her people.

Except for what she discovered through research during the plane ride, Rose did not know much about her client's brothers. As for Brianna, she was more familiar with her. Four previous video conferences leading up to her trip revealed a more conservative yet welcoming woman with impeccable taste and style. She was more likely to drive the Jag parked in the garage, which Rose could see through the open oversized carriage doors. Whatever the case, she would later learn those details and more during her visit to the historic house where she planned to spend the next thirty days.

Tires rolling over gravel made a crunching sound as Rose pulled into the driveway and parked her rented black luxury SUV to the left of the AMG. More crunching and dust filled the air as a car following close behind pulled alongside hers, completing the single row of vehicles, looking more like a luxury dealership than a driveway. "99 Miles From LA," by Johnny Mathis, played over the stereo, and Rose listened for a few seconds before shutting down the engine. Music and mantras helped ease her anxiety and help her feel more centered, and today she wanted to be on point for her meeting with Brianna Morrison, the one name synonymous with art in Europe.

"Breathe. You can do this. You are the descendant of queens, and you belong here," Rose told her reflection as she checked her face in the rearview mirror. She took a deep breath and, in one fluid motion, grabbed her keys and cell phone, and threw them in her handbag before exiting the car. Anticipating Troy would not be too far behind, Rose raised her hand to signal him to stay in place and continued alone up the granite stairs to the landing near the massive front doors. She had already pushed his limits, driving herself to the house so she could fully experience the countryside. And now, the initial meeting with her new clients did not warrant a strong security presence.

Troy had a habit of overdoing it when it came to her security. The last time she came through Heathrow, he almost got them detained for interfering with airport security when they threw out her conditioner. "Hey, that's under the limit," he had yelled at the agent, who ignored his objections. The container hit the trash with a loud *thud*, followed by another as the agent rifled through Rose's luggage. "Hey!" Troy protested, but Rose raised her hand to keep him from irritating the agent further, and he grudgingly backed off.

That was the last time Troy succumbed to her whims of flying commercial versus private. She wanted to have some semblance of normalcy. To walk the streets without a security detail or tracking devices. But there was nothing normal about her life. Rose was the daughter of the wealthiest Black man in the country, and there was nothing normal about that. Like it or not, she knew that Troy—her six-foot-five man-of-steel chief of security—was on task saving her from herself, and from any distractions she may fall victim to.

As Rose made her way toward the house, she noticed that the centuries-old home was well maintained. The modern carriage doors and newly pointed stone walls were evidence of the home's recent renovations. The front doors, which dwarfed her even in her stilettos, opened just as she reached the threshold. Standing about four inches taller than herself, a fine young muscular gentleman greeted her. She recognized his face from her research, recalling the article where the headline read, "Celebrity Chef Marina Mack Spotted With a Hot New Man."

"Hi, I'm Niall King, Brianna's brother. You must be Ms. Ross," he said, smiling down at her.

He was cute and clean-shaven. Inky black, curly hair covered his head; it was slightly longer than corporate, cut neat and tucked behind his ears, starkly contrasting his fair skin and deep Mediterranean blue eyes. She found it peculiar in such a grand house that he casually greeted her at the door in his bare feet. Rounding out the look, he wore dark blue jeans with a tightly fitted, white, silk t-shirt emphasizing the flex in each muscle in his arm as he extended his hand to her. Rose's eyes followed his hand as it reached her own, waiting to shake his. Nothing was lacking with his grip. Strong. Sturdy. Manly. He was the complete package. *I can work with casual*, she thought, trying not to stare.

"Nice to meet you, Niall. I'm Roselyn Ross, but people call me Rose. Your sister is expecting me," she greeted, looking past him into the foyer.

"Welcome, Rose. How apropos. It's my pleasure. Indeed, we're expecting you."

Niall held her hand a few seconds longer than expected while studying her head to toe. Finally, when his eyes met hers, he released her hand.

Although Rose was no stranger to people staring, certain situations still gave her anxiety. At first, she was paralyzed with the fear of having to speak in front of an audience. Over time, she learned to spend extra time preparing for her meetings until she knew the material inside out. She could tackle tough questions when she was focused. A double master's in computer science focused on artificial intelligence combined with art history had served her well in front of audiences. But the dread that something could go wrong always niggled at her, so she got into the habit of meditating moments before stepping in front of an audience. But that was business, and this look from Niall felt different. She wondered whether this was his first time seeing someone like herself up close. How many women with long, textured, brown hair, almond-

14

shaped brown eyes, and caramel-colored skin had he encountered in her profession? Or even in Ireland, for that matter. From what little she knew of Niall, he spent most of his time in countries less diversified than the United States. If bleach-blond, blue-eyed women like Marina Mack were his type, he certainly would have no interest in her, and she was okay with that.

Her recent research revealed that very few people in Northern Ireland were of African descent. Until recently, laws prohibited any foreigners from seeking to gain citizenship. She was surprised to learn that starting in the early nineties, a great migration that lasted about ten years led to enhanced racial tensions in the region as more foreigners tried to integrate into the area. Foreigners that looked like her. This information led to an overflow of questions in her mind. Would she encounter lingering sentiments during her visit? How would her client respond to her? Would she feel the hateful stares of citizens burning through her flesh?

She was careful to prepare herself for the political landscape and moral sentiments she might encounter while traveling abroad. That, coupled with the security briefs from Troy, dictated the number of staff members she brought. It dictated the length of her stay. And her least favorite of all, it dictated how involved her dad was in her affairs. And since her dad's company was known worldwide, safeguards were always in place wherever she traveled. How many people—members of the invisible security detail—had he sent to watch over her? Maybe their recent conversation got through to him. She closed her eyes a second, tamping the thought from her mind, and opened them to refocus on Niall, who was still smiling down at her. Still staring.

What does he see when he's looking at me? she thought.

"Are they joining us?" Niall tipped his head toward the driveway without breaking his gaze.

Before Niall had the chance to invite her in, Rose bent to remove her stilettos. She had been vacillating between keeping them on and taking them off, but opted to follow Niall's casual lead; she quickly undid the ankle straps, slipped them off her feet, and held them as she stepped into the foyer.

"They won't be coming in. My team is going to the gallery for a walkthrough. Afterward, they'll go to the city to get settled. Your sister was gracious enough to have me as her guest."

"She briefed me. The gallery you'll be working in is the building you passed to the left of the driveway. You can access it via any of the doors on this side of the house, then through the courtyard. Brianna felt a short commute would be more suitable for you, in addition to providing you with the comforts of a home."

"The closer, the better. Everything else is a bonus," she remarked in her business voice.

"Great. My brother and I are visiting Brianna and staying overnight. We can help you get settled. By the way, I've heard good things about you."

"It's always nice to hear that. Maybe we can chat over tea when I get settled, and you can tell me more about what you heard." She chose her words carefully, not wanting to send the wrong signals. She was there on business and didn't have time for distractions.

"I'd like that very much. Say, the gentleman you arrived with—your security person—I can tell by how he's canvassing the place he has a trained eye. But I doubt you'll need a bodyguard during your stay here. My brother and I can look out for you when we're here if that's a concern."

Rose's brow furrowed at the thought that Niall may have researched her. The idea of Troy not being around made her stomach churn ever so slightly.

Nine years and hundreds of trips later, Troy's loyalty was old hat. He went with her everywhere. Any media pictures of Rose reveal Troy not too far from her. They were so close that people often mistook them for a couple. Troy was a tall, fierce, fine dark chocolate man who was always well suited. She appreciated how close they had become. But it was not always like that. After his initial assignment, Rose tried to ditch him several times that year. Rebelling was her modus operandi when her parents mandated something, despite the legitimate reasons for their concern. In reality, the childhood trauma she experienced caused her to keep a small circle of friends, so she was initially cautious about letting Troy in. Then, there was the fact that she had separation anxiety following the retirement of her former chief of security. "Rose, it's time for me to hang my hat. I promise you'll be fine," her former advisor assured her, attempting to convince her that Troy was well trained and had passed even the most rigorous tests he could put him through. "Give him a year. If, after a year, you two can't adjust, I'll come out of retirement until we find the right one." Rose agreed. Eventually, she adjusted to Troy. Now, they were virtually inseparable.

"I appreciate the offer, and don't doubt that you and your brother could offer the security I may need, but Troy has me covered for now." Rose attempted to take a step forward into the foyer.

"Forgive my manners, Rose. Please come inside." Niall gestured toward the long hallway.

Rose smiled at Niall when she passed. Walking into the house was like stepping back in time when there were working castles. The finishings were grandiose, and the floors were covered with oversized white marble tiles that were unexpectedly warm to the touch.

Rose stopped and turned to Niall. "Is your sister in the main study?"

"Yes, how did you know?" He stopped short in his tracks behind Rose.

"That's where she took most of her video calls with me. She said it was her favorite room in the house. I had hoped to see it live one day after getting a glimpse of her incredible artwork collection on video."

They entered the room to find Brianna sitting in a chair on the far side, finishing up a call. She was dressed in an olive-green sheath dress and matching heels. Rose wasn't surprised that Brianna had the same signature black hair and blue-eyed traits as her brother, except her hair flowed past her shoulders. However, Rose was alarmed to see how pale Brianna's skin was and how much weight she had lost as the tailored sheath dress hung strangely loose on her.

Still on the phone, Brianna waved them in and nodded her head. "That's fine. Have it delivered to the gallery entrance. I'll—" Brianna paused.

Rose picked up on the gist of the conversation, waved, pointed at herself, and mouthed the words *to me*. She was ready to do business and wanted Brianna to know she had her act together.

"Someone will be here to receive it. The name? Of course, please have it sent to the attention of Rose Ross. Thank you. Sure. Great." Brianna ended her call, pushed herself up from the chair, and stood to greet Rose.

"Welcome to my home, Rose."

"It's a pleasure to finally meet you in person. I hope you don't mind me jumping right in while you were on the call."

"The pleasure is all mine. Thanks for jumping in. So, you had a long journey to get here. How was your flight?"

"It was smooth. Uneventful." Sleepless, she wanted to add, but stopped herself, vowing to remain professional.

"That is good to hear. However, I imagine jet lag will be setting in soon. May I suggest you take a few days to rest, get familiar with the grounds, and visit the city before you jump into work?" Brianna asked.

"Thanks, but I feel fine. A full day's work is the best way to thwart jet lag. Besides, we have a tight timeline. I'm anxious to get started." And she had reason to be. Although she had a head start before arriving, most of the work had to be done in Belfast. Her events usually took six months to several years to create, dependent upon the subject, venue, and budget. Four weeks would be the shortest time she spent curating and executing any exhibition.

"My home is yours for however long you choose to stay."

"I appreciate that. Being here is truly a great honor for me, Mrs. Morrison."

Brianna held out a hand, inviting Rose to sit on the leather daybed, doubling as a couch near a glass-topped kidney-shaped table in the center of the room. "Have a seat. And please call me Brianna," she insisted, returning to her chair as if she were adjusting to a hot tub of water.

Rose did not know how much Brianna's family knew about Brianna's ailment other than she had a congenital heart defect that became exacerbated following her husband's death. Brianna didn't feel she had the strength to pull off the event alone this year, so she handed the reins over to Rose. She also commissioned Rose to retool and breathe new life into the event. It was a big deal for Rose. She would be the first woman of color and the first Black woman to curate this prestigious art event in Europe. Given the good press, this could prove to be a pinnacle moment in her career.

"I'm okay to stand for the moment. After the long flight and the drive, I need to stretch my legs a bit. Please accept my wishes for your speedy recovery."

Brianna nodded. Rose could tell by the subtle squint of her blue eyes she was attempting to mask some pain.

"I would love to have recovered by the day of the exhibition, but only time will tell. In the meantime, there are no words to express my gratitude for having you step in on my behalf. Mia, who I trust dearly, sings your praises. I can't thank her enough for introducing us. She'll be attending the event?"

"Yes, she confirmed with me. We've grown quite close. Did she tell you how we met?"

"She said it was at one of your shows."

"That's right. About five years ago in San Francisco, she attended one of my exhibits on an artist she'd been following. We've been great friends ever since. When she told me about this opportunity, I didn't hesitate to answer the call."

Brianna's phone buzzed. "Speaking of calls, my apologies; I need to take this," Brianna held up an index finger and answered her phone.

Rose looked around. The room seemed more like a library than a study. The long wall to her left housed an ebony-stained wooden bookshelf stretching floor to ceiling, lined with books of various heights and thicknesses. Sprinkled throughout the shelves was an eclectic grouping of paintings. An abstract by Joan Miró sat on a shelf opposite a portrait of a little girl by Mary Cassatt. Adjacent to the bookshelf was an oversized gilded mirror leaned against a striate-painted wall mimicking fabric. In the mirror, Rose could see her reflection alongside Niall's, who was watching her watching him. She wanted to know more about this man whose stare she felt at her core, but she would not allow herself to be distracted. That was not the purpose of her visit. She dropped her eyes and looked at Brianna instead.

"I'm sorry about that, Rose. My doctor is checking up on me. Do you have everything you need?"

"I received your email with the gallery plans and your guest list. I'll schedule time with you later this week to review the proposed theme and run-of-show before we get too far down the planning. My team is doing a gallery walkthrough, but I expect we have everything we need."

Brianna stood and walked towards Niall, who had quietly observed their exchange.

"Perfect. I'm relieved you're here. I know we are in good hands, and the exhibition will be spectacular. You and your team have the full range of the property. If you can find the time, I suggest you familiarize yourself with my private art collection. I sometimes incorporate pieces into gallery showings. You're welcome to do the same. Now, please forgive me. I need to get some rest. My brothers are here helping me, although at times, a little overprotective. Especially this one." Brianna shot a glance at Niall. "But they can make themselves available to you if you need anything."

Rose and Niall stepped aside, allowing Brianna to pass and exit the room. Niall's eyes stayed fixed on Rose's, and his lips slightly quirked up on one side whenever she unintendedly glanced his way. Rose forced a subtle smile to mask the range of emotions she felt. Jet lag was beginning to kick in. She felt the anxiety to impress her client and pressure to deliver a fantastic exhibit on behalf of Brianna and herself.

It all left her feeling exhausted. The room felt like it was starting to spin. Rose leaned back slightly, allowing her shoulder to rest on the trim of the doorframe, but she quickly adjusted her posture to avoid the perception of fatigue. *Breathe*, she told herself.

"Are you okay?" Niall's voice was low and calming. "If you're tired, your room is on the second floor in the front of the house overlooking the courtyard. I think you'll find it very accommodating. I can show you the way." Niall gestured toward the hallway.

"I'm okay. My things are still in the car."

"I'll have someone on staff take care of that. Is that okay?" Niall asked. Rose nodded.

Something about Niall's presence helped her relax. A few seconds of silence passed between them before she spoke up. "So, is there anyone else here I need to meet? Brianna hinted that your brother is here, and I recall seeing two cars in the driveway. I'd like to meet him if he's available."

Niall's lips parted slightly, then curled into a hungry smile. He moved closer, leaned down, and lowered his right hand to retrieve her stilettos while holding her gaze. His scent, an earthy-sweet mix of cardamom and plum, wafted past her. She tried but failed to hold her breath, allowing him to satiate her senses. Rose wondered how many Irish women had fallen prey to the sweet-smelling blue-eyed god gazing back at her.

"No one of particular importance. I'll get your things ready for you," he said before disappearing into the foyer with her shoes.

Rose didn't wait for Niall's return. She had work to do. Art lovers, celebrities, and socialites from across Europe would descend upon that location to witness a spectacular art showing in twenty-eight days. She had magic to work. So, she exited barefoot through the patio doors taking the long-paved path leading to the row of vehicles. There, she met with Troy, whose eyes were fixed on her every move as she powered toward him. Although she didn't know the exact details of things he did or had done to keep her safe, he was the one person she felt completely safe around.

Rose gently placed a hand on Troy's shoulder, which relaxed beneath her fingers. "I suppose Kris is in the gallery?" she asked.

"He went to the gallery to take pictures and measurements and prepare an inventory list. I can walk you over to Kris now. He'll take your things into the house when he's through in the gallery." Rose shifted her weight from one leg to the other. Troy looked down. "Better yet, wait here; let me grab your shoes from the car," he said, taking long strides toward the car.

"Niall sent the staff for my luggage. Just grab my driving shoes from the passenger seat," Rose called to Troy, who was already near the car.

Within a few seconds, he returned and placed the shoes on the ground near Rose. She looked down, wiggled her toes, then stepped into her tan-colored Birkenstocks that served as a pleasant break from her stilettos.

"How are you feeling about staying here versus in town?"

"I realize it's a disruption in our normal routine, but with Niall and his brother here, I'll be fine. This will also give you a little time to yourself after hours."

"I can't take time to myself when it comes to your security. Besides, I'm not here on vacation."

"I just meant things seem low-key here. Consider this. Once I get settled for the evening, I'll let you know when it's time to leave. Later, I'll text you at our usual time to confirm things are good before I crash.

Does that work for you?" Rose knew Troy needed every detail mapped out. Neither of them liked surprises.

"I can work with that."

THE SUN LAY PARALLEL TO THE HORIZON, CAUSING THE FINAL RAYS OF light to reflect against the house, highlighting it in vibrant flows of color. Rose exited the gallery, where she had spent a significant part of the afternoon familiarizing herself with the structure of each room to update her renderings. She wanted to explore the grounds while there was still light, so she walked back through the courtyard toward the main house.

Once inside the u-shaped courtyard, she could fully appreciate the centuries-old home's grand scale. Rose imagined the space as a gathering spot for people to converge throughout the exhibition. She envisioned patrons standing around highboy tables having drinks and networking following the show. Rose looked to see her room perched on the cornerstone of the house and was generous enough to overlook the gallery and the courtyard entrance. Next to her room, in one of the large, picturesque windows, she spotted the silhouette of a man sitting in the window. It appeared his attention was on something in his hand. The glow reflected upon his face told her it was a digital device. *That must be Aedan*, she thought. "Why haven't you come down to meet me?" she asked aloud, knowing he couldn't hear her.

Rose continued walking until her path led her through a slight transition point to the pool area at the rear of the house. Maybe she would string fairy lights on the patio and add some additional lounge seating and coffee tables for when patrons made their way poolside. She contemplated whether to add floating flower arrangements with lights in the pool. "Maybe I can use these," she spoke to herself when she reached a patch of lavender.

She picked a few flowers, rubbed them in her hands, raised them to her nose, closed her eyes, and inhaled. Her mind wandered to her childhood best friend, whose parents grew lavender, educating her about the flower's various uses. Rose liked the scent of lavender so much that she made spritz water with it, and when she got older, she combined it with vanilla and made it her signature scent.

"Rose." The deep familiar voice shattered the silence and pulled her out of her thoughts. When she turned, she saw that Troy stood a few feet from her.

"It's a good thing I know hand-to-hand combat. I didn't hear you coming."

"You didn't notice me because you're distracted," Troy smiled while gesturing his hand for her to lead the way forward.

"I feel a lecture coming," Rose continued walking.

"I'm not a professor. I'm here to protect you. This property is immense, and the woods are quite dense. I need to be with you if you plan on exploring. But you know that already."

Rose turned and narrowed her eyes at Troy. "It feels a little dramatic, don't you think?"

"I know you don't mean that. You're easily distracted when under pressure. It's a defense mechanism. My job is to keep that in mind and ensure you're covered. You say you never want to know what's happening behind the scenes, then stick to protocol."

Rose feigned a frown. "I should have drop-kicked you the second you called my name."

"Next time, you can show me what you got. Are you ready to head in?" Troy looked to Rose for a response.

"I suppose. There's a lot to do, and the best way through this is one day at a time." Rose opened her hands to let the crushed flowers fall to the ground, then reluctantly headed toward the house.

CHAPTER 2

Round Midnight

"When a woman is talking to you,
listen to what she says with her eyes."

– VICTOR HUGO

IT WAS SO QUIET THAT WHEN ROSE STEPPED INTO THE HOUSE, SHE could hear the synchronized ticking coming from the second hand of the kitchen clock and another at the top of the stairwell. It was a reminder of how little time she had. However, she wanted to see Brianna's art collection sprinkled throughout the house. So, she headed up the staircase, dimly lit by antique wall sconces, opening onto a series of rooms. She had read that each room had a distinct piece of artwork that reflected the room's spirit.

Rose opened the heavy, carved, wooden door to one of the rooms and discovered the music room—a room she had read about before, but had not found any pictures of online, no matter how much she scoured. She switched on the light to reveal a sparse chamber with a piano in one corner and several strategically placed velvet chairs in another. The dark absinthe-colored walls were bare except for one. Directly across from the door was a wall filled with music-themed paintings of various sizes—in the center of it all hung a worn, yellow document with faded lettering framed behind glass. A lamp hovering above the frame lit the paper. Rose held her breath and walked over to take a closer look. She recognized the document immediately. She considered this the piece de resistance—a playbill dated March 1750, prepared for the Crow Street Theatre in Dublin. Rose could barely make out the writing, but she knew this was the only surviving playbill for the first appearance of Rachael Baptist, a singer the Irish had dubbed "a black siren." She recalled reading how the documents played a significant role in Ireland's history, promoting what was considered a momentous event at the time. It would mark the first time many people saw a Black woman in Ireland.

"I can't think of a better way to capture the essence of my exhibition on Blacks in Ireland than with the first Black woman who was introduced over two hundred years ago. This document could serve as the centerpiece of my exhibition." Rose knew she needed to get clearance from Brianna on this and grew excited as she envisioned how patrons would get their first reveal.

"I see you found her," a woman's voice spoke from behind Rose. She turned to see Brianna seated in an armchair near the door.

"Brianna, I didn't hear you come in. How are you feeling?"

"Tired of resting. So, what do you think about it?"

"The playbill—I think it's amazing. I'd love to use this as a centerpiece for the exhibition."

"So, you've already started formulating your theme?"

"I have."

"It's the hallmark of a good curator to see a piece of art and know how to present it to tug at the viewer's emotions. And this, my dear, is why you're here. What have you come up with?"

"I'm considering looking back on Ireland's art history, focusing on contributions made by Black and other underrepresented minorities, and following that theme forward to the present. It will be ambitious but bold, and I expect it has—"

Brianna cut in. "It has never been done before. The Irish have a strong sense of family and belonging. The patrons will follow your lead if you tie in something to grab their attention when they enter the gallery. Are you up for the task?" Brianna asked.

"I am. I have a few ideas on how to draw the patrons in. But I think having this playbill in their line of sight will tease them toward the far side of the gallery further into the exhibit. What do you think?" Rose held her breath, awaiting Brianna's response.

"It sounds like a good start. I'd be interested in seeing your renderings. Listen, I brought you here because I believe you are the best curator of our time. You need to believe the same about yourself. I'm giving you a chance to help the world catch up to that notion. The depth and complexity of your past showings introduced us to art in ways that challenged our perception of ourselves and how we relate to others."

"I've learned from the best. Studied people like yourself. I try to apply a fresh lens to everything."

"It's more than that, Rose. I told someone a few weeks ago that you see and present things in a way we haven't imagined. I'm expecting you to deliver on that."

"That means a lot coming from you. But I also feel the weight of your words. It's a lot of pressure."

"Our upcoming exhibition is the most exclusive one-day art event in Europe. Even for me, it's a lot of pressure. But I couldn't think of anyone more capable of handing the reins over to. We need to experience art through a different lens. Now is your time."

"I appreciate your confidence. Going in this direction will be controversial. I'll be shattering many firsts. But like Rachael, someone must pave the way," Rose acknowledged.

"Taking risks reaps the rewards. I only wish I were well enough to watch you work."

Rose lowered her voice. "About that. What have you shared with your brothers about your condition?"

"They know I have an exacerbated heart condition." Brianna clasped her hands together.

"Do you plan to tell them your doctor's recommendation?"

"In due time. I want to get a second opinion. Now, keep that brilliant mind of yours focused on your exhibition plans. I'll be fine." Brianna stood and went to the door. "I'll leave you to it. My resources are at your disposal if you need anything. Goodnight, Rose."

"Goodnight."

FOLLOWING THE DISCUSSION WITH BRIANNA, ROSE DECIDED TO continue exploring art in the rest of the house. She popped in and out of the rooms until she came upon one that she recalled overlooked the courtyard. The door was closed. However, upon further examination, a sliver of light peeked from beneath. *This is Aedan's room,* she thought. Just as Rose was about to knock to introduce herself, she quickly put both hands behind her back and walked away, assuming Aedan would make her acquaintance on his own terms. She crossed the hall to another room she believed was Niall's when she heard the muffled sound of his voice speaking to some unknown person on the phone.

Like a curious cat, Rose headed up the flight of stairs tucked away at the back of the house leading to the third floor, where Brianna had a private suite amongst other family rooms. She got as far as one of the first sitting rooms and noticed an absence of light in Brianna's section of the house, so she refrained from venturing further and headed back to the second level instead.

To her surprise, Niall unexpectedly appeared at the bottom of the stairwell just as she reached the last step. "We all had a late lunch that doubled as dinner. Can I get you something to eat, or would you like me to keep you company?"

"No. I'm fine, thanks. You caught me in the middle of exploring this lovely home and noting the paintings. If it's okay, I'd like to continue. You're welcome to join me." Rose didn't want him to think she was lost or, even worse, snooping.

"I think I will. This room is good to note. It's one of three libraries. There's one on each floor, with the largest upstairs doubling as one of two dining rooms. You passed the other one on the first floor. There's a door hidden in the panel for the service stairs. In each room hangs a famous still life painting that I expect would be of interest to you." He pointed to a large painting depicting a lavish banquet.

"It appears the artist is entirely unapologetic about the spread in this one." Rose leaned in for a closer look.

"Seems that way. It's all relative, I suppose. You never really know until you get the back story."

"You have a point," Rose agreed.

"There's more to see if you're interested." Niall gently palmed her elbow and gestured to the door. The slight touch sent an unexpected rush of electricity through her, which she tried to ignore.

"I was hoping to see the grand library upstairs, and maybe get a peek at that hidden stairwell, but I'll look at that another day. I don't want to disturb Brianna." Rose walked silently with Niall in tow, then turned to him. "You mentioned touring me around the property—I'm curious, are you visiting your sister for the week?"

"A few nights. Maybe more. I live downtown, so it's not a far distance if Brianna needs me. Or if you need me," he smiled. "But just say the word, and I can extend my stay and be available during the mornings and evenings since I did offer my services in lieu of your bodyguard."

"He's my chief of security," Rose corrected.

Niall gestured to a door. "Try this one," he said, ignoring her comment and moving on with the tour.

Rose opened the door and then turned back to Niall. "Troy's got this. We usually stick to our routines. Someone has eyes on me whether he's here physically with me or not. I don't always see them. It's worked well for me so far."

"I won't interfere with that," he said, following her into the room.

"On the other hand, I'm sure Brianna is happy you and your brother are here. What sister wouldn't want her brothers around? During one of our calls, she told me how supportive you both were last year when her husband passed away." Rose walked across the room she assumed was an office.

"I didn't realize you two were that close."

"I wouldn't say we're best friends, but we're open with each other and offer support to one another. So, I felt it might be best to accept her invitation to stay here instead of at a hotel with everything happening in her life."

"I'm glad you two have a connection. Brianna is generous and kind for the most part, but don't let that fool you. She can be very exacting."

"Your sister and I have that in common. We have to be in this industry—especially when curating a show. Everything has to be perfect. I'd love to say there are only admirers of art, but the truth is, most are critics, and that's where expert storytelling through art comes in. I suspect it's the reason Brianna asked me to help."

"She hired you because you're the best in the industry. On that note, you have at your disposal a team of people on staff here to help you stay on track. And as I mentioned, my brother, Aedan, and I can be available on those off-hours at the beginning and end of your day. Just let me know what you need."

"Speaking of Aedan, I haven't met him yet."

"My brother can be elusive at times. However, not much gets past him. Running a small empire doesn't leave him much free time. He'll make an appearance when he's ready."

"And you're not running an empire?"

"Not at the magnitude you're used to. But to your point, I was just checking in to see if you needed anything, and it sounds like you don't. Like my brother, I have some work to catch up on, but don't hesitate to interrupt me if you need anything." Niall waited for her acknowledgment, then left to return to his room.

Rose took a break from her exploration, went to her bedroom suite, and opened the patio doors to watch the sky grow a darker shade of blue against the horizon. She could see Troy below monitoring the estate. She wondered if he still had on his earpiece. Rose retrieved hers from her pocket, turned it on, and placed it in her ear. "Connecting Picasso to MOS," said the automated voice for her earpiece. She knew Troy was likely shaking his head to hear her connect. He felt her alias was a little strange but even stranger that she referred to him as her man-of-steel. Rose stepped onto the deck, revealing herself to Troy as he looked up to pinpoint her location.

"All clear out here. Are you good for the night?" His Barry White voice that she loved so much reverberated in her ear. Sometimes, Rose engaged him in conversation solely to listen to him talk.

"Yes, all clear. It's a lovely night tonight. Do you know why the night sky is blue?" she asked.

"Tell me."

"Because blue light travels in shorter, smaller waves. So, when the gases and particles in the earth's atmosphere scatter light, there's more blue light scattered than other colors."

"Your brain is too big for me."

"Anyway, you should know that Niall and Aedan stay at the house off and on, but are both here for the night. Feel free to head out when you're ready. I'll see you tomorrow after breakfast, okay?"

"Confirmed. Kris is already at the hotel. I have a stand-in taking over once I leave."

"Have a good evening," Rose watched as Troy walked out of sight.

Still restless, she took a deep breath and accepted the warm embrace June in Belfast offered. The sun was long gone, replaced by the moon shining like a spotlight in the night sky, illuminating the entire estate. From her deck, she could easily count the number of dark hedges. Their thick trunks sprouted limbs that stretched over the road like gigantic arms until the branches and leaves intertwined, forming a trestle from the driveway to the edge of the woods. She stood there a moment, taking it all in.

Back inside, Rose opened her laptop. She tried her best to capture all the event ideas floating in her head, allowing them to flood onto the computer screen. When she finished capturing notes, she caught up on email. There was an email from Mia checking in, one from Kris with a link to the art he inventoried earlier, several from her associate curator back in the states, a string of emails from Rick Ross Enterprises, and feedback on her draft legislation to review. Then, there were about ten random emails from people she didn't know wanting to meet with her to talk about donations, which she forwarded to Troy with a note to have his security team review them. Once she cleared her inbox, Rose spent the next few hours on conference calls for Rick Ross Enterprises before finally closing her laptop. She took a deep breath, attempting to control her anxiety and keep her mind from racing so she could sleep. But she couldn't.

Rose had been to many countries with extended stays, but something felt slightly different about this trip. So much was riding on this event. She needed to shape this into the pinnacle event for the Morrison Art Gallery and prove herself as a premier art curator. Brianna was right— this was her moment. And then there was the situation with the board of directors. She had a big decision to make. The clock was ticking, and she had no idea what she would tell her dad.

Day one was seconds away from ending, and day two was about to begin. The moment's stillness was shattered by two short beeps from Rose's watch. It was her midnight alert—her signal to herself to text Troy that she was okay and put his mind at ease. Although it was time when most people lost their battle with sleep, she knew Troy could not entirely succumb to slumber until he had his final check-in. He was loyal to a cause, and they had a long history. "All is good," she texted him. And for a brief moment, she believed it.

Something else caught Rose's attention in the darkness of night's cover. A faint sound was coming from the floor below. Someone else was still awake in the large, stone house. She couldn't help herself; she was curious. Maybe Aedan had finally come up for air. She left her room, went downstairs, and walked past an open door leading to the kitchen. There was a light on, but no one was there. Instead, she could hear the faint sound of fabric rustling. The dim light from the hallway revealed Niall's muscular body as he entered the sitting room carrying something in his hands. Rose was so quiet that Niall didn't hear her walk behind him.

"Looking for me?" she whispered to avoid startling him.

"I was so focused on work earlier that I lost track of which part of the house you wandered into. Which is a bit ironic when I think about it."

"You found me. How can I help?"

"You mentioned tea earlier, so I brought you some. It's chamomile. You seemed restless. I figured it might help you rest. I hope that's okay." He placed a small tray on the kidney-shaped table, then removed a lighter from his pocket and lit the two tapered candles.

Rose could hear Troy's voice in her earpiece, which she forgot she had turned on earlier.

"Is everything alright, Rose?" The Barry White voice inquired.

"Yes." Her response served as an answer for both questions posed to her. Niall was oblivious to any conversation outside of his own with Rose. He placed a tea strainer in the cup, poured hot water, then handed the cup to Rose.

She raised the cup to her lips and blew across the surface. "You're very observant. I get a little anxious at times."

"Well, I'm here to help. I'm not sure if you saw much of the grounds today. But if you're interested, I could show you around if you have time this week. This place has been in our family for generations, and as you can imagine, it's steeped in history." Niall's eyes locked on hers. He shared a few facts she had not uncovered through her research, like the house's ten thousand bottle capacity wine cellar, the location of a secret private lounge, and the date of the most recent restoration.

"You know, that sounds great. I'd like to take you up on your offer. I'm sure it will also help as I put together my plans for the exhibition." She was already formulating a plan of how to use elements of the house's art history to add the personal touch needed to set the event apart from others.

"Don't you give your mind a break from work?"

"Sometimes, but not when I'm in the middle of an important project with a tight deadline. This exhibition is important to Brianna. It's important to me." Rose took a sip of her drink.

"Five thousand miles is a long way to come for a favor. Anything in particular draw you here?" Niall asked.

"I would assume it's by the same token you do whatever you do. Passion. It doesn't feel like work when I immerse myself in art. And the traveling—well, that's just a by-product. But if you're wondering what brought me to Ireland specifically—it was your sister. She gave me the opportunity of a lifetime, and I'm not one to walk away from a challenge." Rose took another sip. "This is nice. I usually have a cup every night." She walked over to the daybed and took a seat. Rose noticed Niall monitored her every move. "You know, Niall, my mother told me once that if you want to know what someone wants, you should just watch their eyes." She pursed her lips and waited for a response.

"I haven't heard that one before."

"I don't mean to be so forward. It's just that you're doing this thing where you... Well, you have this tendency to stare at me." Rose paused, considering what to say next. *Like I'm your favorite dessert*, is what she wanted to say, but instead, she opted to keep that thought to herself. "Is there something I can do for you?" Rose waited for his response, hoping her message landed as intended. She wanted to eliminate the possibility of any distractions during her thirty-day stay, and she knew that meant eliminating the possibility of anything happening between the two that seemed to be brewing in Niall's mind.

Niall flashed a hungry smile. "Nothing. I'm enjoying the beautiful view."

"You sure about that?"

"Absolutely. You may have noticed I don't mince words. So, when I say you're the most beautiful woman I have ever seen, you can take that to the bank."

Rose was at a loss for words. She was trying to check him, not charm him.

"Maybe you're just fascinated with me. From what I can see, there aren't many women like me around here, and the data says the Black population here is small. And as for the art scene, being the only Black in the room is my situation pretty much wherever I go, except within my community or Africa."

"Our demographics are changing—slowly but surely. But back to my point, I won't apologize for staring or stating that you're beautiful."

"No need to apologize. I like your frankness. Now that that's out in the open, did you need anything else?"

"While you're here, I would like the opportunity to get to know you better. Sound harmless?" Niall asked.

"On the surface, sure, it sounds harmless enough. But I'm just here for the art exhibition. I'm not looking for anything new." The absence of his smile told her he got the message. She hoped she didn't come across as too harsh. After all, she was not there to feed into his fascination nor compete with Marina Mack. Rose had a reputation to uphold, and they had to get along for the next month.

Niall nodded, took one step through the doorway, then turned back to address Rose. "I realize it's not the right time for this. If I've done anything to offend you, that was not my intention. Now, I will get out of the way so you can do your job. We'll see you in the morning. Try and get some sleep, Night Owl." He turned and left.

"Good night," she whispered after he was out of earshot.

The beeping in her ear signaled that Troy was done listening and had turned off his earpiece.

———

CHAPTER 3

Between Brothers

"It takes two men to make one brother."

— ISRAEL ZANGWILL

SUNLIGHT FROM THE KITCHEN WINDOW LIT UP THE COUNTER WHERE Niall and Aedan sat sipping coffee.

"What are your plans for this week? I think one of us should be here for Brianna if she returns before Sunday," Aedan said.

"She's not acting like herself. I could have driven her to Dublin. She didn't need to summon Carol before the crack of dawn," Niall remarked.

"Our cousin may have influenced her to some extent, but like you said, Brianna's not herself."

"Yeah, I didn't expect Tom's passing to take such a lasting, physical toll on her." Niall sipped his coffee and looked past his brother to some unknown spot in the room.

"None of us saw this coming." Aedan bowed his head slightly, rubbed the back of his neck, and exhaled.

"I think it's too much for her to handle. Her health, the grief, this house, business affairs—it's a lot, even for those of us in the best of health," Niall admitted.

"We can relieve her of tactical things. I'll have my attorney handle all the business items. We have everything covered if you can handle the house staff, and we'll split our time here at the house," Aedan said.

"And our new guest, Rose?" Niall's eyes shifted to his brother, waiting for his response.

"Right. Another reason for us to split our time here."

"Brianna doesn't know the breadth of Rose's work outside the art scene. She knows about Rose working for Rick Ross Enterprises, but that's it," Niall noted.

"About Rose...I noticed you paying particular attention to her yesterday."

"How do you know anything about what I was doing yesterday?"

"I have my ways."

Niall shook his head. "You're too much, man. Anyway, she's a smart, beautiful woman. It's hard not to take notice."

"Let's think this through. We're obligated to be available to Rose after work. The stakeholder's meeting is tonight. It's a formality following a day of meetings—no talking shop. I could invite her. What do you think?" Aedan asked.

"She hasn't even met you yet. I doubt she'd accept. Besides, I don't want to sit around talking shop with a bunch of suits, so it's unlikely Rose would, either. Remember, she's not here doing business on behalf of Rick Ross Enterprises."

"It doesn't hurt to ask. We could be overthinking this. She may already have plans. Regardless, I still want to know more about her."

"If you're interested in talking to her, invite her to lunch one day."

"Or take her for a drink?"

"Aedan, she's not someone you can treat like your usual flavor-of-the-month."

"Never crossed my mind. This is strictly business."

Niall shook his head. "Until it isn't."

"I'm going to invite her to the dinner. I want to know everything about this woman working for Brianna."

"She's here on business curating a show. Nothing else."

"Which makes her all the more intriguing."

"So, you're intrigued now?" Niall asked.

"Like you said, she's focused. That piqued my interest to want to know more about her. Come on, Niall. When's the last time you or I had to work to get a woman's attention? Have you ever heard the word *no*?"

"Yes, from Rose. Less than twelve hours ago."

"Exactly."

"This is not a game, Aedan. You've read the file I sent to you on her."

"I did. It paints a picture of a brilliant, no-nonsense, hard-driving, ambitious, thirty-two-year-old woman."

"It tells you more than that, Aedan. Did you read the white paper in the file from five years ago? It was initially posted as some business case study but was immediately taken offline?"

"I read the file."

"Then you know she's a big deal. The brains behind the company's original AI algorithm that's the closest to human performance without bias. In the wrong hands—" Aedan cut his brother off.

"That information won't get into the wrong hands. Nor will Rose. Not on my watch. And certainly not while I have you at the helm of the largest private security firm in the UK."

Niall locked eyes with his brother and nodded, sealing an unspoken agreement between the brothers. "I need more coffee," he said.

CHAPTER 4

Night and Day

*"Words are a pretext. It is the inner bond that
draws one person to another, not words."*

– RUMI

ROSE LAID ON HER BACK, WATCHING THE SUNRISE THROUGH CLOSED eyelids, allowing the sun's rays to warm her face. In her mind, she counted down. *Five, four, three, two, one.* Then, in one fluid motion, she sat up on the daybed, forcing herself awake in hopes of summoning the energy she so desperately needed to tackle the day ahead. It took a minute to get her bearings, then, an anxious feeling washed over her—the feeling she got when something was wrong. *Darn.* She realized she had fallen asleep in the sitting room. She placed her feet on the floor, and they touched something furry she did not recall being there. Rose looked down to find a puffy pair of blue slippers. She was disappointed with herself for falling asleep there, and was even more disappointed at the thought that someone could have entered and exited the room without her knowledge as she laid sound asleep. Why didn't anyone wake her? There was no place for this kind of slipping up when Troy was not around.

She sat for a moment to allow her senses to readjust. She inhaled the morning fragrances, a mixture of brewed coffee and cinnamon wafting in the air. "I got this," Rose told herself as she stepped into her newfound pompoms, sent a few texts to her team, and rushed upstairs to clean up. After her shower, she got dressed and then headed down.

Before reaching the kitchen door, Rose heard an unfamiliar, deep, accented voice. It sounded similar, but not quite like Niall. *Aedan.*

"The faint whisper of vanilla and lavender caresses my senses like the light touch of a feather. Can this be our lovely American house guest approaching?" the voice said.

When she entered the room, she found Niall standing at the coffee machine, wearing a curious look directed at who she suspected was his brother. It wasn't until Niall's eyes locked on hers that the look dissipated, and a subtle smile formed across his face. She couldn't help but smile in return. He looked even more distinguished than he had yesterday, dressed in gray slacks and a white shirt. Aedan was seated at the end of the marble counter with a device in his hand.

"Gentleman," Rose addressed the room.

"Ah, the Night Owl is awake. I trust you slept well, but not as well as you would have in your bedroom. Rose, let me formally introduce you to my elusive brother, Aedan."

"Good morning. Please accept my belated welcome and excuse my brother's penchant for nicknames." Aedan got up to greet Rose with an outstretched hand. He kissed the back of her hand and led her to the kitchen counter.

What better way to start the day than having breakfast with two strapping Irishmen in one room? Rose thought.

Aedan was equally striking in his appearance as Niall. He was movie-star cute with a perfectly chiseled face and a cut body. His scent—a hint of sandalwood and brown sugar—wafted in the air around them. Like his brother, she could see the Mediterranean reflecting in Aedan's eyes. Rose tried but failed to look away, holding the counter to steady herself. *Distractions.*

"You're the mysterious brother, Aedan. It's nice to finally meet you," she said professionally.

Aedan flashed a sudden smile. "Likewise."

She held up her thumbs and forefingers, simulating a photo snap. "I'm going to immortalize this moment. Breakfast in Belfast with the King brothers." She smiled.

Niall shot a curious glance at his brother, who raised an eyebrow. They both looked at Rose.

"Don't look at me like you don't both know how handsome you are. You're just not used to people saying it out loud," she admitted. It was as good of an icebreaker as anything else she could serve.

"Now, that's my kind of good morning, Night Owl, and quite unexpected after our brief encounter last night," Niall smiled.

"Oh, about last night. You were—"

Niall cut her off. "Hovering."

"I was going to say *a perfect gentleman.* I hope I didn't come off as curt. I wasn't trying to be."

"No apology necessary. And you're right. People aren't usually forthcoming. Coming from you, it's refreshing." Niall put a plate on the counter in front of Rose.

"The two of you together are rather distracting. But in all seriousness, I'm here until the day after the exhibition. I don't know what I don't know, so I may call you if I need help."

"Well, you certainly know how to break the ice. I love it. In case my brother and Brianna haven't informed you, we'll make ourselves available when you need us. The next few weeks should be quite interesting," Aedan smiled, then slid the serving dishes to Rose's side of the counter.

"Only time will tell. It smells so good in here," Rose locked gazes with Aedan. She wanted to say that it smells just like sandalwood and brown sugar but refrained from doing so.

Niall handed Rose a fork. "Time will reveal all. Dig in."

The art gallery was bustling with tradespeople who wandered in and out carrying furniture, paint, lights, and tools. Rose was meticulous and accounted for everyone's activity on the team. The first order of business was to remove everything from the space, and then have the painters patch, prep, and repaint the stark white walls. Rose planned to allow a few days for the paint and prep work to be completed before reimagining the space.

Across the room, Rose caught Kris' attention and watched as he walked over to meet her.

"How are things coming along? I know it's our first full day, but it seems a lot is getting checked off the list," she asked.

"We're getting through all of today's items and should be able to get a head start on a few things from tomorrow's agenda."

"Good. That works to our advantage." Rose knew her project plan was in good hands. Kris was efficient in his work, which usually kept them ahead of schedule despite the volume.

"It's not just me. You received great recommendations when it came to the contractors here. I'd love to pack some of these men away and take them back with us," he said in a high-pitched voice.

"Hopefully not for selfish reasons," her eyebrows creased, and she offered a playful wink.

"Oh, it's *purely* work-related."

Rose shook her head. "Listen, I have one major change on paint. I'd like the third gallery painted this color." Rose handed Kris a paint card. "The rotunda and the inner room remain white."

"That's a beautiful shade of blue. What's the significance?"

"It's the color of the sky in the early evening when the edge of darkness chases away the sun. The hour you would be heading into town to the theatre."

"Whatever you're planning for that room must be special."

"It is."

Rose pointed out a few more action items for Kris, then retreated to the office to catch up on calls and emails. Exhibitions back in the states and fire drills at Ross Enterprises required her attention. If she wanted to prove herself, balancing it all was non-negotiable.

Rose looked up to see Troy headed toward her.

"How was your first evening?" he asked in a knowing voice.

"Good. Uneventful. Yours? Locate any bad actors?"

"You don't want to know the answer to that."

"You're right. I don't. Hopefully, the contractors cleared their security checks."

"All clear. Regarding the staff, do you need any of the trades to stay late?"

"Not tonight. It's early in the timeline, and everyone has been efficient, which keeps us on schedule. I sent you some emails last night."

"I received them. We're analyzing the content. I expect an update any moment."

"Always on top of things. How's Kris?"

"I thought I saw you two catching up."

"We were just covering the project plan. I meant personally. Kris wouldn't tell me how he felt if I asked."

"He seems on top of things. No jet lag that I can see. No complaints. He's getting to know some of the locals."

"And how are you?" Rose asked, knowing Troy was the one person who could handle any situation thrown his way.

"Nothing to report. I do have a question for you."

"I'm surprised. You usually have a lens into everything."

"Your answer will solve that. Kris informed me your calendar is clear tonight. What time do you think you'll wrap up at the gallery?"

"The last of the contractors will wrap up around five. It may take about fifteen minutes for them to clean up before leaving. So, everyone should be gone no later than five-thirty."

"Will you be going out for dinner tonight or staying in with your hosts?"

"I'm not sure. I missed dinner with Brianna yesterday and thought I should have at least one dinner with her this week. Let me check with her and get back to you."

"Brianna left this morning. She'll spend the rest of this week at her aunt's country home in Dublin."

"Dublin? Are you sure? Everything hinges on booking the artists. I planned to review the list with Brianna this evening before arranging the interviews. What happened?" Rose's eyes widened, and her heart started to race. She didn't like surprises or being out of the loop. As COO of a multibillion-dollar company, she was used to having a tight handle on operations.

"Due to Brianna's mobility issues, she will stay in a one-story house that will allow her to get around unassisted during her recovery. Also, her cousin is there to help. I believe she might also return home with her."

"I could tell Brianna wasn't feeling well yesterday. But the subject of her leaving didn't come up at breakfast with the brothers." Rose pinched the bridge of her nose between her thumb and forefinger. She needed to talk with the brothers to ensure they kept her apprised of Brianna's situation or anything that might impact her event. But right now, she needed to speak with Brianna.

Rose stepped passed Troy and stuck her head out the office door. "Kris," she called out.

Kris looked up and headed straight to her.

"Kris, can you get Brianna on the line? Use her mobile. If that doesn't work, call her landline. Just find a way to get a hold of her." She looked over at Troy, who pulled up his phone and texted something to Kris. "That's the family home where she's staying this week. Come get me when you reach her," Rose instructed.

"Got it. Give me a minute," Kris replied, then stepped out of the room.

Rose's face grew warm, and her heart raced. This event was important to her; she needed it to go off without a hitch. Not having complete control gave her anxiety, and this situation proved why. If Brianna was a decision maker, she needed access to her. Rose walked to the office window and then back to the door. Kris came back in.

"The number went to voicemail, and the lady who answered the house phone, Ms. Murphy, said Brianna was unavailable."

"You told them you were calling on my behalf, right?"

"Yes."

"Thanks, Kris. That's all," Rose said. Rose closed her eyes as Kris walked out.

"Rose, look at me." Troy's voice was deep and deliberate. Rose looked up at Troy. "Breathe. It's *your* event now. You got this. I suggest we stick to our usual morning security briefs during your stay. Have your conversation with the brothers if you want, but no matter what, you and I will stay on track."

Rose knew Troy was right. If Brianna wasn't available, Rose controlled everything moving forward. She had to stay on point and not get distracted. The brothers were a definitive distraction.

"Agreed. Is there anything else I need to know?" she asked, a slight irritation leaking through her words.

"Just that. So, what are you doing about dinner?"

"We're tracking slightly ahead of schedule today, so I have time to explore local restaurants, and there's a place Mia recommended I want to try out. I am assuming you'll be joining me?" She looked to Troy for a response, but his knowing look spoke volumes. "Don't give me that look. I meant, will you be *having* dinner with me?"

"I'll check with Kris to see if he would like to join us. He made some friends during happy hour at the hotel last night, so I have my suspicions he may already have plans."

"Double check with him just in case."

"It's four-thirty now. If I retrieve you around six-thirty, will that give you enough time to finish up here and get ready?"

"It should, barring any unforeseen distractions."

Troy raised an eyebrow. "Distractions? Are you having any issues with Niall? You did a good job of managing expectations with him last night. I can talk to him if you need me to."

"Freaking technology. One day I'll forget to turn that thing off, and you'll hear more than you bargained for." She barked out a laugh. "I think Niall got the message." At least Rose hoped he got the message. His smooth, flirty moves won't work on her. She was there to work, not be his next headliner. He had Marina Mack for that. "I'll see you at six-thirty, Troy. Dress up. We're going to a nice restaurant." Rose gathered her handbag and tablet, and then headed to the main house.

⚜

ROSE WALKED IN THE FRONT DOOR TO FIND THE HOUSE PLEASANTLY quiet compared to the gallery. All the day's bustling and discussions left her feeling dry, so she took a detour to the kitchen to get water before heading upstairs. The sound of her heels click-clacking across the marble floors reminded her to slip off her stilettos. Rose bent to take a shoe off. When she straightened, she almost head-butted Aedan, who had also bent down seemingly to assist her. There was no masking the sudden smile revealing her pleasant surprise. He was dressed in a dark blue suit and crisp white shirt with no tie. His hair was less tousled, but irrefutably fine.

"Em, sorry if I startled you. Let me help you with that." To her surprise, Aedan seemed a little flustered when he held out his hand, which Rose gladly took to balance herself. His hand was warm and strong. She watched as his eyes scanned the length of her body until they met hers.

"Hey. Uh, no, not startled, just thankful I didn't bust your lips with my head. That would have been embarrassing. I'm so comfortable in heels that sometimes I forget to take them off in the house." She fixed her gaze on Aedan and bent to remove the other shoe. Why was this man watching her, and why did he have to be so damn good-looking? She licked her lips, instinctively craving the cold drink of water standing before her. She was going to need some ice.

"I assumed you heard me coming down the stairs. I was just about to head to a business dinner in town. I should have mentioned it sooner, but you're welcome to join me if you don't have any dinner plans. Alternatively, Niall is having dinner at the house tonight if you decide to go that route. Just let us know."

Everything in her wanted to say yes to a delicious distraction. "No, thank you. I wouldn't want to intrude on your business plans. Besides, Troy and I are trying a restaurant a friend recommended." She bit the side of her lip. Mia taught her the trick of controlling her facial expressions to look like she was thinking, not drooling. Rose still needed to work on her technique, especially around handsome men.

"You typically eat with your bodyguard?" He gave her a tell-me-I've-got-it-wrong look.

"Troy is my security advisor. And yes. We do a lot of things together."

"No offense. Just inquiring. I'll be at the Deanes restaurant on Howard Street if you change your mind. Do you have your phone handy?"

"Yes. Can you hold this a moment?" She handed the water to Aedan before he could even respond, tucked her shoes under her arm, and retrieved the phone from her purse.

"Okay, what am I inputting?"

"My number." He rattled off his number, handed her back the water, reiterated his invitation to join him if she changed her mind, and left.

"Okay," she mouthed to herself, trying to synthesize what had transpired between them. "I'm putting you in as Mr. King," she said, typing it into her phone.

THE RESTAURANT WAS FORMAL, QUAINT, AND QUIET. ROSE'S TABLE was at the back, away from the windows, as per Troy's request. Troy was attentive but uncharacteristically quiet. She figured jet lag might be catching up to him. She thought back to the first day he took over security for her. Rose was twenty-three, and Troy was on her dad's security detail. Her father felt Rose needed a personal security advisor, and Troy demonstrated the smarts and the stamina to keep up with her. He proved himself early on when he thwarted a kidnapping attempt on her during a trip to Mexico with her father. Rose didn't know then but found out a few years later that another attempt occurred during a trip to Africa. From then on, Troy's career was on track. Nine years later, he was in sync with her every mood and movement.

The meal was simple yet flavorful. Rose watched Troy as he pushed food around the plate with his fork. "Do you like your meal?"

He forced a smile. "It's pretty good. I didn't know what to expect. How about yours?"

"Mine is good, too. You should eat that before it gets cold." She could tell he was thinking about something, but what? She wanted to probe if a real security threat was looming but decided against asking.

"I will. You should finish yours up, too," he responded.

"Although this is great, nothing compares to home cooking."

"Of course, nothing compares to home cooking, but a good restaurant will suffice."

"Speaking of home cooking, I think I might go grocery shopping tomorrow to pick up some things to make a home-cooked meal. Since we'll be here for a while, I prefer not to eat out daily."

"Let me know if you prefer to shop for yourself instead of sending someone so I can secure the area. Kris could easily pick up things on your list, which is what I'd prefer. It's best to minimize any unnecessary outings. The climate here is unstable on many fronts."

"I understand. Thirty years of civil unrest leaves residue. Let's see how the day plays out. On another topic, what's up with you? You're so quiet tonight."

"I'm good. But I'm uncomfortable with your living arrangements; you being so far from Kris and me is unusual."

"Are you having separation anxiety?" she smiled in a failed attempt to loosen him up.

"Seriously. I have a job to do. Having the proper plan in place is important. And this morning, you saw the impact of not having our early morning security brief. There is more at stake here than your event."

Rose realized Troy was right and didn't want to undermine his authority or role. "I understand what you're saying. I'll be okay. You trained me well, and although the brothers seem a little self-assured, they're certainly harmless to me. The files you gave me say they have martial arts, military, and weapons training, if that's any consolation. If my facts are correct, Aedan was in an elite special forces unit. So, between them and you, I feel like I'm in Fort Knox. What do you think?"

"I've been through the files. The brothers are partners in running several enterprises, including physical security and logistics companies, but I'm still biased toward knowing I'm the most qualified to keep you safe. They don't know a fraction of what I know about how you operate. Just the same, I have a team in rotation in the area."

"You're right. You have repeatedly proven yourself, but I think this is a low-risk assignment. Besides, the whole point of my coming here is to make a name for myself in Europe—it's not like I have accomplished that yet. Let's not overreact. How about this, I—" Her phone rang.

"I should take this."

Troy nodded.

"Hi, Aedan. I didn't expect a call from you so soon. How can I help you?"

Music and talking dominated the background, but his masculine, melodic accent rang through crystal clear above the noise. "Rose. I called to let you know that we finished dinner, so I stopped at Máire's Café and Bar for a drink. I'm checking to see if you're still in town and if you want to stop and have a drink with me before heading back. We can free Troy from needing to drive back to the house, and you and I can ride back together."

"Sounds like fun. Hold a second." Rose muted the phone.

Troy gave Rose a knowing look. "He wants you to hang out for a while in town?"

"I was about to say before the call that I promise to let you know if at any point something feels off or if anyone in the house is acting recklessly. Now, Aedan is over at a place called Máire's. He would like me to join him. You can handle the change of plans, right?"

He looked at Rose. "I disagree with this, but it's your choice if you want to meet up with him. I can send our detail over there now. My hotel is nearby if it gets too late and you just want to stay in town. Just signal and keep your tracker active. But don't think I'm not around."

"Got it. Even if I don't see you, I know you're there. The detail takes over after a certain hour. My tracker's always on, and my earpiece is in. I know the drill." She wanted to roll her eyes, but she inhaled and placed a hand on his shoulder instead.

"He has his driver, right?"

"I expect he does."

"Great, get his driver's number. I'll collect the check so we can head over." Troy signaled the waiter.

Rose could hear Aedan talking. "Rose? Are you there?"

She tapped the phone to unmute it. "Sorry for the wait. We're heading over. What's the address? By the way, can you text me your driver's phone number for Troy? He's not on board with this, which would be no surprise to you."

"Sure. Troy has nothing to worry about. Let him know my security detail is here already. He doesn't need to send anyone. It's all taken care of."

"Got it. See you in a few minutes."

"See you then."

TROY PARKED PARALLEL TO THE OLD COBBLESTONE SIDEWALK IN front of the restaurant. There was no mistaking the matte-black painted building lined with windows. A large hand-painted sign that read

Máire's Café Bar hung just above the entrance. Troy jumped out to open Rose's door before she could reach for the handle.

"From what I see, there's a large crowd inside. I'll walk you in." Troy extended a hand to help Rose. She took his hand and placed the other on his shoulder to balance herself.

"That won't be necessary. I have Ms. Ross." A melodic Irish-accented voice rang out from behind Troy.

Rose instinctively chimed in to defuse Troy, who was inherently on the defense. "Aedan, I'd like to introduce you to my chief of security, Troy."

"You're looking lovely tonight, Rose." Aedan extended a hand to her. "Nice to meet you, Troy. Sorry man, we haven't met before now. Thanks for bringing Rose here tonight. I assure you she will be in capable hands with me."

Troy responded with a nod before turning his attention back to Rose. "Signal me." He tapped his watch and monitored Rose as she walked alongside Aedan through the cafe's double doors.

Rose wasn't surprised that Aedan had already secured the best seats in the house at a booth across from the live musicians. Their table, aptly positioned, had a full view of the bar. The decor was reminiscent of her favorite absinthe bar she frequented in the states. Alcohol bottles glistened under decorative lights lining the mirror-backed shelves against the brick wall. Rose looked around to see a homogenous group of people—not that she had expected anything different. The dimly lit lounge was at maximum capacity, with lively patrons ordering stouts, chatting it up, and laughing. She could tell the band was a favorite with the crowd. She was feeling the vibe, too. Some people danced on stage, others swayed in their chairs, while some appeared to be lip-syncing along. A tall, sandy-haired man dressed in a white shirt and black slacks walked around greeting people before seeing Aedan, then proceeded to their table.

"Aedan." His Irish accent was thick. "Is this the lovely American you spoke of?" He addressed Aedan but looked at Rose.

"Rose, this is Colin. He owns this establishment. We went to secondary school together. Be careful of him. He's quite the ladies' man. Colin, Rose. She's here on business for a few weeks."

"My pleasure to meet you, Rose. Welcome to Máire's. Ignore anything Aedan tells you about me."

"Thank you. Happy to meet you, too. Don't worry. I'll take what Aedan tells me with a grain of salt. I'm sure you have some stories to share about him, too. Your lounge seems like a popular spot, and the band is on point."

"Smart lady." Colin gave Aedan a sideways glance, then turned to Rose. "We have a steady crowd of regulars. And the band, well the lead singer is another mate of ours. Is this your first trip to Belfast?"

"First to Ireland in general."

"Well, I hope you get a chance to take in more of the scene. What are you two drinking tonight?"

"We'll have two Manhattans if the lady doesn't mind," Aedan nodded in Rose's direction.

"Actually, I'll have sparkling water. I try to avoid drinking on work nights."

"Brilliant. Rose, if there is anything you need, don't hesitate to ask. Enjoy yourself, and I hope to see more of you during your stay." He nodded and then went to the bar to place their order.

"Manhattan? You researched me. If it were anyone else, I'd be creeped out but seeing it's your line of work, I'll give you credit for uncovering this detail about me."

"You keeping score? I'm just trying to learn more about the lady who will be occupying my sister's home for thirty days. Em, like you didn't look me up."

She was learning to interpret his speech and could tell he used *em* when he talked fast or got flustered.

"Touché."

"I didn't realize you weren't drinking; I shouldn't have assumed. Are you okay with all this?" He looked over his shoulder.

Rose looked around and shrugged. "This place? It has a good vibe."

"This, meaning me inviting you out tonight. I caught up with my brother today. He said you seemed focused on the exhibition. I thought you might want a break from work this evening."

"He's right. I am focused on the exhibition. That's the only reason I'm in Belfast. But to answer your question, I had a nice evening out with Troy. Although, this sudden change of plans didn't sit well with him. And, about your brother, I thought I cleared things up with him this morning." She pursed her lips, not knowing what direction Aedan intended to take the conversation.

"Honestly, I'm a little perplexed why Troy is so worried. You heard Colin. Most of the folks here are regulars. I doubt there's a safer place than having me by your side."

Rose could tell Aedan was used to stating his opinion and having others follow along with it. Running a multi-billion dollar company, she wasn't used to following anyone's lead.

I can see you're not short on hubris, is what she wanted to say, but instead, she said, "I can appreciate your perspective, Aedan. But Troy has legitimate concerns. There have been a few kidnapping attempts in the past."

"That's an awful situation to be in. I suspected as much, but don't think I'm not discounting your safety. Be rest assured, Niall and I got this. Is there something more there between you and Troy?"

Rose coughed to choke back a laugh. "You and I don't know each other like that." She sat back in her chair, locked his gaze, and waited for his response. His prettiness was about to wear off, along with her patience.

Before Aedan could speak, Colin returned to the table with two drinks. Aedan gestured to him to serve Rose first. He placed a coaster down in front of Rose, put a glass on top, then repeated the same for Aedan. Rose smiled up at Colin. Aedan glanced between the two.

"I don't remember you ever serving me directly. You usually send your staff over for that," Aedan quipped.

"You're not as beautiful as Rose. Speaking of, is there anything else I can get you, Rose? We have quite the selection of small plates."

"I think we're good for now. Thank you," Rose answered.

Colin placed a menu on the table and then turned to Aedan. "I'll be back to check on you two." Aedan shook his head at Colin. Rose watched on as Aedan and Colin passed knowing looks between each other before Colin left.

"Don't fault Colin for being so smooth. You could take some lessons. I'm still waiting for your response." Rose took a sip of her water.

"You're right. I don't know you like that. However, the situation does happen. Niall and I always coach our teams about not falling for their clients. But I've overstepped. I'll let the question go, though. Forget I ever asked it," he said with a small smile. "Are you comfortable staying at the house?"

"Assuming you're referring to last night and the fact that I didn't sleep in my room. I don't know what that was. Clearly, I was exhausted. But yes, the house is great."

"You seemed quite peaceful last night."

Her eyebrow raised. "So, the elusive Aedan made an appearance while I was sleeping. The slippers, I assume that was you?"

"I can't take full credit. Brianna suggested it before she left this morning."

"Brianna?"

"Yes, she said something about women and their heels and giving your feet a soft place to land."

Rose shook her head and rolled her eyes. "Oh great, on top of it all, I had an audience unbeknownst to me. Was I snoring?"

"Don't worry. In case you're interested, there was no audience, no snoring, and no drooling." The slight curve of his lips revealed the hint of a smile.

Rose sipped her drink like water would wash away the awkwardness. "Thanks. On the topic of Brianna…I learned from Troy that she left this morning. Frankly, I was surprised the subject didn't come up during breakfast. Maybe we can use breakfast for morning briefs before we head our separate ways."

"You are all business."

"I'm here on business."

"That's my fault. I should have said something before you left for work. It's a family thing, and I need to remind myself that you're here doing important work on her behalf. Morning briefs sound good." Aedan sipped his drink. His cell phone vibrated on the table and lit up with the letters *AJ*. Rose watched as he picked it up, turned it off, and slid it into his pocket.

"Sorry about that."

"You can take that if you need to."

Aedan shook his head in response. "On a positive note, the fact that you're curating this show for Brianna is the one thing I've seen lift her spirits since my brother-in-law's passing."

"We share a passion—" She paused when Colin walked over to the table carrying a bowl of thinly sliced deep-fried mushrooms.

"I thought you two might want something tasty to snack on with your drinks. Can I get you something else from the menu?" They both shook their heads. "Signal me if you need anything." Colin looked at Rose, and she smiled at him. His gaze stayed fixed on her as he serviced the table behind Aedan. *And there's the ladies' man*, she thought to herself.

Aedan took a sip from his glass, then looked at Rose. "You know Colin was right earlier. You should take time to get to know our beautiful country during your stay. I understand you're focused on your event, but you can take a break to tour. After all, you've come a long way."

"I'll think about it."

"Well, I hope you make time. Also, if there is anything you want to see or do—"

"I know. You and Niall will make yourselves available. Aren't you both busy running your companies? It is plural, right?"

He nodded.

"Then I wouldn't want to impose on you."

"You wouldn't be imposing. It's a benefit of running my own company. I have the luxury of setting my schedule. Besides, there's no one better than one of us to show you around. But you probably know that about me already."

"You're in the business of being elusive. I only know what you want people to know about you." She took a bite of a mushroom chip. "Oh, that's good. Try one." She slid the bowl closer to him.

"Is there something you want to know?" He popped a chip in his mouth. "You're right. These are great. Colin's been holding back on me."

"Nothing at the moment. I'm content enjoying the rest of the evening, drinking and eating these chips. Although you could clarify one thing."

"Anything. But first, I just want to clarify that we refer to chips as crisps."

Rose couldn't help but laugh. "Sorry, *crisps*. Now, two things, actually. Are you coming to the exhibition? I'm only asking because I didn't see your name on Brianna's guest list. And why do they call them crisps?"

"I never miss Brianna's annual show. You can put me down for a ticket. You have attracted quite an impressive lineup of people slated to attend. And I have no idea why they're called crisps. Maybe because they're made differently here. Ours are thinner than the American version."

Rose clinked Aedan's glass with hers. As arrogant as he was, she was surprised to find herself secretly relieved there was no one Aedan deemed worthy of bringing to such a prestigious event. "To Belfast. To Art."

"May I?" He held up his glass.

She nodded.

"This is how you toast in Ireland. May your Guardian Angel be at your side to pick ya up off the floor and hand ya another cold stout from the store. Sláinte, Rose." The heaviness of his Irish accent was in full force.

"And there you have it. Sláinte."

Rose reached her hand across the table to clink glasses with Aedan again.

A sudden movement near the dance floor caught her eye. From her limited view, a man tripped or stumbled onto the dance floor. Rose couldn't make out which. A guy in a black suit seated at the bar immediately reached for the falling guy and helped him up. They appeared to exchange words, then the black-suited guy escorted the other man back to his seat. "Did he pat him down?" Rose asked herself. She caught a brief glimpse of the black-suited man's gaze before he sat back down at the bar.

"Rose." Aedan's voice pulled her attention back to the table. When she looked at him, he nodded his head toward her phone, which displayed a picture of the painting *Young Acrobat on a Ball* with the letters MOS overlaid in white block lettering. The image depicted a young girl balancing on a large ball in a traveling circus. At the same time, a muscular male acrobat looked on attentively in the foreground, which was her tongue-in-cheek interpretation of her relationship with Troy. Rose tapped the screen to make the image disappear, clearing Troy's signal that he and his team had eyes on her. She knew Aedan did not pick up on the private message, but she had her answer. The man in the black suit *did* pat down the man who fell.

"Do you need to get that?" Aedan inquired.

She shook her head. "It's just an app notification."

"May I ask you something I couldn't uncover via research?" he continued.

"Sure."

"I'm curious. Why did you come here?" he asked.

"Is this a trick question?"

"No."

"You mean like here, here?" she pointed down. "I thought we covered all that. When you invited me, it seemed like a good idea. I figured you would be good company." Rose knew that the situation would have been very different if she were back in the states. She had given up the idea of leisure outings with friends, not to mention the prospect of dating. Instead, her schedule was a delicate balancing act of speaker engagements for her dad's company, rushing to kick off an event she was curating, or putting in appearances at charity events. But for now, Rose was thousands of miles away from all that.

He raised an eyebrow, catching her gaze. His eyes revealed everything she already knew before he spoke. Her dad had the same question. "You know what I mean. Here in Ireland."

"You know my story."

"I do. But it feels like there's more. From all accounts of what I know, you are a premier art dealer and an award-winning curator. I mean, making the Power 100 list is no small feat. It sounds like you want something more."

"Not quite. I want to be the best, to snag one of the top three spots on the list. It will serve as global acknowledgment. I want to be known for transforming people's lives through art. I truly appreciate art, unlike those hoarding priceless paintings in a garage waiting for the value to go up. I help represent art so the masses can access and appreciate it. I breathe life and give voice to the stories that most dare to whisper. That is why your sister invited me here and why I came."

"What about Rick Ross Enterprises? It's one of the largest companies in the world. You realize that you'll have to choose one or the other at some point, or have little time left for yourself."

Rose sipped her drink, pursed her lips, and summed up her life. "My passion lies in art, and I have less than thirty days to cement *my* name as the best in the industry or commit to being the face of the company bearing someone else's name."

"It's clear you can handle both, which is what's got you to this point, but you need balance."

"And by balance you mean a personal life."

"It's something to consider. But I'll drop it. Let's toast. Here's to a successful thirty days." Aedan raised his glass, took a sip, and leaned back in his chair.

She smiled and lifted her glass. "Here's to thirty days in Belfast. And to all the newness it brings. Sláinte"

"Sláinte."

"You ready to head out? We can stay longer if you want."

"I have a lot to get done. Let's call it."

Aedan stood and offered his hand to help Rose up from her chair. The car was already waiting when they walked from their table to the front door. He opened the car door, helped her inside, and sat beside her.

"I had a nice time tonight, Rose. It would be nice if we could do this again."

"I had a good time, too. If the invitation is still open for touring, I'd like to take you up on that." Rose stiffened and leaned back in her seat when she realized what she had done. She had opened the door to a distraction.

CHAPTER 5

Unthinkable

"There is a charm about the forbidden
that makes it unspeakably desirable."

— MARK TWAIN

Rose woke to sun rays spying past silk curtain panels to warm her face. She lingered in the bed for a moment, appreciating the stillness in the air. Her mind wandered. She thought about everything on her plate—the event, the board appointment, and Brianna's health. Was she recovering? How would Brianna feel about the recent changes to the exhibition? Rose retrieved her phone from the bedside table and set a reminder to call Brianna. Coincidentally, her phone vibrated. It was a text message from Troy telling her he was downstairs, signaling the start of a new workday. Rose gave herself a morning pep talk, bounced out of bed, and headed for the shower.

She felt surprisingly good following last night's drinks with Aedan. Thoughts of their conversation swirled like confetti in her head. Although the prospect of a casual relationship was looming, she was conflicted. Rose had been down this path before. No matter how lovely the distraction, goals and guys didn't mix well.

After a hot shower, Rose grabbed her stuff and headed down for breakfast, not knowing what to expect. As she neared the kitchen, the familiar smells of coffee and cinnamon greeted her once more. She was not surprised to see Niall standing at the coffee bar, coffee in hand, looking handsome in dark blue business slacks and his signature white button-down shirt.

"Good morning, Niall. You're pretty consistent, I see." She walked over to the counter towards him.

"Here's my Night owl. May I pour you some coffee?" He held up his cup.

"Sure." She glanced around the room. "Is your brother joining us this morning?"

"No, he left a while ago. He should be at the office by now. He mentioned something about staying in the city a few days, but he'll be here Friday." Niall got an empty cup, filled it with coffee, then handed it to Rose.

"I suppose he has a busy schedule," she said as if talking about the weather.

"Client obligations. Were you expecting him for breakfast?" Niall leaned his hip against the counter and watched Rose. She knew by the slight tilt of his head and curious gaze that he was reading her face.

"No. Just curious." Rose sipped her coffee, hiding her disappointment.

"He mentioned you joined him for drinks last night."

"We met up after dinner. Aedan said he wanted to get to know the person proxying for his sister."

"That's understandable. We both do, for different reasons. He's a little guarded—he sees himself as the family protector. We're both like

69

that, but enough talk about us. Are you hungry? Breakfast is hot." He nodded in the direction of the stove.

"I want whatever smells like cinnamon."

"I wish I could lay claim to that bit, but it happens to be buns in the basket on the counter. Lift the cloth and help yourself."

"There are a lot of pans here, but I didn't see any staff around. Tell me you didn't get up to cook." Rose intentionally ignored his comment and seductive smile. She lifted the lid to a blue pan containing a vegetarian omelet, then opened another, revealing pan-fried potatoes.

"I can cook if I need to. But no, I didn't cook this. I had my favorite restaurant prepare it. I gave the house staff the morning off, so I had this made for you."

Rose was surprised Niall took the time to make special arrangements for her. She wondered whether this was how he typically behaved for guests or solely for her benefit. Or were these compliments of chef Marina Mack?

"This was nice of you. I wasn't sure what to expect this morning."

"Usually, I have something simple to grab and go in the morning. But I figured you'd be hungry."

"Light eater?"

"At least for breakfast. But don't let that fool you. With the type of workouts that I maintain, I need to get my carbs in."

"What kind of workouts are you doing?"

Niall's lips turned up in a wry grin. "I'm not sure how you want me to answer that."

"I was just thinking that I wouldn't mind joining you if—" Rose paused, realizing by Niall's ever-widening grin that he was reading a different narrative into her words. She certainly wasn't interested in his celebrity trysts. On the contrary, she was trying to avoid becoming one. Rose put her index finger up, attempting to regain control of the conversation. "I meant that if you are doing any combat sports routines, I would like to join you. Troy makes me train several days a week. It could be interesting to train with someone else. That is, if you're not afraid." Now she was sporting a wry grin.

"Afraid? Maybe for you. But if you think you can handle me, you're on. Would you be up for Muay Thai?"

"Normally, I would say yes to Muay Thai, but I only recently recovered from all the bruising from my sessions last month. I don't want to risk the bad press showing up to the exhibition looking like I lost a fight. But we can do kickboxing instead. That is, if you have time and know a place with equipment. I brought my protective gear with me."

"I'll make the time."

"Well, if you can make it work, let's plan on two days a week in the city after work."

"There's a gym on the ground floor of my building with all the equipment we'll need. I can't wait to see what you got."

"You live in an apartment building?" Rose asked as she walked to the counter where the cinnamon buns were. She placed her cup down and then proceeded to break off a piece of pastry, popping it into her mouth and letting the flavors dance on her tongue.

"Loft," Niall corrected.

Rose stopped mid-chew and looked up at him.

"Seems by that look you've formulated some opinions about me. Care to fill me in on what's happening in that beautiful head of yours?"

"You don't seem like the domesticated type—you know, grocery shop, wash clothes, mow the lawn, do house repairs—that kind of stuff.

71

And I didn't quite peg you embracing the apartment life either. Not with all those strangers milling around. Running a security company and all."

"A big showy house with a circular driveway is not my thing if that's what you're getting at. And no, I don't grocery shop. I pay someone for that. But you're right about my focus on security. Would it satisfy your curiosity to know I own the building? There are only a few units, and I've thoroughly screened the occupants."

"That seems more like what I'd expect. I'm not off track after all."

"If we're done analyzing me, what's happening with you? I know it's only been two days, but how's the planning going?"

"Initially, I was a little freaked out when I realized your sister wouldn't be here."

"Yes, that's unfortunate. My cousin may have influenced that sudden move. But I'm sure you have things under control."

"Surprisingly, we accomplished a lot yesterday, putting us ahead of plan by a few days. I'm beginning my artist interviews to gather material to create my concept. I'm oversimplifying to keep from boring you."

"You could never bore me. Watching you move seamlessly between topics is fascinating. One second, you're talking about curating art, the next business, and martial arts. Besides, although I've supported some aspects of my sister's exhibitions, my schedule prevented me from involving myself in the day-to-day planning, so I don't know all that goes on behind the scenes. I'm looking forward to seeing your final production."

"We're just getting started." Rose went to the cupboard and opened and closed a few cabinet drawers until she located utensils to cut the omelet. She glanced over her shoulder to find Niall still watching her.

72

She plated half an omelet and brought it to the counter, where she sat facing him. "This is good."

Niall was still leaning on the coffee bar counter, his long legs crossed and stretched in front of him. He was thoughtful and handsome. It was hard not to get caught up in his looks, and although she had the best view in the house, she wasn't about to get caught up in his charm.

"These guys do a good job." Niall lifted his chin in Rose's direction, wearing an I'm-secretly-enjoying-the-view smile.

Rose realized that even though she previously rebuffed him, Niall was undeterred. She had caught his eye. He wanted to get to know her better, and she was not mad at him for that.

Rose studied Niall's face for a few seconds, trying to imagine what he was thinking while she pieced together the differences between him and his brother. Although he was neat and clean-shaven, he seemed somehow more relaxed than his brother in his mannerisms and communication style. He also exuded a subtle natural air of self-confidence. Who else would sit comfortably in silence with her? On the other hand, Aedan's mannerisms were more pronounced, and when he walked into a room—one hand in his pocket—his presence filled the space and commanded attention. She felt a little weak at the thought of how distinguished Aedan looked last night in his suit when he greeted her. The strength in his muscles when he accidentally bumped into her before he left the house. The command in his voice when he had her input his number. *Ugh,* she mumbled to herself. Rose needed to clear her head. She didn't come to Belfast for distractions, yet it was what she felt. Distracted.

Niall's lips moved, and his smooth, silky, accented voice stopped her train of thought.

"Rose, since my brother is in the city for the next few days, I'll be back here in the evening after work. I can take you to dinner tonight if you prefer to eat out, or we can have the staff cook something and eat in. I don't want you to feel stuck here by yourself. It's your decision, and I'm happy to take the reins. Also, I'll have the staff make us both a traditional breakfast to eat in the morning. They can have it ready by seven-thirty when you usually head down. Sound good?" He drank the last sip of his coffee and placed it on the counter.

Rose could tell by how he uncrossed his legs and stood straight that he was about to head out for the day. "You may not have guessed, but I'm not the type to surround myself with staff at home. I'm used to preparing my own meals, so I thought I'd whip up something for dinner tonight. Troy can take me shopping to pick up a few things to prepare for dinner. I'll cook for us both if you don't mind."

"You're our guest. I'd never suggest that."

"It's no big deal. I told you, I usually cook for myself at home. I'm not one for eating out when I don't have to. Cooking calms me and lets me express my creativity."

"You sure you don't mind?"

"Not at all. Any food preferences?" She made a mental note to remind Troy of her shopping plans.

"I don't have food allergies, but I'm a vegetarian. So is Aedan, although he won't be here tonight. I thought you should know, in case he didn't mention it to you."

"Noted."

"Great. See you tonight." Niall reached out, placing a hand on her shoulder before heading down the hallway towards the front door.

"Tonight," she echoed.

74

Gallery updates continued ahead of schedule. Trade's people flowed in and out of the space like water around rocks in a stream. Rose was a master curator. She had her hands in everything from paint touch-ups to digitally mapping out potential art placement. She curated her art like she curated her life, travel, and wardrobe, carefully selecting everything for an emotional impact. Rose saw herself as a music conductor, finessing and enhancing the greatness of everything she touched. The real testament to her success would come on the day of the art show. It would be the apogee of weeks of hard work.

But for now, the clock was ticking. Vibrant orange hues of sunlight trickled through the office window, signaling the end of the day was near, but she had a few things left on her list to accomplish. Rose went into the main gallery to find Kris.

"Hi, Kris. Are you almost done for the day?" Kris took his job seriously and was all work all the time when on a project. She needed to prioritize additional work and assign some items to him.

"Just finishing up here. How can I help?"

"I emailed you a list of people I'd like to speak with over the next few days. Most are Black benefactors. I'd like to ensure they receive highlights about the art before the exhibition. I included everyone's availability, so you shouldn't have trouble nailing down the schedule. For anyone back in the states, you might have to push them out a day. I've got dinner plans tonight. I'll keep the call with Dad. But feel free to load up my calendar with the others tomorrow. Also, can you arrange for me to have lunch next week with Kaleb Pierce? He finally agreed to meet me." Rose gave Kris the rundown on Kaleb, explaining his history as a local Black artist, including his rise, fall, and resurgence as an artist, and articulating his work's importance as it translated to the exhibition.

She could tell by the intense attention Kris gave her that he was impressed but not surprised by her knowledge. It was her modus operandi to study everyone as if she were preparing for an exam.

"Sure, consider it done. Are you heading out now?"

"Yes, can you close for me here? I need to get to the market." Thoughts of recipes floated through her head, drowning out her anxiety about cooking for Niall. She had no idea what Niall's favorite dish was or why she felt nervous about cooking. Maybe it was because she hadn't cooked for any man except her Dad and, occasionally, Troy. Any man she had dated usually opted for dinner at a restaurant.

"Of course. Enjoy," Kris said, then went about his work.

Rose hoped Niall didn't see this as a date. They were to have dinner and nothing more. Possibly take some time to get to know each other since their paths were bound to cross daily for the next month. She could also formally apologize for being so curt her first day. At least, that was her plan. Rose began to second guess herself, which she recognized as a symptom of being distracted.

⚘

FRUIT AND VEGETABLES OF EVERY RAINBOW COLOR FILLED BINS AT THE market. An assortment of vegetables tempted their way into her shopping basket, like potatoes, kale, several mushroom varietals, strawberries, cabbage, onions, and carrots, to name a few. Rose could not keep herself from picking items to touch, squeeze, and smell. The market was her muse as a recipe for tonight's dinner began to formulate in her mind.

"I think I got it," she announced to Troy and tossed a few more items into the cart.

"You decided what you were going to cook?"

"It's a spin on a meal I had at dinner last month in San Francisco," she remarked, sounding pleased with herself as they headed towards the register.

Troy scanned the area while Rose placed items on the rolling platform as she described her version of a fish dish reimagined with vegetables. She was getting hungry just telling him about the shitake mushrooms and onions sautéed in butter, truffle oil, and seasonings. "Instead of fish, I'll use a thick slice of Portobello mushroom over the whipped potatoes," Rose said.

"That sounds delicious. I don't think I'll be having anything quite comparable to mushrooms in truffle sauce."

Troy probed her about her meal on the return drive home. She was unsure what he thought about the whole situation and whether she wanted to open that can of worms with him. She reflected on the discussion she had with Aedan the previous night. Was there really anything unusual about her relationship with Troy? Thinking back, she was more relaxed with him compared to how restrained she behaved around her former advisor. Her previous advisor typically stood a few feet away to either side or behind her. It was different with Troy. She tended to link her arm around his when he escorted her around. And besides Kris, Troy was the only other team member she shared regular meals with outside of company events. Maybe she felt more comfortable with him because they were closer in age. Could her behavior be misconstrued? Rose had to remind herself to keep it all in perspective and keep Troy focused.

"Troy, did you notice all the attention we were drawing at the market?"

"I did."

Despite the stares in every aisle they went, they did not let the atmosphere detract them from their mission, nor did they dwell on the topic beyond those few words. Rose was quickly able to brush off the vibe because she traveled so often that being one of a kind was second nature. She knew she had Troy and getting past him to her was almost impossible. Instead, she recognized this was an excellent opportunity to shift the narrative via her work curating the upcoming exhibition and ensuring that Blacks were seen positively in the country.

"Thanks for helping me this afternoon. By the way, I'm supposed to see some sights with Aedan on Friday. He hasn't given me the details, but we'll be away in Dublin for the weekend. Although he suggested that he would be my personal security, I know that won't fly with you, and rightly so. But if you can get all the details and work it out with him, that would be great." She deliberately looked at Troy. Rose could tell by the slight narrowing of his eyes there was a hint of irritation behind his otherwise untouchable mask.

"You want me to follow?"

"I could play naïve and say don't go at all, but that's not what I'm asking."

"I'm not going to ask if you are certain about going because I know what you'll say. But I am going to insist you keep your tracker activated. I may need to return slightly ahead of you on Sunday, so someone will ride back with you—that's non-negotiable. And yes, I will get all the details from Aedan directly. I'll be following, but by no means will I be stealthy."

"I guess that's pretty much impossible for both of us in Ireland when you think about it," she smiled, attempting to lighten the mood.

The wrinkle in Troy's brow eased as she outlined their schedule for the remainder of the week. She knew Troy needed to feel in control of his domain and did her best to ensure he did.

Her goal was to get him over the hurdle of the next two days, knowing that Niall would be hanging around during the evenings while the rest of his siblings were away. She would also have to keep herself in check when she thought about it. Following her last serious relationship, Rose hadn't taken up with anyone—just a few mutual one-night stands here and there. Anything further, she initiated on her terms. She liked her sexual freedom and the ability to choose who she was with and when with no attachments. But she also wondered if she would ever acquiesce to wanting something more.

"We need to stick to our routine," Troy urged, pulling Rose out of her head.

"Don't stress, Troy. Over the next few days, you and I will be inseparable. Kris has me booked solid between work at the gallery and meetings in town."

"He got through the recent list you gave him?" Troy asked.

"Yes. Check your phone. Kris sent the final schedule while we were on the road. I'm booked through the end of Thursday and well into next week. I'm super excited I landed lunch with Kaleb Pierce. Afterward, I have a meeting with Kamal. He agreed to be our MC for the event."

"Sounds like a big deal, but I'm not surprised. You typically collaborate with some of the most important people."

"It is." She reflected on Troy's statement. Seeing her life through his lens gave her perspective. Troy was right. Few people, if any, declined a meeting with her. But Rose wanted to make sure it was a byproduct of her work, and not because she was the daughter of Rick Ross.

"And what about this weekend with Aedan? It seems sudden and unexpected."

"A spontaneous decision. I surprised myself." A surprise was the understatement of the day. She struggled to understand it. To understand her newfound need to have an emotional connection with someone after being single for so long. Being emotionally vulnerable was unfamiliar to her, and not something she took lightly.

The last person she dated was on her father's payroll. She thought about how much time she invested in making that relationship work, only to see it conclude following a conversation about goals and priorities. She never told anyone how disappointed that experience left her. Disappointed that she couldn't make time to simultaneously build her career and pursue a relationship. Disappointed in being distracted. Disappointed that someone else had taken control of a conversation she should have sensed coming. The loss she felt following her last breakup kept her from forming relationships with men who wanted more. Rose was committed to controlling the narrative in every aspect of her life. Caution would hover over her like a storm cloud for the next few weeks. She looked over at Troy, who had just shut the engine off and was halfway out of the car. Caution was an everyday event for him.

"Troy, about tonight..."

Troy got out of the car, helped Rose, and grabbed a bag of groceries. The house was dark and empty. Troy entered first, turned on the lights, did his check, then gestured for Rose to join him.

"What about tonight?"

"What—" she paused, deciding whether to ask her question, then reached her free hand down to slip off her heels instead.

"Did you need help with that?" Troy asked.

"No. I was about to ask—" Rose hesitated again. "What is your impression of Niall?"

"Are you asking me to help you with a risk assessment, or is this personal?"

"You wouldn't allow me to live in the same house with the man or any person if there were risks, and I certainly wouldn't be about to cook dinner for him."

"It's not my place to advise you on personal matters."

"Troy, I'm asking."

"If you must know my thoughts, then fine. I believe Niall is self-assured and clearly interested in you. I don't know enough about him personally to assess how he handled your initial rebuff. It was a cunning move on his part to back off. If he's smart, he'll wait for you to make the next move."

"I think he backed off because I made my intentions clear. I didn't offer up dinner for him to understand it as me making the next move." Rose placed the bag she had on the counter and started removing items. She nodded in the direction of the counter, signaling Troy to do the same.

"I don't have to tell you that you're that rare unicorn that men like Niall—and I suspect Aedan—have been searching for. You have also been searching for the same qualities in a man from what I have witnessed. But you don't need me to state the obvious. They're both playing for your hand. They have drawn you into the game if you haven't realized it by now."

"Sounds like you have given this some thought."

"My job is to monitor, assess, and analyze every move someone makes who's taken an interest in you. Yesterday 12,562 people attempted to contact or research you in some capacity. Thirty-five of those people are in Ireland right now. I know where every one of them is within an inch of proximity to you every second of the day, twenty-four hours a day. So, yes, you can say I have given every move you make plenty of thought." Rose's eyes widened like saucers in response to Troy's words. She unintentionally pushed the button she previously tried to avoid. Rose didn't want to know the inner workings of his job. She didn't want to be paralyzed by fear of what-ifs.

"I'm not sure how to respond to that, Troy."

"Don't. You asked my opinion. Since you asked, I think anything related to the brothers is a distraction. I wouldn't want you to lose sight of why we're here."

Rose felt a mix of emotions. She was surprised and slightly annoyed by Troy's response. Did she want to know what he was holding back from his monologue? Should she be concerned about those thirty-five people? She hated to admit that he was right about distractions. The brothers were distractions in every sense of the word, and she needed to regain focus.

"So, needless to say, you think I'm sending the wrong message having dinner alone with Niall? Have you forgotten how many meals you and I shared? This is not a date."

"My role is to keep you safe so you can focus on your work. Only you can decide what you want from Niall. I think dinner alone with him could be misconstrued. Niall made his intentions known in more ways than one, and tonight provides him a prime opportunity to act on his intentions. And what was the situation with Aedan last night?"

"Aedan and I had drinks—that's all. And I don't anticipate having anything more with Niall than dinner."

"Sounds like you made your decision."

"I can handle Niall and Aedan, for that matter." Rose had heard enough. It wasn't a conversation she wanted to have with Troy. It was equivalent to talking about sex with your brother. She poured out the remainder of the grocery bag's contents on the kitchen counter and started sorting things by order in which she planned to use them. Anything which required refrigeration, she put away accordingly.

"You have great instincts and don't need a lecture from me. You have parents for that."

"I know this is your attempt to avoid saying aloud that you think this guy only wants to get in my pants, and Niall may be under the impression that I'm leading him there."

Troy looked at Rose and pursed his lips.

"Don't worry, Troy. I can handle Niall."

"I'm here if you need me."

"You'll be happy to know that despite any resistance you're getting from me, that is the one thing that gives me peace of mind." The corners of Troy's lips curved slightly, which was rare for her to see. Rose smiled in return, allowing it to cut the cord of tension between them.

The sudden sounds of tires on gravel coming from outside caught their attention. Troy's half-formed smile disappeared.

"I'll be here through midnight, then the team takes over," he outlined.

"Understood. Thanks again, Troy. I'll see you in the morning." She placed a hand on his shoulder, which relaxed beneath her touch.

"No problem." Troy headed out just as Niall reached the landing.

"How's it going, man?" Troy lifted his chin to Niall.

"Good. Long day, but good," Niall responded.

Troy nodded and went outside.

Niall stopped in the kitchen to say hi to Rose and inform her that he had more work to complete before dinner, but offered a helping hand if needed. Rose had things under control and agreed to get him if she needed him.

Rose started prepping dinner; slicing mushrooms and cutting potatoes was a welcome distraction for Rose. The intricacies of cooking helped clear her head of the never-ending exhibition checklist that occupied her thoughts. When she was done prepping, she put things away in their proper place so she could do the final fixing after she dressed.

⚘

WARM, PUFFY, WHITE SUDS FLOWED DOWN ROSE'S CARAMEL-COLORED skin, and she breathed a sigh of relief as she attempted to wash away the pressures of the day. Now, all she wanted to do was eat, drink, and have a relaxing evening on her third day in Belfast. As she got ready, she allowed each movement to ritualistically strip away any thoughts of work, art, and decisions she had yet to make. Effortless was the look she aimed for as she readied herself for the evening. Instead of makeup, she used tinted moisturizer on her face and tinted gloss to highlight her full lips. A few strokes of mascara were all she needed to frame her almond-shaped eyes. She hated dealing with her hair. The impact of mixed races on both sides of her family left her with hair that was neither straight nor super curly, but rather long in tight waves. So, she finger-combed through the thick hand-formed ringlet in her hair—compliments of all her expensive hair products. Rose slipped into a black strapless bra to give her some shape before topping it with a simple black silk slip dress that fell right above her knees, highlighting the results of her consistent workouts. She was happy to be back in her sleeveless dresses now that the last vestiges of martial arts workouts had faded. It was warm, so she put on silk underwear. The final order of business was to slip into a pair of black, four-inch heeled, strappy sandals. She never went anywhere without a pair of heels. Her days were spent living in a man's world, competing with men. Rose wanted people to accept her on her own terms, and she was a woman who liked to look like a woman.

Fully dressed, Rose stood in front of the mirror for one last look before heading downstairs to finalize the meal. The vegetables only took a few minutes to reheat, thanks to her pre-prep. Now, all she needed was her dinner companion.

A knock at Niall's door was Rose's indication that dinner was ready. Although only an hour had passed since he came home, she imagined he was feeling famished. Niall stood in the doorway, looking Rose up and down with a wide, hungry grin.

"You look absolutely stunning, and you smell perfectly delicious," Niall said, enunciating every word.

Rose smiled. "Thank you. I'm heading down now to get our plates ready if you care to join me. I held off on making the sauce, but that'll only take a minute."

"I'm hungry. Lead the way." Niall gestured toward the stairwell. She could feel the intense heat from his eyes on her back as she descended the stairs with him in tow. Closer to the kitchen, savory scents permeated the air.

"Have a seat, and I'll get things ready." She went to the counter and turned on a saucepan with butter.

"Let me help." Niall stood so close to her she could feel the warmth radiating from his body. His scent—a mix of cardamom and plum—mingled in the air amongst the savory smells of her cooking, making her mouth water. Making her hungry for something other than vegetables. Hungry for a man that wasn't hers to want.

"Okay, then. Hand me that flour and truffle oil, and you can use this spoon to place a few scoops of potatoes on each plate." Rose laid a spoon near Niall and took the flour from him. She measured out a few teaspoons into a small bowl, and looked up to find Niall watching her with his one eyebrow raised.

"What?" she asked.

"Um, is that supposed to be doing that?" Niall gestured to the pan with butter, which was beginning to smoke.

"Oh my god. No," Rose exclaimed as the smoke alarm started to sound. Niall grabbed a potholder and fanned the ceiling alarm until it stopped beeping. Rose took the pan off the flame and put a lid on it to suppress the smoke. This was not how she expected dinner to go. She could feel her face grow warm, and her heart started to race. She needed to work fast to recover dinner, knowing Niall was watching. "I can fix this," Rose said and began moving things around the counter until she felt a hand on hers.

"Hey, look at me. It's not a big deal." Niall's voice was calm and low. Rose looked up to Niall. "Follow my lead and time your breaths to mine." Niall inhaled slowly, then expelled a deep breath. Rose followed suit. "That's it," he said, then released her hand.

"Thanks, Niall."

Niall grabbed a new pan from the cupboard. "I'll start the sauce, and you can hand me the ingredients, and we'll do this together."

Rose gathered up all the ingredients and handed them to Niall in order. "You don't have to do this."

"I want to. I don't mind cooking. I just don't do it often. Okay, hardly ever," he quipped.

"Like you said this morning, you can pay people for that."

"I suppose. Now, talk to me about this craving you have for keeping everything perfectly in order and under control. I saw that on your first day." While Niall waited for Rose's answer, she poured some truffle oil over the butter in the pan and added a few sprinkles of flour as Niall whisked the ingredients together.

"I feel anxious if things aren't going as planned. Maybe I'm a control freak. I don't know. I think the sauce is ready." Rose pointed to the pan.

Niall stopped stirring, turned off the pan, and turned to Rose. "I didn't phrase it like that, but I can see you don't want to talk about it. Maybe another day. For now, let's get dinner on the table. How'd I do?" Niall put a little sauce on the spoon, blew on it to cool it down, and offered Rose to taste it.

"For someone who doesn't cook, you did great. Now, let's see if you can complete the dish. Start with the potatoes, layer the veggies over, and I'll drizzle the sauce."

Niall took the spoon and placed two even-sized portions of whipped potatoes on each plate, then mushrooms and onions on top. When he finished, he slid the dishes to Rose to add the sauce, then leaned against the counter and watched her. She felt the strength of his stare as she ladled on the sauce. If watching her was his thing, then she would have to adapt. She couldn't remember any man watching her prepare a meal except Troy when he arrived at her house early to escort her somewhere. "I need to eat before I go, so you may as well have something while you're here," she would demand. Then, Troy would patiently wait for her to finish whatever she was preparing.

"Voilà. Let's dig in." She placed both plates on the table, and they sat down to eat across from one another.

"This looks and smells amazing." Niall cut a piece of the Portobello, scooped up some potatoes in the truffle sauce, and took his first bite. "And it tastes amazing. We make a great team."

"I'm grateful for the help." She took a bite of her meal. "This is good. I didn't know what to expect. It's my first time making this." Rose described the original dish she reinterpreted as Niall ate.

"It's brilliant. You're racking up the titles. Businesswoman, art curator, grandmaster cook."

"Sauce burner. Lifelong learner. But tonight, I had help," Rose said with a smile.

"Don't sell yourself short. Your skills reveal you're more than a learner. I can't think of anyone—man or woman—I've met with your abilities. Would you like a drink?" Niall jumped up to retrieve the bottle of wine sitting on the counter.

"I forgot to open that." Rose was secretly surprised he was enjoying the meal. She suspected he had plenty of professionally cooked meals with Marina, who probably never burnt the sauce. Now, her focus was to get a second chance to make up for being so curt with him on her first day. His dejected look was etched in her brain from when he walked away.

"I'll get it. You've done so much already." Niall opened the bottle. "Would you like a glass, Rose?"

"I have sparkling water. But don't let that stop you."

"May I toast?"

She nodded and lifted her glass.

"Here's a toast to the woman who has officially flooded all my senses with pleasure. May your presence grace us as long as you please. Sláinte."

"Thank you. Sláinte."

She ate a few more bites before noticing Niall had eaten everything on his plate. "I'm a little full. Can I share some of my meal with you?" She cut a heaping piece of her mushroom, scooped up some potatoes and sauce, and held out her fork for him to take a bite, which he did not hesitate to accept. She watched, in a guilty pleasure, as he slid the food from her fork.

"The combination of flavors is unbelievable. I have to stop before I make a pig of myself." Sensual groans unintentionally slipped from his lips. She knew the sound. It was the one she made every time she ate decadent desserts. Niall took a sip of wine. He looked like he was trying to compose himself as much as a man in heat could.

"It was much simpler to make than I thought—sans the sauce. But I need to confess—I didn't make dessert. Although, I did pick up a cake if you have room for some."

"Maybe later," he said with a hungry smile.

"Niall, can you tell me a little about your business? I did a little research, but as I'm thinking about additional vendors for RRE, it'd be good to have an insider view of your enterprise. It would also help to understand what drives you." Rose focused her attention on Niall, pushing away his empty plate. "I'll take that." She gathered their dishes and took them to the sink while waiting for his response.

He stood to join her. "Here, let me help you with that." He placed the remaining items on the counter, grabbed the wine bottle and their two glasses, and gestured for her to join him. "We have a lounge just down the hall with a fireplace if you haven't already explored it. Let's take the conversation there. It might be cozier than hanging around in the kitchen."

Rose walked ahead of Niall until she came upon a series of rooms. When she turned back to look at Niall, he smiled, then tilted his head toward the room for her to enter. She switched on the light and stepped into a massive lounge with an oversized couch and two wingback chairs flanking a large fireplace at the far side. Niall headed toward the fireplace, wine and water glasses in hand, and put both on a side table between the chairs. Rose sat in front of the fireplace while Niall lit the fire before sitting opposite her. Within a few minutes, the fire was blazing.

"This is much better, wouldn't you agree?"

"Depends on what we're trying to accomplish," she smiled wryly.

Fireplace. Check. Wine. Check. Smoking hot guy. Check, check.

"Like I said—something more comfortable. But getting back to your question. I'm president of several ventures with my brother focused on logistics and security. We go into war-torn countries and provide infrastructure and security for the military and foreign civilians. The other company is private security for companies and families. I also own several multi-unit residential buildings like the one we discussed this morning. Aedan previously lived in one of my buildings until he bought his own. So, we both have multi-storied loft buildings near each other."

Rose sipped her wine and listened intently as Niall filled in the information she could not uncover through her research. Niall described how he was attracted to various martial arts at a young age and trained alongside his brother in karate and Muay Thai. He talked about his stint in the Irish military and its impact on fueling his need to protect others. Rose listened as he spoke about the type of combat training he went through and the kind of assignments he received before deciding to resign from the army to go into private business with his brother.

"Hearing about the type of assignments you covered provides more context as to why you and your brother are so hung up on Troy. So, if I need additional security, you have me covered." She lifted her glass and nodded in his direction.

He smiled his familiar hungry smile. "Covering you would be difficult, but a lovely change compared to my other assignments in dangerous remote places."

"I don't understand why I'd be so difficult compared to other assignments."

"We have a strict policy around dating clients. I told you on your first day here that I was attracted to you. If I were contracted to protect you, I couldn't be with you the way I want. The day you say yes to me, I'd have to resign."

Rose sipped her water to hide the rush of heat on her face. Flirting for Niall seemed as natural as breathing. "Well, we don't have to worry about either."

Niall locked gazes with Rose. He had a hint of a smile. "I love a challenge."

Rose ignored Niall. She knew bait when she saw it. "So, is everyone on your team trained to go to dangerous remote places and come out unscathed? Do you still go on those assignments as well?"

"Yes, everyone is trained. I deploy my teams across the globe. Whether or not I go depends on the assignment. I haven't lost a team member or client yet."

"My situation is not so different. When your family is worth what mine is—not to mention having created groundbreaking technological advancements in AI—kidnapping is a daily threat."

"Your situation is not that uncommon. I also have clients like your family. Those are usually the assignments I would personally oversee."

"Sounds dangerous and takes a certain confidence to do that job. One thing is for sure: we both have demanding jobs that keep us busy."

Niall shifted in his chair, took a sip of wine, and tilted his head slightly. Rose could tell by his look there was something else on his mind. And she wasn't sure if she wanted to know what it was.

"Is this why you're single? No time for a relationship." His tone was matter of fact.

"Are you asking a question or making assumptions?" Her eyebrows creased. Rose didn't know whether to be offended or embarrassed. She was annoyed at Troy for being right, even more so than at Niall for being presumptuous.

"Since you put it that way...I'm making a statement."

She opened her mouth to say something curt but sipped her drink instead. She thought about Niall's question and the direction the conversation was headed. She needed to check herself and Niall. "I'm single now, but I am curious how you secured all your information. You and your brother seem to know much more than most people know about me. I'm pretty low-key when it comes to relationships."

"It's my job to know everything about people around me." His tone indicated there was more discussion hidden beneath the surface. She didn't want to tell him this was the second time someone had said those words to her.

"Okay, Niall." She took the bait. "Break it down for me."

Niall's hungry smile returned. "It's straightforward. The fact is, it's a little over a year since you've been in public with a guy." He paused a second as if he were debating something in his head.

She wanted to say, *A month ago, you were out with a celebrity chef,* but held back.

"Go on," she pressed.

"I'm not sure you want to hear this, but the way you showed up at my suite earlier looking like this—" he waved his hands over the length of her body. "You told me you're here focused on the exhibition, which is perfectly fine. But a side of you comes across as very sensual. I think a committed person would be, well—" he paused again, and she knew he was searching for the right word. "Would act differently, more reserved."

Rose choked back a laugh. "Niall. Come on. You said it yourself. I need to have everything in order. For me, that includes how I look. If you perceive me as sensual, you read that into something you like about me. Someone else may perceive me as rude and arrogant. Some people perceive me as disgusting because I'm Black. It's all perception. And at the end of the day, I only know how to be me. Are you saying I would have to be a certain way to be your woman?"

"That's not what I'm saying. You're very captivating. Perhaps accidentally so. Only you can tell me which. I certainly didn't expect it after my experience on your first night here. You seemed pretty intent on putting me in my corner."

She took a sip of her drink. She didn't know what to think about Niall, but she would hear him out before passing judgment.

Niall continued. "If you were vying for my attention—"

"Which you know I'm not."

"*If* you are, you had it long before tonight. So, take caution if you come looking for me again with that dinner-is-served tone you gave me earlier." He barked out a laugh so loud it made her laugh, too.

"Don't blame me because you're a masochist. I've already explained my intent. It's not what you think."

His eyebrows raised. "No?"

"No. I'm a woman who likes looking like a woman. You'll rarely find me in jeans and a hoody or a traditional suit." She crossed her legs, and her foot accidentally dusted Niall's pant leg. His eyes swept down the length of her body, then back up to catch her gaze. She felt the heat in his stare but continued. "But just because I can kick your butt both in and outside the boardroom doesn't mean I want to look like I can." She tilted her head in Niall's direction, who seemed to be amused.

Niall's laugh was even louder than before. "Lady, you have no idea what you do to me."

Rose wasn't sure she wanted to know. "Hey. I appreciate the compliments, the laugh, and the honest conversation. It's refreshing for someone in my position. And a relief to know I hadn't totally ruined my first meeting, but like I said. Please don't read into it. It's nothing more than what it seems."

She caught herself staring Niall up and down as he sat across from her, allowing silence to fill the space between them. He was staring back at her, which was now their thing.

"I seem to be at a loss for words." Niall stood and went to the fireplace, wine glass in hand. "You realize you have me all flustered." He took a sip and then winced. "I need something stronger than this."

"I can't help you with that." Rose didn't clarify which of his issues she was addressing. She didn't want to admit he had the same effect on her.

"I'm not asking for help. Give a guy a chance."

Rose smiled in an attempt to lighten the mood. "How do you know I'm *not* giving a guy a chance?"

"I think you understand what I'm saying."

"You're right." She got up from her chair as if to leave the room but walked to the bar and retrieved a glass and crystal carafe containing amber-colored liquor. She hoped it would suffice. Rose walked back over to Niall. "This is for you. I'm assuming it's whiskey." She poured the contents into the glass.

"I know you're focused on work, but I can't help feeling there's something more you're not telling me about why you've completely closed the door on relationships. Something just doesn't add up when I mull it over in my head."

Rose thought carefully about what to say next. Niall was one of the most powerful men in Belfast, and she knew he wasn't used to hearing the word *no*. She sensed his frustration as he ran his fingers through his thick, black hair in a failed attempt to push it out of his face. He locked gazes with her, and she knew he was planning his next move. She wanted to tell Niall to stop looking at her. She wanted to say he looked sexy when he ran his fingers through his hair. She wanted to tell him everything she wanted him to do to her at that moment. But she also wanted to ask about Marina Mack, what she was to him, and where she was at that moment.

"Here." Rose handed him the drink, exchanging it for the wine glass she placed on the mantel. Niall took a sip of his drink and then tipped the glass to her lips. Rose took a sip. Her gaze remained locked with his. She knew Niall was still waiting for her response.

"I don't know what to tell you, Niall. You know I still have this decision to make that my father's put a tight deadline on, and with the exhibition—"

"No, Rose. You know I'm not talking about work."

"There's nothing else," she breathed in defeat.

"I find that hard to believe, given our current situation." He placed the glass on the mantle.

"I'll let you off the hook. It's me. Maybe I might have regrets later, but I'm not interested."

"I'm not trying to pressure you. If I may—just indulge me for a moment." He smiled, holding his hand out to her, which she surprised herself by taking. Niall drew her close to him—close enough that only a sheet of paper could pass between them. His gaze was still locked on hers when he rested a hand on the small of her back. She could feel the warmth of his hand on her bare skin through the silk fabric. His eyes followed her hand as she reached out to fix the curl he stroked out of place. "You are beautiful," he said finally, pressing his cheek to her wrist.

"So you've told me," she whispered to mask the hitch in her voice.

"Yes. You are a rare bird on an island. And the perfect one for me."

"Niall," she called his name for no other reason than it felt right.

"May I kiss you on the lips?"

She thought about her recent night out with Aedan. The things they'd discussed. Their plans for the weekend. Then, the online post that referred to a photo of Niall as Marina's hot new man flashed in her head. "We're not together like that," she heard herself say as she fought the urge to lean into Niall's lips, which hovered a breath away from hers.

"Then, how about this?" He pushed her natural curls away from her face, touched his lips to her temple, inhaled, then brushed his lips against her ear. Rose tilted her head slightly in a haphazard attempt to avoid his touch. The kinetic energy from his skin brushing hers sent a rush of heat through her body. "Or this?" He dusted a kiss on her neck. She fought the urge to pull him into an embrace. Then, Niall gently brushed his lips against the corner of hers. The side of her lip twitched impulsively, and she felt him smile triumphantly against her face. She knew he took it as his signal. "May I?" he asked.

She lifted her chin slightly in response. Then, in one smooth move, his lips covered hers. Rose hesitated at first, then leaned into his kiss before taking a step back, but not completely out of his reach. She felt the heat of the moment tempting her, but she needed to gain control of herself. She touched her top lip. "That was lovely. Niall. Really. But—"

He cut in. "But what?"

I'm soaking wet, is what she wanted to say.

"I'm not going to your room tonight." Rose watched as the Mediterranean blue color in his eyes went a shade darker, and the crease above his eyes deepened, signaling to her those were not the words he wanted to hear.

"I'm not asking you to."

"Then, what are you doing?" she asked, already knowing the answer to the question. But she wouldn't let him get away without stating his intentions.

"Presenting you with an option. I'm making sure you have no doubt I want to be with you. And I'm not talking about a one-night stand or let's hang while you're here. I want something more. I'm telling you that it must be your decision to come to me. I've shown you my hand, Night Owl. I'm going to kiss you again, hard this time. The next move is yours." Niall pulled Rose close. This time, he didn't allow for any space between them. He dipped his head, pressed his lips to hers, and kissed her. Hard.

Rose surprised herself as she parted her lips to receive his tongue, allowing it to mingle with hers as she leaned into his hard, hot body. The urgency behind Niall's kisses drew her deeper into his embrace. The desire to satiate the pulsing between her legs was overwhelming. But the niggling voice in her head was still there, telling her all this was a distraction. Telling her that she didn't have time for a complicated relationship. Rose pulled her face away and put her hand beneath Niall's chin so they could lock eyes. She refused to admit to him or herself how bad she wanted to take him at that moment.

"I can't do this. I just met you." Before the words left her mouth, she knew it was just an excuse.

"We both know that has nothing to do with this. You're a smart woman. You know everything you need to know about me. More than most people I've known for years."

"What if I did need—" Rose paused. She didn't have to ask. She knew his type: self-made, self-confident, and seriously into her. Simply ripe for her taking.

"To know more?" he finished. "Nothing is closed off to you. For more time? Is that really what you need?"

"To be honest, no. Niall, I have been working hard to ensure that your sister sees me for the talent I bring. I don't want to do anything to undermine why I'm here. I certainly don't want to appear as some easy conquest. To become some caption in an online photo."

"Is that honestly what you think? That I'm looking for an easy conquest? You may not know it, but I'm telling you now, that's not how I operate. I want you. I'm not interested in anyone else. And we both know captions don't reflect the truth. I shouldn't have to explain that to you. Your reputation is not at stake here. Not with anyone and especially not with me."

"I'm glad to hear my reputation remains intact."

"Rose, I'm not a gambling man. But all my cards are on the table. It's up to you to pick them up."

"Honestly, Niall, I don't know how any woman can resist you, but I need to try. Standing here so close, I feel your manhood harden like steel against me. I—" Rose paused. She knew in the end that Niall would walk away frustrated. In the end, she would walk away frustrated.

Niall didn't know it but she couldn't give him what he wanted. She wasn't built for a happily ever after—or she feared she wasn't, at least. Besides, taking his brother up on a weekend of touring was distraction enough.

This time, it was Rose who leaned into Niall. She wanted to be entirely sure of her decision when she placed her arms around his neck, pulled his head down to meet hers, and kissed him with all the passion she had previously held back. He kissed her back gently at first. Then, his kiss became more urgent as their tongues mingled, and he explored every inch of her mouth, sucking and licking until she felt so consumed, she couldn't breathe.

Niall lowered his hand and traced the smooth curve of her thigh, slid her silk dress up and his hand down the back of her silk underwear until it came to rest on her bare bottom. He pressed his fingers into her backside, pulling her close until her body molded around the growing length in his pants. She felt his hand slowly move between them, down her body, toward the warm moist craving between her legs. Rose closed her eyes. Her back instinctively arched in response to his fingers sliding between her folds. She groaned in pleasure against his mouth at the sensation, and the noise caused Niall to pause. He pulled away from the kiss, slowly removed his hand from where she wanted him most and touched his forehead to hers.

"Damn," he panted, then grabbed his glass from the fireplace mantle. Niall tossed back the contents in one shot and returned the glass. "You're so damn wet. You have no idea the things I want to do to you," he groaned. Then, he put his hands on her waist, kissed her on the forehead, and gently guided her away from him. Like a soldier, sword still raised, he retreated.

"Niall," she breathed out his name, still lost in the moment. She held onto his hand before it completely slipped away from her waist.

"Lady. Please forgive me. I'm a little surprised and frustrated. You sure have me all heated for someone who was about to say they don't want me. A few seconds more, I would have had that dress off you. And your body. Oh my god. Your body tells me everything I need to know. So, I'm heading upstairs, and if you don't plan to follow me, I intend to take a cold shower, knock down my email, and go to bed. I would be more than delighted to wake up to you by my side. In any instance, I'll see you in the morning, Night Owl."

Rose bit her bottom lip. She could still taste Niall's kiss in her mouth, feel the sensation his fingers left as they pressed against the slickness between her legs. Rose knew he was right—she was about to tell him I'm not going to your room before she kissed him. All she could muster the nerve to say now was some silly cliché. "It's hot in here. I need some air."

"I'm assuming that means goodnight." Niall ran his thumb along her cheek, kissed the corner of her lips, and walked away.

"I can't give you what you need, Niall. Goodnight." It was the last thing she said as she watched Niall leave the room.

Rose wanted to grab Niall's hand and follow him upstairs. She wanted him as badly as his body showed he wanted her, but instead, she went outside and found her security detail. She needed to walk around the property to clear her head and walk off the throbbing between her legs.

Later, back in her room, Rose texted Troy to confirm she was in for the night. Before Rose turned off the lights, she made the first move with Aedan and texted, "Hey."

To her surprise, he responded immediately with a text. "Hey, you."

"I missed seeing you today. Looking forward to touring Friday," she texted back.

"Thinking about you, too. I can't wait for Friday."

At that moment, she felt she had made the right decision.

CHAPTER 6

Fame

"Without this playing with fantasy, no creative work has ever yet come to birth. The debt we owe to the play of the imagination is incalculable."

— CARL JUNG

ROSE ANTICIPATED BREAKFAST MIGHT BE AWKWARD FOLLOWING LAST night's turn of events. She was first to arrive at the kitchen in time for breakfast, followed a few minutes later by Niall. Contrary to her expectation, he was very upbeat and cheery when he walked in. Of course, he was his usual handsome self in a striped suit, which she both loved and hated equally. He didn't hesitate when he hugged her, followed by a kiss on her cheek. It all seemed entirely benign in contrast to last night. At that moment, Rose realized they would never return to being strangers.

"Good morning, my lovely Night Owl. I hope you don't mind." He reached past her to grab a fried potato from the pan. "As usual, you smell good enough to eat, but I'll behave and have this instead." He examined the potato before popping it into his mouth.

"Good morning, Niall." The side of her lips turned up slightly as her thoughts flashed back to their kiss last night. Rose went to the coffee pot, filled a cup, and handed it to Niall.

"Full day today?" Niall grabbed a plate and loaded it with toast, potatoes, and fresh fruit. Together, they sat next to one another at the marble counter to eat.

"Pretty much. I have back-to-back calls after breakfast. Some of the vendors are still roaming around working. I'm hoping to sneak in time for lunch."

"Like a magnet, you're drawing in some triple 'A' players to this event. Forty-eight hours ago, it was business as usual. Since you landed in Belfast, my email has been on fire with people tracking me down, desperate for an invite. That list of yours must be pretty exclusive. Is this what it's like to be famous?" He took another bite of food from his plate.

"You'd know more about fame than me, but exclusivity is more the pace with this type of show. We have some outstanding artwork to display for a one-night-only event. Attendees were hand-selected from an elite group across the globe. Speaking of invites—" She paused to take a sip of coffee. "Can I expect to see you there?"

"Do I need an invite?"

She let out a tentative laugh. "No, but I should probably ban you after last night."

"Come to think of it, you should," he quipped. "Seriously, if you want me there, just say the word, and I will be there."

"I want you there." She drank the rest of her coffee before continuing. "Dinner again tonight after work? I'm cooking."

"As long as we hold off on dessert." His hungry smile needed no interpretation. "Yes, dinner sounds just fine."

They chatted for a while about the guest list. He showed her a few emails he delayed answering from people asking him about tickets to the event. Rose dictated a response to some emails and suggested he forward the remaining ones to her chief of staff. She would have Kris craft a personal message to each person, thanking them for their interest in attending but providing a gentle letdown with a simple explanation and a link to donate to the arts.

"Niall."

"Don't say it. It's fine."

"No, Niall. About last night—"

He reached across the table, took her hand in his, and kissed the back of it. "It's fine."

She smiled and exhaled. "Thank you."

"Don't take that as me giving up."

"I would be offended if you did." They laughed, and with it disappeared all semblance of awkwardness from last night. After breakfast, they went their separate ways to work—Rose next door to the gallery and Niall into town.

✿

LIKE A FRESH CANVAS PATIENTLY AWAITING ITS FIRST STROKE OF color, so were the bare white walls of the massive gallery awaiting art installations. At that moment, Rose represented the artist standing in the center of the room, sans paintbrush. Kris and the remaining contractors rushed around her like commuters coming and going from the train station as they worked. The current state of her brain mirrored that of a complex algorithm processing incoming data. She stood there mapping art relative to the artist, analyzing space in relation to light, anticipating attendees' needs, and deciding how to incorporate sound to create the ultimate art experience. Since Brianna was out of commission, Rose knew she needed to focus and nail the program's vision. Any deviation from the original outline she previewed with Brianna required flawless execution. She was outside her family's sphere of influence and feeling the pressure. Rose spun around towards the window facing the main road and waved Troy inside.

"Everything okay? You look a little stressed." He asked.

"Not stressed, I'm trying to think, but there is too much going on in the gallery. Can you ensure everyone clears the building for a while, including Kris? Consider it an early break. I have a call to make but come and get me once everyone is gone." She placed a hand on his shoulder. "I'll be fine. Thank you, Troy," she assured before disappearing into the gallery office.

Rose pulled out her cell, tapped the screen, and instructed, "Call Dad."

He answered right away. "Hey, Princess. How's Ireland treating you?"

"Good so far. You still working or winding down?"

"You know me. I just closed my laptop and am about to head up to bed. Great job this morning on the conference call—more specifically, last night. Hopefully, you got some rest afterward. Have you been thinking through your decision? We have to file documents before the end of the month."

"That's what I wanted to talk to you about." Rose knew her role as an officer in a public company meant she and her dad's staff were subject to public disclosures. She had to give their attorneys and communications teams ample time to prepare for their pending press release.

"I'm all ears, Princess."

"You know why I'm pursuing art curation?"

"You told me you want to make a name for yourself. If selected, your first press release as CEO will accomplish that in one shot."

"No. The headlines will read, *Rick Ross' daughter takes over as CEO of Rick Ross Enterprises.*"

"It will say, *The board of Rick Ross Enterprises is pleased to announce the appointment of Roselyn Ross as the new CEO.*"

"But you can't control the narrative in the media."

"That's never been a problem for me in the past."

"That's the point; it's not a problem for *you*, but it's my name getting lost."

"I understand your concern. What are you suggesting? I know you've been thinking about it, and that's a good sign. I was afraid you might be calling to decline the job."

"You're not afraid of anything. Besides, I haven't made a decision either way." Rose wished she had more time.

"You know the deadline. I trust you'll figure things out. If you're wondering whether you can handle both—you have already proved yourself. You built a high-performing team with us and have a strong lineup of successors several layers deep. You wouldn't be the first CEO to perform double duty leading multiple companies and certainly not the last. If you want their advice, let me know. I can have them call you. Tell me who you want to speak with—Jack, Warren, Jeff, or others. Trust your instincts—they haven't failed you. I love you."

"Thanks, Dad. Love you, too." Rose ended the call and stood. She could see Troy standing in the gallery near the front door, watching her through the office window. She opened the door and stepped into the gallery.

"All clear," Troy said from across the room.

"Thanks. I was trying to visualize the event, and there were just too many people milling around. Let's head into the great room."

Rose and Troy stepped into the large, round room. Troy stood near the entrance while Rose went to the center of the room. She walked in a slow circle, looking at the walls and making a mental note of each. After one rotation around the room, Rose stood still, closed her eyes, and tried to visualize how the finished space would look. She imagined herself walking in from the front entrance and passing through the gallery toward the rotunda. She tried to visualize the completed room with a view toward the front and vice versa, trying to experience the space through the patrons' lens. Unbeknownst to her, a visitor entered the room and stood next to Troy.

Troy had his hand out, holding back the visitor to allow Rose to remain uninterrupted. They both waited for her to open her eyes.

"I got this. Brilliant. Freaking brilliant." She held her hands out as if holding up some invisible object. "Oh my god, this changes everything, but it will be amazing if I can make it work. Troy!"

"I'm here," Troy responded.

"I have so much work to do." Rose opened her eyes to find she wasn't alone with Troy. Aedan was looking back at her, smiling, standing tall, dashing, with one hand in his pocket.

His smile widened when their eyes met. "Hi. Am I interrupting something?"

Her face warmed. "Um, hey, Aedan. I was about to, um, what—"

He stopped her mid-sentence. "I came by to see if you were free for lunch?"

"Wow. Uh, sure." Somehow, she managed to walk across the room with grace. Barely.

"Great. Anything you need to wrap up before we head out?"

"No. I think I'm good."

She turned to Troy and mouthed, "What," before heading outside with Aedan, who was confidently leading the way. Troy shook his head uncharacteristically, then tapped his watch.

"Uh, Aedan. Before we head out, can you provide Troy with details of where we'll be?"

"Sure." Aedan stopped walking and turned to face Troy. "I made plans for lunch at the Ginger Bistro. No need to follow us into town, Troy. I'll bring Rose back to the gallery directly following lunch." Aedan turned to face Rose. "Ready?" Aedan placed a hand on the small of Rose's back, led her to the car, and slid into the back seat beside her. "Ginger Bistro," he called out to the driver.

Once inside the car, Rose pulled her thoughts together to form a complete sentence. "Sorry if I seemed a little surprised. I didn't expect to see you until Friday. What happened?"

"A little birdie told me you needed lunch," he teased. "But seriously. I heard it might get a little hectic for you today, so I took a chance and dropped by to give you some respite. I understand the pressure you're under to make the exhibition successful. Besides, I was hungry, and I imagine you are, too. I hope that's alright."

"Give my thanks to the little birdie. Niall, right? I suspect it was him that put you up to this."

"My brother is very observant if you haven't already noticed. He said you were anticipating a busy day and hoping to squeeze in lunch. Neither of us would let a subtle plea like that go unanswered."

She didn't realize Niall was paying attention to every word and was even more surprised he sent his brother instead of making time himself to take her out. For a second, she was suspicious. What game was Niall playing? She lingered on the thought for a second but quickly let it go so she wouldn't miss anything Aedan had to say. "I'm delighted you dropped by. Can we chat about the weekend? Any hints on what I can expect?"

"Anxious?" Aedan asked.

"Like a kid on Christmas morning." She rubbed her hands together. In reality, she despised surprises. They often brought disappointments—like when her ex-boyfriend planned a brief getaway for two at an exotic beach in Mexico early in their relationship. He didn't know she had an aversion to spending time at the beach that stemmed from her past traumas, and that she was not interested in spending time in Mexico on holiday.

"Well, I've been planning something to give you a taste of Ireland. I was hoping not to reveal anything yet to keep it fresh and unexpected. That can't happen if I tell you all the details. So, why don't we agree now that you'll go into this with blind trust? I promise to take great care of you."

"Sure." Submission was not her strong suit.

"I can share a few things to help you prepare."

"I'll take any morsels you can dish out." She forced a smile.

"Alright. We have three days together and will return to the house Sunday afternoon. So, you'll need to pack a light bag. I'm using the word light loosely." Aedan paused. Rose caught his gaze and nodded for him to continue. "I suggest you bring comfortable shoes, preferably flats, which you can pair with equally comfortable clothes. Those four-inch stilettos are more than welcome, but for nights only. You can pair those with a beautiful dress for dinner if you like. Lastly, think about dressing in layers in the event we experience inclement weather from location to location."

"That's it?"

"That's all you get for now."

He interrupted their conversation to ask the driver to double-park alongside the row of cars outside the five-story brick building spanning the entire block. It looked like they were in the warehouse district of every city she had visited. There were several different establishments in the same building as the restaurant they were headed to. The restaurant had signs hung over arched windows, all of which read, *The Ginger Bistro*. Inside, she discovered a quaint room that was long and narrow, like a row house with tables on either wall leading to the rear of the restaurant. The atmosphere felt friendly and relaxed, although her presence still drew attention when they walked in.

"I wonder what she—" Rose heard someone's voice trail off into a whisper as she passed. She knew the end of that sentence was what that Black woman was doing with that hot Irish guy. It was all too familiar.

They took a seat and immediately received a paper menu listing various dishes to satisfy every palette. "Anything to drink?" Aedan asked Rose while the waiter stood by, ready to take their order.

"Water is fine."

"Two glasses of water, please." The waiter placed a couple of coasters on the table and disappeared into the kitchen.

Rose looked back at her menu, quickly eying a couple of veggie dishes. She debated between gratin of roast squash, pine nuts, leeks, parmesan with garlic green beans, or red lentil and carrot dahl with curried cauliflower fritters. She thought about it for a second. Gratin roast squash won. Aedan took pity on her and said he would order dahl to share with her.

"Wow, it was hard to choose just one item. Everything sounds good."

"I like this place because they have delicious vegetable dishes. Belfast is great about having a nice eclectic mix of food. It's one of my favorite lunch spots, but I hope you'll have time during your stay for me to share more lunch spots with you. Being from California and traveling the globe often, I know you are intimately acquainted with eating well."

"I've had my share of great meals," she concurred. "By the way, you missed the fantastic meal I made last night. I think your brother was impressed if I got my signals right. Except for a little hiccup with the sauce." She bit her lip and prayed they weren't the type of brothers that shared *everything*.

"Em, yes. Niall did mention that you did a brilliant job with dinner. He said we could take some lessons from you. Maybe he could, but I consider myself a good cook, too."

"Ouch. That sounds like a challenge. I was apprehensive since I reinterpreted another dish that I had eaten months ago. But if you want to try your hand one day, I'm more than willing to be a taste tester, Aedan. Better yet, maybe the three of us can have a cook-off. That is, since you're throwing shade on your brother and me."

"You're on." He glanced around the room, searching for the waiter but found other patrons staring at them instead. "Does that bother you?" Aedan asked.

"What's that?" She traced a path from his eyes through the room to find a point of reference. "People staring? I'm not naive. I know Ireland has a short history of pluralism and diversity. That's why my art installation for the exhibition has a multicultural focus. As for stares, it comes with the territory, so I try to ignore them. I suspect the same thing happens to you on your trips to India, China, and other places where most people don't look like you. Although not with the same sentiment. Am I right?"

"You're right, but I guess I am more sensitive to it here because you're attracting stares to us. I don't want to make light of the thoughts or sentiments behind the stares, but it almost feels like they think you're a celebrity. You never know."

She laughed. "Yeah, like they think I'm Beyoncé. I can assure you that's not the case. And yes, we both know this has nothing to do with fame, which is the root of your discomfort. Does it bother you? The stares, I mean."

"I'm concerned about you and the extent of the narrow-mindedness behind the stares."

"I'll be okay."

"You know you are breathtaking."

Nothing about those stares made her feel breathtaking. "Thank you. You look very handsome as usual. I think your brother and you won the lottery on good looks in Ireland."

Aedan rolled his eyes. "I'll remind Niall how good-looking you think he is. You're a straight shooter. I like that."

"No time to be anything else."

"How did you get this way?"

The waiter returned, bringing their water and some bread for the table. Rose mouthed the words, "Thank you," before taking a sip of water. Aedan relayed their food orders, and the waiter disappeared to the kitchen again.

"Being unfiltered?"

"That, amongst other things I've noticed."

"You sure you want to know?" he nodded in response. Rose continued. "It was back in San Francisco."

Aedan smiled. "You sound like you're about to cite a novel."

"Funny. It is a long story. Like I said, I was in San Francisco. My best friend and I were hanging out at Ocean Beach one sunny Saturday. We spent the day writing our names on the wet sand and phrases describing how the beautiful day made us feel. We drew hearts with arrows through them and included our initials and those of our celebrity crush at the time. Alongside my initials were GM, another heart had DB, and another had LO. Translation: George Michael, David Bowie, and Lawrence Olivier. Don't judge me," she interjected. "It was all fun and games and bliss. We were fifteen at the time."

Aedan listened intently, watching Rose's face as she looked straight through him, lost in her memories.

"After a while, my friend got restless and wanted to swim. By the time I got to the ocean, I couldn't find her. Eventually, a sneaker wave sucked me deeper into the ocean. I never felt so small nor felt such immense power like the invisible force of the water dragging me beneath. I fought as hard as possible to break free from the water's clutches but got swallowed up by the ocean several times. I don't know who or what was around me. All I could see was water. I could hear the water. Breathe water. Feel water. Taste water. And the horizon kept slipping in and out of view. It seemed like an hour, but later someone told me I was out there struggling for about ten minutes. Eventually, I made it to shore but found no sign of my friend. The emergency crew who came to help searched hours for her before they had to give up."

"I had no idea." His eyes softened but stayed fixed on hers.

"Not many people know the story, thanks to my father keeping it out of the news. His company wasn't as big as it is now, and I didn't have an entourage following me as a kid. I don't know how I made it out, but I did. Surrounding me was a crowd of people hovering, talking, and saying things that I couldn't quite make out, but I remember people saying how strong I was. I remember that." Rose's thoughts drifted to how she felt having her friend ripped away from her life and the years it took her to trust people enough to make a connection. The slight movement of Aedan's hand on the table pulled her away from her thoughts. She straightened in her chair, and he withdrew it.

"Rose, I'm so sorry. I shouldn't have probed, but I'm glad you trusted me with that."

"Now, I live each day urgently as if it were my last." Rose inhaled.

"I'm glad you came to lunch with me, Rose."

"I appreciate you asking."

"I'm also looking forward to this weekend." He flashed his familiar smile. "Ah, look at this." The waiter brought lunch to their table and sat a plate in front of each. Rose and Aedan spent the rest of the hour sharing stories of their youth. She talked about being a cheerleader in high school. They both got a good laugh out of it. Aedan talked about the sports he played—rugby, soccer, and hockey. He talked about why he became a vegetarian after attending a hunting excursion with some friends.

"It didn't sit well with me," he explained. "I thought I had a kill shot, but I didn't. There are some things you can't unsee, like watching an animal run away and bleed out. I haven't eaten meat since. That was ten years ago."

"I know it doesn't compare, but I haven't eaten a hot dog since I saw a movie in school on how they were made. I was eight at the time.

Now I know why your brother made a point of telling me your food preference. Speaking of Niall, why did you choose him to run your companies?"

"Don't tell him, but there's a lot of things he excels at. Besides being a great leader, he is strategic and a fantastic problem-solver. Give him a problem, and he can quickly map out every move you need to make to get to the solution. I've never seen anything like it before. Also, I'm impressed with the extent of his network."

What in the world is Niall up to? she thought.

⁂

BACK AT THE GALLERY, AEDAN DROPPED ROSE OFF AND REMINDED her of their plans on Friday. He kissed her on the cheek before handing her off to Troy, who stood patiently nearby.

"Are you okay?" Troy said with a stern expression.

"Yes, I'm fine. Lunch was nice. It was good to get away for a while."

"Did you need my help with something? You looked a little stressed earlier and seemed surprised to see Aedan. Speaking of which, I plan to talk to him about these spontaneous events. Having you show up in places I haven't cleared is irresponsible. I had half a mind to follow you to the restaurant."

"I'm glad you didn't. It would have been unnecessary. I hear your concern, but everything worked out. You did have some time to contact the restaurant before I arrived. Right?"

"That's beside the point. But yes, and fortunately, Aedan had already established security protocols with them. I sent a team to monitor you anyway."

"I wouldn't have expected anything different. I know you by now. And don't be down on Aedan. He's a good guy. Anyway, Niall encouraged him to pick me up for lunch."

"I doubt it took much convincing. You didn't answer my question. Did you need my help with something earlier?"

"I wanted to brainstorm with you my idea to make the art show more engaging to the crowd both personally and emotionally. But unfortunately, it comes with a few complex security, logistical, and political challenges." She narrowed her eyes and pinched her chin between her thumb and forefinger.

"What's the issue?"

"I have to interview all the artists, so I know how to represent their art in the best light."

"You always conduct interviews with every artist you meet."

"Well, for this show, I plan to change it and curate art pieces that serve to influence the artists we're showcasing. I expect some of those pieces will be hard to acquire for the night."

"I've never seen you not get something you want. People call you to help them when they've exhausted all avenues to acquire something they want. If you can't get it for them, it's unlikely anyone will. How is this different?"

"I'm in Europe. What if the piece is priceless? Maybe Brianna could make a call to the Louvre and get them to hand over something like the Mona Lisa for the evening, but certainly not me. And I am committed to doing this without calling Dad and his team for help."

"You've managed fine art curation in the states. This is no different. So, what do you need to make this happen?"

"Influential connections spanning multiple industries, including the government here, some expedited loan agreements, an international security team with someone to serve as a curator on my behalf, time, and a private jet. If I need to acquire pieces in the states, I have access to the right resources, and no one would deny my request. But here—"

"Unfortunately, I can't divert my team away from Ireland. It would leave you in a vulnerable position. And as it stands right now, I'm the only one on the team here qualified to serve as a proxy for you that knows the international protocols, and I don't plan to leave your side."

"I know, and I can't pull our team back in the states off their project either. On a positive note, we do have a jet, and I might have some level of influence here. These plans are ambitious, but it will be the highlight of my career if I can pull this off in this short amount of time."

"You can do it."

"Did you know that some of the curators at the Louvre threatened to resign when Jackie Kennedy convinced the French culture minister to loan out the Mona Lisa in 1963? The US Coast Guard accompanied the liner, which carried that painting." She closed her eyes and covered them with her fingers. She took a few deep breaths.

"It's an important piece. It garnered that level of scrutiny. But I have an idea: Niall. His company provides this level of support for a living. I am confident you'll figure out how to acquire the pieces you need— you always do. Navigating international security protocols should be no problem for his team. I expect they previously provided Brianna with this level of service. And whoever acted as conservator for Brianna can proxy for you, then you won't have to sacrifice your projects in the states. Do you want to talk to Niall, or do you want me to?"

"Oh my god. That's an excellent idea. I'll talk to Niall." She started to hug Troy but patted his shoulder instead.

"Glad I could help."

"Troy, you're a lifesaver in more ways than one. I'm so excited about this and can't wait to see my plan in action."

"I'm sure it will be amazing."

"I am banking on it."

CHAPTER 7

Do I Move You?

dis·cov·er·y | /dəˈskəv(ə)rē/ | noun: discovery; plural noun: discoveries

1. the action or process of discovering or being discovered.

ROSE OPENED HER EYES TO CAPTURE THE MOMENT BEFORE DAWN when an absence of light in the window left the room blanketed in shades of gray. As she lay nestled in covers drawn taut to her neck, envisaging sunrise, all good intentions to get up and greet the day escaped her. "Get it together," Rose told herself, then flung the covers off and to the side of the bed. "Spending an entire weekend learning more about the country is a lovely treat. Let's see what the elusive Aedan has planned." Curiosity got the best of her, so she jumped out of bed to get ready before making her way downstairs.

Rose entered the room to find both brothers perched on barstools at the kitchen counter, immersed deep in conversation.

"I wrap up the Mercer project today. But between the high-profile clients we signed on for next week, it doesn't seem feasible to take on another. So, who is this AJ guy anyway?" Niall asked, looking at his brother with furrowing brows, one hand pressed tightly around a steaming cup of coffee. He still managed to be sinfully sexy, stern look and all, while sporting his pressed white shirt and black slacks.

Rose stepped further into the room in Niall's view. The second their eyes locked, the corners of his lips curled into a slight smile. Although Aedan had his back to her, she knew his delayed response meant he picked up on Niall's cue to her presence.

"Let's catch up when I get back," Aedan turned to face Rose. Seeing him sparked something in her. She wasn't sure if it was excitement or curiosity.

"Morning, gentlemen. Don't let me interrupt." She walked over to give each brother a well-received hug. Rose inhaled, allowing a hint of their combined spicy-sweet aromas to waft over her before stepping back to savor the sights. She swallowed a smile, thinking of words to adequately caption the scene. *Delicious. Distraction.*

"You're not interrupting. We can table the discussion until Monday," Niall stood and pulled out a chair for Rose. "Aedan is officially off the clock starting now. And so are you, Night Owl. By the way, you look beautiful. Ready to experience all that Emerald Isle has to offer?" he probed.

"As much as I can be, although I don't quite know what your brother has up his sleeve." She turned her attention to Aedan, taking her time to give him the once over. It was her first time seeing him dressed in dark blue jeans and a grey tee-shirt hugging well-hewn muscles, looking more like his brother did when she arrived her first day.

"Good morning. Niall's right. You look fantastic. I haven't seen you in jeans before."

"I could say the same. You did say dress casually. Right?"

"I did, and you're perfect. You'll want to fill up. We have a long day of driving and hiking ahead of us." Aedan slid a plate in front of Rose.

"My brother is a lucky man to spend all day in your company."

"You mean all weekend," Aedan poked.

"Guys, before I put you both on time out, let me say it's nice to have a few days off from work to experience all the beauty Ireland has to offer," Rose chimed. "How about you, Niall? Any plans for the weekend?"

"Nothing major. I'll try and head home early, hit the gym, change, and get to the pub for a bit. Maybe a little later, I'll grab some dinner."

"So, you won't be staying out here tonight?"

"No, not this weekend. You'll be gone. Brianna is away, although she is returning Sunday night, so I'll be back in time for her arrival."

"We'll be back Sunday by four o'clock, Rose," Aedan said.

"How is Brianna?" Rose asked.

"She's doing a little better, everything considered. Brianna is strong." Aedan got up to put his empty plate in the sink. "Now, get some food in you. We have a long drive ahead of us."

"Working on it."

"Remember, Carol is returning with Brianna, so you may want to give Rose the backstory on her at some point," Niall mentioned.

Rose raised an eyebrow. "Oh no, that doesn't sound good."

Aedan narrowed his eyes at Niall. "It's not all that bad."

"Really?" Niall shot Aedan a you-must-be-joking look.

"Every family has one. I'll tell you about her on our way back. It's nothing for us to concern ourselves with at this moment. Right now, I'm looking forward to showing you around Northern Ireland."

"I'm looking forward to it as well."

"Well, I'm heading out. You two have a great weekend." Niall patted his brother on the back. "She is stunning, man," he whispered to Aedan, then left.

TROY WALKED AHEAD OF ROSE AND AEDAN, AND HEADED TO THE CAR as they left the house. Troy held his hand to help Rose as she got into the back seat.

"Although you won't be riding with us, that doesn't preclude you from having eyes on me. Am I right?" Rose whispered to Troy before stepping inside. Troy nodded in response and then released her hand when she sat down. His intense stare told her trailing behind did not sit well with him. But she knew Troy well enough to know that a hand-off had already happened between him and Aedan's driver.

Aedan got in next to Rose. "You ready for this?"

Rose smiled at Aedan. "Ready."

They had only been on the road about twenty minutes before Aedan dropped a few hints about the first leg of their trip. Coast, rocks, and landscape were the only clues Rose had to work with to guess their location. She read that many historical places in Ireland were on beautiful rocky coastal landscapes, leaving their options broad.

"I don't know where we are, but the drive has been beautiful so far." Rose turned to face Aedan and caught him watching her. "How much further is it?"

"You'll know when we get there."

"You sound like my dad, but with an Irish accent." A smirk formed on her face.

He laughed. "I'm certainly not trying to be your dad. Interestingly enough, you haven't talked about him before. Except to say he gave you a deadline."

"Hasn't been a reason to, and I expect you read enough articles about him. He's in the news almost daily."

"I'm sure there's more to him than the public persona."

"Outside of that, he's Dad. Despite the media's portrayal of him as a hard-driving billionaire, he is loving and thoughtful. Honestly, he's the standard of excellence by which I measure all guys. He was everything to me growing up." *He still is,* she thought, her mind drifting back to their recent conversation. Despite the clock winding down for her decision concerning his succession plans, he had been reassuring. "He taught me everything he knew about business, and if he didn't have an answer, he referred me to the right people to fill in the gaps."

"Sounds like a man I would want to meet. I hear the passion in your voice when you talk about him."

"He made me who I am today. You know—"

"I know what?" he chimed in.

"I am sure he'd like you."

"Sounds promising."

"So, are we close?"

Aedan shot Rose a knowing glance. "Almost."

She snapped her finger. "Got it. I think I know where we are now."

"Certain?"

"Pretty much."

"Okay, you get one guess. If you're wrong, you can't ask me where we're going for the rest of the weekend. Or you can have faith in me, sit back, relax, and enjoy."

Rose vacillated between telling what she knew and spoiling his surprise or keeping quiet. The need to control the situation was overwhelming, but she knew Aedan felt the same—they had that in common. But for her, it was more profound. She needed to control the level of angst she felt when she didn't have all the details. "Okay, then. I'll wait until you are ready to tell me." She sat back in the leather seat, propped her hand under her chin, and stared at Aedan through her eyelashes.

He smiled. "Don't look at me with those disapproving eyes and pouty lips. That won't work on me."

"Don't say I didn't try," she smiled wryly.

"Okay," Aedan glanced past her and tipped his head toward the window. "You can look outside now. We're nearing our destination, Clochán an Aifir, or you may recognize it as the Giant's Causeway. That sign marks the visitor's entrance to our destination." He referenced a UNESCO sign in the distance. Aedan leaned forward in his seat to speak with the driver. "Can you pull over near the front? We will have to hike the rest of the way. Thanks."

"Perfect, this was on my list of must-see places."

Maybe this guy knows what he's doing after all, she thought. She would wait and see.

"I have something for you in the trunk." Aedan got out of the car and helped her out. Together, they went to the trunk, where Aedan retrieved a lightweight blue backpack. "Here. Put your things into this. We have some rugged terrain to cross. You'll need both hands free to grip rocks and maintain your balance."

"I see you came prepared." Rose liked a man that anticipated her needs.

"Was trust one of those lessons you had to learn?" he quipped.

"Oh, right. Trust. Relax. Enjoy," Rose listed, reciting her new weekend mantra. Trusting someone other than her family and Troy was proving to be complicated.

"We have about a one-kilometer walk from our current location to the site where we will spend much of our time this morning. All the surface areas will be uneven, so please be careful." Aedan and Rose made a brief stop at the visitor center. Then, they went to explore the site.

On their way, Rose couldn't resist prodding Aedan for information. "Can I ask a question?"

"Of course."

"What made you choose this location to start? I suspect there is a sequence of events about to take place."

"You're right. There is a method to my madness. I thought about how to give you the best experience in our short time together. The sequence will tell a story, provide a historical perspective, and share a glimpse into some of the beauty Ireland has to offer. I know we won't get the chance to see everything in the next few days, but you'll get a taste to keep you interested. Maybe after this weekend, you'll want to explore more of Ireland."

"I'm in."

As they continued walking, Rose soaked in the view of rolling green hills that led to a series of staggering rock formations flowing into the sea. She placed a hand on Aedan's shoulder to balance herself while they navigated the uneven path. He paused a moment, allowing time for her to catch up, then took her hand in his. She liked the rush of heat that sent through her body.

"Your hands are cold."

"It's a bit chilly, but this works." She held up his hand.

"I guess I'm used to this weather. I don't feel the chill." Aedan took off his blue and gray scarf and wrapped it around Rose's neck. They continued traversing toward the main feature. "I chose this site first because it may be the oldest thing you and I will ever see. This site is said to be over sixty million years old. Although there are many interesting tales about how this place came to be, it's a bit scientific, but fascinating. You were born in a country with a lot of volcanos. I'm sure you get this. It is the aftermath of an ancient volcano eruption, and the formations result from the lava burning and cooling."

"As always, I am awestruck by the forces of mother nature." She reached to touch one of the hexagonal rock formations protruding near her. "To think this predates any life or history of people recorded. Imagine witnessing the eruption, lava flowing over the earth into the water—a massive force of nature purifying all in its path, blanketing this part of the earth like concrete fixed in place. I can't even fathom the degree of heat that would have forged this or the sound it would have made during cooling. How long would the entire process have taken? Days, months, years? What happened millions of years ago that only the earth could record?" She sat on one of the columns to take in the view.

Aedan pulled out his cell phone and held it up. "Hope you don't mind. I'll send it to you when we get back in the car."

"Don't mind at all. Come here." She held out her hand. "Let me see that a moment." She took his cell phone, turned on mirror mode, positioned them both on the screen, and then took a selfie. "There. Now we're both in the picture." When she turned to look at him, his face was so close that if she moved a fraction of an inch, she could kiss him. She smiled instead.

"Nice," Aedan wasn't looking at the phone. He was looking at her lips.

"Let's head over there," Rose pointed towards one of the massive formations covered in lichen. She sensed a closeness developing

126

between her and Aedan but wasn't sure how she felt about it or his intentions. Unlike his brother, he held his cards close to his chest.

"Sure. There's a lot more to see. This site consists of about forty thousand basalt columns. As you can see, they are all interlocking."

"Some look like steppingstones, some the height of chairs, the taller ones—"

"Are close to forty feet tall. Pretty amazing, right?" he finished.

"Yes. I've never seen anything quite like this, especially naturally formed."

She was both fascinated and amazed as they trekked further into the site. Aedan told Rose how the Causeway got its name and other associated tales. He shared one of the stories about two giant brothers fighting because each had different loyalties.

"All this hiking is making me hungry," Rose confessed.

"I've got just the solution for that." Aedan took Rose by the hand and led her out of the basalt.

⚉

AEDAN HELPED ROSE REMOVE HER BACKPACK IN THE CAR, WHICH SHE sat near her feet. Aedan retrieved a few moist towelette packs from the console, gave two to Rose, and kept one for himself. Rose opened one to clean her hands and the other to clean her face. "Thank you. I'm pretty sure I touched every stone out there," she admitted.

Aedan washed his hands and face, then took out his phone, which he wiped clean. He unlocked it and handed it to her.

"On our way to lunch, I thought you might want to flip through some of the pictures we took at the Causeway."

"I'm sure they came out great with the natural lighting and scenery." Rose flipped through the pictures. She saw a photo of her standing on a hexagon, an identical one of Aedan, and one with her making a face and hugging a hexagon. Rose continued scrolling and found a picture of her in front of the rolling green mountain landscape. When Aedan took that photo, she thought about the rolling green grass and how it was even more vivid in person than the tourist guide's online depiction. Midway through, she located the selfie they took together. Something about the image warmed her inside. "Look. This picture of us is beautiful, Aedan. It is one of those pictures you see in the movie when the guy and girl break up, and then they look back at some old photo during a flashback to happier times and the music queues, and they go searching for each other years later."

"You got all that from that picture? It sounds so tragic."

"Rewrite. It's one of those pictures in which a mother shows her daughter and says, 'I hope you find what your father I had the day we took this picture.' Then they hug and cry together before the hallmark channel credits roll."

"Em, much better. But I am hoping it goes something like this. 'This picture was the first of many to document the lives of two people who spent a lifetime loving hard, playing hard, and working hard to save the planet and humanity together.'"

Her face warmed at the thought, and it was her turn to flash a sudden smile. "That works, too. Although kind of mushy—I mean, lovely," she teased. Rose hadn't thought about finding love or even the perfect mate. She was focused on work, her goals, and the ever-pending deadlines that succeeded each. She thought about it for a moment and how that fact may have influenced her to let go so quickly in her last relationship.

It was a short ride through the colorful twisting coastal road to their lunch destination on the Causeway's outskirts. Aedan talked about expanding some of his companies into new countries. He spoke about how well Niall was running the businesses and tasked him with thirty percent growth. She was impressed and glad to gain insight into a typical day in his life. She learned how he became the powerful businessman who dominated his competition with Niall by his side, outmatching them on quality, satisfaction, and ethics. Rose imagined, like herself, that Aedan didn't have much downtime. So, she was surprised he was dedicating time away to be with her.

"Having a good time so far?" Aedan asked, pulling her away from her thoughts.

"Of course. I'm glad that I took time off to explore Ireland. I draw inspiration for my work from personal experiences. Then, I visualize how it all ties to the exhibit. I think you caught me in one of those moments when you surprised me during lunchtime earlier this week."

"I was interested to know what stroke of brilliance you devised but expected you'd tell me in your own time. After all, I interrupted you at work. I'll have to remember you're here to do a job."

"Honestly, I'm adjusting to that myself. It makes it hard to set boundaries living and working in the same space. Like I assumed you'd come down to meet me when I first arrived."

"I can explain."

"That's the point. It's not necessary. As I said, it's our circumstances. If I'd been staying at a hotel, neither of us would've given it a second thought."

"Even so, you're due an explanation. We had a deadline to meet the next day. It was late when we wrapped up. By the time I came down, you were already asleep. I think you'd agree I made up for it over drinks the next day?"

"You did. It's why I'm here touring with you this weekend."

"Thanks for your trust."

"Don't thank me yet. In case you haven't noticed, I'm still working on it."

"I appreciate the efforts. How do I get you to the tipping point?"

Rose raised an eyebrow. She was curious to know what his intentions were. Rose hoped he wasn't looking for a one-night stand or a long-term relationship. She wasn't interested in a long-distance relationship with all she had going on. The single life had been working just fine for her, which would continue to be the situation if the stars didn't align. And she was okay with misalignment for now. She needed to clarify that whatever they had between them was limited to her time in Belfast.

"Aedan, I have a question."

"Ask me anything."

"I think I know the answer. But why do you want me to reach the tipping point? Now is the perfect opportunity to help me understand your intentions. Why are you here with me?"

"I'm still trying to figure this out. The more I learn through our conversations, the more I want to know you better. At first, I was just trying to understand the person my sister chose to host her biggest event of the year. Then, somewhere along the way, that quickly evolved."

"Quick is the operative word and an understatement, I might add."

"We have a limited time together, so I want to use our time wisely. One of my faults is my tendency to move quickly. It serves me well in business. Gives me a competitive advantage. At other times, it may not be the best tactic. This is not something I'd normally do, but I'd like to see it through." He waved a finger between them. "Wherever it leads," he continued.

"Admittedly, I'm attracted to you. And today, wandering around holding your hand and hearing you share your country's history, felt unexpectedly good. I don't want to taint that, but the truth is, I'm not looking for a happily ever after. I'm perfectly happy with my current situation and don't intend to make any forever decisions. So, a long-distance relationship is *not* something I see in my future." She had tried that before. It didn't work. "It's important to set the stage so there's no confusion."

"Duly noted. So, you're telling me you're okay with a happy *for now* instead of a happy *forever*. And for you, that means in Belfast."

"Something like that."

"I would caution you never to say never, but I get it. You should also know that I considered all angles before asking you for lunch the other day. If anything comes of this, I'm fully prepared to do what's necessary to make things work. Did I mention my company operates in over eighty countries, including the United States?"

"I know. But there are still many more things I want to know about you."

"Patience. We'll get there."

She put both palms up and moved her fingers in a bring-it-on gesture. "I'm good at surprising others but don't like surprises. I like to know what lies ahead. So, where are we going this weekend?"

Aedan flashed a sudden smile in return. "You're used to being in control. So am I. You're in good hands. Our next stop is a city. We'll see some sites and stay overnight."

Rose took a deep breath and re-played the weekend mantra in her head. *Trust. Relax. Enjoy.* Relaxing and enjoying would come easy. Trust, on the other hand, was a harder pill to swallow.

They left the restaurant and returned to the winding coastal path, heading northwest until they reached another coastal city steeped in history. Now, they were in Derry, where *The Troubles* supposedly began with the Battle of Bogside.

⁂

THE TOWN—ANOTHER SLEEPY, SUNNY, COASTAL CITY—WAS QUAINT yet beautiful. White, puffy clouds dotted the pale blue sky, becoming the backdrop to part of the town bordered by a rocky coast and divided by the River Foyle on the other side. There were ruins high above the hills where waves crashed against the shores. Centuries-old stone mountains covered in moss and grass punctured the horizon. Aedan took Rose to where locals and tourists were milling around, sightseeing, having dinner, shopping, and hanging out in the city's lower elevations. She imagined a town like this would have inspired Charles Woodbury to open a school at Ogunquit to teach students to paint the scenery in a similar setting.

Rose reminded herself this would have been a different picture twenty years prior as she began to understand how complicated Ireland's past was, which contained many conflicts between the Catholics and the Protestants. There would have been fights and bloodshed in the streets of a city divided. The sectarian violence between these groups originated in Derry with the Battle of Bogside. Rose was all ears as Aedan explained how it eventually spread to other parts of Ireland into a significant event called *The Troubles*, which Aedan said subsequently spread like wildfire across Northern Ireland. Issues continued into the early nineties, widening the rift between two groups on separate sides of Unionism and Nationalists. She could only imagine how that impacted Aedan and his family.

Aedan's tone hinted to Rose that, like his brother, he had his own backstory tied to these tragic events, but Rose was reluctant to press for more information. She hoped he would share more when he was ready. For now, they were on an excursion through the city, exploring the various sites where events took place.

"Let's stop here, Aedan. I'd like to grab some water and check out the *tchotchkes*," Rose said over her shoulder before stepping into the store.

"I guess we're shopping now," he quipped and followed her in.

Rose greeted the shop owner, made her way to the cooler, and grabbed bottled water. "You want one?" She handed the bottle to Aedan.

"No, but I'll hold it while you look around."

The store resembled the shops at the airports. A collection of items was neatly organized on shelves by type and size. There were whiskey shot glasses with *Ireland* printed on the front, tabletop displays covered in magnets, stacks of hats, and t-shirts with various slogans hanging on a turnstile rack. Rose picked up a black t-shirt with white lettering.

"This is different. More blacks, more dogs, more Irish." She read aloud the words from the t-shirt, then held it up in front of her as if sizing it.

"A young artist helped make this phrase go viral when she produced a video of this phrase being painted on the side of a house. It's a play on words referencing racist signs on establishments across the UK that read "no blacks, no dogs, no Irish." Were you thinking of buying one?" Aedan picked a shirt from the rack. "This one is more your size. You might get lost in the one you're holding."

"I think I will. Hold that up." She pulled her mobile from her pocket, took a picture of the t-shirt, then texted it to Kris along with a note.

"What was that for?" Aedan took the shirt from Rose, replaced it on the rack, and sat the smaller shirt and water on the checkout counter.

"The artist you mentioned sounds like someone I'd like to profile for the exhibition. The message ties to the untold part of Ireland's history related to people of color I plan to showcase. This artist has a story to tell, and I'm in the perfect position to amplify their message. I sent a note to Kris to track the person down and set up the meeting."

"You're not afraid to tackle complex subject matter through art, are you?"

"Why would I be? Take a step back for a second. Don't you see the irony in this? Irish Catholics struggled to survive in a Protestant world when emigrating to the United States. Finding a job was hard, and as an oppressed race, they resorted to furthering the oppression of their closest social class competitors: African Americans. So, here I am in Ireland with you, and with this t-shirt about social issues both our peoples experienced." Rose flicked the t-shirt.

"Political and nationalistic differences have been at the forefront of our life here for as long as I can remember. I hadn't really thought about race."

"I, unfortunately, don't have the luxury to ignore it. So, I make sure to educate people by telling the truth of the matter through art."

"Point taken. It's fascinating to watch you work. I see why my sister brought you onboard." Aedan paid the clerk and escorted Rose outside. "Any more impromptu stops before we move on?"

"No. It seems we've covered a lot of ground today. It's been heavy but informative, solidifying that my exhibition is in keeping with Ireland's complex history." Rose suppressed her desire to ask what was next.

"Our climate is highly political, and I suspect that will be the case for years to come. On a lighter note, next on the agenda is something less sociopolitical and more relaxing. Before you ask, it's dinner, and if the weather holds out, we can cap the evening with a brief stroll in town so you can see the city lit up at night."

"That works for me."

"So, would you like to get checked into our hotel, clean up, get dressed, and head to a nice restaurant for dinner?" Aedan asked.

"What's the alternative?"

"Grab something at a place that will take us the way we are now." He scrunched his nose and tugged at his t-shirt.

"I feel you. Let's get cleaned up so I can put on heels."

"I was hoping you'd say that." He flashed a sudden smile. Rose knew the look of a man with something up his sleeves.

"Are we headed back now? I know I'm supposed to trust you, but I think that's a legitimate question."

"Yes. I'll send for the car."

Their hotel was a large granite and glass building at the edge of the Foyle River. Several hotel agents rushed to the car to greet them and collect their bags from the trunk when they arrived. "We'll take these to your rooms," a member of the staff informed them.

Aedan placed his hand on the small of Rose's back as they passed through the sliding glass doors leading to the central lobby. It was the first time she felt part of a couple in about a year. Following her last breakup, she didn't see herself as couple material. All her focus was channeled into Rick Ross Enterprises and her art foundation. There was no room left for anything else. Or so she thought.

Once inside, Rose found the minimalist design ubiquitous, like an art gallery. The reception desk, rendered of polished granite, held no hint of its true purpose, save a few pens and two vases filled with orange lilies.

Aedan went to the desk, where agents stood ready to greet and check them in while Rose looked on. His chiseled face had developed a five o'clock shadow. A warm sensation rushed through her at the thought of how it would feel to have his cheek brushing against her skin.

"I asked them to put us on the same floor next door to each other." The sudden sound of Aedan's voice snapped her out of her trance as they headed to the bank of elevators.

She turned to Aedan. "It seems you've forgotten our current arrangements are similar at your sister's house?"

"I hadn't looked at it that way. All the same, I'd feel much better knowing you're only a few steps away."

"You sound like Troy. I am perfectly capable of managing myself. Besides, there are only a few suites on the floor, and Troy will be across the hall."

"I'm just being cautious. Nothing more. And Troy would do the same if I weren't here."

When they reached their floor, Aedan escorted Rose to her suite.

"Here, let me," Aedan insisted as he stepped in front of Rose to check her suite before allowing her to enter. "All clear." He gestured for her to step in.

"What time should we meet in the lobby?" she asked.

"That depends."

"On?" She stepped forward, causing Aedan to walk backward toward the door.

"On how long you think it might take you to get ready. I wouldn't want to rush the process."

"Ha ha. What are you trying to say? Women take a long time to get ready or something?"

"Something like that."

Rose watched as he scanned her from head to toe, as if trying to commit her to memory. "And you think standing there undressing me with your eyes will make the process go faster?" She poked his shoulder with her finger, causing him to step into the hallway.

"Touché. But like I said. I am not trying to rush the process. I did commit to you wearing your heels—and I like it when you wear heels," Aedan's voice rolled low and deep in a way she hadn't heard before.

"Okay, Mr. Take As Much Time As You Need. Give me thirty minutes to pull myself together. I'll meet you in the lobby. Is that enough time for you?"

"Plenty."

Rose used every second to transform her look from casual to captivating. She didn't hesitate when choosing a short silk slip dress and four-inch slingbacks. She had a matching envelope clutch large enough to hold her passport, mobile phone, small wallet, travel-sized bottle of her favorite scent, and a tube of lipstick. A glance in the mirror near the front door and Rose was ready to go.

ROSE ENTERED THE LOBBY TO FIND AEDAN AT THE BAR, STANDING with a hand in his pocket, awaiting her arrival. All eyes were on Rose—including his—as she glided across the room dressed in a silk, green, ombre slip-dress. The beautiful, bronze-colored woman was impossible to miss amongst the sea of homogenous guests.

Rose walked directly up to Aedan with her hand open in a low-five position to her side, not wanting to draw more attention than she already had. Aedan interlocked his fingers with hers, then leaned in to kiss her cheek.

"Rose, you look spectacular. Touring suits you."

"A bit of an improvement from my jeans. You think?"

He cleared his throat. "That's an understatement. Look around—everyone stopped what they're doing to stare."

"Is the dress too much?" she asked.

He leaned in and lowered his voice when he spoke. "It's not the dress that has their attention. It's the beautiful woman working the dress."

Rose looked down to hide the rush of heat forming on her face. Usually, she could shoulder a compliment. But the unexpected whisper of desire disclosed in his voice left her speechless.

"Thank you." She stepped back to drink in Aedan. He was the personification of eye candy, standing there with well-hewn muscles perfectly packaged in his steely gray suit and white silk shirt. She couldn't decide whether to kiss him or lick him. Perhaps both. "You look handsome as ever, Aedan."

"You have everything you need?"

"I believe I do. Am I missing something?"

Aedan's eyes dropped to her shoulders. "Will that wrap be enough to keep you warm? It might be a little chilly outside."

Rose adjusted the loosely draped black wrap on her arms. "It's perfect."

Aedan nodded and held out an arm for her to hold as they walked to the car.

"We don't have far to go, but it's better to drive since you're in heels. I hope you like the restaurant I chose."

"I'm sure it's fine." She lowered her head to enter the car and greeted the driver.

The restaurant, *Browns in Town*, was only a few blocks from the hotel. A large black and white sign bearing the restaurant's name hung above the front door. The building's aged brick façade paired with updated pillars and big glass windows gave it a contemporary feel. Rose and Aedan exited the car into the chilly night air. Before they could reach the restaurant door, a staff member opened it to greet them. Inside the dimly lit restaurant were booths wrapped in dark paneling from floor to ceiling along the inner wall and tables for two bordered the windows facing the street. In one corner was a pianist playing jazz covers. *In A Sentimental Mood* by Duke Ellington was the current song under interpretation. Several sharply dressed couples sat sprinkled around the room. She could tell it was a spot to celebrate special events. Just then, a toast rang out. "Here's to Matt and Dianne. May the world be your oyster."

"Happy birthday Liz, to your health," a voice sang as cheers echoed within the room. Everyone was seemingly in good spirits. There was no hint of turmoil from the past. It was a good night in Derry.

"Are you okay with this table?" Aedan watched as Rose scanned the restaurant.

"Yes, perfect. It is a nice spot. Have you eaten here before?" She watched as Aedan waited for the server to leave.

"Actually, no. I heard about this place from some business associates. But I did check their reviews. I wanted to make sure I took you someplace special."

"I'm surprised you haven't tried this place out yet."

"It's rare for me to take time away from work."

"You need to get out on your own more."

"Well, there needs to be something—or *someone*—worth me getting out more. I hope you've enjoyed the tour so far."

"Everything has been great so far. The coastline reminds me of California. But there's so much more richness in Ireland's history and structures, which go back much further than ours. But California is beautiful and worth touring if you have the chance."

"I've visited before, but mainly for business. I always hear about the 1906 earthquake."

"It's one of the most significant events. Every year on the anniversary, we honor the men and women who lost their lives on that day, which happened to be several thousand more than was initially reported. But that's a whole story in and of itself. I curated an art show one year, assembling the stories of people of African descent in San Francisco who were around at the time of the earthquake. It was pretty powerful." Rose looked down at her menu and then closed it. "I'll have the ravioli, with Malbec. Surprise me with dessert," she said to Aedan, who nodded in response.

"I recall reading about th^at exhibition. Seems it was well received. Maybe our tour will give you more ideas for your upcoming exhibition. Do you feel you're getting a sense of the place and the events that happened in the past?"

"I get the gist. But having been raised in California, it's hard to comprehend living through a civil war in modern times. Our last one was between the northern and southern states in 1861. To this day, there are still people that can't accept the outcome. But Ireland's not the first country I've traveled to that had similar issues to the sectarian violence occurring around the same time as *The Troubles*."

"Oh, where was that?" Aedan asked.

"Croatia. They had it bad in the nineties. There were so many incidents of families torn apart by war. Many people fled the city of Dubrovnik until the terrible times had passed, returning after the war. I can only imagine how horrible it would have been to live through that and return to the country you were scared of before you left. It leaves a lot of personal fences needing mending."

"I lived through something similar here. After the problems, we had curfews for a long time, and some streets were off-limits to Catholics during the day." The waiter interrupted their conversation to bring water and take their order. Aedan looked to Rose for confirmation, and she nodded in response. "We'll have two of the squash ravioli, the Malbec, and for dessert, mousse for the lady, and sorbet for me. You can bring the wine out when dinner is ready." Aedan returned the menus to the waiter before he left. "As I said, going anywhere at night was virtually impossible and risky. During the day, it wasn't that good either. You could be stopped on the street and harassed by the military or someone from the opposition. In my case, by a Protestant at any point."

"I wouldn't do well under those circumstances." Rose pursed her lips.

"It was rough. We were always on guard. Brianna had an incident one day heading home from school alone when she came upon some kids that started taunting her. Luckily, I caught up with her just as one of the kids knocked her bag out of her hand."

"Sounds like a volatile situation."

"It was. The gang turned on me when I reached Brianna and the others."

"Did you have to fight them?" she asked.

"Yes, although it was two against one. Thanks to all my training, I could take them down easily. But one of the blokes pulled a weapon on me. Before he could get it out of his pocket, I kicked his hand so hard I expect I broke a bone or two."

"Remind me not to pick a fight with you."

Aedan raised his hands, surrendering. "I would never lift a finger against you—just tell me what you want, and I'll hand it over. Besides, with your training, I should be the one worrying. Didn't Troy train you on defensive techniques?"

"Some, but I received most of my training before meeting him. My former security advisor was my defensive tactics coach when I was younger. Did Brianna train with you and Niall?"

"Never. Brianna seemed to shy away from strenuous activity, citing exhaustion. Even so, I don't think Brianna had the temperament for it. I believe she's afraid to hurt someone that way, even in self-defense. So, Niall and I were the designated protectors, so to speak. I think you get a sense from the history tour that family and culture are essential to life here."

"I can see that. You and your brother give off that *family only beyond this point* vibe. Niall went as far as to ask me to dismiss Troy when he's there."

The waiter returned to the table with their drinks and dinner plates. He poured a sampling of wine for Aedan to taste and then filled their glasses after Aedan offered an approving nod. Rose and Aedan both thanked the waiter before he disappeared into the kitchen.

"Dismiss?"

"Well, dismiss is such a harsh word. Let's just say Niall wanted me to give Troy the gift of time."

"The situation won't be any different with me. I recall explaining to you earlier this week that Troy's services are not required while we're around."

"That's presumptuous of you, but I'm listening." Rose took a sip of water and watched Aedan's face for signs of resistance. She knew Aedan didn't get to his status by backing down—it wasn't in his nature. Despite his opinion, Rose knew Troy would always have eyes on her.

"I know he serves a purpose, and I respect his work. Niall runs one of my companies solely dedicated to security. So, you can understand there is no need for overkill—we have you covered."

"I understand your point, but Troy is here for me literally and figuratively, so let's table the discussion. Also, that reminds me, I need to chat with Niall about the event when we get back."

"Did something happen?" he asked.

"Not exactly. I had an idea."

"The one I walked in on?"

"Yes, that one."

"I'd like to hear it."

"I plan to enhance the patrons' and the artists' experience and make it profound. My idea is to interview the artist and discover which art pieces inspired their career. Then, I'd showcase those pieces for the one-night-only event. It would be a surprise to both the participants and the artists. How wonderful would you feel if something that inspired your life's work was present during an important day for you?"

"It's brilliant. So, what do you need from Niall?"

"Many artists are inspired by the works of other famous artists that came before them. I expect that could include priceless works of art by Picasso, Basquiat, Van Gogh, Frida Kahlo, Mary Cassatt, and others."

"I see where you're heading. You want to curate the art that inspired the artist. You'll want the team to ensure the art reaches its destination safely, limit access to visitors on the premise, and have it returned intact the next day. Right?"

"Exactly. You sound like you've done this before." She smiled, not because Aedan was on board with the idea, but because she could see her plan coming together.

"We secured a few important things in our past. I'm very familiar with Brianna's shows. Unlike Niall, I get more involved when it comes to Brianna."

"So, I can count on you to arrange for someone to collect the pieces and hand-deliver them to the gallery?"

"We have you covered. I'll text Niall before we return so he can begin assembling a team."

"You realize the art could potentially be located anywhere around the globe at this point, right? I'll map out a list of what I have so far tonight."

Aedan raised an eyebrow. "Tonight? I know you never stop working, but we have other plans tonight. You can work on your list when we return to Belfast."

The waiter returned to clear their dinner plates, which he replaced with their dessert. Rose watched wide-eyed as the waiter placed a glass dessert dish in front of her containing double-layered white and milk chocolate mousse topped with dark chocolate shavings.

"This is pure sin." Rose put a heaping spoonful of mousse in her mouth. "Oh my god, this is so decadent. Are you sure you wouldn't prefer this over sorbet?"

Aedan pointed toward his face, gesturing for Rose to check hers. She wiped the side of her face with a napkin. "Here, let me get that," he said.

Rose leaned towards him. Aedan brushed her cheek with his thumb, leaned in, then pressed his lips to the corner of hers. "There." He groaned and sucked her bottom lip before covering her mouth with his. Rose opened her mouth, allowing his tongue to mingle with hers. Their kiss lasted unusually long for a display of affection in public before Aedan pulled back as if catching himself. "I prefer my mousse on you," he whispered.

Rose leaned back. The passion behind his kiss, combined with the chocolate, made her body tingle. "Mr. King, are you putting the moves on me?" She sure hoped he was, considering how he sat back in his chair, smiling at her like the cat that got the cream.

"I am. I've been dying to do that all night." Aedan reached a hand across the table and held it open. Rose placed hers in his. His hand was warm and strong.

"Between the chocolate and you, I need a smoke."

Aedan smiled. "We both know you don't smoke."

"Okay, maybe not, but if you do that again, I'll need to step out to get some air."

"Speaking of stepping out. How would you feel about a short walk before returning to the hotel? There's a garden lounge at the end of the block and around the corner. It's beautifully lit at night. I think you'd like it."

"Sounds lovely."

They finished the last of their drinks, and Aedan flagged the waiter and paid the bill before they left the restaurant. Together, they headed out, locked arm in arm. The two walked past a few local establishments and went around the corner into the lounge. Aedan informed the staff to seat them in the garden and proceeded through the crowded restaurant outside to an empty patio. The setting was beautiful and cozy. Heaters overhead masked the night chill. The sky was clear enough to see the stars through the string of fairy lights hanging overhead. The terrace had an outdoor stereo system that made it easier to hear the music. Aedan and Rose sat on one of the couches together. A side table with a candle and a bowl of purple-wrapped sweets was in front of them. Aedan offered one to Rose.

"You know, I just had a whole dish of mousse. I think you're trying to send me into overdrive." Aedan opened the candy and popped it into his mouth. A few seconds later, a waiter walked over to take their order.

"Manhattan?" Aedan looked at Rose.

"Sounds good."

He turned to the waiter. "Two Manhattans, please." The waiter nodded and disappeared inside. Aedan turned to Rose again. "It was a good day."

"It was. I had a lovely time." She paused and turned her body so that she was facing Aedan. "Can I confess something?" They were sitting so close that when she crossed her legs, her stilettos gently brushed his lower calf.

"Sure."

"I'm sure I mentioned earlier this evening that you look handsome tonight." Her words were slow and deliberate. "I'm glad our time together has been easy. Natural."

"I like what I hear so far," he said.

"Good. There's more. I haven't been able to keep my eyes off you. I hope we can continue what you started at the restaurant."

Aedan's response was immediate as he leaned in close, put his arm around her shoulder, drew her to him, and kissed her. He tasted like milk chocolate, and she wanted more as their tongues collided. After a few moments, he leaned back so slightly that only the sides of their noses touched when he spoke. "Perfect." He licked her lips.

"You stole my line," she smiled. "Although *yum* came to mind first."

He flashed his familiar smile. "I'd love to do that again, but I see the waiter heading our way." The waiter appeared on cue and placed drinks on the table in front of them. Rose's eyes never left Aedan as he acknowledged and thanked the waiter. When the waiter left, Aedan handed her a Manhattan. "Here's to you, to me, and to exploring something new. I would never have expected this moment to happen, but I am happy for every second." Aedan and Rose clinked glasses and sipped their drinks.

Rose took both their glasses, placed them on the table, and turned to Aedan. "I prefer this." She pressed her lips to his. They explored each other's mouths a while before coming up for air. Rose picked up her glass and took a sip before breaking the silence. "Mmm."

"They did a good job on that, didn't they?" Aedan lifted his chin toward her drink.

"That was for you. I've been wondering what a Manhattan tastes like on you. And your kiss—well, let's just say, I felt it."

"Should I be blushing about now?" The corner of his lip curved up slightly.

She was surprised at the gesture, but wasn't sure why. Maybe because she hadn't seen Aedan blush before or because she had made someone that powerful blush. "Hum. Not unless you're twelve or a virgin. In either case, we wouldn't be here."

"Neither. Thank goodness. I am thoroughly enjoying my adult status tonight."

"You're still getting used to my candor."

"Almost there. And we've officially crossed the flirting line."

"Does it bother you?" she asked.

"No, but what does this mean to you, Rose?"

Rose had asked herself the same question. Was she ready to take the next step with Aedan? She would have to mentally compartmentalize their relationship to avoid being distracted from her goals. "It means we still have tonight and the rest of this weekend to figure it and us out. It means I'm only thinking about you and what's happening now."

"Sounds like you don't know what to do with me."

"That's the problem. I know exactly what to do with you." She smiled wryly.

Aedan dipped his lips to hers and kissed Rose hard. "You know we can't continue like this here. We're about five seconds from getting kicked out."

"I wouldn't mind either scenario," Rose said with a mischievous look.

Nina Simone's song *Do I Move You* came on. "Would you dance with me?" Aedan stood and held out a hand to help her up. She stood, and together, they stepped into a clearing a few feet away to dance. Aedan placed one hand around her waist and held Rose firmly against him while they danced. He dipped his face to kiss her while Rose responded in kind, kissing him back as she stroked the hair at the nape of his neck. Their bodies swayed to the music. The touch of his body enveloped her in warmth.

"Thank you," Aedan whispered against her mouth.

Rose looked up at Aedan. "For what?"

"For taking me up on my offer to see some of Ireland. For being independent, strong, honest, brilliant." He paused for a second. "Sexy."

"Let's finish our drinks and head back," Rose suggested.

"Does this mean you made up your mind?"

"On what I want to do with you?"

"That." He moved her hair away from her face and dipped his head to kiss her neck.

"I told you, Mr. King. I know exactly what to do."

"I'll send for the car."

⚘

Rose sat in front of the fireplace in her hotel room. "I love this suite you picked for me. It's modern but with a feel of the past with historical photos and artwork."

Aedan opened a bottle of champagne he had sent to her room, filled two glasses, and handed one to Rose. "I thought you would appreciate the décor. The art. Champagne." He held up his glass. "I didn't want to go too old-world on you." He tipped his nose in the air. "Your room has a hint of vanilla that I love so much."

"It's a woman's secret weapon to bring a bit of home away from home. That's my favorite travel candle you're smelling. It's spiced vanilla bean. You have to know all my secrets, don't you?"

"Not really. I ask because I'm curious about your motives. Like my brother, you don't leave anything to chance."

"I guess he and I have that in common, but we're not here to talk about him. And I am okay with old-world charm in a hotel. I can think of a few places I have a fondness for." Rose leaned back in her chair, crossed her legs, and sipped her drink.

"Care to share?"

"Is this a test, Mr. King? You know I'll pass. Here goes. The Empress Hotel in British Columbia, the Taj Lake Hotel in Udaipur, and the Driscoll in Austin, to name a few. These are lovely places to stay if you're looking for that old-world feel. Although I have to say I was a little disappointed with the Driscoll."

"Why's that?" Aedan asked.

"I was hoping to see a ghost or something, but all I got was the soundest sleep I can ever recall at a hotel. No ghosts."

Aedan laughed. "You have a funny side to you. You don't strike me as a person that would give ghosts a second thought."

"I'm serious."

"I know. That's what makes it so funny. Are you afraid of ghosts?"

"I don't think so, but I haven't actually seen one. I'll let you know when I run across one."

Rose watched as Aedan tried to suppress a laugh. "Come here." He opened his arms to her. "I don't imagine that there's much of anything of which you are afraid. And I expect you'll agree with me. But just in case, I'll protect you."

But Rose was afraid. She was worried that a real relationship would undermine her ability to achieve her goals. Most of all, she needed to protect her heart. Despite her worries, Rose put down her glass and went to Aedan. He put an arm around her waist and pulled her close to him.

"You're right. Although I'm fascinated by the idea of ghosts, I am more interested in this." Rose put her thumb and forefinger on Aedan's chin and tilted his head down until his lips hovered above hers. Their breaths mingled as he dipped his head and pressed his lips to hers, closing the distance between them. Rose wrapped her arms around his neck, pulling him into the kiss. She felt waves of pleasure rush through her body when he slipped his tongue into her mouth.

Rose melted as Aedan's arm tightened around her waist. The steel between his legs pressed against her body, straining to be free. He slid one hand down her back and past her waist, lifting her silk dress to stroke her bare hips, causing the space between her legs to pulse in response. When Aedan suddenly stopped kissing her, Rose tilted her head and looked up at him curiously. She was wet and ready, and hoped he hadn't changed his mind.

"This is beautiful on you, but at the moment, it's standing between me and what I want." Aedan tugged gently at her dress.

"What do you want, Aedan?" she teased, knowing the answer already.

Aedan reached out with one hand, cupped Rose's face, and kissed her mouth softly before moving downward to kiss one of her breasts through the silk dress, and sliding his hand down her stomach. When he pushed his fingers between her legs to her warm, moist center, Rose gasped and felt her body respond in a welcoming way. Aedan slid his fingers in and out, carefully brushing his thumb against her sweet spot. It took all her energy to keep her legs from giving way.

"Rose, you are so ready for me. I want all of you," he breathed out over her lips.

"Then we have to do something about this." She lifted her arms, allowing Aedan to undress her in one motion. Then, she turned her back to him so he could unhook her bra. Once it fell to the floor, Aedan wrapped his arms around her waist, pulling her back into his chest, then reached up to cup her breast. She leaned down to remove her stilettos, but Aedan tightened his grip, pulling her even closer into him.

"No. Leave them on," he commanded, kissing her neck softly. He slid one hand down between her legs while the other alternated between caressing her breast and squeezing her nipple.

"You're going to make me cum." Rose lifted her head back over her shoulder to take in a kiss from Aedan.

"That's the plan," he panted.

And when Rose came, her body contracted hard against his fingers that were still grasping for more. Aedan turned her around to face him. "Now you're ready."

He removed a condom from his pocket, tossed it on the bed, then took off all his clothes, leaving them in a pile on the floor. Aedan cupped his hands around Rose's face and kissed her hard. His gentle embrace turned urgent as Rose pressed her body into his until she could feel his manhood grow harder against her. He placed his arms around her bottom, lifting her effortlessly, and laid her on the bed.

"I need to take you in for a moment," he said as he lay beside her, propped up on one elbow, staring down at her. Aedan cupped one breast with his hand, leaned in to put his mouth around the other to suck it, and kissed up and down her body, covering every inch. Rose reached down to stroke the length of his manhood and turned her body toward Aedan. "Can't wait?" he asked.

"I need you inside me." She was ready, and the power in her hands told her he was, too. Aedan grabbed the condom, slid it on, and positioned himself over her. Rose wrapped her legs around his waist and guided his rod until the entire length disappeared inside her.

His first thrust was slow yet firm. Rose lifted her hips, allowing his thick rod to fill her completely. She guided his hip in her hands, ensuring every subsequent thrust hit its mark. Then, Aedan lifted her leg over his shoulder and pushed in and out—harder, deeper, faster—until the culmination of pent-up desires to be with each other in a way so intimate and primal shattered into a cacophony of gasps and growls when they came together. Then, it was over, and the room fell silent except for the faint sound of their breathing.

CHAPTER 8

The Nearness of You

"The meeting of two personalities is like the contact of two chemical substances: if there is any reaction, both are transformed."

— CARL JUNG

A NEW DAY OPENED TO EXPLORATION ON DUAL FRONTS. A NEW relationship was brewing between Rose and Aedan, like hot coffee early in the morning. And they were headed on an extended drive southeast from Derry to tour another popular world heritage site, this time in Newgrange. It took Rose a few attempts after having Aedan repeat it for her, but she mastered the name Newgrange, formally known as Brú Na Bóinne valley. She was a stickler about pronouncing names correctly, which came in handy in the art world.

When they arrived at the site, Rose and Aedan walked through a field covered in lush green grass toward a mound of neatly stacked stones forming a semi-circular wall stretching toward the vibrant blue sky and past a long line of people waiting to enter.

"Aedan, can I ask how you got these coveted tickets without us having to stand in *that* line? The people back there don't look too happy about us marching to the front." Rose glanced over her shoulder at the crowd.

"I hate to say no to you, but that's a secret I plan to keep. Besides, I know this is not your first trip to the front. Let's enjoy the tour."

"Sure. This reminds me of Xi'an, China. Those tombs were also hidden beneath green fields, which is how a farmer found them; he was digging a well."

"That's right. Have you been to the Pyramids or Stonehenge?"

"Both, yes." She held his hand as they walked to the entrance, past massive ancient stones carved with repeating circular patterns to meet their guide.

"This site is older than both the Pyramids and Stonehenge. These tombs date back around five thousand years."

Their guide took over the conversation, explaining similarities to Stonehenge and the Egyptian Pyramids as they explored the megalithic tombs. He pointed out that archeologists have yet to determine the reason for the design or method of transporting the massive stones. Rose listened while walking hand in hand with Aedan, mindlessly rubbing her thumb against his palm. Every once in a while, she would take a photo of a circular carved design on a stone formation or snap a picture of Aedan when she caught him watching her. She wanted to capture the slight hint of a smile she was sure most had not seen.

"No one really knows the purpose of this site, but during the winter solstice, it aligns to the rising sun, so there could be a religious significance," the guide explained.

Rose tried to visualize what it would have been like thousands of years ago when the structure was under development. She had so many unanswered questions: Who were these people? What were their beliefs? What were their strengths, their fears, their loves? Every day, she got up and called upon the wisdom of the ancient Africans to guide her to make the best decisions. She called upon them to help her solve the complex algorithmic problem that led to the success of Rick Ross Enterprises. She wondered if her hosts did the same. Did they draw upon the wisdom of their ancestors to channel strokes of brilliance? Rose turned her focus back to the guide, who pointed to a pattern carved in a rock. Although Aedan knew a lot about the site, he allowed the tour guide to drive the discussion. From time to time, Aedan interjected, adding some detail of significance. Rose liked that he allowed himself to be a tourist along with herself.

Rose absorbed all the information like a sponge. She also found time between listening and taking pictures to flash Aedan a flirty smile, a slight squeeze of his hand, or brush against his shoulder—the same strong shoulders carrying the large cut muscular arms that hovered over her in bed last night. The tour took several hours, and her mind overflowed with new information, which she neatly filed away for future use. By the end of the tour, she was slightly spent, thoroughly educated, and surprisingly hungry in ways that had nothing to do with food.

"Are you ready to get on the road?" Aedan gestured toward the car where the driver was standing by.

"Yes. Maybe we shouldn't have stayed up as late as we did." She gave him a knowing smile. "Not that it wasn't worth it."

"Rose last night was everything it should have been." Aedan dipped his head to catch her gaze. Rose nodded in response.

"For the rest of today, you have a few choices. We can check into our next location, get something to eat, and do a little touring. Or we can skip the touring, check into the hotel, eat and chill the rest of the day, catch the sunset, drink, and let things evolve organically. Whatever you prefer, I'm fine with it."

"I'm putting a damper on your plans, aren't I?"

"No, not at all. That's why I'm asking you. I realize that not knowing what comes next is stressful for you, so I'm changing it. This time away is all about you and what you want to do. My plan was for you to have time away from work, see new places you've never been to before, and have some new experiences. I'm completely flexible on how the next few days unfold."

"You've done a good job so far. Okay, let's chill, have a drink, and play the rest by ear."

"We're heading to the hotel," Aedan told the driver as he held Rose's hand and helped her back into the car.

"By the way, Aedan."

"Yes?"

"Knowing how much of a gentleman you are, I am sure you booked us in two separate rooms."

"I did." He looked at her, one eyebrow raised.

"You can cancel the second room. Unless you have any objections."

The corner of Aedan's lips tipped slightly, and then he cleared his throat. "Em. None. Consider it done. But if you change your mind, just let me know."

Rose looked on as Aedan typed something into his phone. "Are you making your own arrangements?"

"No, my assistant manages my calendar and travel arrangements. I will introduce you two if you have time during your stay. He's very efficient."

"He? That's very forward-thinking of you," Rose continued watching him for a moment.

Evidence of the windy day reflected in his tousled hair and caused his black curls to flow across his forehead like bangs, which made him look more like a student heading to a lecture than the distinguished businessman she had come to know. She reached over and combed his inky black hair back with her fingers, then traced a line down the side of his cheek to his chin. Aedan looked at Rose and smiled. She wondered what he thought when he looked at her and why he hadn't settled with anyone yet. Unlike his brother, Aedan wasn't as forthcoming with his feelings.

"What's happening here?" She rubbed the back of her hand over his chin.

"This?" He rubbed his chin between his thumb and forefinger. "I'm letting my beard and mustache grow in—something I do when I go on holiday."

"My dad does the same thing. All our vacation photos show him sporting a beard. Why do some guys do that? If you want to have hair on your face, you should have it whether it's vacation or not. It's on-trend."

"So, you like it?"

"Looks good."

"Maybe I should consider keeping it, even when we're back."

"You're still swoon-worthy if that's what you're worried about," Rose commented with a wry grin. She glanced up at Aedan to find a look in his eyes that was part amused, part desire. She leaned over, took his top lip between hers, and kissed him. Aedan cupped her face, licked her lips, then deepened the kiss when she opened her mouth to him. When they came up for air, they were both panting and flush.

"We're going to have to hold that thought until we reach our destination," Aedan told Rose. She sat back in her seat and licked the evidence of his passion from her bottom lip.

On the short drive to their hotel, Aedan relayed the story of the Battle of the Boyne, which took place in 1690, in which William of Orange, a Protestant, defeated James II, a Roman Catholic.

She was beginning to see a sectarian theme in their tour, which she made a mental note of to discuss with Aedan later. For now, this was a story Rose knew well as she had seen a painting of the battle by Jan van Huchtenburg, who was famous for painting horse and battle scenes.

"I know this story. King Willian III commissioned Jan van Huchtenburg to paint significant battles fought in Europe. I saw the painting. The details were so intricate that I felt I was there."

"I know I shouldn't be surprised because you're an expert in art history. But I can't help but be awestruck by how amazing you are on all fronts."

"Thanks. I'm hoping it will come through in the exhibition. Speaking of which, any additional updates on Brianna?"

"Her condition is the same. I would have expected some improvement by now. The important thing is that she isn't getting any worse, so she plans to return this weekend with our cousin. Niall set up several home visits with her doctor after she settles in."

"It will be good to see her when we're back."

"Her recovery will take more time than the doctor originally expected."

"She's strong. And she has you and Niall to help her through it. Oh, and going back to your previous statement, is this the same cousin Niall was trying to warn me about?"

"The one and only."

"So, be honest with me. Is there anything I should know about her? It seems there might be by the cryptic way your brother spoke about her."

"Other than the fact that she's not afraid to speak her mind, I don't have anything more to say about her. I think every family has someone like her."

"I understand." Rose knew there was a lot he wasn't saying but didn't want to push. "Anyways, my thoughts are with your sister, and I hope she makes a full and speedy recovery. It would be great if she could attend the art exhibition."

"She would love nothing more."

AEDAN AND ROSE HEADED STRAIGHT TO THE ROOM FOLLOWING CHECK-in. Rose began laying out her next outfit for their afternoon of leisure. She had no plans to give up the heels and pulled out a pair of slingback platforms to match her outfit. "These may seem high, but they are so comfortable that I can basically hike in them if I needed to." She dangled the shoes from her fingers as she walked toward the bathroom to shower.

Aedan followed her into the bedroom to continue their conversation. He sat on the tufted bench at the foot of the bed, where he had a full view of the wet/dry shower room. "You know, Rose, that one line in the song by Aerosmith immediately came to mind when you said that. "Walk this way," he sang. "I can see now that's going to be stuck in my head." He watched her as she turned on the water.

She laughed. "Thanks for that. Now it's going to be stuck in my head, too. You know you can't sing, right?"

"I'm hurt." Aedan clutched his chest in a mock gesture of pain. "Don't worry, I won't sing the rest of the song. It doesn't fit this situation. And I won't quit my day job."

Rose stepped out of her clothes and into the hot shower. "What are you wearing later?"

"I believe you refer to it as my conservative look."

"Grey, blue, or black?" She called out from the shower.

"Do you have a preference?"

"I'm just curious. It's really up to you."

"This is going to make me sound like a teenager, but do you have a favorite color?"

"It's okay, we both sound like youngsters at this point, but let's run with it. Blue."

"Any particular kind of blue?"

"Just blue in general. But don't think I expect you to walk around in blue every day. And I'm not trying to be all matchy."

"Another thing you have in common with my brother. On the other hand, I favor gray because it blends so well with other colors."

"Like I said, wear what you want. Or don't wear anything. Either way, you're total eye candy."

"Eye candy? Now I feel objectified," he laughed.

"I doubt it."

"Just a little." He made a gesture with his thumb and forefinger.

"I'm just saying, there's a lot of you under all that clothing. Until last night, I didn't know what I was missing." She raised her eyebrows up and down. "But seriously, Aedan. You have a pretty impressive set of abs. And the way you move—"

He coughed, interrupting her. "This is a first—I don't know whether to be embarrassed or aroused."

"You want me to be honest with you, right?"

"Always."

"You don't strike me as someone that gets embarrassed about anything. Especially not sex. But feel free to be aroused." She smiled as the water ran over her shoulders and down her back.

"That sounds like an invitation."

Rose pushed the glass door open. "Did I stutter?"

Aedan shed his clothes in a heartbeat and stepped into the shower. He pressed his chest against her back, then wrapped his arms around her waist, dipping his head to kiss the curve in her neck. Rose turned to catch his kiss in her mouth instead. She could feel his desire rise thick against her as the water poured over them. Aedan raised one hand to hold her breast, lowered the other hand, and reached between her folds, stroking her softly. Her desire to be full of him again overwhelmed her with each stroke. Rose bent and placed her hands on the shower walls to brace herself to receive Aedan. At first, he pushed in slow, taking his time to fill her before pulling out, then pushing in harder—faster—repeating the motion again and again. The shower echoed the sounds, the water bouncing off their bodies, their groans of ecstasy, and the rhythm of their bodies colliding.

"Aedan," Rose called out, signaling him.

He pushed in deep, giving her what she needed, and pulled out as he reached his own climax, allowing the evidence to cover them. Then, he turned Rose to face him and kissed her deeply, letting the water wash over them as their bodies recovered before stepping out. He dried her off, carried her to the bed, pulled her back to his chest, and held her close, arms wrapped like steel around her waist. They were two titans, spent and satiated.

CHAPTER 9

Say That Again

"Wise men speak because they have something to say;
Fools because they have to say something."

— PLATO

As the car neared the house, Rose and Aedan saw a red sedan parked next to Niall's car and those of Rose's staff. Troy arrived ahead of time and was standing at the gallery's entrance. Rose knew he had been tracking her every move. The driver pulled in close to the main house.

Aedan placed a hand on Rose's knee. "Are you ready for this?" They had moved well beyond the getting-to-know-you phase, and Rose was in a different headspace.

"Ready."

The driver first opened the door for Aedan, who subsequently opened Rose's. She held his hand as she exited the vehicle. Troy was already standing beside Aedan before Rose was out.

"Let me help you, Rose." Troy nodded in Aedan's direction. "Aedan."

"Troy. It's officially the longest you had to be in stealth mode." Rose placed a hand on Troy's shoulder as she passed him.

"It could well be a record," he replied flatly.

"Troy, thank you for the space, man. I'll turn her back over to your watch shortly. But first, I see my sister has returned with my cousin, and I'd like to check in on Brianna and introduce Rose to Carol."

"If no one has mentioned anything to you, I think you should know your sister is in a wheelchair. She was feeling a little too weak to walk," Troy informed him.

"I wasn't aware." He pursed his lips. "I better get right in. Rose, shall we?" Aedan outstretched his hand toward the house.

"I hope your sister is alright. Did Niall or anyone indicate that her condition had worsened while we were gone?" Rose asked.

"No. Only what we discussed." His eyebrows were creased.

As they entered the foyer, they heard two voices coming from the sitting room. Rose recognized Niall's deep, melodic voice, but the second voice was gruffer, less polished. It was a woman unfamiliar to her.

"Here they are," Niall said, announcing their arrival. "I didn't think you two would ever return." He motioned Rose forward. "Rose, meet Carol, our cousin. Carol, this is Rose. Do you recall those recent articles you've been reading about the upcoming exhibition? Well, this is who they're all about." He turned to speak to Rose. "Your PR team has been quite busy promoting the show while you were away."

Rose's eyes went from Aedan to Niall to Carol, whose face looked like she was smelling a foul odor. "Hi Carol, I'm Rose. It's nice to meet you. Both Niall and Aedan mentioned you might be returning with Brianna. They have been fantastic hosts since she welcomed me to her home."

Rose studied Carol's face. It seemed familiar. *She could pass for a less polished version of Brianna,* Rose thought.

"Rose, pleased, I'm sure," Carol said, sounding slightly sarcastic. Her eyes dropped to Rose's neck.

Carol raised a hand to touch the scarf on Rose's neck. But before she could, Niall placed his hand in front of Carol's hand and guided it down to her side. "Uh, Carol," he said, getting her attention. "What are you doing?"

"Your scarf looks just like the one I gave to Aedan," Carol said, averting Rose's eyes and talking to her neck instead. A twinge of tension sliced through the conversations like a knife.

Aedan chimed in. "It was cold. I gave it to her, Carol. Rose and I have been on the road for a few hours this morning. Let's give her some time to unpack and get resettled."

Rose gave Aedan a light touch on the hand. "Thank you. I'll see everyone at dinner?"

"Sure, either Niall or I will come to find you. Will you be spending any time in the gallery?"

"Five minutes max. Just enough time to check in with Kris and Troy. Nice to meet you, Carol. I'll see you two gentlemen later." After a brief nod in Carol's direction and another towards Niall and Aedan, Rose left the room.

Rose was out of earshot when Carol laid into the brothers. "Bloody hell, guys! What was that? Are you two completely lost?"

Aedan's brows creased at the center. He looked to Niall's eyes for an answer, but the reply was a shrug.

As if Carol were no longer present, he openly questioned Niall. "Did something happen before we arrived?"

"I'm just as surprised as you, Aedan."

"I think Niall and I missed something, Carol. What's wrong?"

Carol was marching around the room. "Are you fucking crazy bringing that girl into this house? Have you two learned nothing from our struggles over the years?"

The brothers tried to get Carol to calm down and explain herself. Carol continued her rant without clarification.

"Carol," Aedan demanded. "Carol, can you please keep your voice down? Just tell us what happened. Do you know Rose from somewhere? You need to calm down. Take a deep breath and tell us exactly what's going on."

Carol blew back with colorful language. "You two have completely lost your minds."

Niall jumped in. "My brother failed to remind you to watch your decorum."

"I have more decorum than that girl will ever have."

"Excuse me?" Aedan's brows furrowed.

"And was that the scarf I gave you around that girl's bloody neck, Aedan? I—"

Niall jumped in. "You're about to cross a point of no return, Carol. What exactly is your problem? Rose is our guest. I don't know anything that would cause you to get this riled up. She's more than welcome here."

"Let's try and piece this together," Aedan interjected. "Are you saying you met Rose before and have an issue with her, or do I hear from your choice of words that your problem with Rose is coming from something else?"

"You're bloody right. I can't believe you two can't see past your dicks for one second. Our country has experienced enough unrest of its own. We don't want to continue to encourage immigrants to come here. Take a look at her work and what it represents. It's not the right message we want to spread. We need to protect our culture. How could you let this Black girl—"

Niall stepped forward. "Enough, Carol. I won't have you talking about Rose this way. Don't get me wrong; we appreciate the help you provided Brianna, but I know I speak for her when I say we won't tolerate this behavior. Rose is our guest. We have no issue hosting persons of different backgrounds. If you have an issue, I can arrange for you to stay at a hotel nearby if you can't control yourself. I can make alternate arrangements for Brianna's care easy enough. So, what's it gonna be?"

"First, you don't have to worry about me acting out while I'm under the same roof as *her*," she said as if Rose were an object. "Second. I'm just fine."

"She has a name. It's Rose Ross. Are we straight?" Aedan asked.

"As an arrow," Carol answered without hesitation.

"If I hear one more negative reference or so much as see a sideways glance at Rose, you'll be asked to leave. Now, do you care to explain what happened with Brianna? It seems she has taken a turn for the worse. I understand she's in a wheelchair?" Aedan said, concern coloring his voice.

"I already explained this to Niall."

"And now you're going to explain it to me," Aedan demanded.

"Brianna had a relapse. The doctor felt she should return home to familiar surroundings, which might help reduce her stress level."

"Carol, I appreciate the information and your help while Brianna was under your watch. Niall and I can take it from here. Let us know if you want to make alternate arrangements." Aedan turned to his brother. "Niall, can you keep Carol preoccupied while I check in on Brianna upstairs? Maybe you two can check up on dinner arrangements."

"Sure, no problem." He escorted Carol from the room and with her, left the tension.

AEDAN STOOD IN THE ROOM ALONE. HIS SHOULDERS RAISED AS HE inhaled, then lowered as he exhaled a deep breath as if trying to calm himself. When he was finished, he went upstairs, taking two steps at a time. The first room he visited was his sister's.

Aedan knocked on the door to Brianna's room. "Hey, it's me, Aedan. Can I come in?"

"Aedan, please come in."

Aedan opened the door to the suite, which was twice the size of his. Brianna was sitting on a chair near the window, holding an open book in her lap. Her voice rose slightly above a whisper. "Hey. You look so handsome and relaxed. The creases I used to see on your brows seem smooth now. Barely visible."

"Hey. I missed you," Aedan said as he walked across the room.

"I missed you, too."

"How are you feeling?"

"To be honest, not so good."

"Have you seen your doctor?"

"Twice in the past week."

"And what does he say about your condition? Are you following his orders? Is there something I can do or get you?"

"Aedan, I'm scared. He ran several tests."

"And?"

"And he should have results by tomorrow."

Aedan pulled up a chair to face his sister, leaned forward, and rested his hand on hers. "Don't be afraid; we're all here for you. We'll figure this out and get through it. I'll call the doctor and see what information

I can get." Her face told him she was on the verge of tears. She raised a hand and touched the space between his eyebrows. "What are you doing?" he asked.

"Darn. I made those lines come back."

"I don't know what you're talking about."

"I think you do. They were gone when you first came in. I suppose our lovely guest had something to do with that. She's one of the smartest women I know and pretty damn sexy, don't you think?"

A sudden smile swept across Aedan's face. "Actually, yes. I can't deny any of that."

"I knew it was the right thing bringing her here. I've admired her work for some time now. I hope I'm better on the day of the exhibition. I can't wait to see what she does. It will be the best show of both our careers."

"Yes, a brilliant idea you had bringing her on board. Why don't I have Rose walk you through the details if you're up for it later this week? I'm sure she has a rendering she can show you. But right now, you need to rest."

"I'm okay now that I'm back with you and Niall."

"I'm glad to hear you say that."

She inhaled and exhaled, drawing long breaths in the process. "Speaking of Niall, he mentioned you and Rose were out touring over the weekend. How was it? Did you two make a connection?"

He laughed. "Nothing subtle about you. It was nice. I didn't plan to *make a connection.* I promised to help Rose get to know more about our country. Maybe gain some insights to use in the exhibition."

"Did she get to know more about our country?"

"Yes."

"Our culture?"

"Some things, yes. You seem to have perked up a little."

"I told you, being back here makes me feel better. Don't change the subject. What did Rose learn about you?"

He cleared his throat. "Brianna."

"Aedan, don't make me put it out there."

"Rose learned I'm a good businessman. And a great brother."

"Oh my god, Aedan, are you interested in the woman or not?"

Aedan's eyebrows furrowed. He sat back in his chair. "Seems you're well enough to have dinner with us tonight. I'll have Niall make arrangements with the staff."

"I need to gather my strength. I'll let you know if I can make it. But you didn't answer my question. Are you two an item now?"

"Seriously? Let me check your head. You might have a fever."

"I'm serious. These conversations are good for me." She gently nudged his leg with hers.

"I can't talk to you right now. I have work to do. And since when are you interested in my love life?"

"I'm not. But I do want to see you settle down with someone nice. And Rose sure is nice, isn't she?" Brianna couldn't help but giggle.

Aedan closed his eyes, pinched the bridge of his nose between his thumb and forefinger, then blurted out his response. "Fine. Yes. I can see myself getting to know her better. We get along well."

"And that, dear brother, is what I was hoping to hear. Finally, a real woman comes along that you're interested in. Not one of those I-can't-remember-their-name types."

Aedan shook his head and rolled his eyes. "I never forget a name."

"That's debatable. And besides the point."

"I can't believe you made me tell you that. Did you plan this?"

"No. It is good news. Right?"

"For whom?"

"For me. And for you, right?"

"We're still figuring things out. Let's see where this goes."

"I'll let you off the hook for now."

"Thank you. Please rest, and I'll let you know when dinner is ready."

"Aedan, it's good to be home. I love you."

"Same. We're happy you're back, and I'm happy to uplift your spirits, albeit at my expense."

⁂

AEDAN LEFT HIS SISTER, WENT STRAIGHT TO ROSE'S ROOM, AND knocked on the door.

"Is that you, Aedan?"

"The scent of vanilla and lavender fills my senses," Aedan leaned against the doorframe, undressing Rose with his eyes.

"Hey. Don't act new. Come in." Rose held out her hand to him. "I just finished my shower and was taking in the view." Rose led Aedan to the open patio doors. "It's become one of my favorite spots. Something about the row of dark hedges draws me into this place."

Aedan stood behind Rose, wrapped his arms around her waist, and rested his chin on her shoulder. "This is one of my favorite spots." He pushed her hair back and then kissed her on the neck. "And this." He kissed her cheek. "And this." Aedan turned Rose in his arms and covered her mouth with his.

Rose smiled against his lips, then leaned back to look at him. "Did something happen? You want to talk?"

Aedan shook his head, then dipped back down to reclaim her lips. He slid a hand down the length of her hip and under her dress. He caressed the bare skin on her outer thigh, slipped his hand between her legs, and uttered three words against her lips. "I want you."

CHAPTER 10

Feeling Good

"The past is never where you think you left it."

— KATHERINE ANNE PORTER

ROSE IMMEDIATELY RETURNED TO WORK, ARRANGING INTERVIEWS, reviewing artwork, and updating the design to include her new ideas. Today, she was headed to meet one of Ireland's famous artists making his comeback.

A cool, gentle breeze caressed Rose's face as she stepped out of the car in front of the Gresham Hotel in Dublin. There was an unmistakable lightness in her step as she disappeared into the *23 Restaurant* to meet Kaleb Pierce for lunch. It was old stomping grounds for him, and she envisioned he would have plenty of stories to tell about happenings at his favorite spot. She looked to see Kaleb already seated at one of the tables and headed toward him. He stood and extended his hand to greet her. Rose was amazed but not surprised at how youthful this elderly black gentleman looked as if he had discovered the fountain of youth. Anyone who didn't know him wouldn't think he was a day over thirty. Although she only had an hour with him, a thousand questions ran through her mind.

"It's nice to meet you, Mr. Pierce. I'm Rose Ross. I'm curating the exhibition at Morrison Gallery later this month showcasing some of your pieces."

"Hello, Rose. La vie en rose." His melodic voice conjured the old song. "It's nice to meet you. Please, have a seat."

"Before we start, you must know that I'm a fan of your work. I have several of your pieces in my private collection."

"That's so lovely to hear."

"Mr. Pierce—"

"Call me Kaleb."

"Of course. Kaleb. Before we begin, would it be okay if I take notes during the conversation? I might use quotes from our discussion for articles or in the exhibition. You'll have final approval on the content, of course."

"Sounds brilliant."

"There's been a lot written about you over the years, yet I think journalists have only scratched the surface when it comes to understanding you as a person. You're one of the most important Black artists of our time. I'd like to talk about what inspires you and the mark you want to leave on others. Can you share that moment you realized you had a creative gene?"

"For me, it happened early. I think we were asked to draw a scenario in primary school, and my drawing looked like a loosely abstract representation of the scenario. I don't think the teacher or I knew I was creative at the time, but a pattern emerged by the third or fourth drawing. At some point, I realized I was special and never looked back."

"Do you remember the first drawing you were paid for?"

"I don't, actually. Drawing wasn't making me money, so I focused on other types of art, like music and dance. It wasn't until later in life that I began to explore painting starting with oil on canvas. Once those started to gain attention, people wanted to get their hands on my other works, including old drawings."

"My exhibition will explore perspectives of significant Black artists and other peoples of color who've contributed to Ireland's art history. To date, only the United States has attempted such an exhibition, and unfortunately, as important as the 1976 exhibition was, it failed to include some significant Black contributions to art."

"It was highly controversial at the time. I echoed the sentiment of some of my peers who were notably absent."

"You're the most celebrated Black artist in Ireland. Can you tell me what that means to you?"

"It means a great deal to me. It's recognition for forging my own path. I need to remain true to myself and my craft. I can't succumb to a category. Every piece of art should be as unique as a fingerprint. But in that same vein, you should be able to look at that fingerprint and say, 'That belongs to Kaleb.' I want my work to express the feeling I'm trying to put on canvas. I want to be an example to those who haven't made it to the spotlight. To show them it's okay to be original. I've been fortunate to have risen slightly above the suppressive and systemic challenges."

"By slightly, you mean you feel you haven't achieved the level of recognition you wanted, right?"

"My peers in the art scene in the United States have works of art that sell in the seven figures, if not more. My art doesn't come near that."

"I see. I'm attracted to the brilliance in the structure and feeling behind your pieces. I notice that people just getting familiar with art often want something simple and uncomplicated. Or they steer toward the unattainable. The artist who passed on at twenty-four, leaving a small sampling of their work behind. Sometimes, popularity detracts from exploration of more complex forms of art. In those instances, it drives up the price."

"Exactly."

"So, Kaleb, you've been a dancer, singer, director, and painter. In which art form does your real passion lie?"

"As much as I love all forms of artistic expression, I prefer painting on canvas."

"That passion definitely comes through in your work. We're privileged to showcase your paintings at the exhibition."

Rose did her best to get all her questions in during their hour together, since this would be the last time they would talk before the exhibition. She gained deeper insight into his life and how it translated to his art, allowing her to envision his pieces in new ways. Armed with further information, it was clear to her how to best represent his art and his influencer, Vincent van Gogh.

"Thank you again for your time and for providing a glimpse into your creative mind. I hope my exhibition will do your work justice, make you feel proud, and inspire others."

"I'm sure the show will be brilliant, and I look forward to seeing you again soon." Rose shook his hand, grabbed her purse, and headed outside. Troy stood just outside the door to greet her and walk her to the car.

"Good meeting?"

"Excellent. The man is amazing. A real genius of our century."

"I know you were looking forward to meeting him for a while."

"I believe this show is just what Kaleb needs to bring his work back to the forefront of the art scene."

"Are you okay on time for your next meeting? The studio is about a ten-minute drive from here."

"Yes. I'm meeting with Kamal, but you know that. It should be interesting. Another local Black celebrity I haven't met before, but have heard a lot about."

"Have you decided on your dinner plans tonight? That was still an open item on the schedule."

"Troy, to be honest—" She paused, looking down at her phone. "I'm not sure. I'd like to stay in and spend some time with Brianna, but their cousin is a little out there." Rose used air quotes to emphasize *out there*. "Then I received this text from Aedan about a pop-up. I have no idea what that's about." She hoped it had nothing to do with Marina Mack. Although she had never met the lady, the article she read left her underwhelmed.

"Do you need me inside when Carol's around?"

"No, nothing like that. Although, it's clear Carol is annoyed by me. I need to get to the bottom of that."

"Do you think Niall or Aedan know what's going on with her?"

"I'm sure they do, but if they don't feel it's important enough to share with me, I'll get to the bottom of it on my own. I'm letting you know just in case."

"Let me dig to see what additional information I can come up with on her."

"That would be great."

"Don't worry, I got this. But in the interim, do you need me with you inside? Or do you trust the guys to keep Carol in check?"

"No, I'm good. If anyone needs checking, I can handle that myself. Let's stick to our regular schedule. I'll keep you posted if anything changes."

⚸

THE DRIVER TOOK THE LEFT FORK ON THE ROAD DOWN A NARROW street. He immediately pulled to the side and parked in front of the building with an all-glass entrance. Rose was scheduled to meet with Kamal Davis, a local celebrity talk show host and news anchor. She prepared a brief outlining his role as emcee for the exhibit to efficiently use their time since he was on a break between his morning and afternoon segments at the RTÉ. Rose managed her way through all the security checks. When she reached the receptionist's desk, an intern greeted her and escorted her directly to Kamal, who was seated at the counter in his dressing room. On the counter in front of him lay a half-eaten sandwich, a bottle of water, an iPad, and an array of beauty and makeup products protruding from a kit that seemingly belonged to the makeup artist standing near him.

"Hi, Rose. Thanks for coming down to meet me. I apologize in advance for getting ready while we talk. I have another show in an hour."

Rose sat on a barstool at the makeup counter next to Kamal. "It's good to finally meet you in person. And you don't have to apologize. You're on the job."

"I'm very excited to be your emcee. Your name is coming up in increasingly broader circles out here. So much so, they want me to profile you on one of our future shows if you're open to it."

"I'd be honored. I hope we can make the timing work. I'm only here until the end of the month, although a return visit is an option."

"I'm sure we can make something work," Kamal assured.

"Agreed. Have your team send me a production schedule. Speaking of schedules, here's the run-of-show. I made a few tweaks since we last talked, but I think you'll like it. The program flows well."

Kamal flipped through the pages. "This looks great. I see you added a few additional artists."

"I discovered a few whose works could contribute to the overall story I'm trying to tell."

"Have all the artists approved their bios?"

"Kaleb was the last one I needed. I just came from lunch with him."

"Can you put in a word for me? That man is hard to get an audience with. You appear to be the artist whisperer."

"I have my team to thank for landing the meeting with Kaleb."

"You're being modest. Two words landed that meet: Rose Ross."

Rose blushed, trying to hide her smile. She hadn't realized that Kaleb had been protecting his time by being selective with his interviews. Had the opportunity to meet with her been that significant to him?

"I appreciate the sentiment. Let me know if you'd like an introduction. Also, say the word if you want to get the artists on your show in the next few weeks. It would be great for them to get exposure and good publicity for the exhibition."

"That's brilliant. I'll have my team get back to you."

Rose and Kamal covered a few more items, and Kamal covered his agenda before their meeting wrapped, and Rose headed outside. Troy was patiently waiting when Rose came out. She gave him a slight nod, then noticed he had his cell phone in hand lowered to his side, tapping it with one finger.

"All set, Troy. We can head back to the gallery now. I'm sure Kris has some action items waiting for me. Is that him?" She pointed to his phone.

Troy didn't answer right away. He escorted her from the building and into the car before responding. "Have you checked your phone?"

"It's in my purse. I had it on mute since I entered the building because of the live broadcast in the studio."

"Please check it. Mine and Kris' have been blowing up for the past ten minutes."

"Why?"

"Your guy is trying to reach you."

She laughed. "Be serious. You know I don't have one. Who could be trying to reach me through the two of you? Are you talking about Dad? Certainly not one of the brothers—like you, they seem to know my every move." She shook her head at the thought of three men always having tabs on her. Her life was full of people watching and monitoring her every move—the public knew every significant financial and career move she made. Per Troy, there were thousands of people unbeknownst to her tracking her online, and now the brothers. Then, Troy's voice said one word that pulled Rose out of her head and into the moment.

"Alejandro."

⁂

ROSE WAS STILL RIDING THE HIGH FOLLOWING HER MEETING WITH Kamal. Pieces of the exhibition were finally falling into place. She tried to piece together what Troy was telling her, but with everything going on—all the interviews, meetings, and new staff—the name Alejandro did not immediately click in the way it should have. Rose turned and looked out the car window. A steady stream of people went back and forth between the office building and the adjacent coffee shop for an afternoon caffeine fix. Some people sat in the window bar seats, sipping coffee and looking out the window, lost in their thoughts.

"Rose. Did you hear me? Alejandro is trying to reach you," Troy pressed.

Rose repeated the name in her head. Her eyes widened when she looked at Troy.

"I …" She inhaled, closed her eyes, and felt her face grow hot. When Rose opened her eyes, Troy watched her, waiting for a response. Why did hearing his name make her feel anxious? She thought she had moved past any feelings for him long ago. "Alejandro," she repeated. "What did he say?" She reached into her handbag to retrieve her phone. There were two notifications: one missed call and one text from Alejandro. But why? She hadn't heard from him in over a year.

Alejandro was the archetype of her distraction. He was smart, sinfully sexy, and had a megawatt smile that made women swoon. The last time they had been together was an early morning in London after one of their rendezvous. They woke up locked in each other's arms. By the end of the day, they decided to pause their relationship. It was a day etched like glass in her brain. They went from frequent communication, video calls, text messages, and occasional get-togethers to nothing. At first, Rose was reluctant to agree to the breakup. But she weighed all the variables that were working against them. Alejandro was an international attorney with clients in over thirty countries, which meant he was away from home most weeks. Rose's situation wasn't all that different. She was focused on making a name for herself, independent from her family. And between that and living cross country from each other, there was no way their relationship could work. After the breakup, she decided that anything unrelated to her goal was a distraction. The pain of having someone so important sucked out of her life was not an experience she wanted to repeat.

So, why was Alejandro looking for her now? *Maybe there's a family emergency*, she thought.

"Troy." She tried to find the answer in his eyes.

"You haven't talked with him recently?" he responded.

"No. So what does Alejandro want, Troy? I know you spoke to him. This text says, 'Call me as soon as you get this.'"

"He's in town."

"Okay, so did you let him know I'm overseas? Where is he? At my house? The office?"

"No, *here* in town."

"In Dublin?"

"In Belfast. It won't take us long to get back."

Rose looked at Troy. She was searching his eyes for answers, expecting the sides of his lips to curl into a sudden smile signaling it was all a joke. There was no way this was happening to her. "You're kidding me. Right? Tell me. What *exactly* did he say?"

"He said, 'Have Rose give me a call as soon as she comes out of her meeting.'"

Rose called Alejandro. He answered on the first ring, and she immediately felt vulnerable in a way she hadn't felt since the last time they spoke.

"Hi, Rose. I see you got my message," he said, sounding self-assured in a way attorneys do.

"I did. Hi." Rose bit her lip at his supposition. It was her least favorite thing about Alejandro. His manner of questioning made her feel like she was on the witness stand. Not because he purposely intended to make her feel that way. An attorney at heart—he was born to do his job. But hearing his voice stirred up mixed emotions wrapped up in endless questions. Why was he suddenly back in her life? Now. In Belfast. Rose wanted Alejandro to state his case.

"I got a little carried away. I wanted to make sure we connected. I'm in Belfast attending a meeting that's about to start soon. Do you think you can swing by for coffee or an early drink in an hour? I should be done with the meeting by then. I'm over at James Street South. I'd love to see you while I'm in town."

Rose was at a loss for words. Alejandro randomly showed up in her life in another country as if no lost time had passed between them. She thought they were done after their year had passed with no word. She wasn't mentally prepared to deal with him. "Honestly, I don't know what to say. I'm in Dublin on business and wasn't expecting *you*."

"Rose, I understand. I'm in Ireland on business, too. I know you don't like surprises, but I'd like to see you while I'm in Belfast. That's all." Rose could hear him walking as he talked. She put her phone on mute, took a couple of deep breaths, then turned to Troy.

"He wants to meet with me today. What do you think?" She wanted Troy to tell her to say no, provide her some security-related excuse— anything to help her not experience old feelings again.

"Rose, I don't know what's on your mind, but I understand your dilemma, especially considering everything else you have going on. It's not a security matter but one of the heart, so I can't advise you. If you decide to meet with him, I'll be by your side the entire time. We can make the schedule work. Just let me know what you want to do."

Rose placed a hand on Troy's shoulder, took another deep breath, then unmuted her phone. "Alejandro," she said.

"I'm here," he answered.

"You're right. I don't like surprises. I'm on a deadline, but you're here now. I'll have Troy bring me over before we head back to the gallery. I'm not sure how long your meeting is, but it'll take me over an hour to get back."

"I was hoping we could grab an early dinner. You and I have a lot to catch up on."

Rose recognized the attorney in Alejandro, laying out the facts with his words. There were a thousand things she wanted to say. "I can't—" she started.

"Rose, sorry to interrupt. I just stepped outside for a second to take your call, but I need to get back inside for my meeting. I'll see you soon. We can figure things out when I see you. Okay?"

Rose closed her eyes and breathed out. "Sure." A stream of emotions flooded her in the silence, and it took Rose a second to collect her thoughts. "Troy, what just happened?"

"Alejandro would like to see you."

"Can you tell my face is red?" She touched her cheek.

"You look fine. Where are we headed? It's still your decision."

"You know where. James Street South."

Troy updated the navigator. There were only a few other cars on the road since it was not quite rush hour, which meant they could be there in a little over an hour. Rose pulled down the visor and fixed her face.

"When was the last time you two talked?" Troy asked, looking at the road ahead.

"A little over a year ago. I wonder how Alejandro knew where I was." She found it strange to say his name aloud as if it were an everyday occurrence. Although he worked for her dad as outside counsel, their paths never crossed. She met him only by chance when in-house counsel was tied up with a merger and needed help with another case. He walked into the conference room, smiled at her, and made an instant connection. *I have to resist that smile,* she thought.

"Don't forget, you're planning one of the most notable events in Europe. It wouldn't take much to find you, which is why I have so many eyes on you. Then there's the fact that he works for your dad. One thing is for sure—he timed his trip. Like you, he never leaves anything to chance."

Rose pressed two fingers to her forehead. "You're right. Alejandro likely timed his business to coincide with mine."

"I understand if you don't want to see him. But I thought you two were amicable."

"We were. Or rather, we are. Somewhat. But I have too much going on to try and reconnect with Alejandro. I'm weeks away from one of my most important shows. It's all too much."

"You got this. I won't leave your side. Just say the word when you're ready to leave."

"I am half annoyed yet somewhat curious now to find out why Alejandro randomly showed up here." She was also secretly curious how she would react to seeing him again. It was hard for her following the days of their breakup. Not trusting her instincts around men. Categorizing them as a distraction as a defense mechanism to protect her time. To protect her heart.

THE DRIVE WAS FASTER THAN ROSE EXPECTED. BEFORE SHE KNEW IT, they were back within the Belfast city limits. Troy pulled up in front of the restaurant and turned off the engine.

"Are you good?" Troy asked.

"Yes. I'm good." Rose lied.

"Okay, let's do this."

Troy opened the restaurant door for Rose. She took a deep breath. "Okay, I can do this." She smiled at Troy. He nodded in response.

The restaurant was mostly empty except for two gentlemen sitting at the bar and a couple in the back. Rose saw an opening leading to a small private section of the restaurant and walked toward it. Alejandro was seated at a table and stood when she entered the space, followed by Troy. Rose lingered at the entryway, then looked back briefly to give Troy a reassuring look. She could see Troy's eyes scanning their surroundings.

Three place settings were at the table in front of Alejandro. Rose stepped further into the small room, ensuring Troy remained in view.

"Hello, Alejandro. It is nice to see you again, albeit surprising. You remember Troy." Rose's tone was formal, and her hand was outstretched to Alejandro. Troy nodded in Alejandro's direction. "Is the meeting over?" she asked.

Instead of taking her hand, Alejandro put his arms around her shoulders in an embrace and kissed her cheek. The unexpected gesture, coupled with Troy's sudden movement, made her back stiffen, and she stepped away from Alejandro.

"Rose, it's so good to see you." He stepped back and looked her up and down. "Wow, you look beautiful as always." He flashed the signature

186

smile that once made Rose stop in her tracks, but had no effect on her for the first time. Her attention was no longer on Alejandro but on the man standing in the doorway next to Troy. Rose instinctively smiled. Then, her gaze bounced back and forth between the entrance and Alejandro as she tried to rationalize the connection between these two men in her mind. The last person she expected to see with Alejandro was Aedan.

"Hi, Rose. Sorry to crash your reunion. But I agree. You do look lovely, as usual. I trust your day is going well so far." Aedan went to her with one hand in his pocket. He put the other hand in hers and dipped to kiss her cheek, lingering long enough to make a point, but not enough to send sparks flying. *Awkward* was an understated attempt to summarize her emotions as she stood between her past and present partners. She squeezed down unusually hard on Aedan's hand.

Alejandro spoke up. "Aedan, this is my friend, Rose. The one I was telling you about. Clearly, you two know each other. Rose, you just missed Niall, who helped set up the meeting. I believe he had other business to attend to." Rose faked a smile to mask her feelings. Why were they together? What kind of game were these guys playing?

"AJ here was just telling Niall and me that he was thinking of reaching out to you before leaving town. I didn't realize he had already taken the initiative."

"AJ?" Rose raised an eyebrow and tilted her head toward Alejandro. As a high-powered attorney, specificity was at the center of his work. Nicknames weren't his thing, which meant he was up to something, and she wanted to know what. "It seems he found me. And to answer your question, Aedan, my day has been mostly uncomplicated until now. This leads me to Alejandro. What brings you to Belfast?"

"Please, let's have a seat." Alejandro gestured for them to take one of the available chairs. "I had some business in the region, including some with Aedan and Niall regarding their services. Niall arranged the meeting, and here we are. By the way, Aedan, thank you for the additional insight into your company. I am impressed by the extent of your team's network."

Aedan helped Rose to her seat and sat next to her. His response was brief. "It's my lifeblood, and I have great leaders at the helm like Niall," he said, then took out his phone and sent a text.

"Well, I appreciate you taking on my project. From everything I've seen and heard, I feel my client and I are in good hands," Alejandro said.

Rose was annoyed that Alejandro seemed to be taking everything in stride like this was normal. "So, Alejandro, tell me, what made you choose this time of year to come to Belfast?" She wanted him to come clean on his intentions in timing his visit alongside hers. Especially since they were well passed their one-year break in the relationship mark.

"Like I said, this meeting coincided with other business I'm conducting in the region. King Enterprise's level of service far exceeds other companies I met with, making them an obvious choice to do business with. We just wrapped up the final details before you arrived."

"Niall is reviewing the documents with legal as we speak, AJ. You should have the executed contract by the end of the day."

"AJ," Rose mocked under her breath, unable to get past the absurdity of his newfound nickname. "Then, you already knew I was here and decided in advance to reach out."

"Yes, something like that. I thought it might be good to sync up while we were both in town. It's been some time since we last talked.

I figured we could have dinner or, at a minimum, grab some coffee. I hope that's alright."

Rose crossed her legs under the table. She purposely brushed her foot against Aedan's leg and forced a smile while maintaining eye contact with Alejandro.

Aedan picked up on her signal. "Alejandro, I believe I mentioned that my family is hosting Rose during her stay in Belfast. We're committed to ensuring all her needs are taken care of during her time here. That includes dinner. I've already made dinner reservations tonight at a pop-up restaurant, but I will defer to Rose if she's open to a change of plans. Provided Troy clears it, too." He turned to Rose. "I can cancel if you prefer to take Alejandro up on his offer."

Rose thought about Troy standing off to her side. She knew what he would want her to do. "No need to adjust our plans. We're still on, Aedan. I'll have Kris look at tomorrow's schedule to see if there's time to fit in coffee with Alejandro." She turned to Alejandro. "Apologies, Alejandro, you have to admit you sort of just landed in my lap."

"Then that settles it." Aedan leaned back in his chair.

"Fair enough. I can't expect you to rearrange your life for me. Coffee tomorrow sounds great," Alejandro said.

"I'll have Kris send you an invite. I have other business to attend to if we're finished here." Rose stood, and Troy, who had been standing near the door, stepped across the threshold, and waited for Rose. Aedan and Alejandro exchanged pleasantries. Rose extended a hand to Alejandro. "It is nice to see you again. If you need any recommendations for dinner, Kris can provide some. Enjoy your evening. I'll see you tomorrow."

Rose waited for Alejandro to leave before turning her narrowed eyes to Aedan. "Aedan. What was that? Why would you and Niall neglect to tell me my ex was in town? That was unexpected and awkward, to say the least. And you, Aedan, of all people, I'd expect you had a vested interest to warn me."

"It's only business. Alejandro has a client that acquired our services. As you may expect, I only recently uncovered AJ was *your* Alejandro. He knew you were in town and vacillated between reaching out or leaving following the contract review. He didn't tell us he had decided to reach out; otherwise, I would have given you a heads-up."

"Don't be so matter of fact about it," Rose said.

"Rose, you know I know everything about that man by now, including the fact that he's no physical threat to you. But I don't think you are upset over security concerns since Troy personally delivered you here. I realize you previously had a relationship with Alejandro. Still, everything between us indicates that what you and Alejandro had is finished until you tell me otherwise. Did I misinterpret the past few days?" Aedan held both her hands, tilted his head, and caught Rose's gaze.

"No, you didn't," she said, trying to sound upset and ignore the synapse she felt when he touched her.

"Great, we can talk in the car." He turned to Troy. "Troy, I hate to tell you this again, man, but I can manage things from here. But so you are aware, the plan is to stop by Niall's office, head to dinner, then home. My team is always covering me, which means Rose is covered, too."

Troy's face was expressionless. "If Rose is okay with the arrangements, she'll ride with you. Unfortunately, I still plan to follow. That's non-negotiable."

"Troy, I'll be okay. My tracker is on. We'll be in town for the remainder of today, and I know you have eyes on me." Troy waited for Rose to get into Aedan's car before getting into his own.

Once inside, Aedan gave the driver instructions to head to the office. As soon as they turned the corner out of view from the restaurant, Aedan reached for Rose's hand. She sat facing ahead, processing everything that had just happened. Aedan dipped his head and leaned toward her to get her attention.

"I made a mistake. Let me apologize." Aedan's voice was soft and low. He traced her cheek with his thumb, licked across her lips, then pressed his lips to hers. "I hope you don't mind. I wanted to do that at the restaurant when I first saw you." But Rose *did* mind. She wanted to be mad, not make out. *Damn kiss*, she thought.

"I don't understand why you didn't warn me that Alejandro was in town and that you would be at this meeting. You could have just texted me."

He squeezed her hand gently, holding her gaze. "I wasn't sure he would contact you. By the way, you handled the situation perfectly. Maybe when you're ready, you can tell me the story of you two."

"That meeting, although brief, was very awkward. And why would you want to know more about Alejandro? It seems you already know quite a bit. Besides, I don't want to discuss him right now. I thought you were doing some show and tell thing?" She hated that his kiss got her all distracted. Now that she had a taste of him, she wanted more.

"Unfortunately, we don't have time. We're here." The car stopped. Aedan got out and extended his hand to help Rose from the vehicle.

Rose got out, put her hands inside his suit coat, pulled him close, pressed her lips to his, and kissed him with such a sense of urgency that she even surprised herself. She could feel the hard evidence that Aedan was pleasantly surprised, too.

"Rose," Aedan breathed out her name. He pressed his forehead to hers and licked signs of her passion from his lips. "I'm assuming that's a sign of forgiveness." He lowered a hand to adjust himself. "Let's head inside before I forget I have a business to run. Niall will be waiting for us."

"You still want to go in?" Rose smiled wryly.

"That depends on where *in* is. But we're here now." He tilted his head toward the building.

"Ugh. You and your brother planned this."

"No, actually, we didn't."

"Somehow, I doubt that."

He kissed her on the cheek and turned her around toward the building. "Welcome to our office."

Before entering, Rose paused to look at the massive skyscraper, which stretched half the block and towered several stories above her. Aedan looked on. "I know. Pretty impressive, right? I still pause every once in a while before entering—it's hard to believe this is mine. Come with me. Let's go inside."

Together, Rose and Aedan made their way across the lobby to the elevator bank that would take them to the top floor. The building was alive, with people coming and going. All eyes were on Rose everywhere they went, and those not on her were either greeting or nodding in Aedan's direction. She was in his world now. She imagined people wanted to know who this Black woman was walking in with the chairman of the board.

The elevator was empty when Rose and Aedan entered. She seized the private moment to make light of the situation. "I take it by the stares that this is not how you typically arrive to work."

He flashed a sudden smile. "I guess you can say it's not."

"Never walked in with a Black woman?"

"Never walked in with any woman."

"I guess this is a milestone for your employees."

"If you say so."

"Boss, you have some explaining to do," she teased.

"Cute."

The elevator doors opened to a set of glass doors, which led to the lobby. A well-suited gentleman was seated behind a counter. "Good evening, sir."

"Good evening, Charles. This is Ms. Ross. She'll be my guest for today."

"Welcome, Ms. Ross. Please let me know if you need anything."

"How are things going?" Aedan asked.

"It's a good day. Nothing out of the norm," Charles answered.

"Good to hear. Has Niall's meeting ended?"

"Yes, they're just finishing up in the conference room behind you." Aedan turned around to see a lady and gentleman exiting the conference room next to an office with Niall's name on it. Aedan and Rose made their way there, passing the couple. Niall emerged from the conference room and headed in their direction.

"This guy looks familiar," Rose teased, and Niall looked away from his phone to see her and Aedan coming toward him.

"Hi, Rose. Aedan. Perfect timing." He kissed Rose on the cheek and patted his brother on his back. "I got your message and figured you might bring Rose after the meeting with Alejandro."

Aedan shot his brother a look, warning him not to venture into that territory. "Rose is a little upset with us."

Rose looked between the brothers. "Guys, I have every right to be upset. I don't understand how either of you thought I would be okay with this. Is this a game to you? One of you could have said something to me before Alejandro reached out. How did you know I wasn't heading into the lion's den or something worse?"

"I'd never allow that to happen. It's my job to know all variables in a situation. I know you're not under the impression that either of us would put you in harm's way," Niall said.

"I don't think either of you knows how Alejandro feels about me or how I feel about him—that's an important variable you missed. Wouldn't you agree? Is he harmless? Sure, I'll give you that, but he works for my dad. I don't know Alejandro's intent in coming here, and I certainly don't need more distractions. I can't afford surprises."

"We get it. No one is playing any games." Niall instinctively took a step closer to Rose but paused in front of his brother. Rose could tell he struggled with their unspoken boundaries.

"Rose, it was an oversight. It won't happen again. Let us know if you want either of us to be with you when you meet with him tomorrow." Aedan reached out to touch her hand.

"I have Troy for that. You know, the guy I can trust with every aspect of my life. The first person to inform me that Alejandro was here. That guy." Rose bit back.

"We deserve that. On a positive note, I'm glad you're here. You finally get to see how we spend our time. Or at least how I spend mine. There's no keeping up with Aedan."

"Why did you want to bring me here?"

"That was my idea. Aedan texted me from the restaurant, saying Alejandro had contacted you. I knew you don't like surprises and wasn't sure how you'd feel about him being here. So, I suggested Aedan bring you over, and you could get familiar with some of the team you'll be working with since you were in town."

"You don't need a monologue to say you're saving me from Alejandro." Rose shook her head at Niall.

Aedan's eyebrow raised. Rose recognized his signal that the conversation was entering murky waters.

"How about this. Niall will show you around. I have a quick meeting to jump into, and then I'll come to find you so we can head out to dinner. Niall won't be joining us. He already has dinner plans this evening."

"Date night? Something newsworthy, I suspect?" She smiled a wry grin up at Niall.

"Plans. Let's leave it at that," Niall answered.

Together, Rose and Niall made their way around the building. Niall introduced her to the teams sitting in the open space work areas. He explained how the teams were structured based on the client's needs. Niall gathered the group supporting the exhibition in the large conference room to meet Rose. She used the time to give them a high-level overview of the project plan and how she intended to leverage their services. She was impressed at the caliber of talent in the room. Everyone expressed excitement about working with her by the end of the meeting.

After the tour and impromptu meetings, Niall used the downtime to catch up with Rose privately.

"Great view," Rose pointed her chin toward the wall of windows.

Niall walked across the room and stood next to Rose. "Well, this has been an interesting day. I wish I could have been there with you at the restaurant, but I had an important meeting to attend."

She wanted to ask why, but was not interested in revisiting their former conversation. "I heard—something about reviewing legal documents. I had Troy with me anyway."

"Troy. Where is he now," he asked with a twinge of sarcasm.

"That doesn't sound like the Niall I know." Rose caught his gaze reflected in the window.

"I didn't mean to come off like that. You know you don't need Troy around when you have us."

"By us, you mean you and Aedan. I don't see your point. Troy escorted me to the meeting with Alejandro—you know, the meeting, the one you should have told me about in advance," she repeated, still bitter.

"I know. I'm—"

She cut him off. "You're just reminding me of who you are. I understand, but it sounds like you don't like Troy."

"I have nothing against him. He does his job well. He's looking after you."

"Doing his job well is an understatement. He's saved my life on many occasions. So, then tell me. What exactly is the real issue?"

"I'm more interested in what you're doing. Are you interested in Aedan? Why did Alejandro want to see you? Do you still have feelings for him?"

"That's right; you guys know a lot about my past from your research like I'm some homework assignment." Rose emphasized the word *research* with air quotes.

"It's my job."

Rose turned to face Niall. He was still looking at her reflection in the window. "*I'm* not your job." She watched Niall close his eyes and purse his lips. At that moment, she sensed he was holding something back.

"You wouldn't have hired me for the exhibition if I wasn't good at it."

"Not good enough to alert me to Alejandro's sudden appearance." She turned back to catch his gaze in the window.

"I deserved that, but that doesn't discount that I know what I'm doing."

"True, but you really want to know whether I'm interested in you? I think we are well past being coy, don't you think? This book is open. What's your question?"

Niall turned to face Rose. They stood close enough that his hand brushed against hers when he turned. Rose turned too when she felt a flush of heat pass through her—the same heat she felt the night they kissed by the fireplace. She fought the instinctive impulse to grab his hand.

"You're right, Rose. I don't know where you stand with my brother. All I know is when I'm around you, I have an overwhelming need to reach out and kiss you. May I?" Niall's eyes locked with hers.

"I've suddenly become some new habit of yours. You kiss me every day."

The sides of Niall's lips turn up slightly. "When you put it that way, it seems I have developed an addiction. I didn't see you this morning— you left early. And that's not the type of kiss I'm referencing. May I?"

"No, Niall, we're not doing this. And to respond to your comment, I left early this morning because I didn't want to deal with your cousin, Carol. Please, ask your question."

"I think I have my answer."

"I don't believe all you wanted to ask me for was a kiss. Ask your question."

"Are you sleeping with my brother?"

"Yes," Rose blurted out. She stared at Niall.

The subtle twitch in his eye revealed her response was not what he wanted to hear. "Have you developed feelings for him?"

"I enjoy his company. But no, I'm not in love with him if that's what you're asking. We're just exploring our connection. Now, don't expect me to elaborate more than that. I don't even know why I told you that much."

"I'm not asking for details. And, like it or not, my brother and I appear to have broken through your tiny, trusted inner circle and vice versa. You know you have our confidence."

"Did you study psychology, too?'

"No."

"That's a relief."

"Do you love Alejandro?"

"I thought the inquisition was over. But no. Alejandro and I dated, and we ended our relationship amicably. I suppose if I loved him... If I loved him, we would still be together."

"What about Troy?"

Rose touched her forehead. "Niall. Seriously? Are we doing this?"

"You said to ask. I'm asking."

"All personal questions?"

"It's probably the only thing I don't know about you. And you said it yourself—I need to understand all the variables."

"You're cocky."

"I know what I want. I'm smart."

"Okay, I'll give you that. You're smart and cocky. But right now, you're annoyingly handsome."

He barked out a laugh. "That's a switch. But I'll take any little compliment I can get from you. No matter how sideways it is. So, what about Troy?"

"There's nothing between Troy and me. There never has been. He makes sure I stay out of trouble. I know him as well as he knows me, but that is its extent. I'm sure you know your brother already asked me about him. Didn't he tell you?"

"He did, but I wanted to directly look you in the eye and hear your response."

"You have it. What's next?"

"Nothing. I wish I had whatever it was you're looking for."

Rose laughed, then cupped Niall's cheek in her hand and gave him a quick, friendly kiss on the lips she hoped would satisfy him. "That's funny. You have it. But something tells me I need to take a chance on your brother."

"Which means no chance for me."

"We had this discussion. You'll be the first to know. So, I think we're done here. Where's your brother?"

"Turn around. He's in the hallway heading towards us." Rose inhaled. She forgot the offices were like glass bubbles. She hoped he hadn't seen that kiss. Maybe not. Aedan was smiling when he entered.

"You two must be talking about me." Aedan stood next to Rose. Niall's eyes went from Rose to Aedan, then back to Rose.

"We were. Rose was sharing how excited she is about your dinner plans tonight."

"Did she convince you to come along? I don't know why you declined the invite. These pop-ups are a rare experience."

"I'm okay, Aedan. Events like that are meant to be experienced with someone special."

"And your plans don't include someone special?" Rose asked. He had her curious.

"No. I'm in the exploration phase," Niall quipped.

"It appears you two have been discussing more than me, but I'll stay out of that. By the way, Niall, I told AJ you'd execute that agreement today."

"It's here." He tipped his head toward the desk. "You know me. I need to weigh all my options before signing on to something new." Niall half-smiled at Rose.

"Rose, are you ready to head out? I thought we'd stop by one of the local galleries before they close." Aedan held out a hand to her.

"That sounds good. I'm ready. Niall, thank you for the tour and for allowing me to spend some time with your team. I can check this off my to-do list, and I'll see you later." She gave him a hug and kiss—this time on the cheek.

Niall whispered in her ear. "I meant to tell you that you look beautiful. Have a nice time."

"See you later, man," Aedan called out to Niall.

"Later, Aedan."

※

BETWEEN WALKING THE MAZE OF FLOORS IN THE GALLERY, VIEWING art, discussing her ideas for the upcoming show, and getting through an intimate seven-course dinner with strangers, several hours quickly slipped away before Rose and Aedan made it back home. The house was dark except for the entryway. The only sounds were the faint click of the door latching behind them and a large clock ticking. Rose placed a hand on Aedan's shoulder to balance herself when she took off her heels. Aedan broke the silence. "I think Carol and Brianna have turned in for the night."

"Seems so. I'm not ready to turn in for the night yet. Care to join me near the fireplace for a drink? I feel like I've been switched on all day and need to unwind."

Aedan gestured for Rose to lead the way and followed her into one of the rooms. Rose headed toward the wingback chairs.

"Rose." Aedan held a hand out to her, and she turned to walk toward him. "I'll take those." Aedan took her shoes and placed them on a table near the door. He took both her hands, pulled her toward him, and then dipped his head to kiss her long and slow. Rose indulged in the passion behind his kiss, then tried to pull away.

"Not yet," he breathed across her lips. Rose looked up and pressed her lips to Aedan's. His response was urgent and needy as they savored their desire to be close to one another until they came up for air. Rose pulled her face away from Aedan and caught his gaze. She was beginning to understand that although he was not big on articulating his feelings, he didn't lack in showing them given the opportunity.

"Why Mr. King, I see you're not one for PDA, but you're quite the kisser behind closed doors. I'm going to need that drink with ice." She peeled away from Aedan's body, which was hard in all the best ways, and went across the room. He followed and lit the fireplace.

"Anything specific you want to drink?" he asked.

Rose was already seated in one of the wingback chairs facing the flames forming in the fireplace. She was already flush with heat and wet with desire. "Sparkling water."

Aedan poured himself honey-colored liquid from one of the crystal decanters, then sparkling water over ice, and handed her a glass before sitting in the chair across from her. "I needed that kiss. We haven't had a moment alone aside from our time in the car," Aedan said.

"I'm not complaining. Your kisses leave me heated in all the best ways." Rose locked eyes with Aedan.

"Okay," he said with a low, slow growl.

"Dinner was great. But yes, we haven't had much time together today. Although it was nice to mingle with Irish celebrities. You must know someone to have secured that invite."

"A client."

"You don't talk much about your clients. I don't believe I've heard you mention any of them by name."

"We take the stipulations of our confidentiality agreements seriously amongst all the other details. We're known for our integrity."

"I picked up on those signals from Niall today when you asked about a contract earlier."

"He's serious about his work."

"We all are. But I am glad today is over." Rose took a sip of her drink.

"Anything wrong? You're not still upset about Alejandro?"

"No, nothing is wrong. I almost forgot about Alejandro until you mentioned him. Just glad to have this moment to unwind." She raised her glass in the air before taking another sip. Aedan copied her, raising his glass.

"So, you don't have an issue meeting him tomorrow?" Aedan stretched his hand across the chair's arm, holding the drink, and swirled the liquid in the glass.

"No, not at all."

"I can go with you if you'd like me to."

She laughed tentatively, unsure whether Aedan was serious. "I don't think that would go over well with Alejandro. Are you worried about how my meeting with him will impact what's between us?"

"I wonder how close you two really were. If Alejandro's visit will ignite a familiar spark. So yes, I wonder what impact his presence here will have on us. Rose, I don't normally date. I don't hang out with the women I've been with, and I certainly never brought anyone home with me."

"What do you do with them?"

"I think you know. We go back to her place or to a hotel. I get what I want and leave. I don't know how to do this." Aedan waved his hand between the two of them. "But something about you makes me want to try. Despite you telling me there is no chance of a long-distance relationship, I like where we're heading. I like being with you."

"How about this. I'll keep my meeting with Alejandro by myself, and I promise to text you right after. Troy will be with me the entire time, so don't worry about me getting whisked away."

"It's not like that, but I'll back off and let you do your thing and wait for your call. Don't bother texting. Call me."

"Deal. By the way, I was drawing the other day and thought you'd like this." She handed him a petite gold leaf picture frame from her bag.

"What's this?" He flipped the frame over to reveal a drawing she made of the rock formation at the Causeway.

"It was the first place we toured. The shapes and texture of everything we saw were so natural and inspiring. I know now why artists feel the need to capture real life. Art imitates life."

"I don't think I knew you were an artist." He studied the drawing. "This is beautiful, Rose. It was so chilly that day I had to hold your hands to warm them. You darn near touched every rock. I'm glad you agreed to go with me."

"Same."

"Rose, I have one thing I'd like to discuss that Niall brought to my attention."

"Sure." Knowing Niall, she realized it could be anything. She braced herself, then her phone buzzed. The initials RR appeared on the screen. "I need to take this." She held up her phone.

"By all means. I can step out," Aedan offered, but Rose held out her hand, urging him to stay.

"Hey, Dad. Did I miss a meeting or something?" Rose held the phone up to FaceTime her father.

"That would be a first, wouldn't it? I met with the board. One of the members put forward another candidate for us to consider. I'm not convinced they're viable, and I'm sure most of the members would agree."

"What does that mean for me?" Rose sat back and crossed her legs.

"For us. More pressure. If I need to secure another qualified name for the list, I can, but you know I don't want to. The vote is in two weeks. I need to know your decision before then."

"You'll have it. I just need time to think and get comfortable with my decision."

"So, you've decided what you want to do?"

"You'll have my response before the deadline." She watched as her dad pursed his lips and nodded at the screen. "I know that face, Dad." He always gave her his full attention, but she could tell he had somewhere to be as the screen went from the back of his car to the airport tarmac.

"I've got a flight to catch. I'll trust you'll make the best decision for everyone. You have my full support, whatever you decide. I love you." Rose placed two fingers across her lips, then ended the call.

"No pressure there," Aedan chimed in.

"Right? Like I don't have anything else going on in my life."

"Your dad said he trusts you to make the right decision. If you need to talk about it, I'm here."

"I still have time before the board meets. So, you were mentioning something about Niall."

"This may sound trivial after all that, but Niall sent me a text after we left to say you were feeling guarded around Carol. I don't want you to feel that way about anything or anyone. I know Carol can be a little contentious but tell me what I can do to help."

"I can handle contentious, but there's no reason for her to be that way with me."

"She can be on a different track than the rest of us. For the most part, we tolerate Carol. What do you need from me? Tell me."

"She gave off the vibe she didn't want me around."

"Forget Carol."

"Aedan, this is important. I'll be worried about her until I have to step back on a plane and head home. I have a lot of work between now and the exhibition, and as you can see, I'm up for consideration for a highly publicized position. I can't be distracted by Carol."

"Like I said, don't worry about Carol. The political unrest we've experienced here has her guarded about different people."

"And by different, you mean she doesn't like anyone who doesn't look like her."

"She's confused."

"That's not being confused, Aedan. That's a choice. Don't gloss over it."

"That's particularly pointed."

"You know by now I mean what I say."

"I hear you. I'll deal with Carol. I'm not sure what happened. Did you hear her talking to Niall and me the other night?"

"Carol's reaction to me was denotative of who she is, but nothing I haven't seen before. I have no interest in what she said to you two last night. She's your cousin. You may want to have more than a surface discussion with her. Get clarity on where she's coming from."

"I'm definitely going to talk to her for all our sakes. How about this. I will be on sight while Carol is still here. No more spending half my week at home and half here. I can help diffuse some of the tension."

"Thank you. I appreciate Niall bringing it to your attention. Speaking of which, your brother put me through the third degree today."

"An attempt to get to know you."

"Oh, so you knew he would do that."

"That's how he is. He turns over every stone, asks questions no one anticipates, and leaves nothing to chance."

"Then, you know what he asked me?"

"Knowing Niall as well as I do, I have an idea. Are you offended by anything he said?"

"No. I wanted you to know we talked."

"Look, Niall's a good guy. I trust him with my life, my company, and with you. I'm not going to tell you what to think about him or how to handle him. Just trust your instincts."

"I always do."

"Great. Are you done with your drink?" Rose nodded in response. "Would you like a refill?"

"No. I'm ready to head upstairs."

"I get it. You've had a long day. Here, I'll walk you to your room." Aedan stood and held out a hand. When Rose stood, her eyes locked with Aedan's. He had a hungry look in his eyes that she wanted to satisfy. She stood on her toes and put her lips to his ear.

"I was hoping to get time with the chairman of the board," she whispered. Aedan turned his face to meet hers. His lips hovered just above hers so close that one slight move would close any distance between them.

"You found him," his breath mingled with hers.

"Any chance I could see your boardroom?"

"You just want to *see* my room?" The corners of his lips turned up into a half-smile.

"I believe we have some unfinished business, Chairman."

"You're not too tired, are you? What I have planned could take all night."

"No."

Aedan covered her lips with his, and with that, he ushered her into his room.

CHAPTER 11

Distraction

"Desires dictate our priorities, priorities shape our choices, and choices determine our actions."

— DALLIN H. OAKS

On Rose's second day in Belfast, she awoke in the sitting room with slippers that Aedan, whom she hadn't yet met, had left for her. That seemed a stark contrast in time to waking in Aedan's room, in his bed, wrapped in his arms. Although it wasn't the first time they woke up together, this time felt slightly different. She had crossed an invisible line, not recalling when she stepped over from a situationship to a relationship. Rose looked down at Aedan—who was still asleep—and watched him briefly before waking him with a kiss on the cheek.

"Good morning. It's time to get up." Her voice was barely above a whisper.

"You make a beautiful alarm clock. I could get used to this." His voice was deep and groggy, but his mind was on point. "Are you ready for another round?" He tightened his grasp around her waist and pulled her so close the pressure of his hard steel pressed against her made the place between her thighs throb in response.

"We have to get ready for breakfast. I need to get started early. My schedule is pretty tight now that I'm meeting Alejandro." She writhed in his arms in an attempt to resist his body beckoning her.

"You didn't answer my question. But this is what I'm going to do. I'll let you try and convince me to get up, and then I'll make love to you. Afterward, we'll have a shower, then we'll get ready and go to breakfast."

Rose rolled her eyes. "Come on. I have to get ready."

Aedan didn't move. He just laid there, holding Rose tight against his body, watching her lips move while she made excuses. She knew he was waiting for her to make the next move.

She smiled down at Aedan. "Don't look at me that way—you are not making this any easier. I'm going to take my shower. You can join me."

"I'm not ready for a cold shower yet. Are you?" Aedan rolled Rose on her back, dusted kisses on her neck and cheek, and then hovered over her lips. His warm breath against her skin and the look in his eyes like she was all he ever needed was the final match that ignited a fire all through her body. She smiled and then pulled his face down to hers.

* * *

Despite their morning activities, Aedan and Rose were the first to breakfast, followed by Niall. When Carol walked in, Rose and Niall were at the table eating while Aedan was at the refrigerator, getting them all orange juice.

"Good morning, Carol. I trust you slept well?" Aedan said.

"Good morning. I did. I see you are all up very early," Carol observed.

209

"Good morning, cousin. We all have packed schedules. Morning is the only time we're available to coordinate our schedules before the day gets hectic. Have a seat and join us." Niall gestured to a chair.

"Sounds like some new tradition, albeit not a *family* tradition. I'm just here to grab something to take to Brianna for breakfast in bed. You all carry on with your *routine*," Carol said.

"Brianna already has her breakfast. We brought back the staff full-time following her return. That's one of the topics we cover in our morning syncs. But don't let that stop you from checking in on her to see if she needs anything else," Niall said.

Rose feigned a smile. "Carol, feel free to join us. Aedan was just about to pour us some orange juice. Weren't you, Aedan?"

"Carol, would you like a glass?" Aedan held up the pitcher.

Carol scowled. She looked thoroughly annoyed with them all. "No. I'll just go check in on Brianna." Her curt response reflected her disdain. Carol turned on her heels and marched out like a toy soldier before anyone could say bye.

"Doesn't seem like she's interested in playing in this sandbox. Why is she continuing to stay here?" Rose asked.

Aedan rejoined them at the table and poured everyone a glass of juice. "She says she wants to help out with Brianna. But I have to be honest, I haven't seen the value since she's been here. I'm hoping Carol will get her act together. Niall and I went ahead in the interim and hired a nurse to provide in-home care until Brianna recovers. So, the house now has a full staff."

Niall swallowed his piece of toast and then cleared his throat. "You know why she's here. To cause trouble under the guise that she's helping. I warned you about her, Aedan."

"We just need to keep an eye out on her. If she can't be hospitable, I will personally ask her to leave. Brianna will understand," Aedan explained.

There were some things Rose wanted to say to Aedan, but she kept her mouth shut to stay out of their family affair. Besides, Aedan committed to dealing with his cousin, and she trusted he would do just that when the time came.

Rose, Niall, and Aedan sat together for a few more minutes before each had to go their separate ways. Rose started to head out the door with Aedan before doubling back to say something to Niall, but Carol had reappeared and had his attention. Niall caught a glance at Rose and nodded. Rose smiled back, then went outside where Aedan was waiting alongside Troy.

"Troy. Both Niall and I will be in the city until late. Rose has a meeting later with Alejandro. You'll have to keep a special eye out on her," Aedan said.

"You know Kris and Troy have my every move mapped out, Aedan."

"Can you give me a few seconds with Rose, Troy?" Troy nodded and stepped back a few feet. Rose gave Troy a look, knowing he could do better than that, and watched as a partial smirk grew on his face. She couldn't help but smile in response.

"Don't tell me. This is about Alejandro." Rose frowned at Aedan.

Aedan put his hands around Rose's hips, drew her close to him, and kissed her with a lovemaking fire that made her drunk on desire. His rod rose against her body. He pulled her closer. It took all her focus to keep from walking him back upstairs.

When Aedan came up for air, he breathed out her name. "Rose. This is about me showing you how much I want you. We'll finish this tonight. Call me if you need anything. Have a good day." Aedan kissed Rose on the corner of her lip, then got in his car and left. Rose could still taste him and feel the lingering sensation from having his hard body pressed against her. It took Rose a minute to center herself.

When she was ready, Rose and Troy walked to the gallery. Through the window, Rose could see Kris busy at work with the rest of the staff. Aedan, Niall, and Kaleb were simply color-coded names on a calendar to him. Nothing more than data points tied to an intricate set of activities that needed to get done. Alejandro was a name Kris had not seen on the calendar in more than a year. But he was more than a name on the calendar for Troy. When Rose and Alejandro were dating, he was subject to wearing a tracking device. Tracking devices were earmarked for family and boyfriends, someone who could be used as a proxy to gain access to her family if they couldn't get to her. After Rose and Alejandro broke up, Troy no longer needed a stealth security detail on Alejandro. This time, when Kris added Alejandro to the calendar, he highlighted his name with a red bar, not green.

Troy cleared his throat. "I checked the schedule and see you're still on with Alejandro today. What exactly are his intentions? You know he consumed a lot of your time when you were together. I'd hate to see you repeat the past. It feels like this is yet another distraction from your purpose in Belfast. After all, we both know his trip is not a coincidence."

"I appreciate the feedback. I think we established yesterday that Alejandro's trip was aptly timed. I plan to find out why," Rose said.

"Putting the attorney on defense?"

"Something like that. I want to know why he's here and why now. But first, I need the Cliffs Notes version on what he's been doing the past year and a half."

"The man's a workaholic like you. I doubt anything significant has happened, but I'm sure he'll drag out his time with you just the same. We need to keep you on schedule. Speaking of schedules, Kris is heading toward us with a frantic look." Rose and Troy were a few feet from the gallery door when Kris came running out with a tablet in hand, stylus pointing at something.

"Rose, you have fifteen minutes before your first artists' interview, which should last one hour. The next one starts immediately after that, then the next meeting is moved to the city, so you have a short window to get there. That gives you only fifteen minutes this morning to inspect and sign for the pieces Niall's people delivered ten minutes ago. I don't know what you said to that man, but I never saw anyone get us access to work this priceless as fast as he managed to. I need you in the gallery now. This man still has that thing locked on his wrist."

"Kris. Breathe. We got this. Let's take a look at the piece."

Rose, Kris, and Troy walked into the gallery, where a member of Niall's staff stood holding a large black leather case with a silver chain running from it to a stainless-steel bracelet on his wrist. "Thank you for your patience," she paused, allowing time for him to state his name.

"Hi, I'm Ben. Ms. Ross, we put this on a plane as soon as we could."

"Thank you, Ben. I appreciate it. You didn't have trouble getting through customs, I take it?"

"No. Mr. King secured letters from both governments and official papers from the museum." Ben unlocked the case and gave it to Rose with documents to sign. Rose opened the case and inspected the piece sitting in a bed of grey foam cut precisely to its dimensions. She would later have Kris lock it in the walk-in vault, where she temporarily housed all the priceless art until the exhibition.

"This is breathtaking." She took a step back, admiring the piece. "When you dust off all the experiences you have accumulated over a lifetime and put them on canvas, you have art. Then you know for sure that art is life. It feels surreal that this piece connects me to someone else's past life. Anything else you need from me, Ben?"

"I have everything I need, Ms. Ross. I will be on my way if things are to your satisfaction."

"Thank you, Ben. Kris will show you out." Kris escorted Ben to the door where Troy stood watching. Rose pulled out her phone. She wanted to be the first to let Niall know the piece had arrived. Before she could unlock the screen, her phone buzzed. It was a text from Niall.

"Night Owl. Ben confirmed you received your art piece. I'm almost in the city—text me if you need anything. Have a great day."

Rose's response was swift. "You delivered. IOU." She received a blushing smiley face alongside a writing hand emoji in return.

"You know that man's brilliance makes him a special kind of sexy. Yes. I said that out loud."

"You certainly did," Kris giggled.

"Well, I'm not stating anything I haven't told him already."

"Oh, and here I am, thinking I'm getting a scoop. Back to work, lady. Your first interview will be here shortly."

※

THE RIDE TO THE CITY SEEMED MUCH SHORTER THAN ROSE remembered. Maybe it was because the route was familiar, or perhaps it had something to do with her upcoming meeting with Alejandro. The thought of his name conjured old memories for Rose of their time as a power couple. She felt he was the perfect glove that fitted so well on her hands when they were together. But over time, gloves lose their shape and don't fit well anymore, pulled and stretched from every angle. Now, sitting in the car moments away from seeing Alejandro again, Rose took a deep breath, trying to tamp down old feelings.

"Are you ready for this?" Troy asked as the driver pulled up to the pastry shop where she and Alejandro were meeting for coffee.

"Of course. We're just having coffee and catching up. Everything is fine." That is what she wanted to believe, but she was giving herself a pep talk. *Resist his sexy smile, forget former feelings, and don't get distracted.*

"I'll be standing here watching by the car if you need me."

Rose walked into the café alone. The sweet smell of baked cinnamon buns filled her senses as soon as the door opened. Alejandro had already arrived and was sitting at a window seat. He was breathtakingly handsome and impeccably dressed in a black suit and white shirt. His signature top two buttons were undone, revealing a glimpse of sun-kissed, brown skin. When Alejandro stood to greet her, his thrilling smile she remembered all too well lit up the room. Rose took a deep breath and held out a hand to shake his—just as she did the day before—but once again, he gently pulled her to his chest, giving her a familiar embrace instead, and kissed her on the cheek. Over his shoulder, she could see Troy in full view just outside the window, leaning against the car, watching the entire scene unfold before him.

"Hi, Rose. Sorry about surprising you the other day. I know you don't like that, and I should have contacted you as soon as I decided to come to Belfast. Please, have a seat. I took the liberty of ordering for us. Old habit. I hope that's okay." Alejandro pulled out her chair.

"I'm okay with you ordering. Surprised to see you is an understatement. How have you been?"

"I'm good. Business is great." The waitress came over with two pastries and two cappuccinos. "I hope you still like these?"

"This is perfect. I'm glad to hear business is still going strong for you."

"If we can hold off from talking business a second to pay you a compliment. Lady, I hope you know you look amazing."

"You look great too, Alejandro. I didn't mention it the other day, but I noticed you let your hair grow longer. It looks good on you. I didn't realize your hair was so curly." She took a sip from her cup.

"It's a new look for me—I'm glad you like it. Listen, I'm delighted you could make time for me today. Kris informed me your schedule is tight leading up to the exhibition. And from all the buzz, I hear this is the hottest ticket in town."

"There is nothing like creating a capstone event. But I'm sure you caught up on all the publicity surrounding it; otherwise, you wouldn't be here. That is how you found me, right?"

"I did read a few articles highlighting the event. But no. I knew you were here before I arrived." He smiled wryly.

"Then, I'll assume, reading between the lines, that you and my dad had some discussion that led you here. How'd you come to hear about Aedan and Niall?"

"I'm the attorney. Shouldn't I be cross-examining you? I met them recently. Until now, I didn't have the opportunity to fly to Belfast and execute the contract. We'll be doing business together, but I guess they have already shared the details with you?"

"Actually, no. Aedan and Niall don't share information about their private business dealings. You know, NDAs and all that."

"There's that."

"How long are you in Belfast?"

"Five days. I arrived a few nights ago."

"Then you're here for a few more days. I'm surprised."

"Surprised?"

"The other day, you seemed rushed to get ahold of me, contacting Kris and Troy. You left me with the impression that you'd be leaving soon." Rose took a sip of her cappuccino and licked her lips when she felt the sensation of tiny foam bubbles. She looked up to catch Alejandro staring at her tongue. "What made you decide to look me up here versus back in the States? I assume that passing through California is still part of your business routine. Sorry, it's been over a year. I guess I'm trying to figure out why here, why now?"

"When we were together, did you recall me ever not being in a rush to see you?"

"No."

Damn attorney, she thought, then took a bite of her pastry and washed it down with more cappuccino.

"Nothing has changed. When I learned you'd be here, I didn't want to miss the chance to catch up in person and express how impressed I am with your work." Alejandro flashed her one of his signature smiles.

"I'm not sure what to think about that. The Alejandro I remember has a purpose behind every action. And every inaction is an action in itself. Maybe you can elaborate on your impeccable timing. That way, we can move past this point of the conversation and get to catch up if that's really your intention." Rose checked the time on her watch. She felt anxious about falling into familiar habits with him and was doing her best to resist his sexy smile.

217

"That's the straight shooter Rose I remember. I'll get to the point. Yes, I timed my visit to yours. And to answer your previous question, yes, I frequently travel to the Bay Area. I thought about getting together, but my schedule was so compressed—I didn't want to rush our time together. It felt reminiscent of bad habits that led to our break. I couldn't put you through that again. Recently, your name came up in a discussion I had with your dad, and that is how I knew you were here."

"But why try at all? We mutually agreed to go our separate ways. I'm fine with our decision. Aren't you?"

"Not anymore. If I had a chance to replay that day, I would do it differently. I'm the one that initiated the separation. I was wrong, and I am sorry."

"Don't blame yourself. I played an equal role. But you did finally move on, didn't you? At least, that's what I would expect of you. You're a good catch. Aren't you dating someone?" She knew he was a one-woman type of guy, but she asked the question on the off chance that he'd changed.

"A compliment. It's good to know you still think positively of me."

"No one has ever accused me of being dishonest. You are prime material when it comes to guys, but I digress." She smiled wryly.

The waitress returned to the table to see if they needed anything else, but Alejandro shook his head, which the waitress understood as a cue to disappear behind the swinging kitchen doors. The coffee shop was quiet and peppered, with a few people getting their late afternoon fixes. For once, there were no prying eyes. Only Alejandro, staring intently at her across the table, and Troy, her sentinel, standing by outside—never too far away.

"No, I dated someone for a minute, but I'm single now." She liked that he was still a one-woman type of man.

"What's your definition of a minute?"

"A few months."

She laughed softly. "That's not dating. You were just scratching an itch."

"I won't deny it. It was just sex. And if I'm honest, I wasn't really dating her."

"And I suppose that minute ended recently or within the last few months?"

"Nothing gets past you. I always loved that," he said, evidently growing nostalgic of their relationship.

"But you didn't come here to talk about how perceptive I am. You came here to see if there was a possibility of us getting back together, right?" She sipped her coffee in between talking. Rose wanted to demonstrate she was in complete control of the conversation. She wouldn't get corned into something by his savvy lawyer tactics. And she certainly wasn't going to be wooed by his sexy smile. Not this time.

"Honestly, I'm here to catch up. I want to know what's been going on in your life. And yes, explore the possibility of us again. But only if you want to. It would be good to have lunch or dinner occasionally when I'm in California. I don't want to lose our friendship, whether or not we're a couple. We have a connection that neither of us can deny. Make sense?"

"I get it. But you didn't have to come to Belfast for that."

"Are you seeing someone?" he asked.

"I'm exploring possibilities."

"So, there's a chance for us." Alejandro leaned forward, reached across the table, and touched his fingertips to hers. A shadow was cast across the table by someone passing outside the window. Rose thought Troy might be interceding but looked to see Carol heading passed the cafe and down the street. She pulled her fingers away.

"I didn't say that."

Damn, she thought. Rose certainly hoped Carol didn't see his hands touch hers.

She grabbed her phone and texted Troy three letters: "WTF?" Troy returned her message, saying Carol just happened to be walking by, spotted him, peered into the window, and left.

"*Geez,*" she articulated the words in her brain that she hoped would transmit telepathically to Troy.

"What's that, Rose?"

"Oh, sorry. Nothing. Just a text. I'm listening."

"I miss you. Those first few months after we separated were rough. I hadn't realized how deep the emotional connection I felt was until I reached for the phone to call you about something and remembered we weren't together."

"You could have called me anyway. We didn't say we couldn't talk."

Alejandro sat back in his chair. "Then there was the time I made dinner arrangements for us, but I changed the reservations when I finally realized what I was doing. Or when I saw a bracelet in the jewelry store window and went in to purchase it for you. At that point, I was questioning if we had made the right decision."

"You mean you were questioning *your* decision."

"Exactly." Alejandro opened the palm of his hand, inviting her to take it. His eyes fixed on hers, and then he unleashed *the smile.*

"And you came here looking for some validation from me."

"Possibly."

Rose glanced out of the window a second, then back at Alejandro. She thought she was immune to his captivating smile, but thoughts about when they were together flooded her mind. She wanted to say yes. She squeezed her thighs, and the soreness between her legs reminded her that she was craving one man.

"Alejandro, I can't give you any. That day we talked it over, we both agreed. I moved forward from that day and every day since. We committed to our work, and I'm focused on mine. We discussed this."

"We could try."

"At this point, friends will have to do for now. Honestly, Alejandro, I'm still riding the wave of our aftershocks." She said it.

The absence of his smile signaled it was not the answer he wanted to hear. Rose saw a mixture of desire and pain in his eyes at the sound of her words. She felt herself projecting the same, finally admitting out loud something she'd been holding inside for the past year.

"I'm sorry," he said.

"There's nothing to be sorry about."

Alejandro withdrew his empty hand. "Are you happy? How are things?"

"I am happy. Just like you, my business is also thriving. I am completely immersed in the art scene," Rose said.

"That's good to hear. I understand you will be in Belfast for a while. Are you enjoying your stay?"

"So far. I've mostly been focused on work, conducting artist interviews, curating art, reviewing pieces, and pulling together the event," she said, happy for the change in topic.

"Have you had a chance to see Ireland and check out any sights? It's a beautiful country with a lot of history here."

221

"I did a little sightseeing over this past weekend. And you're right. It is a beautiful country. I hope to get in a bit more touring before I leave. What about yourself?"

"I've been here before and took in a few sights but nothing too extensive. I have a local contact if you need to arrange additional tours."

"That won't be necessary. I'm pretty well taken care of here."

"Your team or Aedan and Niall?"

"All of the above. Don't worry. Things are good." Rose finished the last of her coffee and pastry. A few taps on her phone signaled Troy that she was ready to leave. "Listen, Alejandro. It's been great catching up with you. But I have a compressed schedule, and I need to head out to my next meeting. I'm glad we did this."

"Glad you accepted."

"The next time you're in California, don't hesitate to reach out so we can have dinner together or something."

Alejandro stood to help Rose from her chair and gather her things from the table. "Sorry again for springing this on you."

"I'm working on forgiving you."

"I'd love to get together again before I leave. Would you be able to fit in dinner tomorrow?"

"I'll let you know. I really need to head out right now." Rose tried to give him a quick hug, but Alejandro held onto her like it was a final goodbye. She could feel his body heat through her blouse. She tried to flush old memories of him from her brain, peeled herself away, and turned towards the door where Troy was patiently waiting.

"I hope to see you again before I leave town," Alejandro called out.

Rose looked over her shoulder. "We'll see. Goodbye, Alejandro."

Rose left the café, got into the car, pulled out her phone, and tapped the call button on the screen.

"Hi, Rose. Are you okay?" Aedan asked on the other end of the line.

"All good. I'll see you tonight."

⁂

ROSE MANAGED TO BREEZE THROUGH SEVERAL BACK-TO-BACK MEETINGS following her time with Alejandro. Now, she was about to get into the car and head back to the house. Although the tiny bits of time between meetings allowed Rose to download with Troy on her encounter with Alejandro, she still needed to consider Alejandro's request to have dinner. Troy held the car door open, waited for Rose to get in, then joined her.

"Ready to head back?" Troy asked.

"Yes."

"I did some research following our discussion about Carol." Troy took out his phone, swiped the screen a few times, then handed it to Rose.

"What did you find?" Rose pinched the screen to expand it. "Is this what I think it is?" Rose read the screen aloud. "Let them eat cake. Why direct provision works." She turned wide-eyed to look at Troy. She had an inkling that Carol had issues, but now she had confirmation. This was not something that she could keep from Aedan.

"It's a blog post written by Carol about her campaign to keep direct provision alive and recommendation for further restrictions imposed on Black immigrants," Troy explained.

As research for her trip, Rose had read about how thousands of Black immigrants to Ireland were placed in the direct provision system.

"What the hell, Troy? This references the government program from our research where people are not allowed to work or cook traditional foods for their families under the guise that the program helps them learn the language and ways of the country. For many, it's equivalent to living in jail. Carol is siding with a system designed to keep control of a specific group of people. Not to mention exposing herself as a bigot. Hasn't she learned anything from her country's recent history?"

"How do you plan to handle this?" Troy asked.

"I need to see if the brothers know anything about this. Thank you for the information."

When Rose and Troy arrived at the house, it was quiet yet well-lit. Troy went in ahead of Rose to check things out. Neither Niall nor Aedan had returned from the city, so Troy would remain with her until someone returned. And although Carol's car was outside, there was no sign of her. Rose hoped that would continue to be the case.

"A staff member is in the kitchen finishing up," Troy said, leading the way.

Rose tipped her nose up. The air was filled with the scent of rosemary and onions. "Dinner smells good. They must be waiting for Niall and Aedan to return. You're welcome to join us for dinner if you want."

"No thanks, I'll eat later at the hotel."

"Can you take Carol with you?" she whispered, then bent to take off her shoes.

"No. But I can give you a hand with that." He grabbed her purse and shoe and lent her his arm to balance herself.

"Here. I'll take this. I need to head upstairs anyway to change clothes before dinner."

"You look good in that."

"I'd feel better wearing something else," she said, heading upstairs. Carol came out of her room as Rose reached the top of the stairwell.

"Good evening, Carol. I'm just about to change before dinner," Rose said, stepping past Carol. She found it odd that despite the King family tradition of dressing up for dinner, Carol was casually dressed in simple slacks, a black cardigan, and flat shoes.

"I'm surprised to see you. I half expected you'd stay in town with your Arabic friend," Carol said.

Rose blinked. "I think I miss understood you."

"I saw you and your boyfriend at the café today. Does my cousin know you are out with another guy?"

"I don't owe anyone an explanation about my personal affairs. And it's not flattering to speak out of ignorance. However, your cousins are very familiar with my *friend*, Alejandro, who is Latin and one of the most powerful international attorneys. I strongly urge you to rethink defaming anyone I know, especially him," Rose said, trying to keep calm.

"I see."

"Suddenly short on words?"

"I guess I—"

"You might want to get your facts straight before approaching me in the future. I don't know what your issue is, but I need to change clothes. See you at dinner." The conversation ended abruptly. Rose went to her room and closed the door before Carol could utter another word.

It didn't take Rose long to freshen up and change. Going through the motions of getting ready helped her put Carol's conversation out of her mind. A sky-blue silk slip dress that came just above the knees and strappy sandals was just the look she was going for to help her feel confident. A spritz of vanilla and lavender oil, and she was ready. The clicks of her heels signaled Troy that she was descending the stairs. Patiently waiting—his presence meant that Niall and Aedan had not arrived yet.

"You look great. The guys aren't here yet, but—" just then, the front door opened, and in walked Niall, who stopped in his tracks at the front door when he saw Rose. He was followed by Aedan, who had to push past him slightly to get into the house. Aedan looked to see what he was looking at and froze, too. Troy continued. "Did you need me in here while they're getting settled?" He held her hand as she reached the bottom step.

"Thanks, Troy, I'm good. Are you sure you don't want to stay for dinner?"

"I'm sure," he said, then nodded at the brothers on his way to the door.

Aedan was the first of the brothers to find his voice. "Is it possible that you look even more amazing every time I see you, Rose?"

"Hi, yourself."

"Hi." He prompted Niall, whose mouth was slightly ajar. "What do you think, Niall?"

"Good evening, Rose. My brother is right. You look beautiful. I think I'll eat here every night as long as you are here."

"I appreciate the compliments. However, you two can either stand there and stare at me and starve, or we can all head to the dining room to eat. I prefer to eat, so the faster you two get washed up, the sooner we can start." She gave Niall a quick hug, a kiss on the cheek, and a gentle nudge towards the stairs before turning her attention to Aedan. His look was all fire and passion as he bent to kiss Rose.

"Upstairs," Rose said when they came up for air. Aedan flashed a satisfied grin, caressed her cheek, and disappeared upstairs.

It didn't take long for Niall and Aedan to pull themselves together before dinner. When they walked into the dining room, Carol was already at the head of the table, sitting in silence, giving Rose the slow burn with her eyes. Aedan sat next to Rose, and Niall sat on her other side. "This should be interesting," Rose said under her breath.

Aedan started the conversation by commenting on the day's local news and talking in-depth about local government sanctions that could impact their operations. Rose was full of questions about Aedan's plan to thwart the government from affecting his business. Throughout the meal, Carol was uncharacteristically short on words. Except from time to time, her only comment was, "Oh, that's interesting." She seemed to be waiting for the perfect time to press the right button.

Aedan's attempt to include Carol in the discussion was apparent to Rose. "Carol, did you have a chance today to speak with the nurse on duty before she left?" he asked.

"Yes, I returned from the city early enough to connect with her. Brianna did well today but still required assistance with some basic tasks. I checked with her earlier to see if she was feeling well enough to have dinner with us. She said she wasn't up for it though, so we had dinner brought to her room."

"Sounds like nothing has changed since I talked to her earlier today. You said you went to the city. You could have stopped by to have lunch with Niall and me. Did you do some shopping?"

"No, I wasn't shopping. I went to have lunch with some of our relatives that I hadn't seen in a while. Didn't Rose tell you I saw her out with her boyfriend earlier?" Carol asked.

Niall's raised eyebrows and Aedan's grimace signaled Rose that damage control was necessary, but before she could say anything, Aedan jumped in. "Rose's meeting is none of our business."

Rose bit back the urge to say something.

"Aedan, I thought you would want to know who she's holding hands with when you're not around," Carol said.

"Carol, that's enough. Rose's business is just that. Hers. We have no interest in gossip." Aedan appeared apathetic to Carol's comments.

Rose pursed her lips. She was disappointed Aedan didn't state he already knew about the meeting.

"Carol, we had this conversation earlier about you being misinformed. Niall and Aedan know about my meeting with Alejandro, who happens to be a business associate of theirs. And as Aedan so nicely put it, my business is my business," Rose said sternly.

"But now that you're involved with my cousin—" Carol paused and waved a finger between Aedan and Rose. "You two are an item, right? Then that makes it his business. Which makes this family business."

Rose pressed her lips together. "That's not how this works. But since you're interested in discussing other people's business, let's discuss the bigoted propaganda you posted about enacting additional restrictions on Blacks in direct provision to further strip them of their culture. If you have something to say, now is your perfect opportunity in front of your family."

"You're right. I think our government is not doing enough. If these people want to be here, they need to assimilate to our culture and how we do things here," Carol asserted.

"And by *these people*, you mean Black people like me," Rose said.

"You don't mean that, Carol," Niall interjected.

"I do," Carol confirmed.

Rose adjusted herself in her chair to face Carol. "Do you even hear yourself? The people are coming here in need of protection. You have just under forty direct provision centers. How many of those are embedded within the communities?" Rose paused a few seconds and waited for Carol's response. "Your sudden silence speaks volumes because you know the centers are located in places to keep the people separate from the country where they now live. So, saying they need to assimilate is a ruse. But your post didn't stop there. You called for special restrictions on people of African descent. Hence your issue with my presence. Your passive-aggressive behavior and sideways glances speak volumes, and I scratch my head, wondering what century this is."

Aedan slid his chair back from the table. "Carol, I'm a little disappointed to hear all this. I think Niall and I need to take this offline with you to better understand how you got to this point. From the discussion tonight, it seems your thinking is not aligned with our family beliefs," Aedan said.

"There was a time when you had the same beliefs," Carol shot back.

"Protecting my family from physical harm and political persecution during civil unrest is not remotely the same as racism," Aedan retorted.

"Aedan is right, Carol. We told you the other day that if you have a problem being here, we won't blame you for returning home. We appreciate the support you've provided Brianna so far. However, we won't put up with you bringing this divisive thinking here and insulting our guests. You have a right to your opinion, and we have a right to live free of it," Niall said.

"I'll continue this with you two tomorrow," Carol said and stormed out of the room.

"Rose, I assure you my beliefs directly oppose Carol's. I'll see to it that she leaves here tomorrow," Niall said.

"Carol is out of line," Aedan added.

"It seems Carol hadn't previously brought you up to speed on her ideology. It puts me in an awkward position. I have some work to do, but I'm open to discussing it later tonight, Aedan." Rose said.

"I meant it when I said I need to hear her out. She's always been challenging, but this doesn't feel like the Carol I know. Something's changed, and I need to get to the bottom of it," Aedan explained.

Rose looked at Aedan, unsure if she fully recognized the man who'd recently occupied her bed.

CHAPTER 12

Trust in Me

"Let there be spaces in your togetherness...."

— KAHLIL GIBRAN, *The Prophet*

RISING ACROSS THE NORTH ATLANTIC, THE SUN MADE ITS WAY TO Belfast, and another day was born. Rose blinked several times until her eyes adjusted to the sliver of light coming through the curtains chasing away the night. Alone with her thoughts, reliving last night's conversations left her feeling empty. Getting out of bed to deal with Carol was the last thing she wanted. "Your uniqueness is your superpower. You got this."

Pulling herself together was hard, but she did just that. By the time she had her shower, she had decided to put her blinders back on like they were on her first day and focus on her event. However, the green leather pencil skirt, low-cut white silk shirt, and nude spiked heels would ensure that she looked and felt good.

A consummate trooper, she put a smile on her face and went to the kitchen for her morning ritual with the guys. Hug, coffee, eat. She didn't know if she wanted to rehash the discussion about Carol, but Rose prepared herself for whatever the day would bring. She hoped Aedan would not act apathetic to the Carol issue. It was all too much of a distraction from her real purpose of being in Belfast. She needed to get through the next few weeks. Rose needed to refocus.

As he had done several times before, Aedan announced her before she entered the room. "Come on in, Rose. The scent of vanilla and lavender are always welcome here."

True to his nature, their conversations from last night were long past him. But Rose couldn't forget that she was considered the unwelcome party and the target of Carol's microaggressions, and his silence on the topic felt like acceptance. She had expected Aedan to talk with her privately about her feelings, but he didn't. At a minimum, she wanted to know the timing of the conversation he would have with Carol.

Niall looked up from his phone just as Rose entered. "Man, I don't know how you do that. All I can smell is coffee."

"You need to slow down and concentrate, Niall. You could be missing out on something important." Aedan looked at Rose. "Good morning, Rose."

"Good morning, Aedan." Her tone was cordial but lacked its usual warmth.

"Good morning, Night Owl—although I don't think I can call you that this morning. You retired to your room quite early last night. Work stuff, right?"

"Morning. I'm good. I had a conference call on the west coast to attend. Sorry, I can't hang out with you two for breakfast. I have a ton of work to plow through today. The exhibition is getting closer and closer. I'll just take this and go. And don't worry about dinner tonight. I'll grab something before I leave the city." Rose poured herself a cup of coffee and took it with her as she slipped out of the room just as quietly as she entered. No goodbye. No kiss on the cheek. There was no lingering backward glance at the two Irish gods sitting with stunned expressions. When she opened the front door, Troy was already waiting.

"Morning, Troy. Can you help me with these?" She handed him her purse, portfolio, and coffee. When she reached back to close the door, she found her hand in someone else's and looked back to see Aedan.

"Give me a minute, Troy," Aedan said. This time, Troy didn't back off. He stood inches away from Rose, waiting for her response. Rose nodded—their private signal for Troy to stand by her side.

Aedan turned Rose to face him. The strength in his stare seared her skin as he slowly scanned the entire length of her body, sending a warm sensation between her legs. This was the side of Aedan she was avoiding. The beautiful rock-hard businessman who knew what he wanted and went for it.

"Did you want something?" Rose heard herself say, resisting the heat sandwiched between them. Defying the innate urge to disregard everything she stood for and give into her desires. As she awaited an answer, Aedan dipped his head and kissed her. It was gentle at first—a quick lick across her top lip, a suck of her bottom lip. Then, a more urgent kiss formed as he opened her mouth with his tongue. She instinctively mingled hers with his, sucking and licking into him until they came up for air. All the while, his body grew hard as steel against her.

"That," he said, his mouth hovering above hers. Taunting her.

"I would say back me up against the wall and take me, but I won't. I need to focus on my work, and we—" Rose gestured the short distance between them. "We need to talk about Carol."

"And I can't do either right now. I have to go, but I'll be back tonight. I can handle Carol." Aedan brushed her bottom lip with his thumb and then looked over her shoulder. "Thank you, Troy," he said before disappearing into the house.

Rose didn't know what she expected Aedan to say, but she knew it was not the response she was looking for. Despite her objection to Carol, Aedan had yet to deal with her. At that moment, Rose felt herself pulling away. She remembered when her relationship with Alejandro ended; it was at a time when they both had a lot of work pressures. She remembered feeling something had to give. She remembered feeling distracted. So, when Alejandro suggested a break, she took it.

"Rose." The sound of Troy's voice pulled her out of her head. Troy handed Rose her coffee and escorted her to the gallery. Once inside, Troy cleared his throat. "Are you going to tell me what just happened and what caused you to summon me before you finished breakfast?"

"I was hoping not to get into it. If Carol doesn't leave today, you will move your things into the house, which I think you should do anyway. I need someone from my team here to watch my back."

"Knowing what we know about her, what could possibly be her motivation to stay?" Troy asked.

Rose shook her head. "That's the question we would all like to see answered. Carol could be doing it out of spite or simply because she knows she has a family advantage. Either way, she expressed what side of the fence she was on last night."

"Things went that badly last night?"

"Disappointing. Hopefully, we'll all find some reasonable resolution to what is happening soon. But I have to ask, don't you find it odd that I'm here trying to spread educational awareness through art while Carol is amping up her propaganda, then somehow found her way to Brianna's house? It got me thinking that Carol was the most likely person who declined that call we placed to Brianna on my second day, and I heard from Niall that Carol influenced Brianna to leave the house without first notifying him and Aedan. At this point, I'm not sure what Carol is capable of. The event needs to go off without a hitch, and I don't have time to monitor media, watch out for precious art, and myself while Carol's around. And the guys—well, let's just say it appears they're blind to her antics. Or maybe because she's family, they're ignoring it. That's where you come in."

"No, this is where I get to do my job. From now on, only I make security decisions for you without anyone's interference. Don't worry about the gallery—that's covered."

"You were right all along. I need to let you do what you do best. You'll find no more changes to your plans from me."

"Just so we are clear, wherever you go, I go. Wherever you stay, I stay. If your host has an issue, we will move you to a hotel in the city. Are we aligned?"

"Perfectly. Now, back to business. A few people are coming here today for their interviews, and Kamal is coming for a preliminary walkthrough. The rest of the day—"

"We are in the city," he said, finishing her sentence.

"Yes, but I need to add dinner with Alejandro. I got so wrapped up in Carol and her mess that I almost forgot he was leaving soon, and I promised to let him know whether I was available for dinner before he traveled. Given the circumstances, tonight is as good a night as any for dinner with Alejandro."

"It's your kickboxing night with Niall."

"He hasn't seen me in full force. The way I feel, today would be a full impact day. I wouldn't want to take my frustration out on him. Cancel."

"You have a restaurant in mind for dinner?"

"Yes. But let me get a hold of Alejandro first to confirm he can make it. Once I have that and my coffee, I'll add everything to the calendar. I'll see you later."

Rose went into the gallery office, and Troy conducted his rounds. She took a sip of her coffee, pulled out her cell phone, and sent a message to Alejandro.

"Morning. You still in town?"

Oh, shoot, she thought. *It's only seven in the morning.* She didn't know whether he would be awake.

Too late. He was awake. Alejandro texted back. "I'm here. Call me."

A second after she hit the phone icon, his phone rang. Alejandro answered halfway through the first ring. "Good morning, Rose. It is early, even for you. Everything okay?"

"Morning. You're right. I'm still having my coffee. I didn't realize the hour until it was too late. Sorry about that. Technology makes it too easy to connect."

"No problem. What can I do for you?"

"I was just following up on our conversation from yesterday. You mentioned having dinner together before you flew out. I was about to text you to see if you were available tonight."

"This is a pleasant surprise. Tonight is good. Does six o'clock work for you? Did you have a particular place in mind?"

"Six works. There is a place I wanted to try out. I'll text you after I make reservations."

"How about you tell me the place, and I'll make the reservations. Dinner's on me."

"Sure. Thanks. I have to go now—I need to get through some other work before my first interview arrives. I'll send you the details. See you at six."

"Great. Rose, before you hang up, I just wanted to thank you for reaching out and setting aside time with me."

"See you later."

"Enjoy your coffee."

Kris walked into the office as she ended her call. "You're in super early this morning. I just wanted to check to see if you were okay?"

"I'm fine. While you're here, will you put together some clothing options for me to change into later today at your hotel? I'm having dinner with Alejandro tonight. I don't want to look too corporate if you know what I mean."

"Sure thing. You're not going to the gym before dinner?"

"No gym tonight."

"Are you wearing those shoes to dinner, or would you like me to provide a few options to choose from?"

"Let's include shoe options, too. Thank you, Kris—I appreciate it."

"Will you be staying overnight?"

"I don't have plans. But as usual, grab my overnight bag."

⁂

THE DAY WENT BY LIKE A STEADY BREEZE. SEVEN ART PIECES ARRIVED and were installed, three artist interviews were conducted, and one mini crisis was averted—all in a day's work. Kris was on his toes, making things happen as usual, and no one got past Troy that wasn't on the calendar. Even the commuter traffic within the city was lighter than expected. So, Rose had enough time to stop at Kris' hotel room to relax and get changed before dinner with Alejandro.

"I'm looking at the calendar, and Alejandro got promoted to yellow. What happened there? Not that I object. He's one of my favorites," Kris said in his high-pitched voice, drawing out the *A* and over-emphasizing the *T.*

"It's not like you to pry," Rose said, surprised by his question.

"I know, but I'm looking at this long list of good-looking men parading around here, then the alpha male miraculously returns to the stage after more than a year. At this point, you all have me curious."

"You have a point. I forgot how much you liked Alejandro."

"I didn't just *like* him. I was sitting in the cheerleader section, watching every move he made when you two were dating. I was afraid to raise my pom-poms, fearing they'd block my view, and I might miss something. That man is gorgeous," he said, emphasizing every syllable as he spoke.

"I don't disagree. Like To'ak, he's top-shelf candy—and I love chocolate, but that's not why I'm having dinner with him. He happens to be working out a deal with the brothers in town, and you know the rest."

"Well, you'll get no eye-rolling from me. Just know I'm rooting for Alejandro on the sidelines. What does Troy think?"

"Well, he didn't make you red-box him, right?"

"No."

"There's your answer."

"Okay, it's time for you to stop gabbing with me and get to the restaurant. I should get ready, too. I'm going dancing tonight," Kris said.

"You make friends everywhere you go, don't you?"

"I try."

"Well, have a wonderful evening, and thank you for letting me share your space to get ready. See you in the morning." Rose made her way to the elevator. Her phone buzzed just before she stepped in. Assuming it was Kris alerting her to something she had left behind in the room, she reached into her purse and pulled out her phone to discover a text message, but not from Kris.

"You canceled tonight. Everything okay?" the text from Niall read.

"In the elevator. Will call from the car," she texted back.

Rose looked up when the elevator doors opened to find Troy waiting for her. She briefly touched his shoulder, and he escorted her to the car. Rose scrolled to Niall's name on her phone and pressed the call button. He picked up immediately.

"Niall here."

"I sure hope so since that's who I called. I'm responding to your text," she said in her business voice. Distant voices and laughter came through from the background on Niall's end.

"Night Owl. Can you hear me? Sorry about the noise. I'm grabbing a drink with some friends, but I wanted to talk to you."

"I can hear you just fine." Rose found herself raising her voice to match his.

"Great. I just wanted to connect with you before it got too late. Aedan seemed a little upset following your quick exit this morning. I realize our conversation went a little off track last night, and no one has heard from you since this morning—rather, Aedan and I haven't—so I had to find you and clear the air."

"Clear the air?"

"I talked with Aedan after you left. I told him that based on what I saw last night, it could be perceived he didn't take a real stance against

Carol. And I mentioned it was likely disappointing that he didn't take you up on your offer to talk later. Maybe you can reach out again to talk with him. What time will you be back tonight?"

"I'm not sure. I'm heading to dinner now." In her head, she didn't know what her plan was. She only knew she wanted to stay as far from the brothers and Carol as possible for the night to clear her head, even if that meant staying overnight at a hotel.

"I'm assuming that's why you canceled on me. Anyways, I just wanted to connect with you before it got too late."

"I appreciate the olive branch, Niall, but I really need to go now."

"Enjoy the evening with your crew."

"I'm meeting Alejandro for dinner." Rose knew she didn't need to clarify with Niall, but she had been transparent about everything since she met him.

"Then, let's catch up when you return," Niall responded.

The ride to the restaurant was short. Upon arrival, Troy escorted Rose from the car and into the restaurant. Inside, Rose found Alejandro waiting in the receiving area.

"I was surprised but pleased you decided to join me for dinner," Alejandro said.

"You're an attorney. You'd already worked through all the scenarios. Nothing surprises you."

"Earlier this week, it seemed you were taken aback by me being in Belfast. And our coffee chat was brief, so I didn't think you had the time."

"Be honest. You thought I didn't want to make the time."

"I hoped that wasn't the case."

"Well, I'm here now."

This could be a big mistake, Rose thought as she drank in the delicious distraction standing before her. She shivered when a former memory of the titan beneath the suit flashed in her head. Rose was upset with Aedan and thought putting some distance between them might help, but what stood between them now was a man she knew all too well and one she was desperately trying to resist.

"Mr. and Mrs. Rodriquez, I have your table ready." The sound of the waiter's voice pulled Rose out of her fantasy. She glanced up at Alejandro, who had a full-fat cat grin. He didn't bother correcting the waiter. Instead, he placed his hand on the small of her back, sending a familiar sensation through her body. They walked through the dimly lit restaurant, passing rows of well-dressed diners sitting at white linen-covered tables until they reached a quiet spot in the corner.

"Is this table okay with you? It gives us a good vantage point to take in the view of the restaurant."

"It's fine," Rose said, studying Alejandro.

"If you haven't had a chance to review their menu in advance, I can make a few suggestions."

"Sure. Maybe when the waiter returns, we can hear about the specials."

"No change in your food and drink preference, I assume?"

"None except I try not to drink on work nights, but I'll have something tonight."

"I am curious to know more about what else, if anything, has changed."

The room seemed quiet, as if everyone there were awaiting her response. Rose didn't have an answer she thought could satisfy Alejandro without sounding curt. A defense mechanism she would purposely deploy more for her sake than his. Alejandro was another lovely distraction she didn't need.

Rose slid her silverware off her napkin and placed the napkin on her lap. When she looked up, the waiter had returned. He put some bread and dipping oil on the table and lit the candle in the center. Light from the flickering flame created a soft glow illuminating Alejandro's signature smile. He fixed his gaze on Rose, and she forced herself to look away, not to be lured in by his charm, to ignore her body's instinctive craving for him. All she wanted at that moment was a drink and a piece of meat, and reaching across the table was the fastest way to get both.

"May I take your order?" the waiter asked.

"We'd like to hear the specials," Alejandro said.

"Today, we have fresh Haddock baked in lemon and rosemary and thin-cut ribeye drizzled in truffle butter with Yorkshire pudding."

"May I?" He looked at Rose. She nodded in response. "We will both have the ribeye. I'll have a cup of loose-leaf tea and a Manhattan for the lady." Alejandro smiled at Rose. The server confirmed their order and then vanished into the kitchen.

"At first, I felt a little awkward about dinner with you but darn it, when you go around smiling like that, it's like old times." He was a beautiful man and easy to be with. Rose wanted to add, *Can you dial back the wattage a bit? I'm having a hard time focusing*, but she held back.

Alejandro laughed. "That's my Rose. Bold and honest. I still get embarrassed by your unexpected compliments."

"One of my flaws—I can't help myself. Besides, it's a good icebreaker; you get to see my sameness, or lack thereof. I have questions of my own for you."

"What's on your mind?"

"Are you about done wrapping up your business here in Belfast?" she asked, attempting to rein in her libido.

"For the most part. I have a few meetings that take me through the end of the day tomorrow."

"That leaves you with an extra day before you fly out."

"Are you keeping track?"

"No, just remembering what you told me. What are your plans?" Rose asked.

"Originally, I planned to take in some sights. There are a few places I wanted to get to while I was here. However, yesterday I thought about bumping up the timeline to fly out."

The waiter returned with their drinks. "Your order will be up shortly. Is there anything else I can get you for now?"

"No. Thank you," Alejandro responded, then the waiter disappeared into the kitchen again.

Rose took the brandied cherry out of her drink. "It doesn't sound like you changed it." She took a sip of her drink.

"I haven't yet."

"Yet?"

"I was just about to book an earlier flight when you reached out about having dinner. I didn't expect your call. Your call made me rethink my plans, so I left my options open. What made you decide to reach out?"

"You asked me, I have time, and I didn't have a reason not to."

"I don't understand. You need a reason not to see me?"

"No, actually, I don't. I just meant we're still friends. I'm not trying to avoid you. Despite working through the aftershock, I have special memories of our time together." Not to mention some of the spicy memories she was doing her best to suppress.

"They were good times for me, as well. I got used to having you in my life. Recently, I've been thinking about where I went wrong—my personal version of aftershocks. At some point, I went on autopilot. I was driving so hard—living life one legal brief at a time—that it didn't allow me to give more of myself," he explained.

"I wouldn't lament over it. I was in the same situation. We fit perfectly together during the time we were a couple. We're a few years older and following the paths we were meant to take separately."

"Yes, but I wish I had done a better job nurturing our friendship."

"See, that's the thing—real friends can spend time away, live their separate lives, and come back together, picking up as if no time has passed. We have that, and I would challenge anyone who said anything different." She raised her glass. Alejandro did the same. "Here's to friendship. May the tie that binds us never break." She clanged his glass.

"To friendship," he echoed, then lowered his glass. "Can I ask you a personal question?"

"I do reserve the right to plead the fifth." She took a sip of her drink.

"I'll allow it. But seriously, when I asked you the other day if you were dating, you said you were exploring possibilities. Would that be with Niall or Aedan?"

"What makes you think it's one of them?"

"Because they both act like animals marking their territory around you. Watching how Aedan moved in sync with you was interesting. Did you notice how he tended to speak on your behalf? And Niall, before he left, I asked him something about meeting you, and his reaction was more defensive than his brother's."

"Are you building a case?"

"Not at all. Just stating the facts."

"It's their modus operandi. Some of it is cultural, some training. You know, the military, special forces. They can't help themselves."

"I am a man—I know the feeling. It has nothing to do with military training or otherwise. I'm sure people saw me react the same way a few years ago."

The waiter returned with food, placed their dishes on the table, and then disappeared into the kitchen. Rose took a sip of her drink and looked around the room to see no empty seats. The place was lively. Everyone was immersed in conversations. Waiters and waitresses were buzzing, serving dishes, pouring wine, or taking orders, appearing and disappearing to and from the double swinging kitchen doors.

Rose refocused her attention on Alejandro and said a name. "Aedan."

"Aedan?"

"Yes, I've been spending time with him—getting to know him better. But there is nothing serious going on."

"You may want to inform him it's nothing serious, and while you're at it, think about letting Niall off the hook."

"I won't lie. Every move the brothers make is calculated. So, while they're pissing circles around me, as you alluded to, I've intentionally set expectations around my purpose for being in Belfast—the exhibition. Are they distracting? Yes. Have I given into a bit of the distraction? Admittedly so. But it's nothing I can't handle."

"I would argue that you have more work to do with Niall."

"I got this." Rose hated to admit he was right. Niall's persistence had a life of its own. But now Alejandro was pissing circles. She pushed food around her plate with a fork while processing his words. Alejandro was watching her and smiling. She was surprised to see it wasn't his standard, sexy as sin smile that she'd resisted since they sat down. This was the smile she had seen him use in the courtroom. His deductive reasoning smile was the one he unleashed when all the facts were playing in his favor. "You know I know that look, right?"

"Just as well as I know you. You don't stop working on something until you get what you want. This leads me to believe that although you're *exploring* things with Aedan, you've stalled for whatever reason. Did something happen? Does he know you're here with me, or is this part of your plan?"

Rose shifted in her chair. "I'm here because you asked me, and I want to be here. Like you, I value our friendship. I didn't have any special plans tonight. And no, I didn't tell the guys where I was going or who I was having dinner with until Niall texted me on my way here. I'm sure by now he's shared my whereabouts with his brother. But that's neither here nor there—I have no attachments."

"Good to know you're here because you want to be. Although it sounds like you're trying to convince yourself of something."

"Just stating the facts."

He looked at her plate. The food was neatly separated into sections. "Are you planning to eat that or play with it? It looks good, but it's going to get cold. Eat."

She took a bite. "It is good. I haven't had a bad meal since I've been here."

"And I'm sure all your restaurant choices have been thoroughly researched or come highly recommended."

"You know me too well. But you can't blame me. I would not want to waste time or money on a bad meal. That's how you get sick traveling. I don't have time for that."

"That's right, and you have a big event coming up. How's the planning going? You're a big deal in the art scene, but I'm sure you are used to it," Alejandro stated.

"So far, things are falling into place. I came up with some new ideas, and they seem to be working out great—it adds a little extra work on my part, but it's all good. I'm meeting with some cool artists and doing my best to deliver something that does justice to them and the influential artists who came before them. It'll be something no one has seen before when it's all done. I'm super excited, as you can tell."

"Your voice rings with enthusiasm. I can't wait to hear how it turns out."

"Right. You're leaving soon. Usually, I'd say that's okay, but you went out of your way to time this trip. I'm curious to know how you missed the event date."

"Can I plead the fifth for now?" Alejandro sat back in his seat with one hand resting on the table, slightly gesturing as he talked.

"This might be your only chance to come clean."

"A risk I'll take," he said.

"Pleading the fifth only makes you look guilty, and as it stands right now, your whole trip is suspect to me. But it is nice to see you again."

"Does that mean you forgive me?"

"For planning your trip to coincide with mine instead of dropping in when you travel through my city?"

"No."

"Is there anything I can do to make up for it?" Alejandro leaned forward slightly, reached across the table, touched her hand, and smiled. Rose wasn't giving in. She swallowed a smile.

"No. Don't even try. Better yet, I'll tell you when I think of something."

"Just let me know."

"I am disappointed you won't be here for my event. Why didn't you plan your trip closer to the actual exhibition date?"

"It didn't seem like the right thing to do. I didn't know how you would even receive me randomly showing up in Belfast. It could have been a real disaster, and I care too much for you to do anything to disrupt your work. The past year proved that. So, I put enough distance between the time I needed to conduct my business and your event. As I mentioned, I was planning to return home sooner, thinking you might not want me around."

"I appreciate your honesty, but it sounds like excuses."

"It's the truth. In hindsight, it was an error in judgment on my part, not planning around your event date."

"Needless to say, you're right about me needing to focus. That's my cue to you that I need to get going. I have a lot of work to do tomorrow." Rose pushed her plate away from the edge of the table.

On cue, the waiter reappeared, checking in on them, inquiring about dessert, and clearing the table. Rose let him know she did not want any dessert. She was proud of herself for resisting the literal and figurative offerings before her. She wasn't sure how the night would end with Alejandro. Now that he was looking down into his cup, she could break free of his smile, which was her personal kryptonite.

"You seem suddenly preoccupied," Rose said.

"I'm reading the tea leaves. They say our friendship is eternal." Alejandro looked at Rose and smiled *the smile*. She both loved and hated his silly sense of humor and sexy smile. Rose inhaled.

"Seriously, Alejandro, the tea leaves tell us it's late. Before I head back to the house, I have a stop to make."

"No time for an after-dinner drink or dessert?"

There's that word again, she thought.

"Unfortunately, not. You'll have to make your way to the Bay area more often."

"Looks that way." Alejandro's hand went up, summoning the waiter back to the table. He requested the bill. The waiter disappeared and then reappeared with the receipt from behind a podium.

"Thank you, Alejandro. It truly has been a lovely, relaxed evening."

Alejandro stood and helped Rose from her chair. Her final sentiments were a gently cupped hand on Alejandro's cheek, a quick kiss on the lips, and a warm smile.

"I'm glad you had dinner with me, Rose. You can be sure I will inform you as soon as I get to California for a visit. Trust me." She nodded, waved him a kiss, and navigated the maze of tables back to Troy.

IN THE CAR, ROSE USED THE TIME TO UNWIND WITH TROY. "YOU KNOW that wasn't as awkward as I expected. Unlike our meeting yesterday, tonight felt almost—" She paused, unsure of what she was feeling. "Normal." She exhaled.

"Are you okay?"

"Perfectly. I had forgotten how easy it is to be with Alejandro."

"To date?"

"As a person and as a friend. He really is a good guy. You know, he wanted me to stay out a little later for drinks."

"I'm at your disposal as late as you need me. Were you thinking of taking Alejandro up on his offer?"

"I thought about it. But the way we left the conversation was fine. I don't want him to read anything else into it beyond what it was—a lovely evening between friends. Besides, it's later than I planned to stay out already. Now, let's get your stuff

"Sure. We're almost there. Just a few blocks."

"That's right. You and Kris are minutes from all the cool shops, museums, and eating places. I could have stayed in town during the trip if I didn't need to spend so much time at the gallery." From the window, she saw the now dark entrance to shops she had frequented during the day to meet with artists or to have coffee.

"We're here. You'll have to come up with me. I can't leave you waiting in the car."

"Of course."

Troy helped Rose from the car, and together, they went to the top floor, where he and Kris had separate suites. Rose put her purse down on the coffee table in the living room and wandered around the space. "This is pretty cool, Troy."

Troy headed toward the bedroom, talking over his shoulder. "I'll get my things, and we can head back out. I know it's late."

Rose was still examining the space. "Hey, you've been holding out on me. Nice accommodations."

"It does the job."

"Don't be modest." She walked over to the patio window. "Wow, look at this—what a beautiful view. The city is spectacular at night. It gives me an entirely different perspective of Belfast."

Troy abandoned his clothes hunting project to stand next to Rose and take in the city's view. "You're right. It is a great view. I've been so focused on the job that I haven't spent the time to take it in like this."

Troy went back to gathering his things. Rose walked around the room, examining all the items, like the large console, which housed his impromptu bar. She smelled the flower arrangements, flipped through the books, opened liquor bottles, smelled their contents, recapped, and repeated with another bottle until she settled on Tullamore D.E.W. Irish whiskey and poured herself a glass. "Take your time. I'm having a drink. You have quite the collection here. Where did you get all this anyway?"

"What's that?"

"All this alcohol." She sniffed the contents of her glass and then took a sip. "Mmm. That is some good whiskey."

"I picked up a bottle at the grocery store, and the rest Kris brought over. He said his new friends brought them by for a dinner party they were having, but I don't think they realized that he doesn't drink."

"I knew he didn't and thought you didn't drink either."

"I have a sip sometimes but never when I'm on duty. Ensuring you're free to move about as you please is my number one priority."

She did feel free around him. Rose took another sip. "Wow. This is top-shelf good. I need to frequent Kris' parties. So, this is how you guys live when we travel."

"Sometimes, on longer trips like this one. We try to make the best of things. Did you think we were ordering room service every day?"

"Well, you're with me most of the day. You eat what I eat." She sauntered over to the patio door and slid it open for an unfiltered view of the cityscape—drink still in hand. "Oh shit!" she said.

Troy stopped what he was doing and rushed to the patio to see what was happening. As he stepped out, Rose stepped in, running drink first right into him—her body bouncing off his pecs. Troy grabbed her shoulders to help keep her steady. Rose looked up to speak but discovered her lips perfectly poised to meet Troy's. She hovered a second, allowing the warmth of their breaths to mingle before she stepped back. His eyes were wide with concern, apparently oblivious to her dilemma and his whiskey-drenched shirt. Or was he? She let the moment pass; their professional ties unbroken.

"Are you okay? What happened out there?" Troy said, still holding her shoulders.

Rose's initial response was laughter, but the drink's effects produced a sound more like sleep apnea than a laugh. "Sorry. I stubbed my toe and tripped." Troy helped her back in and out of the cold. Rose was looking at Troy, pointing at his whiskey-soaked shirt. "I would say grab yourself a drink and join me for a nightcap, but seeing my drink is all over you, I need one, too." She looked down and pulled her soaked dress away from her skin. "And a t-shirt, please. This thing is a mess."

"You had me worried for a minute. Here, I'll take this," he said, clutching her glass. "Is your toe okay?" he asked.

Rose looked down and wiggled her toe in her strappy heel. "Seems fine. I think the shoe took the brunt of it. Probably a little scuffed."

"They look okay. Feel free to wash up and grab something from my dresser drawer, or I can have the driver bring your bag up."

"I'll just grab something from your things." Rose headed to the bedroom but quickly came back out. "Actually, I have an idea. I'll just stay here tonight, if you don't mind. You need to monitor my comings and goings regardless of where I am. Besides, it's too late to make the trek back to the castle tonight. I can sleep out here in your living room. I have extra clothes, so I have a few outfits to choose from tomorrow."

"If that is what you want. I'll call the driver now to have him bring your things up. You can have my room, and I'll sleep out here. Deal?"

"Deal. After I get cleaned up, you'll have a drink with me, right?"

"Yes. But only if you stay inside, away from the balcony. I think that first drink went straight to your head."

"Maybe, but I don't have anywhere else to be tonight, so it doesn't matter." She kicked off her heels before disappearing into the bedroom.

Troy used the time to contact the driver, requested the hotel staff bring up some additional bedding, and refreshed her drink. This time, he poured her something smoother: Jameson. By the time he finished, Rose had re-emerged barefoot, wearing his gray workout tank top with white lettering on the front that spelled out *legends are made* coupled with a fluffy white bathrobe, compliments of the hotel. She was swimming in the shirt, which looked more like a dress on her long, lean body.

Troy stood and waited for Rose to sit. Then, he handed her a drink as if passing the baton before heading into the bedroom to change his whiskey-stained clothes. She could hear him talking from the open door.

"You're right. It is good stuff. Try that brand I poured for you. It goes down smoothly. I'll have one with you after I change." A few minutes passed before Troy returned dressed casually with quads bulging from well-worn blue jeans and a gray t-shirt clinging like a second skin to muscles pushing to get out.

"Is there anything else you need? I can order room service if you are still hungry. Or dessert?" He sat in the oversized upholstered chair across from the couch where she was outstretched. Her painted toes tapped the air to imaginary music.

"I passed on dessert earlier." Rose smiled at her own inside joke. "I think I'm good. Your bar seems well stocked with drinks and snacks. I opened some chips—I need to get some carbs to absorb this alcohol."

"That's a good idea."

"I appreciate you letting me crash here. I didn't really want to go back tonight." She didn't want to deal with the brothers, figure out what to tell her dad, or think about the event. All she wanted to do at that moment was relax and have a drink.

"No problem."

"It's funny. Since you've been working for me, I don't think we've spent the night in the same room. Let alone have a nightcap."

"I'm not your man. I'm here to protect you."

"When you put it like that—"

"Technically, we won't be in the same room, so your record still stands intact." Troy's lips pressed together into a tight smile, seemingly pleased with himself, she suspected.

"I could comment on that, but I need to remember to have some decorum even as I lounge here sprawled half-naked in your t-shirt on the couch. Didn't you say you were having a drink with me?"

"I did," he said as he got up and made his way to the console to pour himself a glass. He brought the bottle back with him and sat on the end of the sofa near Rose's feet. He clanked her glass. "Here's to firsts."

Rose followed up with, "To firsts," followed by a series of other toasts. "To Belfast. To the view. To old friends, to new friends..." and on and on.

"Do I have to cut you off the alcohol?" Troy quipped.

"No. I'm just having a good time and letting loose. Usually, I don't get to do this on work nights or when I'm out in public or around others.

Lately, I've been so focused on work that it is a rare treat. I know I'm safe in your hands." With that, she repositioned herself on the couch, leaning her back on Troy's shoulder, her feet now facing the edge of the sofa.

"You never have to explain yourself to me."

"I appreciate that. Troy?"

"Yes, Rose."

"Are you dating anyone?"

"My days are focused on you. And when I leave you, I leave you with twice as many eyes on you on my behalf. My nights are spent monitoring everyone else's activities who I've assigned to focus on you."

"And those 12,562 people."

"Them too," he said.

"That's a lot. Speaking of people focused on me. I forgot to tell you earlier that Alejandro had a few things to say about the brothers."

"I'm not surprised. Alejandro is a smart man."

"He felt they were marking their territory and asked that I let Niall off the hook." She air quoted *marking their territory.*

"He's right, and you know it—we both see the behaviors he described. I'm curious. Did something specific happen between them?"

"No. Just more of the same. A bunch of questions about me and familiar posturing during their discussion led Alejandro to the conclusion."

"Attorneys—always drawing conclusions. But in this case, he's right."

"Don't remind me. But there's a caveat."

"Talk to me."

"Well, these guys have their convictions about family, politics, and culture. They'll err on the side of the family. I got mixed messages the other night when they got backed into a corner."

"Are we talking about Carol?"

"Don't get me started. I might drink up all your liquor and lose myself."

He poured more whiskey into her glass. "Like you said, you're with me. Lose yourself."

"That's one of the benefits of having you around—to watch over me and potentially catch me if I fall. Literally."

"Falling, as far as you are concerned, is considerably more complex. I got your back. And Carol's no threat. Anyways, we're back on track with our routine."

The alcohol was kicking in. Rose began confessing to Troy like he was a priest. "I'm so sorry about that. That was a huge misstep on my part. When we set out to come here, I brought you and Kris with specific jobs in mind, and somehow, I got blinded by Irish eye candy and lost sight of my welfare. It's funny because back in the States, this would have never happened."

"You don't need to say anything. I'm here, so you don't always have to be on guard."

"No, I do. I want you to know that I respect what you do and that you're empowered as my security advisor to set me straight regarding my safety. Don't worry if I think you're right or wrong—just be right and make sure it sticks."

"I can commit to that."

"You know... you were right."

"You just told me that."

"No, about having a worthy opponent. Think about it. What's the difference between Aedan, Niall, and Alejandro?"

"They all seem equipped to handle being with you."

"However, with Aedan and Niall, we have shared knowledge and experiences that make it easier to relate. Like positions of power within a corporation, wealth, expert fighting, and tactical training. You know, it makes the man beneath the suit even more appealing. It's the difference between a man who needs to pay to have his car fixed and one who could fix his own if needed. They have a lot going for them. Best of all, their Irish culture inherently makes them more passionate about family and those closest to them. Albeit to a fault in Carol's case."

"You have a point, but I wouldn't disregard people that don't check all those boxes."

"I'm just saying you were right. Those qualities are the reason we were all so intrigued by each other. And maybe I am also attracted to the sexy accent... and the dark hair, chiseled face, and Mediterranean eyes don't hurt either."

"Aren't you supposed to be upset with Aedan or him with you? I can't remember which." Troy poured himself another drink and refreshed hers.

"Are you tipsy?" Rose asked.

"Hardly. And not around you. That was a legitimate question you are avoiding answering."

"I'm going to pull an Alejandro and plead the fifth." Rose made a sloppy mock zipper motion with her fingers in front of her face.

"Let me know if you're getting tired."

"Not yet. Let's stream some music. I see your speakers over there."

Troy reached over to grab his phone from the coffee table. "Sure. Anything in particular, you would like to hear?"

"Here, you can use mine." She swiped her screen to a music app and handed him her phone. "I have some classic jazz from the forties and fifties."

"True renaissance woman."

"You, of all people, know I have an eclectic taste in music."

"Honestly, I'm not sure any of these guys deserve you."

Rose shrugged her shoulders in response while Troy connected to the speaker. The voice of Etta James came on clear and slow, singing, "Trust in me." Troy sat back so Rose could continue leaning against him. Together they sat listening while the song played.

When the song ended, Troy clanked his glass against Rose's. "To trust. Cheers."

"Thank you, Troy. For everything."

⁂

MORNING CAME MUCH FASTER THAN ROSE WOULD HAVE LIKED. HER head hurt, the room was too dark for her eyes to adjust, and she forgot where she was for a moment. The fluffiness of the pillow and extra softness of the bed was a gentle reminder she was at the hotel in Troy's bed. A flash of light and billow of steam emerged from the bathroom door to reveal a tall, dark, muscular silhouette.

"Good morning, Rose. I took the liberty of ordering breakfast for us. It should be here in thirty minutes. Your schedule is tight again today, so I had Kris stop by to prepare your clothes. Everything is pressed and ready for you to choose from after your shower."

"Good morning. It seems you thought of everything." Rose's voice was deep and crackly. "Wow, you're a lovely sight in the morning." She rubbed her eyes.

"Good to hear. It's time to get up," Troy said.

Rose sat up, then collapsed back onto her pillow. "Uh, my head hurts."

"I'm done in the shower. There's some ice water on the nightstand next to you and some ibuprofen. I thought you might need it after last night. I'll be in the other room when you're ready for breakfast." With that, he turned on the lights in the bedroom and shut the door behind him.

Rose conjured all her energy to get out of bed and ready before breakfast arrived. When Troy said Kris had all her things ready, he meant everything. Outfits were lined up in the closet with shoes as if she were at home. He laid out all her toiletries and makeup on a towel in the bathroom, making getting ready a snap. When she emerged from Troy's bedroom, he was at the table waiting for her.

"You look refreshed."

"Thanks. I don't feel refreshed. But I feel slightly better than before I got into the shower." She sat at the table across from Troy. "Never let me drink like that again."

"I learned something about you," he smirked.

"What's that? Are you laughing at me? Oh god. Did I say something stupid?"

"No, nothing like that. After a few drinks, you get sleepy. One minute you were lying on my shoulder talking, and the next, you fell asleep mid-sentence."

"Oh great, I bet that was attractive. I don't even remember going to bed."

"I put you there."

"Ugh. I have a hangover." She propped her elbow on the table and laid her head in her hand.

Troy poured her a cup of coffee. "You might need a few of these before we head out. Sorry about getting you up so early. I had to account for the drive to the gallery, or I would have let you sleep in a little longer."

"That's right, I have to commute in today. Oh, and it's your last commute day since you'll be staying at the house now. I need to let them know back at the house."

"That's all taken care of."

Rose and Troy finished their breakfast and then returned to the gallery, arriving before the brothers left for the morning. Instead of heading to the main house, she went to the gallery to begin work while Kris and a staff member took her and Troy's things into the house. Troy held his usual post near the gallery's main entrance, checking in the contractors as they arrived. When Kris returned, he wasn't alone. Niall was with him. He informed Troy he wanted to check in on Rose. Troy escorted him to Rose, who was on the phone. When she saw Troy, she held up a finger, so Troy escorted Niall to wait in the gallery until Rose finished her call.

"Gentleman," she greeted upon entering the room.

"Niall came to check in on you," Troy announced.

"Thanks, Troy. Niall, come in." Rose led Niall into the office. Troy stood on the other side of the threshold in full view.

"Night Owl. I thought we would connect last night when you returned from the city, but you didn't come home. Are you okay?" His tone was soft and calm. Rose knew he was trying to diffuse any tension she might be feeling.

"Hey, Niall. I'm fine. I had a change in plans," she said, matching his tone.

"I'm not going to probe, but if there is something you want to tell me, you can."

"There's nothing to tell. It was too late after dinner to drive back. If you are referring to Troy staying at the house moving forward—I have to follow protocol. It's there for a reason."

"We told you we would handle Carol."

"And I trust you have. You're a man of your word."

"And you don't need Troy twenty-four hours a day."

"He's doing his job. I'm sure you can understand that."

"And I'm doing mine," Niall retorted.

"I'm not sure what you mean by that, but if by your job you mean taking care of Carol, you have your work cut out for you. But I trust you have that under control. And is Aedan still sticking to his familiar family theme regarding her?"

"He's doing his best to keep the peace. Although Carol grabbed his ear again last night before she left, it perked mine up too when you didn't return."

"What now?"

"Continuing her rants about you dating Alejandro. Now she's upset about the increased press the exhibition is getting."

Rose choked back a laugh. "Niall. As long as the press is good, then that's good for me, your sister, and the foundation."

"I agree."

"But you're concerned about what's happening with Alejandro. And I don't understand why anyone cares what happens between Alejandro and me. I'm not trying to be funny. I'm trying to understand your concern. I'm your sister's guest and the architect of the most important European exhibition. When I am done here, the only thing that will matter is whether I delivered to Brianna's expectations and achieved my goal. Why does Alejandro matter?"

"You know why. And there was a bit of truth in Carol's previous story about Alejandro, albeit out of context. He had been your partner in the past. As you can imagine, Aedan is wondering what's going on."

Rose took a deep breath. "Be honest, Niall. I don't think your brother is that vested in what's going on between Alejandro and me, or he'd ask me himself. He didn't have an issue asking previously. But I can see him being concerned about something else. There's something you're not telling me. Is this about you and me?" She looked at her watch and then back at Niall. "Niall, it's late for you to still be at the house, isn't it? Besides, I need to get back to work. You'll have to excuse me. I have a celebrity walkthrough I need to prepare for. And a decision I need to make. Troy will show you out."

Niall took a step closer to Rose and held her hand in his. Rose saw Troy approaching and held her other hand up to de-escalate the situation.

"I realize you didn't come to Belfast for anything other than Brianna and the exhibition. But you're here now and in our lives. We can't dial back the hands of time. I wouldn't want to anyway. I'm just going to say that if my brother is who you want, you need to talk to him."

"Niall. What is—" Rose started to talk, but Niall cut her off.

"Talk to him."

"Niall, I have nothing to share beyond what you already know to be the facts." Rose nodded to Troy, who immediately made his way over to them. It was Niall's signal to leave.

He let go of her hand, turned to leave, then came back in. "I promise I dealt with Carol. I've sent her on a family assignment. She won't be returning. Do me a personal favor and have dinner with us. Brianna would like to eat with the family, so we are arranging to have it in the library on the third floor. She specifically asked you to attend."

"Have a good day, Niall."

"I hope to see you tonight."

After Niall left, Rose addressed Troy. "Did you hear that?"

"Every word," Troy said.

"I can't figure out what button Carol pushed from Aedan's past that allows her to influence him so easily."

"Do you like him?"

"I like him, but I don't like his approach to dealing with this situation."

"You don't have anything to prove or disprove. Aedan should ignore Carol. And if he is interested in you, he will do just that. And if he doesn't, move on."

"You sound just like my parents when I used to come home, whining about some dude I was crushing on."

"Well, your parents are smart people."

"I can't talk to you anymore. I have work to do," she teased.

"You didn't respond to Niall about dinner with Brianna tonight. Are you planning to attend?"

"Yes. I can't let all this drama interfere with my relationship with Brianna. She's the reason I'm in Belfast."

"Don't forget that."

"She's a wonderful lady, and I have no intention to let her down. I'm glad she's feeling a little better."

"And your dad? Any intent in letting him down?"

Rose sighed. "I'm still mulling over my decision. I still have time. By the way. Most tradespeople scheduled for tomorrow are here today, putting us a day early. I think I'll use tomorrow to do some touristy things, so be prepared."

"Always."

THE REST OF THE DAY WENT WITHOUT INTERRUPTION, ALLOWING Rose and Kris to work effortlessly and meticulously in planning every detail of the event. Kamal did his walkthrough with the lighting specialist on hand. Detailed renderings were designed to show where every painting would be placed, and where every holographic image would be projected. The playlist had been tirelessly worked and reworked. Rose was incredibly proud to have commissioned a memorable, one-of-a-kind gift for every person who would be in attendance. It all seemed to fall into place for the event—she just wished her personal life would follow suit. Time was still on her side. She finished the day's work early enough to have time for tea, catch up on the happenings back in the Bay area, get some rest, and get ready for dinner. When she emerged from her room, she was dressed in a sky blue backless embroidered swing dress gathered at her waist. A single string of pearls adorned her neck like a choker, and a second strand draped down her bare back. Rose looked down a second to check herself and, when she looked up, almost walked headfirst into Niall.

He stopped short in his tracks to avoid the collision and watched her. "You're going to keep doing this, aren't you?" He looked at her as if she were exactly what he had been craving.

Rose smiled and took his hands in hers, drawing him close enough to dust a kiss on his cheek. A hint of cardamon and plum wafted past her. "Good evening, Niall. Tell me, what am I doing?"

"Making dinner simply the best meal of my day. You look delectable."

"About my temperament earlier—"

"You don't have to say anything," he interrupted, studying her face as if it were his first time seeing her. She liked the way he read her eyes every time they locked gazes.

"It's good to know that I have at least one fan. I was just about to head upstairs to the study and have a drink before dinner. Were you headed that way?"

"I just got home. Give me a few minutes to freshen up, and I'll join you. And Rose, you never have to apologize for being yourself around me."

"Sure."

Niall disappeared into his room, and Rose headed across the hallway to the stairwell leading to the third floor. Once there, she went into the study that overlooked the property at the rear of the house. She was drawn across the room to a wall of wooden patio doors stretching floor to ceiling, opening onto a massive deck overlooking the property. She opened one of the doors to get an unobstructed view and heard a glass clink. Rose turned toward the sound. A large stone fireplace flanked by built-in shelves full of books and family photos was to her right. Two leather cigar chairs were positioned near the fireplace, one occupied. Rose walked over to speak to the occupant—someone she knew from experience would have already sensed her presence before entering the room.

"This is a first. You didn't announce my presence. It seems I've fallen out of favor with the chairman." She walked around the chair to stand between Aedan and the fireplace. In doing so, her dress accidentally brushed his hand resting on the arm of the chair. His finger twitched slightly as if he were going to reach out.

"Good evening, Rose. You're a little early for dinner. The staff is still setting up," Aedan said formally. She imagined this was how he spoke to all his clients.

"I came early to have a drink before dinner. I see you already have one." She nodded toward the half-empty glass on the side table between the chairs.

"It's been a long day. I needed the time to unwind. Here, let me get you one." Aedan stood, went over to the big roll-away bar cart, poured a drink, and handed it to Rose. "Feels like I haven't seen you in a while, although it's only been a day. How have you been?"

"Good. Work is going amazingly smooth, and we're all super excited about the big day." Rose took a step closer to Aedan, closing the distance between them. She sipped her drink and looked up at him over her glass—searching for the guy she met in Dublin, unguarded and uninhibited in ways he previously repressed. Instead, she found Aedan, the restrained, elusive businessman.

"Sounds like things are going your way," he answered flatly.

"On the surface. However, there is this cloud looming that I cannot rid myself of."

"And that cloud is me. Niall suggested I sit down and talk it out with you. Maybe we can set aside time to talk after dinner, Rose."

"Until then, I suppose we sit—or stand as it were—in awkward silence while you pretend nothing has passed between us, as if the intimacy we shared never happened. We're both adults. We can talk this out."

"Rose, I told you in Dublin, I don't know how to do this." He lifted his chin between them. "I need to think about the King family and my role as head of the family," Aedan said.

"I hear what you're saying, but I have to admit, allowing your cousin to misguide you is a side of you I never imagined existed—to ignore the facts. And if you're committed to doing this, learning how to communicate is part of that. *This* feels one-sided when it comes to that. I'm almost inclined to believe something else is bothering you."

"We should talk after dinner."

Rose took a step back. She was stunned by his response and upset for allowing herself to be distracted.

"We should talk now," she insisted, acutely aware his obstinance was on par with hers.

"I don't want to set the wrong tone for dinner. We can talk later."

"Never miss an opportunity to say what you feel, and you will have no regrets." Rose left Aedan standing at the fireplace, walked over to the patio doors, took a sip of her drink, and looked toward the horizon. She was finished with Aedan for the moment and attempted to clear her mind when she saw a man's reflection come up behind her.

Had he changed his mind?

A hand came around her waist from behind, and she felt a warm breath on her ear that came with a whisper. "He'll come around soon enough." Rose turned, surprised to find Niall standing so close that his aura wrapped her in an invisible hug.

She squinted and searched his eyes for unspoken words of reassurance that everything would be okay—that she wasn't making a mistake. Niall's eyes softened, and he smiled, saying without words, *I'm here.* It took all her strength to suppress the urge to lean into the kiss suspended in the silence between them. She didn't know whether the urgency she felt was for him or lingering feelings for the man watching from across the room. Instead, she took a step back and handed Niall her drink.

"Here. I'll need this more after dinner." She half smiled and took a seat on the couch.

Niall made use of the drink and took a sip. "Give it time," he said.

Rose looked to the far side of the room where Aedan watched their exchange. His eyes darted between her and Niall, then back to Rose. She knew he was trying to decipher the dynamic between the two. The room went silent for a while before they heard footsteps approach. It was Brianna's nurse with a message. Rose was happy to learn that Niall hired a team of nurses to be available twenty-four hours a day for Brianna. Now, one of them was searching for Rose. The nurse explained that Brianna had overextended herself for the day and would not be able to have dinner with them, but would have it in her room instead. She requested Rose visit her before dinner.

"Thank you. Please let Brianna know I'm on my way."

"I'll walk with you if that's okay," Niall said, helping Rose from the couch. Rose nodded in response.

Together, Rose and Niall walked down the long landing in silence until they came to Brianna's room. Niall ushered her to the threshold, then returned to the study. The nurse was standing near Brianna, sitting at a small table. Brianna gestured to Rose to come to the table and sit down. Then, the nurse left.

"Good evening, Brianna. The nurse indicated you were not quite up to the additional activities tonight. I was looking forward to our conversation over dinner."

"Thank you for making yourself available. I did my best to pull it together for dinner."

"You don't have to thank me, and don't worry about us. Your health and recovery are paramount. I'm just happy to have a little private time with you. I've been working hard to ensure you have a signature event."

"That's what I wanted to speak with you about. My brother tells me things are coming along brilliantly, and I have received the email briefs you sent. I'm very impressed with what I've seen so far, and I know this will be one of the most memorable events Europe's ever seen. The last brief outlined significant changes to your original plans. Brilliant idea to tap into the artists' influencers. I can see how you're showcasing the complete arc of the artists' stories. And the idea of this being the first to showcase all persons of color will cement your place in the history books. Bravo."

"I wanted to run that by you before I made the change, but we didn't have a chance to sync because of your relapse. I'm glad to hear you like the changes. Is there anything you want to make sure I include that I haven't or anything you would like me to rework? We still have time for changes."

"No, the brief you sent along with renderings left me wanting to expedite my healing process to be by your side. It is your show now. The new perspective you bring is exactly what this exhibition needed."

"I have to credit the fantastic team I assembled, and Niall and his staff have impressed me beyond expectations."

"I am so glad you've found a way to include him in the project—he's one of the best. And Aedan is pretty incredible, too." She paused a moment. "Which leads me to ask… have you noticed he's been a little apathetic lately? Any insight into what's going on with him? I'm asking because I told him he should consider getting to know you better if I can be so forward to say."

Rose's face warmed. She cleared her throat. "Aedan's a great guy, and

I have an interest in getting to know him, but I think he's trying to sort out a few things." She smiled, not wanting to out Brianna's brother.

"A few things? I don't know what he's trying to do, but I don't want him to miss out on being with someone special and, for once, someone I approve of. I think you two would be magic together."

"Are my cheeks changing colors? I thought I was the direct one."

She laughed. "You and I both realize life's too short to go without speaking what's on your mind. Whatever's going on with him is a brief setback. Go to him and make him talk to you. Ask him, 'Do you want to be with me?' I am sure the answer is yes. Then ask, 'Then what will we do to make sure nothing comes between us?' Don't let him get sidetracked. And give him time to course correct."

"I appreciate your concern and advice. I will broach this with him. Now, don't expend all your energy on this topic. Take time to relax, heal, and let me know if there is anything I can do to help you."

"You are doing precisely what you are supposed to be doing. I am grateful to have you working on the event."

"I feel the same way."

"Then, we must think of something to send to Mia for bringing us together."

"Let's."

"She will be in attendance, right?"

"Absolutely."

"Wonderful. Thank you again for visiting me, Rose. I see a member of the wait staff hovering. I'll let you get to your dinner. Tell my brothers to behave, and I'm sorry I cannot join them."

Rose got up from the table and placed her hand on Brianna's before turning to leave back to the study.

When she returned, dinner was being set on the sideboard. Both Niall and Aedan were seated across from each other at the fireplace. They both stood when she walked into the room.

"How was Brianna feeling?" Aedan asked.

"She seemed well, but her energy was starting to wane near the end of our conversation. She sent her apologies for missing dinner. Are we ready to eat?" She gestured her hand toward the table.

"Ladies first. I'll sit next to you if you don't mind." Niall pulled out a chair for Rose.

"Sure. This table is much too big to sit on opposite sides," Rose observed.

For the first time during her visit, dinner was formally served. A staff member walked around the table with a food dish serving Rose, Niall, and Aedan. The gesture was repeated for every platter. Rose led the dinner conversation, ensuring she kept the topic light.

"Niall, I mentioned to Brianna the amazing work your team is doing in supporting the event, and she reaffirmed I made the right decision to go with your team. Although, I do detect a twinge of bias on her side. I handed you some pretty demanding assignments. We still have much more to do but thank you in advance."

"You presented us with some challenging deliverables. We had to think through how to make it happen in such a short time, but the good news is we made it work."

"May I ask how you persuaded the Louvre to release that piece without sending one of their staff?" Rose asked.

"I called in a marker. That's all I can say."

"Hum. That is impressive. If I need your help when I return to the States, would you send your team across the pond?"

"Of course. Just let me know what you need."

"Are you done with interviews?" Aedan interjected, trying to insert himself into the conversation.

Rose turned to face him when she spoke, ensuring he knew she was interested in a dialogue with him. "Yes. I did the last one today. However, if I need more information from anyone, I can follow up via email or phone."

"What's the reason behind conducting all the face-to-face interviews?" Niall inquired, re-gaining control of the conversation.

"It's similar to why you interview face-to-face before making a hiring decision. Interviewing is an art. You ask a series of questions that lead to more probing questions, and you pick up body cues to make sense of the conversation. When I try to help represent the artists' work in the most favorable light, I need to know what motivates them and what makes them happy, sad, or anxious. You get all that reading the person, not their words. You know, reading the non-verbal cues as they talk."

"Do you have a psychology degree amongst your long list of credentials?" Niall asked.

"No. Just plugging information into an algorithm as a way of analyzing people."

"Have you developed a profile of us?" Aedan asked.

She laughed, caught off guard by the question. "I will leave it to you to show me the true you." Rose looked around at her dinner companions. Aedan rested his thumb and index finger on his chin and nodded.

"I'm pretty sure I have revealed the true me, wouldn't you say?" Niall flashed his signature smile.

Rose turned to Niall. "I'd say you've been consistent. I appreciate that in a person. Your brother, on the other hand, is quite elusive. I think you said those exact words the first day we met." Niall nodded, and Aedan pursed his lips.

"Rose, if you're interested in additional sightseeing this weekend, I plan to participate in a charity event hosted at the Crom Castle. We would take a private helicopter to fly in and stay overnight if you are up for the experience," Niall suggested.

"I've read about that place. Wouldn't it be better to take that young lady you were with the other day? Or better yet, take your brother. I expect something this exclusive means there are some very influential people in attendance you'd want to network with for your business."

"There's no young lady I'm with. But you're right about the attendees. Why don't you come with me, and I'll introduce you to them? It would be great if Aedan could attend, but he already has a commitment and won't be back by then. Besides, I prefer your company as my plus one over my brother for an event like this." He looked to Aedan for confirmation.

"Niall's right. I need to travel for business. You should go, Rose. Sounds like you're on track with the exhibition. The trades don't work on the weekend. I think you'd enjoy it. Besides, it would be advantageous to network with this group of people. Some of them may already be on the invite list to attend your show," Aedan said.

"I have the guest list, Rose, if you want to review it or need more time to think it over. Just let me know. I'm not obligated to take anyone, but I thought this might be one thing that you'd appreciate attending," Niall remarked.

"Sounds like you two planned this. Weren't you both committed to being *around* this compound?" Rose pushed the food around her plate.

"That's the plan. One of us will always be around during your stay. Originally, I was planning to donate money, and still will if you don't want to attend, but I feel this is the perfect event to attend during your visit. It will certainly elevate the guest list having you there."

"You're trying to butter me up, but it does sound intriguing."

"Just say yes," Niall urged.

"Only if you agree to introduce me to people you know will support the exhibition."

"Done—that settles it."

The rest of the dinner was uneventful. Rose didn't broach any controversial subject with the brothers, nor did they. Aedan maintained a neutral tone with Rose as if there was never any passion between them. He seemed to be waiting for an opportune time to deal with his issues. After dinner, the three remained in the room together for a nightcap. Rose finally got that well-deserved drink she passed on earlier and spent time discussing work with Niall while Aedan stood out on the deck, taking in the night air. Whenever Niall and Rose were out of Aedan's earshot, Niall suggested Rose speak with Aedan. Rose tried, but Aedan seemed stuck in his head and not ready to talk. So, for now, she held firm to her olive branches.

"Gentleman. Dinner was great. Thank you for the company, but I have some work to do before turning in for the night. Aedan, if I don't see you in the morning, have a good day. Niall, I will check in with you before Friday to get details about Crom. Cheers and goodnight." She raised her glass, nodded in their direction, took a sip, put down her glass, and left.

From her room, Rose signaled Troy that she was in for the evening. She placed her phone on its hands-free stand and FaceTimed Alejandro, who immediately picked up the call. Rose paced the floor while she talked.

"Good evening, Alejandro. I hope this is not too late to call."

"Rose. It is great to hear from you. Wow. Even better to see you. You look beautiful—formal dinner, I suppose?"

"Yes, I just came from dinner with the family here."

"What can I do for you?"

"I've been thinking about what you said."

"I said a lot of things. What part?"

"About you vacillating between staying for the duration of your trip and leaving a day early. What did you decide?" she asked.

"I decided to stay on the off chance that I'd get to see you again."

And there it was—the Alejandro she knew. Sure that things will go his way. Rose stopped pacing and looked directly at the screen. "Then I think you'll like what I have to say. I have the trade work stable enough to work under Kris' guidance, so I decided to take tomorrow and spend it touring with you if you still want to do something together."

A moment of silence passed before Alejandro spoke. "Well, that's good news. I can make one call tonight and update the plans to include two. I have to ask—is everything okay? Is there anything else I can do for you?"

"I'm good. Things are great. Thanks for allowing me to join you on such short notice."

"Well, you've made my day. I hope to do more than that for you tomorrow."

"No pressure," she laughed.

"Can you be ready around six-thirty in the morning?"

"No problem. I'm up early every day. I'll see you in the morning. Goodnight, Alejandro."

"Goodnight, Rose."

It was getting late, but Rose was restless and warm as she slipped out of her dinner dress and into a silk nightgown. The moonlight wooed her onto the balcony. There she stood, staring into the night sky, thoughts wandering back to broken conversations of the day, disappointed by Aedan's apathy. *I could find Aedan now and force a conversation,* she thought, her train of thought fractured by the sudden sound of her phone vibrating on the table inside. She went in to retrieve it and stepped back onto the deck.

"Hey Troy, what's up?"

"Rose, I thought you were finished for the night, but Niall checked in and said he needed to talk with you. Did you want to meet him in the library or have me send him to see you?"

"I'm out on the deck. Send him in."

"I'll let Niall know he has ten minutes."

"Maybe less. You and I need to leave by six-thirty. We're traveling with Alejandro for the day."

"I'm sending him in now."

Within thirty seconds, Niall appeared at her door. Rose watched as he closed it behind himself and strolled strong and confident across the room to join her on the patio. At that moment, she fully understood the meaning of a sight for sore eyes. "Seems I'm capped on time," he said, holding her gaze.

"We're all playing by Troy's rules. Where did he stop you?"

"He didn't. You do realize this is my domain expertise. I know the rules. My first stop was Troy."

"I just saw you no more than fifteen minutes ago. I can't imagine what you'd want from me."

"Do you want me to respond to that, or do you want to know why I'm here?" The corner of his lip curved into a half-smile.

Rose rolled her eyes and shook her head.

"You left so early. If you wanted to talk privately with my brother, I would have stepped out. I'm here to urge you to talk to him. Give him a chance to set himself straight with you."

This was not the conversation Rose wanted to have with Niall. She was prepared to talk about their impending trip, the exhibition, or even the weather. She was not prepared to discuss Aedan.

"He didn't even attempt to talk with me. Why am I handing out olive branches anyway? I'm not at fault here. Your cousin and your brother are behind this mess. I understand Carol has some issues, but your brother—" She breathed out, allowing the action to calm her. "Well, no words can adequately describe my disappointment with him. I've done my share of reaching out. I'll be focused on the exhibition and enjoying my remaining time in Belfast. If Aedan wants to talk and set the record straight, he knows where to find me," Rose said.

"So, you don't plan on reaching out to him at all?"

"You mean, reach out *again*? No. I showed up here tonight and demonstrated my willingness to engage in a discussion. To resolve this, Aedan needs to meet me halfway if he feels I'm worth his time. Remember, I didn't come to Belfast for him, and I'm not chasing any man. I certainly don't need the distraction."

Niall stepped closer to Rose, looked over the deck railing, then back at her. "Your words aren't falling on deaf ears with me. If my brother can't clear his head to take the time to fix things with you, I'm walking through the open door. I stepped aside before, but you know how I feel. I told you the extent I'd go to have you. The things I'd give up."

Niall put a hand around Rose's waist and used the other to trace an outline of her lips with his finger. Rose stared at the moonlight reflecting in his eyes. He dipped his head to her face and hovered over her lips so close that one slight move would seal a kiss. She knew he was waiting for her to make the next move. She felt like Eve in the garden of Eden, enticed to satisfy her hunger with a taste of forbidden fruit. She knew giving in would be wrong, but she couldn't deny she was drawn to him. Rose closed her eyes, allowing Niall's signature scent of cardamon and plum to saturate her lungs, and she relaxed into his arms. She didn't stop him when he pressed his lips to hers. And when he parted her lips, his warm tongue searching for hers, Rose instinctively wrapped her arms around his neck, pulling him deeper into their kiss, giving way to a pent-up passion for having some part of him inside her. They held each other so tight that her feet lifted away from the floor when Niall straightened his back. They stayed that way a few moments before Niall gently lowered her and pulled away as if tempering himself.

"There's a hungry look in your eyes, Night Owl. It's the same look I saw earlier this evening in the library and just now before I kissed you. I know part of you wants me in ways you won't allow yourself to say aloud. But you have to tell me, Rose. Tell me I've got it wrong. Tell me you've changed your mind. Tell me you want *this*." He dipped his head and kissed her again, but this time, when he pressed his body against her, she could feel the hard length of his desire. Niall lowered his hands, slid them down her back beneath her hip, and pulled her body to his growing passion. Then, he moved his hand between them and reached beneath her silk gown, sliding his fingers in the space between her folds. From the way his fingers glided across the surface of her skin, she knew that she was wet in a way that would welcome him fully. His kisses grew more urgent as he stroked her. Rose knew if he plunged his fingers into the warm wetness awaiting him, her body would explode with ecstasy, and there would be no turning back. She reluctantly put her hand on his. Niall stopped, released a low pant in her ear, and pulled away slightly to look at her.

"You want me to stop, Night Owl?" he asked in a soft, low voice.

Rose nodded.

"I'm a patient man. I won't take what's not mine. The next time I see that look in your eyes, I hope it's for me and not my brother. And that you have come to me to satisfy your hunger. You need to know that when you do, I'll take what's mine and won't hide the truth from Aedan. Although I don't want to leave, I will."

Rose wrapped her arms around Niall's neck and whispered in his ear. "You're right. I won't put into words what I want you to do to me when you kiss me and touch me that way. We just—" She hesitated a moment. "Niall." She looked up to face him.

"I'm here, Night Owl." His voice was firm but low.

"You need to leave. I'm struggling to—" Rose paused for a moment and chose her words carefully. "Let's say goodnight. We can talk this weekend on our way to Crom. Goodnight, Niall."

Niall dusted his lips against hers, peeled himself away, and opened the door. "Lock this behind me," he said before disappearing into the hallway.

Rose sent a quick text to Troy. "He's gone. See you in the morning." She closed her eyes and exhaled.

CHAPTER 13

Better Version

"The thorn from the bush one has planted, nourished and
pruned pricks more deeply and draws more blood."

— MAYA ANGELOU

NIALL CLOSED THE DOOR TO ROSE'S BEDROOM AND HEARD THE LATCH
click on the other side. "Niall." The all too familiar voice shattered the
silence.

Niall turned to find Aedan standing at the top of the stairwell.
Watching. "We should talk," Niall said slightly above a whisper to avoid
alerting Rose to the situation outside her door.

Aedan tipped his head toward the stairwell and descended the
steps with Niall in tow. Niall followed his brother in silence until they
entered the kitchen. Aedan walked across the room and then turned to
look at Niall.

"Bloody hell, Niall. You're my brother. My confidant. This is a
conversation we should never have. How did we get here?" Aedan's
voice was stern and unforgiving.

"It's—"

"Don't dare say it's not what you think. You smell like her, Niall. It's
exactly what I think." Aedan curled his fingers into a tight ball at his side.

280

"I was going to say it's complicated. You know I've been attracted to Rose since her first day here. You called me on it."

"As I recall that day, she said no to you. And despite the tousled hair and wrinkled collar you're sporting right now, I suspect she said no again tonight." Aedan looked to his brother for a response. Niall nodded. "Then, for Christ's sake, man—if not for mine—leave the woman alone."

Niall started to take a step toward his brother but stepped back. "She's hurting, Aedan, and I can't help but want to make things better for her."

"How are you making things better? Offering yourself up to her behind my back? Was this your plan all along?"

"You know perfectly well it wasn't. You heard every word I said to Rose in the library. Tell me. How many times did you hear me ask her to talk to you tonight and vice versa?" Niall looked down at his brother's hands, then back up. Aedan uncurled his fingers. "You stood there silently watching me negotiating a truce between you two, and you didn't step in. She went to you earlier, and you turned her away. For what? For some sense of family loyalty you feel for our cousin, Carol? What is this thing with you and Carol anyway? She may favor our sister, but you know she's not Brianna, right? Don't let your propensity to protect Carol prevent you from being with the woman you want," Niall lectured.

Aedan went to the refrigerator, retrieved a water bottle, opened it, then turned to his brother. "I'm trying to sort this out the best way I know how. But that's not an open invitation to you to make a move on Rose." His voice boomed, enunciating every word.

"Silence is not working in your favor. I can't stand by and watch what you're doing to her. And I can't change the way I feel. I know you're my brother, I love you, and I'd do anything for you. I don't want this to come between us. So, I'm telling you to step up or step aside."

"You're supposed to be protecting her," Aedan said.

"I am."

Aedan's eyebrow raised. "From me?"

"That's not what I meant."

"If you weren't my brother, this wouldn't be a conversation."

Niall nodded. "You're right."

"Then get your shit together, Niall. Do your job and let me decide how to manage my love life."

CHAPTER 14

Detour Ahead

"The truth is too simple: one must always get there by a complicated route."

— GEORGE SAND AKA AMANTINE AURORE LUCILE DUPIN,
Letter to Armand Barbès, 12 May 1867

THE CAR WAS FULL OF CHATTER, DROWNING OUT THE FAINT SOUND OF classic jazz playing across the speakers in the background of the large luxury sedan. Troy turned his head toward the driver to get a better view of Rose in the back seat as she and Alejandro reminisced about events from their time together.

"You're right, Rose. It's been a while since we've all been on the road together," Troy said, joining the conversation.

"This trip reminds me of when we drove from San Francisco to Carmel that time—minus the Irish scones. Remember, Alejandro?" Rose asked.

"Fondly, of course. But that day started foggily, and it wasn't until we were almost to our destination that it cleared up," Alejandro recalled.

"Yes, and I think it took us an extra forty minutes, too. So much for scenic driving," Rose commented.

"Well, the sky was clear on the return trip, so we got to see most of what we missed on the way."

"It helped us make record time returning. You had one of your first big exhibitions the following week, Rose. Seems Alejandro has established a trend." Troy's eyebrows furrowed, his eyes squinted, and Rose could tell he was processing his own words.

"I've already broached that subject with him, Troy. His lips are sealed. By the way, thanks for bringing breakfast and coffee, Alejandro," Rose said.

"Glad you've enjoyed the breakfast. It's the least I could do after getting you two up so early, to then sit in a car for several hours," Alejandro said.

"So, what's on the itinerary? I am super excited about seeing more of Dublin. The quick business meetings in and out office buildings didn't cut it." Rose turned slightly to face Alejandro.

"You need to have all the details, don't you? It will be a fast-paced and jammed-packed day, especially since we have to head back tonight, but I promise, it will be memorable."

"You may as well tell me then."

"I'll give you some hints. Our day will contain art, alcohol, literature, religion, and retail. Not necessarily in that order. Along the way, we will also stop to eat."

"Gee, thanks for the Cliff Notes version." Rose rolled her eyes.

"Don't worry. We're almost there. Trust me. It'll be fun."

"You didn't give me any hint on how to dress, so I hope this outfit works with your plans," Rose looked down at her embroidered mesh lace top, which she wore over a matching blush-colored tank and black stretch skinny denim jeans. "I brought a matching blazer and high heel sandals to go with this for dinner. I can put on a chunky necklace to dress it up if needed, but for now, I assume these Chuck Taylors and a moto jacket will do."

"You look perfect. I'll let you know when you can add the finishing touches—most likely before dinner."

"You have me curious."

"We'll have a great time. Our first stop is coming soon. We're heading over there. St. Patrick's Cathedral." Alejandro leaned closer to Rose and pointed out the window.

"That's a massive cathedral. And an impressive spire. I can't wait to go inside."

Once parked, Rose and Alejandro exited the car and made their way through a mix of tourists and parishioners milling around to get into the cathedral. Troy followed close behind. Rose walked down the center aisle past rows of wooden benches. There was a sense of calm in the space, even amongst the crowds. Her eyes were drawn to a series of large, pointed arches that formed a path down to the altar. Several panels of stained-glass windows hung above the altar, with one representing St. Patrick's likeness. She found more stained-glass windows at the cathedral's west end, which artfully depicted St. Patrick's story via the thirty-nine images. During their tour, neither Rose nor Alejandro spoke, but instead, Rose used the time to take in all there was to see in the grand cathedral. Although the lighting was dim, she did her best to take pictures of items, including the various Celtic grave slabs on display allegedly used to cover St. Patrick's well, which he used for baptisms. There was a lot to see and take in, but their day was full, so they spent over thirty minutes exploring the cathedral before heading back to the car.

"I see why you chose the cathedral first. A nice, quiet way to get the day started. It was beautiful yet spiritual." Rose walked alongside Alejandro to the car. She thought back to when they were a couple.

Back to when she would loop her arm around his as he walked with his hands in his pocket. He still walked with his hands in his pocket, but she didn't feel compelled to loop her arm around his this time. When they reached the car, Alejandro put his hand on the small of her back, guiding her in and pulling Rose back to the present. She didn't know what to expect or how she would feel being around Alejandro again. One thing she knew was when he smiled at her the way he was now—it still made her happy. Each smile helped lessen the waves of aftershocks she felt and moved toward rebuilding their friendship.

"It was beautiful. Are you happy I added it to the list?" he asked.

"Of course. What's next?" Rose could resist his smile for the moment but not her need to understand the whole picture.

"Patience," he quipped.

"I'm working on it."

"Rose, I can't deny you anything." He shook his head in surrender. "Our next stop is a must-see. It would be fitting to spend a few hours exploring The National Gallery. The museum has undergone extensive renovation and has a pretty impressive art collection."

"Only a few hours?" Rose's eyes widened.

"We have many more things on our list to see today—you only gave me one day to work with. I had to drop several things from the list as it is."

"You're the one heading back across the pond tomorrow, not me. You know I could spend all day at The National Gallery. However, you're right. There aren't enough hours in the day. So, are you going to tell me what items you dropped from the list?"

"Why? So you can try to squeeze them in?"

"No, just want to know what I'm missing."

"I'll tell you after dinner. Look. We've reached the gallery." He smiled, then got out of the car to help her before Troy did.

Together, they spent the next hour mostly in silence, walking through the spacious symmetrical rooms in the gallery while viewing paintings from world-famous artists. Each room had a distinctive style and shape.

"We have to stop here." Rose stood in front of a large-scale painting that spanned over eight feet wide by ten and a half feet tall.

"Besides the exquisite detailing depicted in the fabric on the woman's gown, jewelry, and lace, what should I know about this lovely piece?" Alejandro looked at the painting of a woman who appeared to be meeting a king on his throne.

"This painting is called *The Visit of the Queen of Sheba to King Solomon*. It was painted by Lavinia Fontana, the first female to achieve her status as a painter, and on many other fronts, including the first woman to paint large-scale paintings and nudes. She was masterful at painting intricate details. Look at the jewels in the maid's hand. The detailed pattern on the Queen of Sheba's robe. It's impressive. Did you know this painting was salvaged from the fire and has been restored several times?" Rose turned to face Alejandro and found him studying her instead of the painting.

"What?" She smiled back.

"I'm listening," he said.

Rose touched his chin to guide his head toward the painting. "What's happening here?" She rubbed his chin. "I've never seen you unshaven."

"Trying something new. Tell me more about Lavinia." He took her hand from his face and held it at his side.

"I'm still taken aback by how different you are. Long, curly hair, facial hair."

"Rose. We were talking about—"

"Lavinia. I know. I know. Okay. Speaking of hair."

"Rose Ross." He gently squeezed her hand.

"No. Seriously. Lavinia painted a portrait of a girl who had werewolf syndrome."

"Hypertrichosis."

"Exactly. Although I don't know how you know that. The painting was called *Portrait of Antonietta*. Antonietta's entire face was covered in hair. She lived in France and was part of King Henry II's court, as was typical for that time for people with curious ailments to be part of the court. Lavinia's portrait of her was so detailed, but when you see it, you realize she handled the portrayal with great care and tenderness."

"You're definitely in your element, but I need to keep you moving." Alejandro let go of Rose's hand and put it around her waist to gently guide her to the next painting.

Rose was engrossed in each piece, carefully studying each. Before they knew it, it was time to leave.

"You know, Alejandro, we could stop the tour right here. I think visiting art galleries is simply the most beautiful thing."

"I'm glad you enjoyed it. There's so much to see in this gallery. I wish we had more time to experience it, but we have a full schedule today. If I weren't leaving in the morning, I would have arranged for you to have more time and stay overnight."

"It's okay. Where to next?"

"Okay, this one is a must-do while in Dublin."

"That could be anything."

"Think beverage."

"Beer!"

"You got it. We're heading to the Guinness Storehouse."

"You know I haven't eaten since early this morning. If I didn't know you better, I'd say you were trying to get me drunk," she teased.

"You know from experience that the only thing I want you drunk on is *me*." Alejandro flashed his signature smile. A rush of heat ran through Rose's body, remembering their last time together as a couple.

"Don't worry. We'll have lunch while we are there, too," he said.

"You really do have this schedule nailed down. I'm impressed." She was surprised at how well he knew her and how easy it was to be with him.

"Just wait. I'm just getting started."

The city was so concentrated with sights of interest that it did not take long to reach their destination. Once inside the building, they learned how the beer was made and sampled several glasses of the dark ruby red-colored beer. It was more than enough for her to feel the side effects. Rose held onto Alejandro, trying hard not to lose her balance.

"Alejandro. We need to get lunch."

"Feeling a little woozy?"

"Let's just say I can't be held responsible for any actions I take beyond this point. I am free of my inhibitions," she said with a wry grin.

"Oh, it's a good thing you're with me. I'm a gentleman."

"I'm not," she laughed.

"Funny, but let's table the jokes for a moment and focus on getting you some food." Alejandro led her to the restaurant. He took the initiative, ordering her something loaded with carbs and a glass of water.

When their order arrived, Rose filled her mouth with French fries, and in between bites, she amused herself with corny jokes that Alejandro laughed at. She was sober enough to tell he had been studying her. She wanted to know what he wanted from her, but she wouldn't be the first to broach the subject.

"In all seriousness, today has been wonderful. Packed, but a beautiful day. Was this how you anticipated the day would go?"

"Honestly, Rose, I didn't know what to expect. I'm glad you're enjoying yourself, and I'm happy to spend time with you, as usual. Have you put any more thought into our previous conversation?"

"You mean the discussion about us getting back together?"

"Yes."

"Alejandro, to be honest, I haven't thought about getting together with anyone."

"You sound frustrated."

"I sound buzzed and a little pressured," Rose retorted.

"No pressure here. I'd never want you to feel that way."

"It's not just you. My current situation is weighing on me. I have a lot going on and feel distracted. I'm getting pulled in many directions. Once the show is over, I'll have more time to focus on personal matters. But for now, I'll tour, have some fun, and get back to work next week."

"I can help with the tour and the fun part."

"You're doing just fine. Now, can I get a sip of your drink, please?"

"I cut you off as soon as we completed the tour. I can't have you walking around slurring your words."

Rose narrowed her eyes and feigned a frown at Alejandro.

"Okay, maybe after you eat a little more. However, I don't think you'll want to hang around here drinking if you knew where we were heading next."

"I'm listening, but can you outline the rest of the day for me? You know I'm not so good at this piecemeal thing. It makes me a little anxious." She huffed.

"We are headed to Trinity College to the Old Library to see the book of Kells. Then I thought you might like to head over to the Merrion for Art Tea. We can peruse the hotel art collection before heading out for some shopping on Grafton Street while we're there. You'll have plenty of time to find some unique new things for yourself. Then, we'll finish the evening with dinner at Patrick Guilbaud. How does that sound? You up for it?"

"You're right. Let's skip the drink."

They both inhaled their lunches and headed for the car. Alejandro was very conscientious with their time at each site to ensure Rose had the opportunity to experience everything on the itinerary. Spending time with Alejandro felt easy and familiar, and she was happy to be rebuilding their friendship—smoothing waves a little at a time. Rose filled her camera with cherished moments from each place. She picked out items to remind her of their day in Dublin during her shopping excursions. The day served as a happy distraction from the looming deadline her father had given her. On the drive home, they used the time to download on the day.

"Alejandro, I have to give you your props."

"I'm listening."

"After you laid out the schedule, I was doubtful we could get through everything. A few times, I wanted to linger a little longer, like at Trinity College and the museum, but you kept us on track. Kudos to you."

"It was difficult because I also wanted to stay a little longer at a few places, and I like watching you enjoy yourself. But I kept reminding myself of my commitment to you," Alejandro said.

"I had a good time." She reached across the seat and cupped her hand around his, giving it a little shake. Alejandro flashed his signature smile in response. "So, are you looking forward to heading home in the morning?" Rose asked.

"I have mixed feelings."

"Why?"

"I have some business I need to deal with back in the States, but after reconnecting with you…let's just say I could have planned better," Alejandro explained.

Rose relaxed in her seat. "I didn't realize how much I needed this—needed the time to repair the invisible rip between us. Looking back, we could have handled our break much better than we did."

"I didn't know what I was doing, but I learned from my mistakes. We can start rebuilding from here. Whatever that looks like."

"Then you need to let me know when you are back in the Bay area, and we can get together for drinks or something."

"I can commit to that."

Alejandro and Rose used the time to catch up on email for the remainder of the drive. It was late, and the trio had been up all day, walking and roaming. Rose had her shoes off and stretched her legs sideways across the car floor until they almost touched Alejandro's. When they finally arrived at the house, Troy allowed Alejandro to help Rose out of the car so they could say their goodbyes. Rose gave Alejandro a hug and a kiss on the cheek.

"Thank you again for being such great company and for allowing me to share the day with you. It was nice to spend quality time together. Your smile warms me. I almost forgot how good it felt."

"I guarantee we'll never lose what we have between us. Enjoy the rest of your time in Belfast, and I will see you in California."

"Call or text me before your flight pushes out from the gate so I know you're en route."

"I will," Alejandro said before getting back into the car. Rose stood in the doorway, with Troy by her side, waving until the car disappeared out of sight.

※※

It was a perfect day for a trip. It would be Rose's third one since she arrived in Belfast. If she had to rate her past trips with Alejandro and Aedan, compared to her impending trip with Niall, on a scale of one to ten, the journey with Niall would rate ten before it even started. She relished the thought of flying to Crom Castle on a private helicopter to stay overnight and rub shoulders with the Irish elite. However, this trip would likely be the most awkward of the three. Rose could not deny her attraction to Niall; she knew she would have to work hard to stay focused. She intended to expand her network and ensure her name was associated with the art education and philanthropic work of the Roselyn Ross Foundation.

Rose and Niall did not have far to go to catch their ride. Brianna's property had sufficient space for the pilot to come to them, which benefited Troy, who could monitor her activities until the last moment before they left the property.

Like any helicopter ride, it was noisy. Rose spent most of the ride either looking out the window at the landscape below, talking over her headset to Niall, or attempting to communicate using hand signals. Rose pointed out sights from the view below she wanted him to see, and Niall pointed out landmarks of interest to her. The brilliant blue sky, yellow sunlight, and rolling green landscape were vivid as fresh paint strokes on canvas. When they got closer to Crom, Niall directed Rose to look at the aerial view of the extensive grounds she would soon be walking amongst. She made a mental note of her surroundings as Niall pointed out the lake waters of Lough Erne surrounding the property.

Once they landed, several event staff members greeted and helped them at the aircraft. One of the staff gathered their overnight bags, loaded them onto a small cart, and took them to their room in the West Wing.

Niall took Rose by the hand, leading her across the lawn toward the building. She looked around, taking in the view of the grand castle and vast property in the backdrop. Dotted around the building and strategic points around the property, she noticed the excess of security personnel.

"Niall." She squeezed his hand slightly to get his attention and get him to stop walking for a moment. "I haven't seen this much security in one place since I went to the White House with my dad. Is your president here?"

Niall stopped and turned toward Rose. When she caught his gaze, Niall half-smiled in a way she had seen Troy do when he split his attention between her and a visual security sweep. "Niall?" She gestured her hand toward the castle.

"Our former president is here. I'll introduce you two tonight." Niall's eyes softened, and with his free hand, he pushed away a lock of hair partially covering one of her eyes.

"When I saw the current and former presidents' names on the guest list, I wasn't sure either would actually be in attendance." Rose knew from helping expand Rick Ross Enterprises' global presence that getting to know members of the highest level of government was the fastest way to establish herself in any country. And if she was seeking to make her mark in Europe, this was the ideal opportunity to do it and the perfect prelude to her exhibition.

"Then I'm glad you came. Let's head inside." He nodded toward the castle.

Niall and Rose made their way towards the castle and went directly to their room to freshen up. She was excited about the upcoming events, including a welcome lunch, networking and silent auction, concert, and dinner.

"I hope you're okay with the arrangements. We happen to be staying in the same room."

"That's not an issue. As I recall, room options are limited here. Besides, we have double beds."

"Just checking."

"I feel privileged to be amongst this small group of distinguished guests. Thank you again, Niall, for deciding to attend and inviting me. I don't think I would have had this type of experience if you hadn't. Shouldn't we be getting ready now?"

"Let's do it. Time to meet Irish society and prepare for a memorable weekend."

Niall and Rose changed from their travel clothes to formal attire appropriate for the welcome luncheon. Rose put on a pastel pink butterfly embroidered midi-length dress similar to the blue one she wore at the house. This time, she wore matching pink pumps. Niall wore a gray suit with a white shirt, one button open at the top, and no tie. Rose slipped a matching pink handkerchief into Niall's lapel pocket, looping her arm around his before they left, and headed towards the luncheon area.

The luncheon room was long and narrow. A succession of tables ran lengthwise across the room to accommodate seating for twenty-four. The tablescapes consisted of candles and pastel floral bouquets set in antique blue and white porcelain vases. Only twelve of the twenty-four guests in attendance, including Niall and Rose, were invited to stay overnight. Rose made a mental note of every guest from the invite list she needed to meet and started checking off that list as Niall introduced her to those who attended the luncheon.

Following lunch, Rose and Niall strayed into the silent auction room. They each received a glass of champagne at the entrance. Once inside, they walked around, inspecting various antiquities dotted across the room. Each item had a label describing the item and the corresponding number to bid at the auction. Rose circled the room once to catch a glimpse at each piece before bidding on a miniature, still-life painting of a vase of roses. As other guests filled the room, Niall introduced Rose to them. Actors, government officials, musicians, and some of the wealthiest Northern Islanders were gathered in one place, making small talk for a cause. Rose and Niall continued making their way around the room, talking and networking with the guests. The sudden appearance of black-suited men was Rose's signal the former president was making her way into the room. Niall placed his hand on the small of Rose's back, guiding her to turn around when the former president walked in.

"You ready for this?" Niall asked as he crossed the room with Rose.

"Absolutely." Rose was surprised that the former president had already focused her attention on Niall and was heading toward them.

"Mrs. McCray. How lovely it is to see you again."

"Indeed. It's been almost a year, Mr. King. As you look around, you can tell I still have a lot of work to do on being stealthier with my security detail, as you suggested." She smiled a genuine smile and turned to look at Rose. Niall picked up the cue.

"Madam, I'd like to introduce you to my friend. This is Ms. Roselyn Ross, head of the Roselyn Ross Foundation. She will be curating the Morrison Exhibition this year," Niall said.

The former president held a hand to Rose. Rose was impressed that Niall noticed her need to decouple her name from her dad's.

"Hello, Ms. Ross. It's a pleasure to meet you. Your reputation precedes you. Your contribution to the arts and humanities through your philanthropic work is unmatched."

"Mrs. McCray, it is an honor to meet you. I feel I am just getting started. I aspire to be amongst women like yourself doing extraordinary things. I can only hope to create a lasting legacy."

"You are well on your way. I've seen your work. It speaks volumes. Look around. I imagine the crowd that has suddenly descended upon us is more for you than me, which is our signal to make the rounds. However, I'd love to continue our conversation and have you over for lunch. I'm not sure if you have time while you're here or if you have another visit planned—but let's get something on the calendar," the former president said and lightly touched Rose's arm.

"I'd like that a lot. Thank you," Rose responded before the former president got pulled into another conversation. "This is an awesome event, Niall. I never thought I would have the chance to meet the former president, let alone expect an invitation to have lunch with her."

"It's rare for someone like her to go out of her way for an introduction. Seeing that you are the only one she made a point of meeting, you've already made an impression."

"I think she was making a beeline for you if I recall clearly."

"Using me to get to you," Niall smiled wryly.

Niall introduced Rose to a few more people in between conversations with the guest who sought her out.

"I suppose my name is making its way around Ireland."

"In the best way. Now you understand what I was telling you last week," Niall said.

"I didn't doubt you." Rose knew Niall never said anything he didn't mean, and when he made a statement, he had facts to back it. She just needed to tamp down any self-doubt and start believing it herself.

Once they finished networking and bidding on auction items, everyone moved into another room where chairs were positioned in a semi-circle. At the open end of the circle was a white baby grand piano. Once everyone was seated, the place went quiet, and a young pianist came into the room dressed in a simple mauve swing dress with matching ballerina flats and sat on the piano bench. She announced herself as Maria and told the crowd the three songs she would play: Ludwig van Beethoven's *Moonlight Sonata*, Wolfgang Amadeus Mozart's *Rondo Alla Turca*, and Franz Liszt's *Hungarian Rhapsody No. 2*. Rose looked around the room. Everyone appeared transfixed on the pianist as if they were holding their breath during the concert. Maria's piano skills were flawless, and after she finished, Rose and Niall introduced themselves and learned that the young artist started playing the piano at age three. Rose and Maria instantly connected, agreeing to stay in contact.

Following the mini-concert, Niall, Rose, and the other guests went back into the long narrow room set up for dinner and spent the next hour and a half eating and talking their way through several courses. Rose made deeper connections with those she had met earlier in the day, and by the end of dinner, there was not one person with whom she had not made a personal connection.

When Rose finished her final conversation, she instinctively sensed Niall was no longer nearby. The feeling of missing someone was new to Rose. She looked around to locate Niall and caught his gaze across the room as he talked with a couple. His hand immediately opened at his side. Rose walked over, placed her hand in Niall's, and joined the conversation.

"Rose, the governor has asked if we wanted to join him and his wife for a nightcap in a few minutes. Do you think you might be up for it?"

"Your honor. You didn't tell Niall we had this conversation earlier? One would think you're trying to influence me." Rose smiled at the governor.

"A little persuasion never hurts. You can't fault me for wanting more time with the most popular guest here tonight," the governor said.

"You're being too generous. Your invitation is tempting but pulling double duty working on the exhibition and RR Enterprises before flying here this morning has me a little spent. We should get some rest to be fresh for all the activities tomorrow. What do you think, Niall?" Rose asked.

"You are right. I didn't think about that. Well, sir, we have our answer. Thank you for the invitation, but we will retire now and see everyone bright and early for breakfast," Niall said.

The governor and his wife said their goodnights, then Rose and Niall headed to their room. Once they reached their bedroom door,

Rose rushed past Niall into the room and stood in front of the dresser, taking off her earrings and laughing.

"Okay, let me in on the joke," Niall said.

"There is none. The governor's persistence was a little—" Rose paused a second, trying to find the right word before Niall jumped in.

"Obvious is what his behavior was. He clearly has a thing for you. His wife didn't seem to care either," Niall said.

"She didn't say a word. Just looked at me and smiled. I don't know if you wanted to have that nightcap, but I needed a break," Rose added.

"No, and thanks for the save with the governor. I learned tonight that not only do we finish each other's sentences, but you're good at reading my signals."

"I don't know if I got your signal, but I'm not one of those who end up as the last person at the party," Rose said.

"So, what do you think? Was it what you expected? I know establishing your brand is important to you."

"Pretty much and more. It was the perfect opportunity to make new connections with these people. Can you help me with this?" She turned her back to Niall.

He blew on his hands to warm them, surrounding her with hints of cardamon and plum, filling her senses with forbidden desires as he slowly loosened the dress. She closed her eyes and exhaled. *Focus,* she told herself.

"I'm looking forward to tomorrow. What should I expect?"

"Tomorrow should be more relaxed, and it's a short agenda. Everyone will be heading back home after lunch. It's up to you what time you want to leave. It is a beautiful castle. We can take some time to explore the grounds if you like."

Rose slipped out of her dress and clutched it to her chest, concealing her underwear as she stood in her heels, then turned to face Niall. He looked down the length of her body, then back up and met her gaze with hungry eyes.

"You're a lovely sight. I wish I were my brother right now." His confession lingered like the longing between them.

"Shall I deconstruct that statement?" she asked.

"Doesn't it all get back to the same point in my head?"

"Hand me that, please." Rose raised her chin in the direction of a robe on the bed. Niall wrapped the robe around her shoulders, took the dress, and laid it over a chair. "Thanks."

Rose stepped closer to Niall, put a hand on his shoulder, and leveraged him to balance herself as she slipped out of her heels. "I don't know anything about your head," she smiled wryly. "Just be glad you're you. I like you, but I am not so happy with your brother now."

"I'm not complaining, but I'm glad there are two beds."

"Don't worry. We'll behave ourselves," Rose said.

Niall took off his suit coat, laid it across the chair, and unbuttoned his shirt. "I have to. Until you tell me differently, you're my brother's girl. I can't say I regret acting on my feelings the other day, but I admit I was wrong. Besides, there are other things I need to consider, but I won't go into that."

"Anything else is none of my business." Rose hoped it wasn't Marina Mack. She hated the idea Niall could be attracted to someone so opposite her. She hated that she cared about what he was doing with Marina. Rose went into the bathroom, retrieved her makeup remover wipes, and started removing the makeup from her face. She looked in the mirror, surprised to see Niall leaning against the door, watching her. He caught her gaze.

"You're beautiful, you know that?" he said.

"You won't let me forget. Does your brother know about your attraction to me?"

"He knows more than you think. I told him I made my feelings known to you and that you won't have anything to do with me. I also told him that if he didn't get his act together, I'd make you forget him. This is new for me. I never wanted anything my brother had, but when I think about it, he and I are very alike. Our passions around work and protecting family, but how he lives his life is different than mine, and when it comes to relationships with women—well, that's where we differ. Then there's you."

"Aedan, who? But seriously, Niall, I'm trying to figure this out myself. I didn't come to Belfast looking for a man. You know my story. Seen my faults. I'm equally to blame for the situation we're in. I need to get myself together." Rose half-smiled, stepped past Niall, and went back into the bedroom. She tightened her silk robe and maneuvered out of her bra and underwear. "So, your brother is usually short on words. I'm sure he had an interesting but pithy response." She looked to either side of his face. "I don't see any bruising, so I don't imagine he punched you. Anyway, you two don't seem the type to do that to each other. So, I'm curious. What happened?"

"It was a heated discussion. And you're right, we don't fight like that."

"I gather that discussion took place recently. That's why you're so tempered today." Rose tilted her head, waiting for a response.

Niall removed his cufflinks and put them on the dresser. "Partly. There are other things at play. But connecting with these people this weekend is important to your success. I'd never do anything to jeopardize that. So, for now, let's focus on getting you staged for the exhibition," he said.

"So, this whole Crom thing is exposing you to yet another side of me. Can you handle it?" Rose asked, wondering if she could handle it herself.

Niall shook his head. "This is going to be a long night."

"Don't be so dramatic."

"Seriously, Rose, the other night was real. Every touch, kiss, and lingering glance across the room is real. You only have to say one word for proof."

"Don't worry. I'll play nice. I wasn't lying when I said I was tired. I'm going to bed." Rose stood on the tip of her toes, leaned into Niall, stroked his curly black mane, and pressed her lips to his cheek. "We can talk until one of us falls asleep first." She walked to one of the beds, pulled back the covers, and got in. "I got dibs on this bed. Turn off the lights when you're finished."

Rose watched as Niall stood in the center of the room and removed his shirt, pants, socks, and underwear before disappearing into the restroom naked and reappearing the same way. She watched each muscle in his arms and legs flex as he moved until he sat on the bed, and everything godlike and incredible disappeared beneath the covers.

"I just want you to know one thing," she said.

"What's that, Night Owl?"

"That watching all that," she said, drawing circles in the air with her finger, "was simply amazing." A huge grin cracked across her face.

Niall shook his head. "You are too much. My brother has no idea what he's doing."

"I think he does on several fronts. Despite what you told him, he trusts you. Anyway, I'm coming down from my high talking about him."

"What are you talking about? You only had a half glass of champagne the whole night."

"No, but your display gave me a temporary high."

"Okay, tell me *goodnight, Niall*, before I have to come over there."

"Goodnight, Niall. Thanks again for today," Rose said.

"Sleep well, Night Owl."

A BUZZING SOUND SHATTERED THE SILENCE IN THE DARK BEDROOM, leading Rose to reach her arm out from beneath its warm cocoon covers towards her phone on the nightstand. She opened her eyes and strained to focus on her cellphone. *Buzz, buzz, buzz* again, the sound signaling for attention. It wasn't her phone. She called to Niall in the darkness. "Hey, Niall." No response. She called out a little louder. "Niall." No response. She used the flashlight on her phone to guide her way out of bed and over to Niall's. Rose sat on the side of his bed and gently shook his shoulders. "Niall. Wake up. You have a call."

"What? You need something?" Niall reached out and held her hand.

"No, Niall, answer this." She placed the vibrating phone in his hand.

"What time is it? Hello?" he said, sitting up in bed to answer the phone. Rose turned on the nightstand lamp and studied his face as he talked.

"I'm sorry, what did you say happened? When? Okay. Where is she now? Of course." When Niall hung up, Rose immediately peppered him with questions.

"Who was that? What did they want? Is everything okay?"

"That was the nurse. Brianna is in the hospital, their running some tests. We need to leave and go to her. What time is it?"

"It's about five a.m. Shall I call the pilot?"

"No. I'll call the pilot. We need to get ready to leave. Pack your things."

"Give me twenty minutes. I'll get your things ready, too." Rose reached over and gently cupped her hand around Niall's cheek before getting up. He was developing a five o'clock shadow, and his face was rough.

Within fifteen minutes, Rose had showered, dressed, and packed her and Niall's overnight bags while he was in the shower. Niall walked back into the main room nude, towel drying his hair with one hand and tapping the screen on his phone with the other.

Rose purposely cleared her throat. "Clothes? I laid out yours for you." Rose pointed to the clothes neatly laid across the bed.

"Oh, sorry. I can't find Aedan." Niall reached for his clothing.

"Was the nurse able to get a hold of him?"

"No. The hospital couldn't reach Aedan either, so they asked me to try."

"Okay, so let's assume he's out of cell range or in the air. Wasn't he also traveling this weekend? When was he planning to return?"

"He planned to get back on Monday morning."

"So that's tomorrow. I don't know where your brother is, but I am sure when he receives the message, he will respond." Rose noticed Niall struggling to button his shirt and focus on his phone simultaneously, so she stepped in to help him. "Let me get that."

"Thanks. The pilot just texted he's ready."

Rose finished fastening the last button, brushed a wet curl away from his eyebrow, and kissed Niall on the cheek. "You look like you needed that."

"I did."

"Now, let's get to your sister. You never know; Aedan might be there by the time we arrive."

Niall grabbed both their bags, and they made their way to the helipad. This time, no cheerful voices rose above the roar of the aircraft. Instead, Rose reached over and held Niall's hand as they sat silent for the duration of the ride.

⁂

UPON ARRIVING AT THE HOSPITAL, ROSE AND NIALL WERE immediately taken into a small, pastel, green-colored room with paisley cloth-covered chairs that served as the waiting area. Rose scanned the room. Besides their presence, nothing unusual stood out except that there was no sign of Aedan, and neither of them had any indication he had received their messages. Since their arrival, they didn't know much other than Brianna was weak; they were waiting for test results to determine if surgery was needed, and her situation was severe enough that they were not allowed to see her.

Rose sat in one of the seats as they waited for more information. She looked on as Niall paced the room. After watching Niall wear a hole in the carpet for several hours, Rose broke the silence.

"Have a seat next to me, Niall. Your sister is in good hands." Rose held out a hand to Niall. He placed his hand in hers and sat in the chair next to her. A few moments later, a woman in green scrubs with a name tag came to meet them.

"Hi. I'm doctor O'Connor. Are you Mrs. Morrison's family?"

Niall stood and walked toward the doctor. "Yes. I'm Niall King. Brianna's brother." He turned slightly and reached a hand back toward Rose. Rose got up, took his hand, and stood by his side. "This is Ms. Ross."

"Mr. King, your sister was admitted after she passed out. Mrs. Morrison was experiencing a condition called Bradyarrhythmias. In essence, her heartbeat was slower than normal. You may have noticed that she had a bout of severe weakness leading up to this."

"Recently, she used a wheelchair to get around because she was so tired," Niall explained.

"That's due to her low blood pressure. Your sister has a pre-existing condition that has become exacerbated, causing irregular heartbeats. We performed surgery to implant a device under her skin to regulate her heartbeats."

"You put in a pacemaker? Is this permanent? Will she be able to function as normal? How is she?" Niall peppered the doctor with questions. Rose could feel his hand tightening around hers.

"Mr. King, your sister's disease will require her to wear a pacemaker indefinitely. We will closely monitor her post-surgery, but eventually, Mrs. Morrison will find she has more energy than before. I'll have the nurse outline the timetable for replacements. Due to your sister's type of heart disease, we will keep her here for a few more days to monitor her, but once released, it will be about four weeks before she returns to normal activity levels."

"Can I see her now?" he asked.

"She's in recovery. I'll have someone come get you when she's stable. Do you have any more questions?" Niall shook his head, then the doctor left the room.

After an hour, Rose felt her stomach growl. They hadn't had time for breakfast in all the commotion and flew straight to the hospital, landing on the hospital roof helipad.

"I'm going to get us something to eat. Ugh, and I forgot to let Troy know we're here," Rose said while texting something on her phone.

"I'm not sure I can eat, but okay. Don't worry about Troy. I'm sure he's here," Niall said in a voice that sounded resigned.

Rose's phone buzzed with a response to her message to Troy. "I'm here." The text confirmed Niall's prediction.

It didn't take long for the food to arrive, which Troy collected from the vendor and brought to Rose. Rose spent time over lunch trying to ease Niall's mind while they waited. He was in for a long day if he planned to stay overnight.

"Niall, if you want, I can stay with you at the hospital tonight or at least until they allow you to see Brianna. I'll send Troy back to the house."

"It's been a long day and far from being over. I think you should head back to the house with Troy, get some work in while you can, and get some rest. I will be fine here. Once Aedan gets his messages, I'm certain he'll head straight here. Besides, there is no telling when we'll be allowed to see my sister."

"I wish there was something I could do to help."

"You are helping me. But we're in the same situation. There's nothing you or I can do now but wait. At least I can be here when Brianna stabilizes. I'll message you when I get more information. You have a lot on your plate—I'll be fine," Niall said.

"Are you sure?"

"I'm sure, Rose."

Rose texted a message to Troy before heading back down to the lobby. He was waiting for her near the elevator when she reached the floor. "Hey, Troy, sorry I was gone so long. We were waiting to see Brianna, but they weren't allowing visitors yet. Niall plans to stay overnight. He'll message me if her status changes." Rose walked in tandem with Troy as they headed out the door to the car.

"How are you holding up?"

"I can't believe this is happening. Brianna didn't seem headed down this path the other night when I met with her."

"The human body is complicated that way."

"So true."

"Still no word from Aedan? I didn't see him come through here."

"Nothing," Rose said.

"I suspect he's managing a client. He'll be here when he can."

⁂

MORNING CAME AND WENT IN THE NOW QUIET GRAND HOUSE. ROSE, Troy, Kris, and the team of contractors spent all morning working at the gallery. Rose checked in with Niall to see how Brianna was doing from time to time. During her last call with him, he indicated Brianna was still resting, and the doctors still hadn't allowed him to see her. She also learned there was still no sign of Aedan.

"Troy, Aedan still hasn't shown."

"That's unlike him, but I am sure there's a logical reason."

"I'm worried. Niall needs some respite from that place. I think I'll bring him a change of clothes and a real meal. What do you think?"

"I think he would appreciate it, especially if he's adamant about not leaving the hospital."

"Surely, he is waiting to see his sister and ensure she is out of danger. Also, I doubt he'd leave even after seeing her until he knows Aedan is there. Come with me. I'll have the staff get something ready for him. Double-check everything before it gets loaded into the car."

Once inside, Rose and Troy organized the staff activities. It didn't take long for things to be ready before they were on their way back to the hospital.

"This is great what you're doing for this family despite the daunting task you already have," Troy said.

"I've grown to care about Brianna and her brothers in a short time. I trust they would do the same for me if things were reversed."

"I hope you're right. You know I'm inherently suspicious of everyone. Maybe that's why I'm in my line of work."

"We're here," she said, looking out the car window, ignoring Troy's comment.

It wasn't long before they were out of the car and back in the waiting area. Niall was still pacing the floors. "Niall. How are you holding up?" Rose asked.

Niall stopped pacing long enough to talk to Rose and Troy. "I'm a little tired, but okay. I still haven't been allowed to see her yet, but they said soon."

"I brought you some fresh clothes and a home-cooked meal. If you want to go into one of those rooms to take a shower and change, I can wait here in case the doctor comes out."

"Thank you, Rose. I know I'm repeating myself, but I appreciate all your help. You're right. A quick shower will help me feel better and pull it together." Niall took the bags that Rose had brought him and disappeared into one of the adjacent rooms. Rose sat in one of the paisley chairs while Troy stationed himself at the door. A few moments later, the main door opened. Aedan came bursting through so fast he was five seconds away from being tackled by Troy. They eyed each other for a second before Aedan turned his attention to Rose.

"Rose, is Niall with Brianna?" Aedan asked.

"Hello, Aedan. No, they haven't let anyone in to see her yet. Niall slept here last night, so I brought him a change of clothes. He's just freshening up. He did his best to try and reach you. We both did."

"I was dealing with a covert situation for a client that led to me not getting the messages, or I would have been here sooner. Where's the doctor?"

"I only just arrived myself. Niall may have more information for you. Here he is now." She gave a pouty look to Niall, walking up from behind Aedan.

"Aedan, man. Where have you been? We've been trying to reach you for a while. The doctors haven't let me see Brianna because they're still trying to stabilize her. She had some complications following surgery, but she should be fine." Niall brought Aedan up to speed on everything the doctor told him to date. Rose looked on. Aedan's strained face was revealing, compared to the usually controlled look he had about him. Rose felt compelled to comfort him but didn't dare overstep their boundaries.

"Gentleman. It doesn't seem I can be of any use to you, so I plan to return to the gallery. If you want me to bring you anything—more food, clothes—just let me know. I'm happy to help."

"Rose, thank you so much for being here over the past two days. Your presence has been reassuring. You knew just what I needed," Niall said.

"Rose, I appreciate you for supporting Niall through this. I would not have wanted him to go through this alone. I'm sorry I couldn't be here sooner," Aedan expressed.

"Guys, no need to thank me. Please call or text me when you have an update."

Niall walked over to Rose and hugged her before she left with Troy.

Later that day, Rose learned that the brothers were allowed to visit Brianna. The doctors reiterated that it would be at least four weeks before Brianna would return to normal activity levels. Two weeks after the art show.

CHAPTER 15

Just Fine

"It isn't positions which lend distinction,
but men who enhance positions."

– AGESILAUS II

THE HOUSE WAS STILL. ONLY THE SOUND OF BIRDS SINGING IN THE trees surrounding the driveway shattered the silence. Rose opened her eyes and closed her eyes a few times, adjusting to the morning light streaming through the curtains.

"I have to give Dad my decision." She whispered and blew out a breath tamping down her anxiety. "You are your father's daughter, the master of your domain, and everything will be alright," Rose said. And with that, she got up and prepared to greet the day.

Everyone was at their usual spot in the kitchen. Niall stood near the coveted coffee maker with his prized possession in hand. Aedan was sitting at the breakfast counter, swiping something on his phone. He didn't look up when Rose entered, but she knew he was aware of her presence in the way he always was.

"Rose. Have a seat near me." Aedan looked away from his phone, caught her gaze, and held a hand to Rose the same way he did the first night they kissed.

She wasn't surprised to find herself instinctively placing her hand in his because she hadn't closed the door on him. When Rose showed Aedan Carol's blog post titled *Let Them Eat Cake*, he committed to handling the situation. Aedan stayed true to his word and dealt with Carol in addition to the media outlets where the posts ran. By the time he was done, the outlets had issued updates to their posting policies. However, there was one thing missing. Rose was still waiting for an apology from Aedan. Like herself, he was headstrong. But she wanted him to be accountable for not initially believing her, being complacent about racism, and setting aside facts in favor of family.

"I don't suppose you're trying to put the moves on me." Rose squeezed Aedan's hand. The slight curl of his lips told her he was suppressing a smile.

"I wanted to talk. Is that okay?" Aedan tipped his head toward his brother.

"I'm fine with Niall hearing our conversation. Just like you and Niall, there are no secrets between us." Rose winked at Niall.

"Say what you have to say, man." Niall shook his head.

Aedan positioned himself to face Rose, put his legs on either side of hers and held her hands. "Rose, I know things have been a little strained between us lately, but you know I care about you. I didn't forget that today is when you tell your father whether you plan to succeed him. How are you feeling?" Aedan circled his thumbs on the back of her hands. Rose looked down at Aedan's hands, then back at him. The strength in his stare struck an unexpected chord of desire in her. She tried to focus on what he was saying, to recall his initial failed attempt to push past his privilege to understand her concerns. But his proximity, soft touch, and the scent of sandalwood with brown sugar made her want to dismiss it all and lean in to kiss him. He only had to say two words: *I'm sorry.* Rose inhaled and tapped down her desire to take what she wanted.

"I know you care in your own way. And yes, I have a call scheduled with Dad at four o'clock today. I feel good about my decision."

"I want you to know that I support whatever you decide to do."

"We both do," Niall chimed in.

"I appreciate the sentiment, guys. I really do."

"Do you want me to be with you when you make the call? I can clear my calendar to be available," Aedan offered.

"No, I need to do this alone," Rose insisted.

"I respect that, and I'm here if you need me. We both are." Aedan nodded in Niall's direction. Rose looked past Aedan to where Niall stood. His partially open mouth told her he had something to add, but he held back.

"I won't be able to spar with you tonight. Following my call with Dad, I need to visit the artists working on souvenirs for the event."

Aedan stopped circling his thumbs. "Rose, does Troy know about your change in plans? We're only a week away from showtime, so an increasing number of people know that you're in Belfast. That and the pending board decision make this a volatile time for you." Aedan released her hands and leaned back in his chair. He looked at his brother, then back at Rose.

"He's right, Night Owl. Can someone run the errand for you, or have them put the portfolio online for you to view?" Niall asked.

"Guys, calm down. I need to physically inspect and approve over twenty art pieces, and that's not something I can do over video or online.

"Where is this place you're going?" Niall asked.

"It's some warehouse district for artists. I can have Kris text you the address if you want to know the exact spot."

"I think I know the district," Aedan said, then turned to his brother. Niall's brows were furrowed, and he shook his head briefly in a silent signal to Aedan. If Rose had blinked, she would have missed it.

"Is there something wrong, Niall?" Rose asked.

"It's a blighted district, is all. I'll give Troy a heads-up," Niall said.

Rose pursed her lips. The last thing she needed was Troy trying to convince her to change her plans just weeks away from her show. The souvenirs were an essential portion of the exhibition. Rose felt her face go flush as her heart began to race.

"Night Owl." Niall's voice was pronounced. Rose knew it was a deliberate attempt to keep her thoughts from spiraling. "It's okay. Go inspect your art. I'll talk to Troy. Now, I have to get going. Will we at least see you at dinner tonight?" Niall put his empty cup in the sink and walked over to Aedan and Rose.

"I'll be here," Rose said. Niall bent to kiss Rose on her cheek, then directed his attention to Aedan.

"Don't be late for dinner, man." Niall patted his brother on the shoulder and then left.

"Does that bother you?" Aedan asked.

"Does what bother me?" Rose's eyebrows raised as she waited for a response.

"My brother hovering."

"I hadn't really thought about it since my first week here. I suppose I'm used to it now. It's a sign he cares." Thinking back, Rose couldn't pinpoint a moment beginning with her first day in Belfast when Niall wasn't showing signs he cared.

Rose walked into the gallery's rotunda, the only room of three which was less than two-thirds finished. The souvenir paintings she planned to inspect later today would be the final touch to the room. Rose spied Kris in the middle gallery. He was following the photographer around, taking publicity shots. Besides her immediate team, Troy had assigned one security person per room permanently stationed during the day while Rose was working. Rose knew his hands were full between her and the priceless art that had arrived. But she still needed to get her hands on one final piece.

Rose walked into the gallery office and tapped her earpiece. "Troy," she said. Within seconds, Troy, who was standing outside the gallery door, came inside.

"Everything okay? I can have someone escort the photographer out if he's finished," Troy said.

"Everything's fine. You wanted to know when I was done in the main gallery. I'll be in the office until it's time to head to the city."

"Then I'll be right here when you're ready. You want this open or closed?"

"Partially open is fine." Rose sat at her desk, pulled up a contact on her phone, and pressed the call button. She could see part of Troy's foot across the room as he sat near her office door.

"K-Cee here," The smooth deep voice said on the other end of the phone. Rose loved how singers sounded like they would break into song even during everyday speech. "Is this my girl wonder?" K-Cee announced as if giving a shout-out.

"Hi, K-Cee. It's Rose. I hope the family is great. I don't want to take too much of your time, but I need a favor." Rose squinted her eyes when she said the word favor. Although she was only calling in a marker, it felt strange to ask a musical genius for a favor.

"Anything. I think I owe you about, what, a hundred or more by now?" he said. And he was right. Rose had helped K-Cee and his wife procure several priceless art pieces, including the one she needed to borrow for her show.

"I'm in Ireland curating a show, and one of the Black artists I'm showcasing was influenced by Basquiat. Specifically, his Mecca painting. I would love to include it in the exhibit, which is a one-day event." The words flowed from her lips as if rehearsed.

"Just tell me when your crew is coming for it. I'll have someone here."

"Thank you, K-Cee. I didn't know how you'd respond." Rose exhaled, relieved one crisis was averted.

"I told you—I owe you plenty. While I have you on the phone, I have a room where I think a piece from Toyin would make a lovely addition. When you return, could you have a look and pick out a piece that would fit the space?"

"Does it have to be Toyin, or are you thinking something with her breath of style works?"

"Her work is brilliant, but I'll let you decide what should fill the space. I trust your eye on this."

"I appreciate the confidence. And thank you again for Mecca."

"I'll catch ya back in the States. Good luck with the exhibition. I'm sure it'll be great."

THE DAY WAS RUNNING SO SMOOTHLY AND AHEAD OF SCHEDULE THAT Rose could release her team early for the evening. Kris stepped into the gallery office to catch up with Rose.

"Tell me you like what you see," Kris said.

"I love everything. Once the rotunda is done, we're done."

"Did you want me to go with you to approve the art?"

"No, I have it covered. You should head back to the hotel. We have a little over a week left. Take advantage of the time and enjoy yourself while you're in town." Rose sat back in her chair and crossed her legs. Their conversation ran close to her time to call her dad, but she wanted to hear Kris out.

"You know it's hard for me when I know there's unfinished business. At some point, you'll have to trust me with art approvals," he pressed.

"Next time, but I will supervise to give you pointers if curating is something you're aiming to make a career. However, I need to call my dad right now, and you need to have some fun. Now get to it." She could tell by the smile on his face her answer was met with satisfaction. "And close the door behind you," she called out to Kris, who was already heading out.

The phone only rang once before Rose's dad picked up the call. "Princess. I swear I can set my watch by you. How are you?"

"Good. A little over a week away from the big day."

"Brilliant. And what news do you have for me?"

"I've put a lot of thought into this. You know I really want to make sure I continue your legacy while creating my own mark in this world, right?"

"Yes. I told you, I support you one hundred percent in that and will do my part to help you get there."

"Good. So, this is what I want to do. I'll continue my work as president of the foundation and as owner and curator for my gallery, but I'll hire an associate curator to work for me. That will ensure I can continue my work in those areas without compromising my work at the enterprise."

"So, you plan to pursue a career in the arts," he said.

"There's more. As for the CEO position, I will put my name forward but with a caveat."

"I'm pleased to know you decided to throw your name in the running, but what's the caveat?" Her dad's voice was stern and questioning.

"I'll only put my name forward as a candidate if the board commits to rebranding the company as Ross Enterprises."

"Ross Enterprises. Let's be honest. They may not go for it. Our brand is worth billions. Without a strategy in place, we could lose a lot of money. Besides, I have something else to tell you," he said.

"Let me guess. There's a forerunner," Rose sighed with disappointment.

"One of the other candidates dropped out. The board asked me to submit two names."

"Your second choice—the person we talked about."

"Yes."

"I wasn't anticipating that, but at least I know now you've leveled the playing field. Anyone you put forward will be tough to beat. This brings me to the second part of my argument. If I'm not appointed, whoever is named CEO will be named CEO of Rick Ross Enterprises, so the company name will remain unchanged." Rose paused to listen for a reaction on the other side of the phone. She knew updating the brand wouldn't hurt him but not updating it would stifle her ability to bring her name to the forefront.

"How do you keep us from losing money on the rebranding?" her dad asked.

"If selected, I'll use my appointment to signal a new direction in the market in conjunction with the latest product launch. We'll push out the timing to align with the change. Then, the name change becomes part of the broader strategy and company direction. If done right, we won't lose the equity built into the Ross brand. We'll be emphasizing our position as market leaders in innovation."

"I can see that, but the board has to see it, too."

"If you can see it, they will."

"Rose. I didn't get to where I am today without knowing the right moves. And you, Princess, inherited that. I'll put your name forward with your contingencies."

"Thanks, Dad." Rose smiled. It was the first time she understood the breadth of her father's trust in her abilities and commitment to secure her personal legacy.

"Now, Rose, go smash that event of yours," he encouraged.

Rose felt confident this was the next right move. Now, her final fate rested with the board and whether they thought she was the best candidate to lead the company into the future.

⚘

"I'm not sure I understand what's happening over there, but we're pulling up to the building," Troy announced. Rose nodded in response, shoulders going up and down in time to the music blasting in the car.

"I'm feeling the vibe. Like Mary J. Blige says, 'I'm just fine.'" Rose snapped her fingers and swayed to the music. She knew Troy disapproved of her letting loose whenever he needed her to focus on what he was saying. But she was feeling good. Mecca was secured, she had a good call with her dad, and now she was about to approve the final art pieces for her exhibition.

Troy got out of the car and went to open the door for Rose. She held Troy's hand as she stepped out and took in the scene around her. The multi-unit artist loft complex was a six-story brick and limestone building spanning the entire block. The street, a mix of commercial and residential buildings, was dotted with run-down cars on both sides.

"I guess this does look like the poor side of every city I've been to." She summed up the scene.

"Just goes to show we're all the same," Troy said and escorted Rose into the building. "Kris called ahead and arranged for your viewing on the first floor. They have an event space, so you have room to work."

Rose looked around the lobby, which was nothing unusual. There were three elevator banks and two doors, one on either side of the building concealing stairwells. Rose headed to her right towards the only door not leading upstairs.

"Yeah, Troy, like the fact the artist space was on the third floor didn't have to do with the sudden change. You know your fingerprints are all over this." She nodded to the gentleman standing near the door. Troy opened the door, and Rose walked into a large, wood-paneled room with eight faux wood rectangle tables arranged end to end in pairs forming a square in the center of the room. Standing near a wall of windows facing the street was a thin, young, Black woman with braids twisted in a ball on top of her head, who stepped forward when she spotted Rose.

"I wasn't sure what order you wanted to see these in. Everything is dry, so you can arrange the paintings as you like. By the way, I'm Natasha," the woman introduced.

"Natasha, nice to meet you. I'm Rose. This is Troy." Rose gestured to Troy. "I hope his staff wasn't too intrusive."

"Not at all. They helped me bring everything down and get set up."

Rose walked closer to one of the tables and picked up a painting to examine it. It depicted a couple sitting in a field of grass. "The detail is so incredibly realistic. This could almost be mistaken for a photograph. This is beautiful, Natasha."

"Thank you. But you should know, your staff emailed me three more guest comments to translate to paintings, so those will be done by Monday."

"Monday? I was hoping to have all the paintings hung by Monday. Do you happen to recall what the depictions were?"

"No, but I can go upstairs and get the writeups."

"Don't bother. If you can have everything ready by Monday at nine, that could work."

Rose walked around the tables, carefully inspecting each piece before ending back up where she started. "Do you have some white printer paper handy?" Rose looked around the room and walked toward a table that contained a small, gold-leaf box, a bottle of cleaning solution, and a roll of paper towels.

"I have some upstairs. I'll get it."

"This will do." Rose held up the paper towels. She pulled a long stream of towels off and held it out to Natasha. "Let's put a line of these under the paintings. I need to see how they'll look against a white backdrop since that's how they'll hang. I'll start on this side. You can do those." Rose rolled out some paper towels, placed paintings on top, and then recentered them on the table. As she went around the tables, she picked up a few paintings and replaced them with others until she had rearranged all the paintings. She took out her phone and snapped a few pictures when she was done.

"These are perfect, Natasha. Before you take these back upstairs, would you make sure to order these by number, starting with this painting as number one?" Rose pointed to a painting of a Sankofa. "You can gauge by this grouping where to add the ones you're still working on. I'm sure those will also be lovely. Feel free to write on the back of the frame with a pencil. Is this the box guests will take their paintings home in?" Rose picked up the gold-leaf box and examined it.

"Yes, each one fits perfectly inside with space at the top for the card Kris sent me a sample of."

"They're more beautiful than I anticipated. I'm pleased with what I've seen today. You should be proud of your work."

"I'm grateful for the opportunity. I'll have these all prepared and hand-delivered to you Monday." Natasha pulled a pencil from her pocket and began writing numbers on the paper towel near each picture, starting with the Sankofa.

"Just have them ready by nine. Someone will be here to pick them up. I expect you'll have more work coming your way following the exhibition. Prepare yourself."

Rose put the box on the table and walked toward Troy. He opened the door, stepped into the inner lobby, and waited for her to join. Rose pulled out her phone to text someone.

"Rose. We have a long drive, and I'm committed to getting you back in time for dinner. You can handle that in the car."

"It's Mia." Rose started a text and stepped outside.

She looked up from her phone to find Niall standing near her driver and Ben with his back to the vehicle facing the street. Niall flashed a quick smile and winked. Rose smiled back and tried to push down the warm feeling his sudden presence supplied. He was strong and sexy, and she liked having him around. She liked how he made a point of standing so close that she had to look up at him when they talked. She knew it was a power move, but she wasn't mad at him for that. And she liked how his constant hovering kept his brother in check. She wondered what it would have been like to have chosen him over Aedan.

Rose opened her mouth to say something witty but thought better of it. She closed her eyes to soak up the moment, allowing the sun to warm her skin. Suddenly, the sound of screeching tires, shots slicing through metal, and a crash pulled Rose out of her head. She saw a car jump the curve headed towards her. Another had crashed into parked cars across the street.

"Rose. Go to your car." The unexpected sound of Aedan's voice reverberated above the noise. He was running toward the car on the sidewalk.

Rose felt the force of Troy's body as he stepped in front of her, fending off some guy who bolted from the vehicle. It was a move they had practiced many times, and his signal to her that he was in control and would get her to safety. She moved away from Troy and the car. Within a second, Troy had the man on the ground and cuffed. He ushered her passed Niall, who had a masked guy on the ground at gunpoint. Aedan was on the opposite side of the vehicle, pulling someone out. Ben had his gun pointed at the occupants of the crashed car. Rose went to her car. The suited gentleman she recalled from the restaurant emerged and called to her.

"Hurry, Rose."

Rose was steps away from the car when she caught a glimpse of something to the right. A shot rang out as she saw Troy leap on a man. She could hear scuffling as she got into the car before the door closed.

"Are you okay, Ms. Ross?" the gentleman asked.

"Yes. I'm fine." Rose took in the chaotic sight outside the window, heard the sirens, and watched as police descended upon the scene in a matter of seconds. Then, she heard Niall call out.

"Take her, Troy. I'll deal with this."

The car door opened, and Troy got in. "Go," he yelled.

⚜

THE SMELL OF FRESH LAVENDER WAFTING THROUGH THE AIR, BIRDS chirping, and the warm sun on her skin briefly transported Rose's thoughts far away before the events of last night started to creep into her head. When she arrived home last night, tired and stressed, she'd confined herself to her room. She vaguely remembered Aedan sitting in a chair at her bedroom table, checking on her as she went in and out of consciousness after having taken something to help her sleep. She recalled him telling her that Niall was handling things with the authorities. Whenever Aedan stepped out and back in, she could see Troy's silhouette outside her door. She remembered closing her eyes one last time and opening them as the sun peeked into her room. Now, the sound of talking brought her back to her tablemates.

"That's a good question. I don't know why we haven't done this before now, Aedan. Maybe you should ask Rose. We seem to be following her lead," Niall said.

Rose focused and looked around the table. Niall, Aedan, and Troy watched her, waiting for a response.

"What? Uh, I don't know, guys. Now that I've seen you all in action, maybe I'll spend more time outside in the garden. Troy, what do you think?" She looked across the table at Troy. He pursed his lips and shook his head. "And there's your answer. But seriously, guys, what happened out there yesterday?"

"Some low life hoping to cash in," Aedan said.

"Troy had been tracking someone showing interest in you since you arrived. He's been able to keep your location off the radar until you arranged the warehouse trip. Once you told Aedan and me about it, I alerted Troy, but the information had already hit the dark web, so we got into position in case someone made an attempt."

"And they did," Rose said.

"And failed," Niall added.

"Rose, this is closer than any attempt to date. Are you sure you're okay?" Troy asked.

Rose squeezed her eyes shut, then opened them. "I don't know. I suppose time will tell. Like you said, I've never been through this before. I'm not sure what I'm supposed to feel. I think I slept off any leftover emotions. Yesterday felt like our training sessions but worse. I tried to keep my head from spinning and stay focused like you taught me," Rose confessed. She hated feeling out of control.

"It's okay, Rose. Nothing could prepare you for the real thing. You just have to let the training guide your actions. That's why Troy makes you practice maneuvers repeatedly, so you don't have to think in the moment. You just act," Niall said.

"Like second nature," Rose concurred.

"That's the idea," Aedan said.

"It was still scary. I didn't anticipate how loud it would be. There were a lot of shots fired. Did anyone get hurt?" Rose asked. Aedan looked at his brother, then at Rose. She got the feeling he didn't want to answer the question.

"I wounded the driver of the car that crashed. I needed to take it out of the equation. Ben fired strategic shots into the vehicle to make sure no one exited. That freed us to manage the second car without incident," Aedan explained, his eyes on Rose the entire time.

"And what are you not telling me?" Rose systematically looked around the table at Aedan, Niall, and finally Troy. "Troy?" Her question hung heavy in the air.

Troy touched his shoulder briefly, then returned his hand to his lap. "They were determined to get to you, Rose."

"He took a bullet for you," Niall blurted.

"A flesh wound." Troy's brows furrowed, turning to Niall and giving a stern look.

"Wait! What? You got shot, Troy?" Rose's eyes widened like saucers.

"It's fine, Rose. I'm here," Troy said with certainty.

"But I didn't even notice when you got in the car. It's all a blur. I-I—" Rose felt herself spiraling. She closed her eyes, forcing herself to hear what Troy had said: *I'm here*. She opened her eyes. "Thank you, Troy."

"It's not over, Rose," Troy said.

"You're safe for now. No one's going to attempt anything so soon. They may even give up. Everyone's in custody that attacked yesterday, and the authorities were able to trace and detain those involved in the dark web scheme, but—" Niall got interrupted.

"The source person—the one who alerted them to your location and the original mastermind—is still out there. Until we have those two, this is not over, Rose," Troy said.

"Tell me the plan, Troy," Rose urged, although she knew what came next.

"Continue your prep activities as normal. No unexpected changes to the schedule. Until you board your plane, someone will be by your side inside and outside any building. No exceptions. Preferably that means one of us at this table. We'll find them, Rose. Whatever it takes. We'll find them," Troy assured, trying to offer some semblance of peace of mind.

Rose looked around the table at her companions. As she caught each gaze, they nodded in response. She felt safe for the moment, but still had an exhibition to host and a pending board decision to await.

CHAPTER 16

Ladies and Gentlemen

"I owe you the truth in painting, and I will tell it to you."

— PAUL CÉZANNE, 1905

To say Rose was busy was an understatement the week fol-lowing her garden talk with the guys. She checked and double-checked every detail in preparation for the art show. Her duties required her to play the supportive friend to the brothers while they split their time between work, the house, and the hospital. The sudden need to reset Brianna's device came as a surprise to everyone. They anxiously awaited word on when she could return home and begin the healing process. Despite the double duty, Rose still had no closure on her relationship with Aedan. And as for Carol, the brothers made good on their com-mitment, and she conveniently and permanently disappeared after hav-ing stirred up so much trouble. On the other hand, Alejandro stayed true to his word and loyal to her, checking in once a week to let her know he was in her corner while she was miles away from home base.

Now, on her twenty-ninth day, Rose was on the verge of showcasing the culmination of several weeks of work and meticulous curating to art enthusiasts worldwide. She stood in the doorway and took a moment to take in the scene. Kris was in full glory as he bustled around, ensuring every item was in its place, that there wasn't a speck of dust anywhere, and that all the artists and celebrity staff were on their way. Everything was on point, including the gold-leaf programs she had printed with a picture of Brianna in honor of her work and the commissioned art pieces for guests. Rose was happy to see Niall partnering with Troy on security. She caught Niall's gaze across the room. He smiled and winked in response, which was her indicator that he was headed her way when he wrapped up the conversation with Troy. They had only known each other for a few weeks, but Rose was surprised how she and Niall could interpret each other's unspoken signals the way she'd seen him do with his brother.

"Niall, I can't believe the day is here," she expressed when he made his way over.

"You made it happen," Niall congratulated.

"It wasn't easy to get to this moment."

"You should be proud. Things have come together nicely. You make it seem so effortless."

"I'll be on edge until it's over."

"Well, just a few hours from now, you will host some of the most prestigious people in the art community. I predict your name will be on everyone's lips following this event."

"I can only hope you are right."

"Brace yourself."

"Niall, I wanted to—" Rose paused mid-sentence. Her phone flashed *RR* across the screen. She saw that Troy was still across the room, so she grabbed Niall's hand. "I have to take this. Will you?" Niall nodded and stepped outside with Rose so she could take her call. She hated needing an escort every second but agreed to Troy's heightened protocols.

"Hi, Dad," Rose greeted.

"Rose. I'm calling to wish you all the best on your exhibition tonight. People have been calling me all day asking why they weren't invited to the most exclusive event this year."

"What'd you tell them?"

"They need to know Rose Ross, and the best way to do that is by supporting her work with the foundation. I also said a five-million-dollar donation might get a meeting with you." She heard her dad laugh in the background.

"Dad," Rose protested.

"Rose, the real reason I called is to say congratulations. You have been selected as the next CEO."

Rose blinked, processing his words. "I didn't expect a decision this fast. What did they say about the contingency?"

"It was a tough decision. We went back and forth on the details, but the board approved your proposal to rebrand the company name. The press release goes out on Monday, naming you as my successor effective January first, and stating that I will begin transitioning my role. As part of your new role, you will also be named to the board of directors. Congratulations, Princess."

Rose closed her eyes and breathed in. When she exhaled, she opened her eyes to find Niall quietly watching with a half-smile on his face. Rose knew he had no idea what the call was about, but she wanted him to know. She wanted to shout the good news to him. Instead, Rose instinctively held a hand to her side, and Niall's hand filled hers.

"Dad, that's fantastic news. Thank you for being my mentor and the best dad ever."

"You make both easy. Congratulations again, Princess, and enjoy the rest of your day. We'll debrief when you're back. I love you."

"I love you," Rose said and ended the call. She looked up to Niall, who met her gaze with anticipation. "I've been named CEO. They agreed to the rebranding." She smiled at the thought of her new title. Then, a wave of nerves hit when she realized the transfer of power coming her way—the thing that made her dad one of the wealthiest men in the world and a household name. She closed her eyes.

"Are you okay?"

"Yes, just the weight of it all hit me suddenly," Rose confessed.

"You'll be an amazing CEO. Congratulations are in order, Night Owl. I suppose tonight is the last night I'll be able to say that. I'm not looking forward to saying goodbye."

"You don't have to. We can do business together now that I know your team's strengths. I wouldn't be here on several fronts if you weren't."

"I'm doing my job."

"You keep saying that. Your job is to protect my art. What are you not telling me?" Rose looked down. She forgot she had been holding Niall's hand. She loosened her grip to let go, but he laced his fingers through hers and tightened his grip.

"Just a second. I am going to kiss you before you completely disappear from my life to become the CEO of Ross Enterprises. Consider this my congratulations. Are you okay with that?" Rose nodded. Niall put his free hand around Rose's waist, drew her close, dipped his head, and pressed his lips to hers. She was surprised when he didn't try to open her mouth with his tongue the way he did in the past when they both felt unbridled passion. His kiss was tender, and in a few seconds, he released her, but not before she felt signs that his body wanted more.

"I see you haven't tamed the beast," she smiled wryly.

"Unfortunately, it's a natural by-product of having you around." Niall adjusted himself and led Rose back to the gallery.

A SPOTLIGHT IN THE NIGHT SKY VISIBLE FROM AS FAR AWAY AS THE next city reflecting the Sankofa symbol surrounded by a simple frame signaled guests they had arrived. The fairy lights wrapped around the row of dark hedges lit a path for the long line of luxury vehicles that led up to the building. Guests passed through several layers of security before being admitted to the art gallery.

Inside the foyer, guests received a glass of champagne. Rose stood at the opposite side of the room near the arched entry leading to the rotunda. She waited until the foyer was full of people before removing the velvet rope to provide access to the exhibition's first room.

"Here we go, guys," Rose told Troy and Kris. She stepped a few feet into the room and looked at the black sky through the dome windows.

The night sky juxtaposed with the white room illuminated by lights encircling the border where the walls touched the windows achieved its dramatic effect. The room was bare save for a single row of evenly spaced, small, black framed paintings surrounding the room. A card describing the image and bearing Natasha's name was neatly placed near each painting. The introduction label painted on the wall beside the entrance summarized the exhibition: "Out of Africa, Past, Present, Possibilities: Reaching back in time to bring forward this exact moment. This exhibition by Rose Ross explores the previously unacknowledged first Black Africans in Ireland and their contribution to its history and art. As reflected in the first painting, the symbol of Sankofa, a bird with its head facing backward and feet forward, represents how past artists influenced today's artists in this exhibition. The word Sankofa translates 'to go back and get.' Throughout the exhibition, you will see art representing historical events and a modern view presented by the artist today. And in this rotunda, the walls showcase the possibilities you hope to manifest. Each painting in this room is an artist's translation of your words in response to the question, 'What one thing would you bring forward from your past into your future?'"

Rose stood in the center of the room, flanked on either side by Troy and Kris, watching guests as they explored the paintings. The wait staff walked amongst the crowd serving hors d'oeuvre and refilling glasses. The atmosphere was lively. Soft jazz played in the background, and guests strolled around the room, viewing the art, while others surrounded Rose to make small talk.

"I suppose you know all our deep, dark, secret desires by now." A familiar female voice said from behind Rose. She turned around to face her friend, Mia, who air-kissed her.

"Only yours. That's because you're so predictable. But no, it's anonymous. I asked the team not to share anything with me until after the show. I wanted to experience everything like the patrons. It's so good to see you. You look amazing as always." Rose examined her friend.

"So do you. How are you holding up? I swear you outdid yourself with this. And in the timeline—You are a miracle worker."

"Thanks, Mia. It's been a whirlwind, but here we are."

"This is brilliant. I don't know how you do it. And…" Mia lifted her chin toward the entrance. "I see you've had plenty of distractions. I need details, but unfortunately, I fly out in a few hours. Promise we'll catch up when you get back to the States?"

Rose looked across the room to see what Mia was referencing. Niall was standing in the doorway. "Sure. Let's catch up next week. Dinner. My place. I'll cook. Now, go with Kris so you can get a sneak peek at the new art." Rose gestured to Kris, who came to collect Mia.

Rose watched as Niall walked across the room toward her. At the same time, her cell buzzed and flashed a green checkmark, signifying the last external guest had arrived.

"It's official. You have a full house. How do you feel?" Niall asked.

"It's surreal to see everything finally come to fruition. Even more so to know that I was able to pull together some of the most significant representations of art consolidated in one show." Rose closed her eyes and inhaled as she felt the weight of her words.

"This art show will be referenced for years to come. You've also brought together a pretty impressive guest list to witness it."

"I know I sound like a broken record, but thank you again, Niall. The lengths your team went to get this art here were extraordinary. My head is spinning just thinking about it."

"Glad to assist."

Niall's cell buzzed before he tapped his earpiece. Rose looked down at her phone, which was also buzzing. In her peripheral view, she saw Troy step toward her.

"Rose, sorry for the fire drill. You have an unregistered guest at the first checkpoint. I'll need you and Troy to accompany me for a minute," Niall said and led the way toward the door.

"I doubt anyone I know would show up unannounced, except my dad. Who is it?"

"A photo should be coming across your phone now." Niall kept walking.

"It's Alejandro," Troy said.

"Are you expecting him?" Niall asked.

Rose shook her head. "Not at all. But let him through."

"The element of surprise seems to be his modus operandi," Niall said.

"There is no point in arguing with you on this one. Let's go." Together, they went to the entrance to wait for Alejandro's arrival. Niall had to bypass security with his bio-signature, then Troy, and finally, Rose.

"May I?" Alejandro walked over to Rose with outstretched hands, oblivious to the scene he had caused.

"I'm always amazed how you randomly show up as if it were Wednesday in Wyoming." Rose leaned forward a little to let him hug her. She would not be distracted by his sexy as sin, stop-me-in-my-tracks smile. "I'm delighted to see you, but I thought you had business to attend back in the States. What happened?"

"I know how important the show is for you. I couldn't see you doing this without friends by your side."

Annoyed as she was, Rose couldn't be mad at him for that. "Welcome. Having you here is a wonderful surprise. Please, take the time to meet the artist and enjoy the show. I have a few things to take care of and will catch up with you shortly."

Rose and her entourage walked toward the gallery floor. The guests mingled, talked, walked around, viewed the art, and searched for their inspired pieces. "Councilman. I'm shocked by your tenderness. It's quite unexpected," Rose overheard someone say about a painting, indicating the exhibit had the intended effect on the guest. Rose looked around the room to discover someone was noticeably absent. She gestured to Niall and Kamal to follow her to the gallery office.

"Is everything okay? How can I help?" Niall asked.

"Yes, in a moment, I'd like to open the show formally. But it appears everyone is here except your brother. I know I saw him earlier. Did he leave?"

"Aedan went to the hospital to fix the live feed to the show for Brianna. It's working now. He should be here momentarily. Give him a few minutes."

"Great. During the opening welcome speech, I want to recognize Brianna. It would be good to have an update to know what tone to set. Hopefully, he'll show soon."

"He will. We should get back to your guests." Niall placed his hand on the small of her back, led her to the gallery with Kamal in tow, and then resumed his duties.

Rose gave Kamal final instructions. She found Kris and ran through the room opening sequence once more. By the time she finished, Niall was signaling her to join him across the room. He informed her that Aedan had arrived, and that Brianna was stable and on the path to recovery. Rose breathed a sigh of relief, straightened her dress, smoothed her hair, and then re-took her place next to Kamal, anxiously awaiting the cue to start. Rose looked into the crowd and caught a glimpse of Aedan as he appeared in the entryway. He grabbed her gaze with a look that was a mix of duty and desire, and Rose smiled, then exhaled.

"Kamal—" Rose started to signal Kamal to begin the show but looked back to Aedan when she saw someone walk into the entrance near him. Her eyes darted between him and the woman who appeared.

She could tell Aedan was unaware of the situation. Confusion washed over her face. "Troy," she called out. "Is that who I think it is… Brianna? God, no, it's—" Before she could finish her statement, Troy's hand was in front of her, guiding her behind him. She caught a glimpse of Aedan as he turned, following her eyes to the entrance.

"It's Carol. Follow me," Troy said, charging toward the door without alerting the guests. By the time they reached the other side, Aedan had escorted Carol out. When Rose got to Carol, she was flanked on either side by the brothers and Ben.

"What are you doing here? How did you—" Rose heard Aedan say.

"Get in?" Carol smirked and held up a program. "Everyone always said I could pass for Brianna. Who's gonna keep her from her own event at her house, for Christ's sake?" she laughed.

"What the hell are you doing?" Rose tried to push past Troy, but his powerful arm wouldn't allow her to get close enough to Carol.

"Before my dear cousin here pushed me out the door, I was about to educate your guests on why looking back on the past is a mistake. I believe the government changes I proposed will make a stronger future Ireland," Carol said with conviction.

"Enough, Carol," Aedan exclaimed. "Ben, have your men take her to the authorities." Aedan took Carol by the wrist and handed her to Ben. Ben started walking away with Carol.

"Oh, don't think this is over," Carol called over her shoulders. "I know I'm not the only one looking for you."

"Ignore her, Rose. She's done on several fronts. Ben's got this," Troy assured.

"You need to get back to your guests," Niall said.

"Niall, make sure the gallery is secure. Prep Kamal that the show's about to start. Troy, give me a minute with Rose, please." Aedan turned to Rose and cupped her face with his hands. "Are you okay?"

The feeling that the world was closing in on her fell away at the touch of Aedan's hands. Troy, Niall, and Aedan were right. She needed to pull it together and get back to her guests. She remembered what Niall told her about allowing her training to kick in—to guide her. She had everything within her at that moment to move forward. She always had.

Rose nodded. She closed her eyes, took a couple of deep breaths, then opened them. "I'm good."

"Tell me what you need," Aedan urged.

"Just this." Rose looked into his eyes, stealing strength from his stare. "A chance to catch my breath. Let's go."

⁘

BACK INSIDE, ROSE LOCATED KRIS AND KAMAL IN THE CENTER OF the room. The guests were busy just as they had been before she left, oblivious to the situation with Carol. Rose tapped Kamal on the shoulder. "I'm ready," she told him.

"Then, I guess it's showtime," Kamal whispered.

Kamal stepped in front of the microphone. The spotlight was on him. The music lowered, and a hush went over the room. "Patrons. Welcome to the Morrison Art Gallery and the Northern Ireland Patron of the Arts Annual Exhibition. This year's theme is Out of Africa, Past, Present, Possibilities: Reaching back in time to bring forward this exact moment. And, in a moment, I would like to bring to the stage a young lady who spent much of her life dedicated to learning, curating, and educating the world about art and its long history. Her name is synonymous with art history for her commitment to making art more accessible to everyone. Ladies and gentlemen, without further ado, I give you the founder of the Roselyn Ross Foundation, owner of the Rose Ross Art Gallery, which bears her name. She is this year's exhibit creator, curator, and hostess for tonight. Please join me in welcoming the incomparable Roselyn Ross." Kamal stepped aside, allowing Rose to approach the microphone and address the crowd. Everyone clapped, but the room went quiet when Rose began her welcome speech.

"Thank you, everyone, for coming. I want to say a few words before we open the doors to the rest of the exhibition. I am excited to be here today, yet humbled to have been asked to curate this event. About a year ago, I was hosting an art show at my gallery in San Francisco when a dear friend of mine, a serious patron of the arts and a person who happens to be here today, Mia Monroe, came to me with an idea. Mia, please wave to the crowd." Mia, standing behind Rose, took a step forward and waved. "Well, that night after my show, Mia invited me for a drink to talk about life and goals, and mainly to catch up. But during that conversation, Mia spoke about the incredible art scene in Belfast. That conversation introduced me to Brianna Morrison's effort to bring the arts front and center to the people in Northern Ireland. By the time we finished our conversation, I was probably a little tipsy." The audience laughed. "Well, to be honest, a little more than tipsy, but most certainly impressed by what Mia had shared with me. I told her that night I had to meet Brianna. Fast forward two months and several video conferences later, not only had I met Brianna virtually, but Brianna asked if I could curate and manage her next annual Northern Ireland

Patron of the Arts show. Of course, I wanted to say yes right away, but I didn't want to appear overly anxious, knowing this was one of the most prestigious showings in all of Europe. So, I asked her to give me a day to respond. That was the most productive and informative twenty-four hours I have ever spent. To say I researched everything about Brianna is an understatement. This woman changed people's lives through the work she was doing. I knew I had to produce her next show right then, and when we talked again, I said yes. I think I even impressed her a little with my newfound knowledge. She, too, was sold. Fast forward several months, I got another call from Brianna letting me know that not only did she want me to produce her show but that I had carte blanche to do whatever I wanted, including reimagining the event. And in her request, she asked that I do something that has never been attempted in Europe before." Rose took a deep breath, then continued. "I was up for the challenge. However, what I didn't know at the time, which I learned later through subsequent conversations, was that Brianna was not well and had carefully selected me as her delegate. It was a position she had never bestowed on anyone in the history of her art foundation. Please know that I did not take on this great role lightly. Every week and up to this moment, I have dedicated my time to ensure I pay tribute to the art world in every detail. Every moment we share this evening is a culmination of that. Friends, let me just say that Brianna is not here today because she is in the hospital recovering from a condition trying to dim her spirit. I'm here today representing her and want you to know that her spirits are up, and she is on the path to recovery. This show is dedicated to Brianna and her efforts to enlighten us about the world's greatest art and artists. This show is dedicated to all the influencers whose works you'll see on the wall, both living and not, who allow us to experience their dreams and pave the way for us to create new visions, and visual stories to share with others. May your eyes see through the lens of the artist's interpretation of their world on canvas. When I was a child, I saw many pictures and works of art. But it wasn't until I went to see the King Tutankhamun exhibition at the museum of modern art and looked right into the eyes of the figure painted on pottery, on gold, and on the walls of the tombs did I understand the beauty of those creations. It was the day my eyes opened to art and its expressions of life. I say this to let you know that my early influences were those unknown artists from several thousand years ago, who created images depicting life in the afterworld for the pharaohs. I chose the symbol and word *Sankofa* to bring the language and wisdom of my ancestors forward to the future. In the next room of this exhibition, each of our featured artists represents works of the present. Alongside their art is the art of others that awakened them—their influencers. Look around. Each piece of art encircling us now is unique to a person in this room. Before you leave tonight, you will be allowed to collect your art piece and, with it, the potential to manifest your desires. Now, please turn your attention to the door opposite the entrance." Rose gestured toward the inner gallery, and everyone turned. The adjacent room was dark; however, the main gallery was fully lit, giving everyone direct sight to a dark, steel blue wall with one item hanging on it—the playbill that previously hung in the main house.

"Housed in that room is the art that tells the story of the first Africans in Ireland—a story that everyone here is responsible for bringing forward to future generations. So, everyone, let me welcome you to the twentieth annual Northern Ireland Patron of the Arts exhibition. May your eyes be opened to new possibilities. May you find or rediscover your influences, and most of all, may your senses be so overwhelmed with beauty that you spread the word about the importance of art in our communities wherever you go. On behalf of Brianna, her family, and the Rose Ross Art Gallery team, welcome! Please enjoy the show."

The crowd cheered, and the music started. Rose took a moment to nod toward Troy and Niall, who were at her side. "This is it," she whispered as the guests circled her.

CHAPTER 17

You Don't Know What Love Is

"Love is the whole thing. We are only pieces."

— RUMI

ROSE ATTEMPTED TO SCAN THE ROOM FOR HER ENTOURAGE, BUT THE swirl of people circling and vying for her attention prevented her from doing so. People congratulated her, asked her to autograph their invites, and others wanted to talk about art. She did her best to give each person who approached her attention. It took a while, but the crowd surrounding Rose finally dissipated, and she used the opportunity to catch her breath. Niall, who had been standing guard, broke his silence.

"That was a beautiful welcome speech. Brianna would certainly be proud."

"I tried to speak from my heart. Although it took a second to pull myself together, following your cousin's stunt."

"You did fine. Forget about Carol. She's being dealt with."

"You're right. Focus on the here and now."

"This is quite the crowd. You've done a great job connecting with everyone. How do you feel about the show?" Niall scanned the room for a second, then locked eyes with Rose. As much as his focus and attention annoyed her at first, she had come to appreciate that he always made her feel she was the only one in the room when he held her gaze. It was the one thing she would miss most about him when she left tomorrow.

"I only make it look easy. But I feel okay. Relieved. You should be relieved about Brianna, too."

"I am. It makes working tonight a little easier. I only wish she could have been here to see it."

"I'm hoping Brianna was able to watch the live stream your brother set up. If she didn't, my team is putting together a summary on the website. Kamal is also writing an article, plus he's airing a special segment on his show next week featuring video highlights of the event."

"That all sounds fantastic." He reached his hand out to Rose, and she took it. "Watching you work solidifies everything I love about you. Speaking of work, I hate to leave you, but I must return to my duties. Besides, you have company coming." Niall took a step forward and kissed her forehead.

"Later, Niall."

As Niall disappeared into the crowd, Alejandro took his place beside Rose. She looked up at him and smiled. "You're such a wonderful wild card showing up like this."

"I'm sure you knew deep down I could not miss this event."

"Maybe. So, what do you think so far?"

"Seriously?"

"Yes. What do you think?" She could always count on him for an unabridged opinion.

"I believe you've outdone yourself and anyone else, for that matter. Well done!"

"A little heavy on the personal bias, but I'll take it."

"No. Alejandro is telling the truth," Aedan's deep, melodic voice came from behind Rose.

"Aedan. I thought I saw you looking at the art across the room," Rose said.

Aedan opened his hand to her in a familiar gesture, and this time when she took it, he dipped his head and pressed his lips to hers. Rose swallowed a smile, uncertain about Aedan's renewed interest in her or whether he was just marking his territory.

"I was but couldn't resist the opportunity to pass along my compliments before the crowd descends upon you again. You've done a fantastic job. There are no details left without your signature."

"I still have a way to go before this is over, but I'll take both your compliments," Rose said.

"Rose, I was wondering if I could get a few minutes to chat with you alone?" Aedan turned to Alejandro. "I hope you don't mind, man. It will only be a few minutes."

"Sure. Rose, are you okay?" Alejandro looked at Rose and waited for her acknowledgment.

"Alejandro, I'll catch up with you shortly." Alejandro nodded and left. "Okay, Aedan, you have me alone."

"Sorry about earlier. Are you okay?"

"I'm okay. I know everything is being dealt with."

"Rose, the last several weeks have been nothing short of tragic—at least for me." Rose's face was expressionless, waiting for Aedan to make his point and unsure of the direction he was headed. "I got wrapped up in some misplaced loyalty and let it get in the way of us. I don't remember when it happened, but I messed up. I—" He paused a second and circled the back of her hand with his thumbs. "I let you slip right out of my hands. I had complete control to change the situation, but I didn't act. Instead, I withdrew. I kept silent. Several times, you held out a forgiving hand, and I couldn't take it. I couldn't bite back my need to be in control. To do what I've always done. All the while, you remained true to yourself despite my behavior. In my family's hour of need, when Brianna went critically ill, you stepped in to help my brother and me. You did it knowing you were under no obligation to do so. You did nothing wrong. It was all me. I was wrong to pretend I didn't care. I apologize for the things I did and didn't do. I hope you can forgive me."

"Aedan. Stop. I know how difficult it is for a man like you to tell me those things. You have no idea how long I waited to hear you say *I'm sorry*. But now that you've said it, I realize it's not enough." Rose looked around to ensure no one was eavesdropping on their conversation. "Can we step in here for a moment?" Rose pointed toward two open, black curtains leading to the dark screening room exhibit, which had one bench in the middle of the room. Aedan nodded and held her hand as they walked into the room and stood in the back corner.

"Rose. I'm sorry."

"Aedan, I know you stepped in and rectified the situation, but would you have done that if I hadn't said anything or if I weren't Black?"

A video projected on the wall showed people painting the side of a white house with black lettering. The voice-over was of an Irish-accented woman citing a poem as a woman humming a tune played in the background. "No blacks. No dogs. No Irish," the artist said on the soundtrack.

"I would have said something to Carol." Aedan turned briefly to look at the screen, recognizing the video.

"You would have said something to protect your family from ridicule, not because it was wrong. Don't you see your inaction allows racism to be normalized? You can't turn a blind eye to injustice. You have to stand up for the marginalized. This is not about family loyalty. It's about everything you and I discussed during our holiday in Dublin. About this." She pointed to the video on the screen. "Don't you understand that you need to stand for something? People like us don't have an option to not act against injustice. And when you care for someone, you protect them. And when they're wrong, you let them know. And hopefully, they'll course correct."

"I understand. Rose, I made a mistake and realized the extent when I went up against the media outlet. I know I'll never experience certain things because of who I am and what my privilege brings. I am committed to doing better moving forward." Aedan held both her hands and her gaze. "I'm asking you to believe me and to forgive me."

Rose looked deep into Aedan's eyes, which were the color of the midnight ocean in the absence of light. She could sense his desire to have her back entirely, hear the sincerity behind his words, and feel his heat summoning her as he drew her close.

"I forgave you a while back, but I was waiting for proof you realized the breadth of your error. I've seen the things you've done to show me that you understand." Rose reached up to push away a strand of stray hair from Aedan's face. The simple gesture triggered a reaction in Aedan, and in one motion, he dipped his head, pressed his lips to hers, and kissed Rose with unfettered passion. Rose immersed herself in the kiss but pulled away when the singer humming the tune on the video ended, and the credits rolled.

"Aedan, I have guests. And you need to walk that off." Rose gestured to the evidence of his desire. "And I didn't say I'd jump back into a thing with you." Although his kiss made her want to do just that. She needed to think carefully about her next step. Aedan pulled her body to his.

"I'm making sure...."

"I know. You're making sure I know that you want me. I had started to doubt that. I'm sure you can understand why. But I need to get back to my guests, and you need to take care of this." She lowered her hand between them. "We can talk later after the guests are gone. Maybe we can grab some tea afterward?"

"Sure. I will find you later in the house."

"Then it's settled," she said, leaving the screening room to rejoin the rest of her team and guests. Alejandro wasn't too far behind and joined her when she went to take pictures with the artists.

"Everything alright? Seemed like Aedan needed more than a few minutes."

"Yes. I'm okay, Alejandro. Why? I don't look okay?"

"Quite the opposite. You're beautiful. Smile." He gestured for Rose to turn toward a photographer who snapped a photo.

"I don't know why I'm telling you this, but Aedan said he wants to be with me." Rose looked at the camera and smiled.

"I thought you were exploring him during your time in Belfast. Are you saying you're considering something more?"

"Nothing has been decided."

Alejandro put his hand up, signaling the photographer to pause, and stepped aside with Rose. "Rose. Let's be clear. I love you more than just a friend. I may not have said it in those words before, but I stepped aside at your request several weeks ago to allow you to figure out what you wanted to do. I love every ounce of you and have for many years now. It took me a while to put a name to my feelings, but if you decide to be with me, you know I'm one hundred percent committed to you. I promise to stand by you unconditionally as a friend, lover, or husband—whatever way you'll have me. That will never change."

She kissed Alejandro on the cheek. "I may have misread your intentions, but I am clear on your feelings. I don't doubt anything you're telling me." Rose squinted her eyes and pressed her lips together.

"What's that look about?"

"I have a lot to think about, wouldn't you agree? Normally, I'd be overwhelmed by everything, but now, I'm going to take my time to think through my options."

"No pressure from me. I'll never be too far away whenever you decide what you want to do."

"So, when are you flying out?"

"Tomorrow morning. I'm only here to attend your event."

"I'm cleared to fly out tomorrow night. I am grateful you came to support me. If it's okay with you, let's catch up after the crowd thins out."

Rose continued making her way around the event, completing her photoshoot list, and even squeezed in time to dance with Kris, who was decked out in his purple embroidered jacket and matching purple pants. Troy's ever-watchful eye was tracking Rose's every mood and movement. Niall was intermittently in and out of the event due to his responsibility for overall security. He briefly took a few minutes break, enough time for Rose to share that his brother had come to make amends with her. Niall wasn't surprised and was happy that Rose felt relief.

His parting words to her were, "I'm waiting for that look to be mine."

Rose smiled back at him before slipping into the private office while Kamal engaged the guests with art trivia. "Okay, patrons, you just saw his portrait in the other room. What was Tony Small known for?" Rose heard Kamal ask the crowd.

"Come on, Troy," she said. Troy followed her in.

"You've already had a full night, and it's not over yet."

"Troy, it's been a whirlwind. The Carol situation was a hot mess."

"She's being dealt with. You'll never see her again."

"Thank God."

"The art patrons are circling, but it appears your male constituents are circling even harder."

"You saw that?"

"You know I don't miss anything."

"They're getting serious about their intentions."

"And that's not what you wanted?"

"No. That wasn't my intent coming to Belfast."

"I admit it all seems to be coming at you pretty fast. However, it doesn't mean you have to act on it. Stay focused. There's a time for everything. Even distractions."

"You're right. I just need to get through tonight. But I don't want to lose the right person in the process."

"You can't lose something that isn't yours. Whatever is yours is yours."

"Look at you getting all philosophical. But seriously, Troy. I need you to do something."

"Tell me."

"I may need to go into the city after the art show later tonight. I realize it's not on the agenda, but I need you to take me."

"Do I need to send a team ahead? I am assuming this has nothing to do with the event."

"That's what you need to tell me. After Carol's stunt and all the other stuff, I don't know. I figure as long as I have you, I'm good."

"Planning to be out late?"

"Possibly."

"Overnight?"

"We'll see."

CHAPTER 18

Breathless

"When you reach the end of what you should know, you
will be at the beginning of what you should sense."

– KAHLIL GIBRÁN, *Sand and Foam*

AFTER THE GUESTS LEFT, ONLY ROSE'S INNER CIRCLE REMAINED. NIall was outside with his team ensuring everyone cleared the property. Kris, not wasting any time, was in the office packing. Aedan was in the office on a call with the doctor to get an update on his sister. Previously buzzing with people, the gallery was quiet and empty except for Rose and Alejandro. Rose used the quiet time to reflect on the night's events as they strolled around the gallery to get a closer look at the paintings.

"So, Alejandro, what do you think about the show? It's hard to fathom that it's over," Rose said.

"I'm so proud of you. I can only imagine the sense of relief you must feel."

"I didn't tell you about the crisis we had."

"Niall briefed me. I figured you'd tell me when you were ready," Alejandro said.

"She's not worth a second breath. It's strange, you know, when you put so much energy and time into something, and it's all over in a matter of hours. And you see the results of your work, but it all went by so fast. I remember the first day I walked into this building and every little change I made to get to this point."

"Everyone can tell you put your heart and soul into the event. Tonight, you created something your guests will remember forever."

"You're biased, but I like the sound of that." Rose turned away from the painting to look at Alejandro. His pointed gaze and absence of a smile told her he wasn't bullshitting. She knew Alejandro was not in the habit of placating people because his reputation was built on his word.

"Was it everything you expected it to be?"

"It was better than I had envisioned, but you never know how it resonates with others. Their reaction is nothing I could have predicted. Speaking of unpredictable, I hardly expected to see you, but I'm grateful you made the trip."

"Does that mean you've forgiven me from my last trip?"

"This is still a wild stunt you pulled. But maybe," she said, leaning toward a painting to get a better look. "You know my friend, Mia, bought this piece tonight. I hope you got a chance to meet her. She's a lovely lady."

"We talked briefly. I see why you two are so close. Mia said something about having a flight to catch."

"Mia has great taste—look at the vibrant use of colors set against the gray backdrop," she said, pointing. "You know we sold every piece showcased tonight."

"What's left for you to do now that this is over?"

"Here? Not much, really. I saw Kris packing up. I have a few things to gather and some clothes to pack, then head back to the States. Why?"

"Why don't you fly out with me in the morning?"

"There are some things I want to do before I leave. Besides, Troy banned me from commercial flights."

"One phone call can get you an earlier clearance, and we can fly private together. Troy can't complain about that."

"Actually, no. It is a beautiful sentiment, but I planned my schedule this way for a reason. Besides, I want to see if they'll let me in to see Brianna." She stepped away from the painting and walked around Alejandro, avoiding his gaze. Avoiding his seductive smile.

"It's a long flight. I just thought you'd like company. I know I would." Alejandro turned away from the painting to face Rose.

"Let's make the best of our time together now. If you didn't want to fly alone, you should have left with Mia."

"You know my thing is for you. Do you think you can drop by later for a nightcap? I can wait for you to finish or pick you up later if you'd like."

"You're persistent in pushing this agenda, aren't you? Maybe I'll pop by for one drink, but don't quote me. And I don't need a ride," Rose said.

"Fair enough. I don't want to inconvenience you, but I would love to see you if you can make it. Otherwise, I guess I'll wait until one of my trips to the Bay area."

"You never answered my question, you know."

"What question was that?"

"I asked you a few weeks ago, why here, and why now?" Rose watched as Alejandro's lips formed a straight line across his face, not smiling and not frowning. She knew the look.

"That's simple. You." Rose shot him a *no-shit Sherlock* look. Alejandro put up his hands in mock surrender. "Before you say it, it's a fact. I'm here because of you. Troy alerted your dad shortly after your arrival of a credible threat. With the pending board decision and the significance of your upcoming exhibit, your father demanded more protection for you. Since no one in the company could know, and to avoid a leak to shareholders, I offered to come here and make additional arrangements; selfishly, I wanted to see you again. That's the truth of it."

"You said you had clients here. Did Troy know about any of this?"

"I do have clients here. No, Troy won't know until after the contract expires or unless you tell him now that you know."

"Who else knows about this? Is your agreement with the brothers?"

"That's not my story to tell."

"It is if you value what we have. Your choice." Rose didn't know what to think about this new information. It wasn't her dad's first time inserting himself into her affairs. She knew he was protecting her as well as his best interest. There was no separating the two. But the thought of the brothers being in on it confused her. Rose needed to think hard about her next move.

"Niall structured and executed the agreement." And there it was. Rose flashed back on every instance when she told Niall looking after her was not his job, and he went silent or redirected the conversation. He never lied to her, but now she had her answer to why he dialed back the charm. She wondered if Marina was still in the picture.

"Let me guess, he signed under his own entity, not Aedan's."

Alejandro briefly touched his hand to hers. "Rose, before you light into anyone, think about what I've told you. Clearly, we all care for you. You can't blame anyone for that."

Rose took a deep breath and processed Alejandro's words. She hated to admit he was right. He was her voice of reason, and this situation was bigger than her.

"Seems I made my choice, and this is what comes with it, but it doesn't mean it doesn't sting all the same. And I won't be the one to tell Troy about this. You owe it to him to have that discussion as soon as possible."

"I'll call him tomorrow. I suppose, on that note, I should be going now. Have you changed your mind yet about coming with me?" He dipped his head to kiss her cheek.

"Let me walk you out."

⁂

THE NIGHT WAS STILL YOUNG, AND ROSE HAD A LOT OF INFORMATION to process. Pent up with restless energy, she tossed a pair of stilettos in one of her many bags sprawled across the couch in her bedroom. It is not how she wanted to spend the night following her exhibition, but she needed to digest Alejandro's revelation. Stepping away from her luggage, hands on her hips in a Wonder Woman pose, Rose looked around the room. *I need a drink to get through this*, she told herself and headed towards the door. Unbeknownst to her, Aedan was on the other side. She hesitated a second when she saw him.

"I'm sorry. I didn't mean to startle you."

"It's okay. I was just about to head down for a drink."

"I was about to go to the city, but I remembered I owe you that tea, so I came to see if we were still on for our chat."

"Were you headed home or just out on the town for a while?"

"I was headed home. Join me for a drink before I leave, will you?"

"Sure, but I need something stronger than tea after tonight's events." Rose closed the door behind her in a failed attempt to conceal her mess.

"I'll make you something to drink in the downstairs library."

"Sure."

They both made their way into the large room Rose had become familiar with during her stay. She sat in front of the unlit fireplace while Aedan filled two glasses with whiskey and handed one to Rose. She inhaled and reflected on the fun, sexy, and profound conversations that previously took place in front of the fireplace during her brief time in Belfast.

"To an amazing exhibition. Cheers." Aedan took the seat next to her and clinked his glass to hers.

"Sláinte." Rose took a sip of her drink. "I am ecstatic to hear Brianna is on her way to recovering soon. It was a terrible scare for all of us. I was hoping to see her before I left. Do you think they'll allow me in?"

"They're still only allowing family, but I'll call the hospital in the morning to ensure they let you see her. She still has a way to go, but it seems the worst is over. I plan to keep a close watch on her, so that's part of why I'll be staying in town for the time being until she leaves the hospital."

"That makes sense."

"And I realize you won't need me here after tomorrow. I did plan to drop by after my visit with Brianna to see you off."

"That sounds so final."

"That's not my intention."

"I wish you were clearer with your intentions. Don't forget, playing the I-don't-feel-anything-chairman-of-the-board act got you where you are right now. Maybe a different approach might help this time." Rose swirled an ice cube in her glass.

"Like?"

"Just talk to me. I'm the woman you've been sleeping with who's about to get on a plane and leave tomorrow. Tell me what you're thinking, Aedan. I can handle it."

"Then let's talk about that. When you talk like that, I want to get you home and give you something you'll feel well into next week. I can't get enough of you, Rose. You saw evidence of that when I kissed you tonight. I told you in Dublin that I want you in my life and bed. Nothing has changed, Rose."

Rose crossed her legs to contain the involuntary throbbing she felt at the thought of Aedan giving her something to remember. She knew from personal experience he could make good on his promise.

"I'll admit. I felt that kiss tonight, and the old me would say, take me upstairs right now and make me feel you into next week. Because you do give good love." Rose closed her eyes and opened them again. "But as much as I want to feel you in me and forget about everything, I can't, Aedan. You and I have been on this delicate dance getting to know each other since my second day here. For a while, we seemed to be, as you would say, getting along brilliantly. No commitments. Then things evolved in more ways than one. And for a minute, I was wrapped up in the newness of you. I got caught up in the challenge of having you and got distracted. It happened so fast that when we went off the rails, it jolted me back to reality and allowed me to refocus on my original purpose for being here." She took a sip of her drink.

"I could have prevented us from derailing, but—"

Rose held up an index finger. "It gave me the time to reflect on the situation and get my head out of the clouds. I'm not saying I regret anything about us or where we were headed. I was having a good time. You're a powerful man, and I like that. But, when you pulled away, it allowed me to come up for air, and in doing so, I saw another side of you that I had to sort out. When you owned up to your mistake, that showed me a deeper level of you. We talked about this very thing during my first week. I didn't plan on having a long-distance relationship. At the time, I was okay with the short term and walking away after thirty days. Something I saw in you made me rethink that, so, I opened myself up to the possibility of… more."

"That sounds encouraging," Aedan said.

"I'm trying to say that I need a little more time to figure out whether you and I are right together. Or you can take me upstairs, give me the fuck of my life, and walk away."

Rose watched Aedan cringe. "I deserved that."

"That's not all. I want to know what this *thing* is with you and Alejandro."

"You mean when I kissed you? I told you. I'm making sure you know I want you and can give you what you need. You don't need to go anywhere else for that."

"Not that." Rose shook her head. "Your security agreement."

"Alejandro told you?"

"Yes."

"Then, I'm sure you have the whole story. You can't fault me for protecting you. I've been transparent with you all along that where you go, my team goes. That's been the situation regardless of the agreement. And you've made it clear you don't want to know what's happening behind the scenes. You can't have it both ways, Rose. It doesn't work like that." Rose bit her tongue. She didn't want to admit he had a point. The image of the failed attempt flashed in her mind. She recalled how in control Aedan was when he called her name and instructed her to get to safety. The tactical advantage he orchestrated in mere seconds saved her life. This was not her domain. Not her battle. And it wasn't over.

"You're right. I'm sorry. But I still need to think about us."

"And I'm okay with that. But while you're thinking about us, I'd like to give you something else to consider."

"Not that again." Rose shook her head.

"No, but I'm glad it's on your mind." He flashed a sudden grin. "I was going to say that Brianna is in for a slow recovery. She has several commitments through the Foundation to work with disadvantaged students in the final stretch of learning art curation, including accompanying them to museums. She would love it if you represented her for the four-week commitment. The sessions are only on Saturdays, and the students were chosen from around the globe to participate. It would mean you would need to return to Belfast before the end of summer. There is also the potential to fill in for Brianna at a few other key events dependent upon her recovery. You would have a full range of the house while you are here. Tell me you'll consider."

"That's a big commitment, and with my recent appointment to CEO of Ross Enterprises plus my foundation work, I will have to dial back on the number of art commitments in the US until she's better." Rose flipped through the calendar on her phone. "There are some things I can postpone to make the timeline work, but I can't be sure until I contact a few people. Let me get back to you."

"The fact that you're willing to rearrange things is a start. You can take up some office space in my building to run Ross Enterprises from here. I'd love it if you could let me know as soon as you decide. It would mean a lot to her and me if you could do this."

"I'll talk with Alejandro about the potential of setting up an entity here. This could be a win-win for me to expand the company footprint as part of the rebranding. I'll let you know. You said you were heading back to the city. May I ask what time?"

"My things are in the car. I'm heading out following our discussion. Of course, I had hoped you'd join me."

"Don't write me off yet."

"I'm not. I'm waiting for you to make the next move."

"It's getting late. I feel all talked out and need to process everything, plus I have tons to do before I leave. If you need to head out, don't change your plans on my behalf. Troy is here amongst all the other security people. If I need you, I know where to find you." Aedan stood and reached a hand down to Rose. She stood and combed her fingers through his hair. "You need a trim. But seriously, you'll know where we stand before I leave." Rose leaned in and pressed her lips to his. He was sweet and familiar, and she missed the fire she felt inside when they were together. His hands wrapped around her hips, pulling her close until her body molded to his desire rising against her. Instinctively, Rose wrapped her arms around his neck, held him tight for a moment, then slowly pulled away from the kiss. The niggling feeling of being distracted was overwhelming. Her heart started racing. She needed to get away to think. To get perspective. To breathe.

"I missed this," Aedan whispered in her ear.

"It's been a while. A few days and a couple of words change things. You should get going now, Aedan."

"I understand. Remember, if you need anything—"

She stopped him before he turned to leave. "Aedan."

"Did you think of something?"

"Have you seen Niall? I want to thank him again for his help. He and his team were fantastic. That's not news to you, but I couldn't have pulled off my last-minute changes without him."

"He should be at the loft by now."

"I didn't realize he was also heading home tonight."

"After he wrapped up here, he went to the hospital to visit Brianna and planned to go home afterward. If you need him here, I can—"

"Don't bother. I just wanted to say thank you. Oh, and Aedan."

"Rose."

"I miss this, too." She waved her index finger between the two of them.

"Goodnight, Rose."

⚶

THIRTY MINUTES AND TWO DRINKS LATER, ROSE WAS STILL SITTING in front of the fireplace when Troy intervened. He reminded her of her dad's imposing figure standing in the doorway. As a child, when she was in trouble for something or a serious talk was in order, her father would stand quietly at the door until she sensed his presence. Then, he would talk until they had dissected the situation and resolved why she did what she did and how she planned to rectify it. And now, although she wasn't in trouble, she was at a crossroads. Could she do everything she wanted and make a relationship work this time?

"Come in, Troy. Join me for a minute."

"I have news," Troy announced.

"News? Is Brianna okay?"

"Not about Brianna. We got the person, Rose."

"What? How?"

"When Carol made that statement about it not being over, that made her a suspect. The authorities seized her phone and computer; someone had been monitoring her activities because they couldn't access yours."

"Because my digital footprint is hidden for my protection."

"Right. Carol confirmed someone reached out to her, but by then, she had already been asked to leave by the brothers."

"So, she was going to help them. This is unbelievable. Do Aedan and Niall know?"

"They will shortly. The authorities will brief them."

"Then, without her, how did they find me?

"The warehouse. Without access to you, they were forced to expand their efforts and put out digital trackers to places you might leverage for your exhibition. General contractors, suppliers, etcetera. It was hardly likely for you to turn up in a paint store, but when one of the trades put in your commissioned art order, it came up on their radar, and they put a tracker on Natasha, unbeknownst to her. They knew she was expecting a visit from you and waited."

"It was too late by the time I told the brothers, and the information was already out there."

"Exactly."

"Jesus. I had no idea. Oh god, am I in the clear now?"

"Yes. There's a sting happening halfway across the globe as we speak. When you wake up, this will be done and over."

Rose blew out a breath and downed the last bit of her drink. "What a day. Thank God it's over. Where's the team?"

"Niall's team is already in flight returning the priceless treasures to their owners. Kris has all our gallery items packed and ready to go. We are set for a nine o'clock pick-up tomorrow, and the rest of the paintings are wrapped and ready to ship to their new owners. We just have your things here to pack up."

"In addition to solving crimes, sounds like you've all been extremely busy."

"We didn't want to wait until the last minute, which brings me to you. Rose, I realize you have a lot of personal things to process, but do you have time to lounge down here?"

"Not really."

"But you're making the time."

"Something like that. What's in your hand?" she asked.

"One of your gentleman callers left this behind. It's one of the commemorative gifts you commissioned. I thought you'd want it."

"Don't be a snot. What's with this nineteen-century 'gentleman callers' stuff? Which gentleman?"

"Did you just call me a snot? I'm not going to ask how many drinks you had. And back in the day, gentlemen did present a calling card. Consider this one." Troy handed the painting to Rose. "They're all personalized."

Rose turned over the miniature painting. "I'll take it to him tonight while I'm in the city. I might not get to see him again for a while. And for the record, I haven't had enough to drink after what you told me."

"Back to your original issue. Did you decide what you wanted to do?"

"Despite what you think, I made good use of my time down here. So, yes."

"What's on the agenda tonight?"

"First, I need to finish packing."

"Kris is still on-site; he can help with that."

"After I pack, we are headed to your hotel in the city."

"Why my place? And how do you even know I kept my room after coming here?"

"I know you. You always have a contingency plan. Besides, the brothers are back at their places. I can take all my things to your hotel and leave from there tomorrow."

"Did you still want me to escort you out tonight?"

"Yes."

"You'll let me know immediately if you change your mind?"

"Of course."

THE PACKING WASN'T AS BAD AS ROSE EXPECTED WITH THE HELP OF Kris, who stepped in to help her finish. Troy put everything in the SUV and waited downstairs for her to get ready for the final trip into the city. Rose took her time to get prepared, ensuring every detail was flawless. Tonight, she chose a champagne-colored silk slip dress that rested slightly above her knees, a silk kimono duster with a large pink and champagne cherry blossom pattern and matching high-heel strappy sandals. One glance in the mirror, and she was ready. Troy stood at the bottom of the stairs waiting.

"You look amazing. Can I be transparent?"

"I've never known you to be anything but."

"For the first time, I don't want to take you to another guy's place tonight." He held out a hand, helping her down the last few steps.

"You think I'm making a mistake."

"I think a lot of things. Mostly, I want to keep you safe—whatever form that takes."

"I appreciate your candidness. You're entrusted to stand by during the most intimate times of my life. The lines of protection get blurry."

"If we go to the hotel first, my instinct is to let that be your final destination until we fly out. Our last detour put you in harm's way."

"You were there. No one could even get near me."

"Still, they tried. Here's the plan. I will take you to your destination. Then, I'll bring your extra things with me to the hotel afterward."

"Sure, Troy."

"Are you ready?"

Rose nodded.

Together, Rose and Troy headed out. She expected he might be reticent under the circumstances, but he was more his usual self than she had predicted.

"Does he know you're coming?" Troy asked.

"No."

"Not a clue?"

"He seemed resigned the last time we spoke."

"And you're certain he will be there?"

"I seriously doubt he'd be anywhere else."

"Do you need anything from me?"

"I'd like you to walk me to the door and don't walk away unless you're comfortable with my decision." She looked to Troy for a reaction but didn't find one. "This is your statement to make, Troy. No one gets near me unless you clear the way for them."

"I understand."

They drove a while before pulling in front of the ten-story steely gray modern stone building. Troy helped Rose out, grabbed her overnight bag, and walked with her to the bank of elevators in the lobby just past the reception desk. When he pushed the up arrow, the center elevator opened immediately. Once in the elevator, Rose pushed the number ten button and stood face-to-face with Troy. Although no words passed between them, their eyes spoke volumes.

She leaned in and kissed his cheek just before they reached their floor. "I'm in your hands."

Troy nodded at her just as the bell signaled their arrival on the tenth floor. The doors opened onto a large entryway that could have doubled as a swanky boutique hotel lounge. There was a set of leather swivel chairs to the left and another set to the right in front of oversize framed mirrors rising floor to ceiling. The smell of roses wafting from a vase on a console near a set of doors filled the air. They walked across the room to the double doors. Rose raised her hand to knock, but the door opened before touching it. The face looking back at her took a few moments to process the scene, then looked past her to Troy. Troy nodded and handed him Rose's bag. The small gesture told him all he needed to know about Rose's visit.

"Thank you for bringing her to me, Troy."

Rose turned to Troy and mouthed the words. "I'll see you in the morning." He nodded again before he turned and disappeared into the elevator.

Rose struggled to find the right words to say. She reached in her purse to retrieve a small painting of a Night Owl perched on a rose bush. "You left this at the gallery."

"Has my Night Owl come home to me?" Niall held her gaze.

"I'm assuming I'm not interrupting anything, like a cooking lesson or something." Rose searched Niall's eyes for a response.

"I see what's happening. You think I'm with Marina. She's a client. You know I don't sleep with clients under my protection. Besides, she's not my type."

"I'm under your protection." Rose stuck her chin out and held his gaze. She was surprised when he flashed a hungry smile. She supposed he'd be surprised his secret was out, maybe go on the offense. Instead, he held his hand to her and led her into a massive loft. Niall dropped her bag inside and closed the door behind them. Rose began to walk towards the wall of windows overlooking the city, but Niall held her hand and turned her toward him.

"You didn't answer my question. Has my Night Owl come home to me?" Niall's slow sweep of her body with his eyes showed Rose a smoldering ember of desire ready to burn, and she knew the one word to release the blaze.

"Yes." Rose smiled up at Niall.

Niall pulled Rose close and bent his knees slightly until he was at eye level with her. The simple gesture showed Rose he wanted her full attention on whatever came next.

"My agreement expired one minute after I left the gallery this evening. The imminent threat is over. You said yes. Now, I'm going to kiss *my* woman for the first time." Niall snaked his arms around Rose's waist, pressed his lips to hers, and kissed her with all the fire she knew he previously withheld. His sense of urgency was matched by her own as she sucked and licked and returned his kisses until she couldn't breathe. Niall groaned and pulled away.

"It's going to take all night to do all the things I want to do to you. Are you ready for me, Night Owl?" he said, sliding his hand beneath her dress and between her folds. She felt her body respond instinctively to his touch while his fingers wallowed in her desire.

Rose started to groan, but Niall swallowed it with a kiss. She broke the kiss and panted out his name. "Niall. I'm…"

"Don't worry. You'll cum when I'm ready for you. Don't move." Niall removed his fingers and licked them. "You taste like heaven," he said, then pushed past her kimono, lowered the straps of her dress, and let her clothes fall to the floor around her feet. Niall picked Rose up, and she straddled him as he carried her into his bedroom. After Niall laid her on the bed, Rose watched as he slowly undressed, finally freeing hard proof of his desire.

"I'm forewarning you. I've been waiting a long time for this. I'm vacillating between going in hard and fast or taking my time." Niall placed a hand on either side of her head, looking down at her.

"Twenty-eight days, to be exact. We can slow it down later." Rose reached her hand over to the side table, grabbed a condom, and handed it to Niall.

Within seconds, his straining shaft was sheathed. Niall lowered his face to kiss her. Rose positioned him at her entrance, and before she could wonder what it would be like to have him inside her, Niall pushed in, and she was full. Full of him and his desire to be with her. Finally, full of everything she had been craving.

ROSE WAS SATIATED AND SPENT AFTER SEVERAL HOURS MAKING UP for the lost time. She laid on her back, fingers interlocked with Niall's, and savored the moment.

"Were you surprised to see me?" Rose propped herself on her elbow and faced Niall.

"How could you think anything else?"

"I'm glad you didn't give up on me."

"At first, I wasn't sure what to think when I saw you and Troy on my security monitor. It could have been a goodbye visit." He took a deep breath, then paused before releasing it.

"Thank you for acknowledging Troy."

"I have only respect for the guy. He has a tough job with no true end-of-day."

"It's not my intent to put anyone in a tough situation," Rose said.

"At least with me, he'll never have to worry about you." Niall tightened his fingers around hers. "Does my brother know you are here?"

"I plan to tell him tomorrow."

"No. He'll know tomorrow when I tell him." Niall studied her face as if it were his first time seeing her, as if reclaiming something he'd lost.

"Don't be hard with him." Rose sat up against the headboard and looked down at Niall.

"He's a King. He can take it."

"No, seriously. Don't go in there with a hammer. If I take your sister up on her offer, I have to see more of him."

"What offer?"

"To fill in on some of her commitments until she's fully recovered."

"This night keeps getting better. You do realize you'll get no sleep tonight, right?"

"I hadn't planned on it."

Buzz, buzz. Rose looked around for her phone but remembered all her things were near the front door. The sound was from Niall's.

"Do you need to get that?" she asked.

"It's just a news alert." Niall reached over and picked up his phone. "An article."

"Not another Marina headline." Rose frowned.

Niall scrolled through his screen. His eyebrow raised. "It's about you."

"Yeah, probably a narrative piggybacking off Ross Enterprises' press release. It'll die down in a few weeks."

"I don't think so. This is something new. It's an article citing our Taoiseach. Reporters must have caught up to him at another engagement tonight. It says, *'I had the opportunity to attend the Northern Ireland Patron of the Arts Annual Exhibition. This is my tenth year and by far the best year. When the exhibit opened, I was at once immersed in the event with an art piece inspired by my words. Our host, master curator, Rose Ross, took us on an exquisite yet pointed journey, surfacing hidden art gems from our diverse history, and introducing us to emerging talent. Ms. Ross masterfully told the history of Ireland through a lens we seldom—if ever—see, juxtaposed with an ambitious collection of the world's most treasured art pieces. Rose Ross delivered a brilliantly executed exhibition that was breathtaking to behold.'"* Niall handed his phone to Rose. She shook her head. The proud look in Niall's eyes told her everything she needed to know about the significance of the article.

"I might need extra security tomorrow."

Niall shook his head. "You're safe with me."

"Then you're all I need." Rose laid back next to Niall and placed a hand on his chest.

"I would say you have no idea how long I've waited to hear those words, but you know exactly how long," he expressed, brushing hair from her face. "I am curious. How did we get here?"

"A very windy road."

"I was with you from the beginning. What brought you full circle?"

"I don't have a short answer to that."

"We have all night. I'm certainly not going anywhere."

"It came down to the fact that I missed you. I looked for you after all the guests had gone home. I assumed you were busy. So, I returned to the house, fixed a drink, and tried to relax. The whole time, I was hoping you'd walk into the room looking for me. When I talked to your brother tonight, I found myself looking for you in his eyes. When Troy handed me the painting, I willed your name on it. When I went to meditate and clear my head of all the noise, only thoughts of you remained. I knew Aedan was not the man for me, and Alejandro and I were only meant to ever be friends. It dawned upon me that you and I never had to try. I couldn't solidify those other relationships because I had already imprinted on you. From day one, it was you. By day three, well, that sealed it. You knew it, too— why else would you step back and send your brother to me countless times? I know now that you wanted me to get him out of my system. And Alejandro, he didn't seem to faze you. Somehow, you knew he had long been out of my system."

"You and Aedan were working too hard to make a go of it. He lost you when he didn't fight for you, and poor Alejandro would never recover from an intentional break."

"You knew all along what I was subconsciously suppressing. I thought about our time together at Crom. Looking back, it's obvious that being with you was so natural. I should have made my choice that night. I wanted you that night." She bit her lip. "Okay, that naked walk you did may have had something to do with the wanting part."

"It wasn't the right time. I wasn't going to push for it to be either."

"I get that. It took some time, but I am here now."

"You are. My Rose." Niall rolled Rose on her back and kissed her.

CHAPTER 19

As We Lay

"The gravitational pull of love has a sense of urgency
that cannot be rebuffed."

– RITA A. GORDON

IT WAS ROSE'S FINAL DAY IN BELFAST. SHE OPENED HER EYES TO SEE golden rays of light streaming through space in silk curtains shrouding the window, finding solace on her face. Instinctively, her hands stretched in the direction of light. Fingers, elbows, shoulders, back, and hips embraced the innate tropism pushing through her body toward the sun. Her shoulders raised, her back arched, and she inhaled, slow and long, allowing the air to replenish her lungs.

Rose propped herself on her elbow to look at the finely sculpted face beside her. A slight hint that her man was still asleep came in the subtle movement of his powerful pecs slowly rising and falling and the sure breaths that followed. The four dimples that usually formed above his brows when he was awake were now calm as a mist-covered lake. She smiled, reflecting on the past thirty days, recalling every moment that coalesced to deliver this moment—that brought her together with *this* man.

Her body edged closer to his like a magnet's invisible, unyielding pull. Her fingers glided down the side of his temple, tracing a strand of silky black hair behind the curve of his ears to more soft curls awaiting their turn. They continued, caressing the natural loofah on his cheeks and chin that had charmingly brushed her face so many times before. But this time, when she touched him, everything felt different. They *were* different. Intent on reaching their mark, her fingers continued without hesitation until they reached his slightly parted lips. A sudden smile and kiss on her fingers signaled he was awake. And with that, he turned to her, and his lips launched their own voyage. Rose linked her fingers with his and watched as he slowly traced a path of kisses from her hand, arm, shoulder, neck, and eventually covering her lips. She could feel the warmth of his breath mingle with hers when she parted her lips to clear a path for his tongue, urgently seeking to claim hers. It wasn't long before his body enveloped hers, signaling he was awake in more ways than one.

"Morning. You have a call to make," she whispered against his lips.

Niall exhaled a deep breathy, "After," in response, then positioned himself between her legs, slowly pushing the entire length of his manhood where she desired him most. The sheets' sudden movement caused a picture frame clinging to the bed to fall to the floor. Its significance was a symbolic climax of events she had never anticipated. The end of a journey that began as a favor for a friend in Belfast.

Six Months Later

Everlasting Love

"Love makes your soul crawl out from its hiding place."

— ZORA NEALE HURSTON

"ALL CLEAR," TROY ANNOUNCED, GESTURING TOWARD THE PLANE'S door.

Rose got up and headed toward the front of the plane. She shivered, then buttoned her coat, shielding herself from the brisk cold wind that whipped past her from outside. Rose took Troy's hand as she stepped onto the metal stairs leading to the tarmac. A wide grin spread across her face as she looked below to find Niall looking up and smiling back at her. He was dressed in a black suit and white shirt, looking every bit of the billionaire book boyfriend type of beauty she remembered. Rose's body buzzed with excitement at being back with her man. When she reached the last step, Niall took her hand, drew her close, dipped his head, and kissed her with all the passion she knew he had saved up over the past few months.

"Night Owl," he breathed out in a whisper and touched his forehead to hers. "Let's go," he said, leading her toward one of three SUVs waiting for them.

Rose released a sigh of relief when Niall got into the car, closed the door, and sat next to her. In the last few months, she worked hard on her transition plan with her dad in anticipation of becoming Ross Enterprises' next CEO. She was looking forward to having the Christmas holiday off to be with Niall before stepping into her new role in January.

Rose turned toward Niall. "We need to work on your panty-wetting hellos," Rose smirked.

"Yeah, I could say the same." Niall took her hand and placed it on the bulge in his pants. "I'm suppressing the urge to pull you across my lap. We'll be home soon enough." He brought her hand to his mouth and kissed it.

"So, tell me. How hard was it to pull yourself away from work for the next two weeks?" Rose asked.

"Aedan's on point while I'm away, and since signing a deal with Ross Enterprises and a few additional new clients, I ended up promoting some people. So, we're covered. I'm not saying that I don't expect an urgent call to come in, but the plan is for everyone to go through Aedan. If he reaches out to me, I'll know it's critical."

"Which you know he won't. He's pushing himself too hard," Rose said, knowing she was partly to blame.

On her final day in Belfast following the exhibition, she and Niall walked over to Aedan's loft to talk about Rose's decision to be with Niall. Aedan was disappointed and suspected she was teetering on her decision because of how he had behaved during her final weeks in Belfast. Aedan expressed sensing Niall had a deeper connection to Rose, but at the time, he didn't want to admit it until they came to see him. He was sad to lose her but pleased she was still a part of their lives. During one of her follow-up trips to fill in for Brianna, Rose had time to talk extensively with Aedan. To reconnect and clear the air. He thanked her for helping him move past his player stage. But now, she could see he was burying himself in work. Rose knew Aedan was yearning to have something more with a woman—something like they had. He just needed to find the right woman.

"It's all good, Rose. People like Ben have stepped into more prominent roles within the company. What about you? Wait, before you answer…." Niall pulled Rose onto his lap, cupped her face, and kissed her. The kiss was long and slow as if he were savoring her. When he was done kissing, he pulled her tight to his neck, and she listened as he took deep breaths.

Rose pulled away and caught his gaze. He had a look she couldn't quite place. "What is it, Niall? Is something wrong with Brianna?"

"No. Why would you think that? She's perfectly fine. It's been years since I've seen her with this much energy. And although she's feeling better, you know she's still waiting on your decision on whether you'll host the exhibition again next year."

"Then what is it?" Rose traced her fingers across his face as if trying to memorize his features.

"I… I can't do this, Night Owl. I mean, I can… I'm trying to say that I want to know you're mine, Rose. To know in all certainty, you're in this for the long haul. Because I can't imagine my future without you in it. I fell in love with you the day I met you. You're it for me. I'm not trying to scare you away with some grand proposal, but I want to know if I'm it for you. The rest we can work toward at our own pace—together." Niall pressed his lips to hers.

Rose smiled against his lips. "Hey. Look at me," she said, her voice soft and low as their breaths mingled. Niall's smile was tentative as he awaited her response. "So, there's this guy. He's super tall, strong, and a bit overprotective but sexy. He says he loves me, and I love him. His name happens to be Ni—" Before Rose could finish, Niall pressed his lips to Rose and kissed her hard. She weaved her fingers through his hair, holding him tight, and deepened the kiss. They stayed like that, locked in each other's arms, kissing and holding each other until the car stopped.

"I love you, Night Owl. Let's take this inside," Niall said, then slid her off his lap before getting out of the car. He helped her out, grabbed her bag, and excused the staff before he and Rose got into the elevator.

Rose turned to face Niall as they rode in the elevator. "So, before you professed your love for me, I was going to tell you something."

"What's that?" Niall raised an eyebrow.

"I poached my cousin, June, from another company to replace me as COO," Rose said.

"So I heard. Seems you instructed the team to add June under my entity for protection. I signed the documents last week. You know you could have used King Enterprises' global entity." Niall looked at Rose. She had a sly smile on her face. The elevator doors opened, and Rose stepped out.

"I have my reasons," she called over her shoulder.

"Wait. June will be here to execute some contracts with Aedan while we're gone. You little matchmaker," he laughed, opening the door.

Rose stepped into the loft. Niall sat her bag down, closed the door, and helped Rose out of her coat.

"I get a new nickname, I see," Rose teased.

Niall took Rose by the hand and led her to the bedroom. "No. You're still my Night Owl and the love of my life," he said, placing a kiss on her neck.

Then, they both began grabbing and pulling at each other's clothes until they lay in a heaping pile at their feet. Niall picked Rose up and lowered her onto the bed. He hovered over her with hands caging her in. Rose pulled his face down to hers and stole a kiss.

"I love you, Niall. Now, show me what I've been missing."

Niall lowered himself to Rose and made love to his woman—the love of his life.

ACKNOWLEDGEMENTS

——

WRITING AND PUBLISHING THIS BOOK WAS A PERSONAL AND EMO-
tional journey. I want to acknowledge and thank the people who stood
by my side and helped me on my journey. To Cassandra, thank you for
being the first person to read my rough draft and gently guiding my
hand down a better path. To my sisters, Bess and Nina, thank you for
tolerating the constant talk about this book. Sorry for the wait, but here
we are. Thank you, Mike, for enduring the quirks of my creative process.
To my BFF, Sandra, I would do it all over again too. Love you forever.
A special thanks to Deborah for being there through all the seasons of
my life. Shout out to Natalia, my friend, whom I can always count on
for words of encouragement. Our souls are connected. To dear Megan,
the person I can always call for perspective and positivity. I feel lucky to
have had you in my life all these years. Thank you to the award-winning
creative artist, Magdalena. Your future is brighter than the sun. Thank
you, Sana, for patiently reading and editing every line and helping me
shine. And finally, to Ashbinah and her husband–Thank you for believing in me. There was a moment I was lost and taking my last breath, but
you found me and gave me air.

Thank you all.
Rita

ABOUT THE AUTHOR

Photo by Abigail Huller

Rita Gordon is a California native living in the Bay Area and a San Francisco State University graduate. *30 Days in Belfast* is her debut novel, providing a glimpse into her love of art and travel. Rita is also an avid reader. She has amassed an extensive collection of books that fill the rooms of her house. When not reading and writing, she spends her time traveling, drawing flower designs for her coloring books, or volunteering in her community.

To learn more about the author, visit **ritaagordon.com**.
Stay in touch!

Subscribe to her newsletter:
https://www.ritaagordon.com/subscribe-page

Follow Rita on:
@rgordonshaw

Goodreads:
https://www.goodreads.com/author/show/21524163.Rita_A_Gordon